HMB

To Jack
From Mary -

Ch[illegible]andon.

THE MAN ON THE WHITE HORSE

THE MAN ON
THE WHITE HORSE

By

WARWICK DEEPING

McCLELLAND & STEWART, LIMITED
PUBLISHERS   TORONTO

T. H. BEST PRINTING CO., LIMITED
TORONTO, ONT.

Contents

CONTENTS

Modern Names of Roman Cities, etc., Mentioned in This Narrative

Calleva	.	Silchester
Pontes	.	Staines
Londinium	.	London
Venta	.	Winchester
Aquæ Sulis	.	Bath
Regnum	.	Chichester
Corinium	.	Cirencester
Verulamium	.	St. Albans
Deva	.	Chester
Ratæ	.	Leicester
Rutupiæ	.	Richborough
Isca Silurum	.	Cærleon-upon-Usk
Glevum	.	Gloucester
Sorbiodunum	.	Salisbury
Eboracum	.	York

THE MAN ON THE WHITE HORSE

CHAPTER I

The Finding of Guinevra

¶ IT was Geraint's dog who heard the sound. Head up, collar bristling, body quivering, he stood with his muzzle pointing south. Geraint, riding ahead of the wagon and its guard of spears, reined in, and held up an arm.

He spoke to the dog, and the big boarhound looking up at him, whimpered, and stood sniffing the air. From the road a stretch of grass rose gradually to a beech wood, a black wood powdered gold and green and steeping its summit in the sunlight of a May morning. The sky was blue; the grass full of flowers; a little warm wind came out of the south. The stillness was absolute, the stillness of grass and of trees.

Geraint sat watching the wood—its grey trunks and the blackness within were mysterious and mute. His men had taken their spears from the wagon, and stood leaning on them, their faces turned towards the wood. There might be nothing there—or there might be death. Their lord had loosed his sword in its sheath. The dog's legs quivered.

Suddenly a jay screamed. They saw the bird go bustling and scolding among the tree tops. Again there was silence, but a silence that had become sinister. That dark wood held something—but what?

A cry. It rose, held for a moment, and broke like the plume of a fountain into a scattering of words. They were mere little sounds in the silence, distant and yet somehow distinct, like fingers plucking wildly at the strings of a harp. And the voice was a woman's.

Geraint turned in the saddle.

"Martin—a spear.—Caradoc, and four of you, come with me. The rest—on guard here."

He set his white horse at the green slope and went up it at a canter, his men running in a bunch at his heels. The beech trees were old trees, and within the droop of the outer branches the trunks rose like the grey pillars of a vast temple. Last year's leaves lay here in bronze. A greenish light filtered through the young foliage. Ahead Geraint saw nothing but the crowded trunks.

But there were sounds, and he rode on with the hound beside him, and his men's feet pattering over dead leaves. A splash of sunlight marked the break of a little glade. The grey trunks dwindled.—He saw—what he saw.

A girl, a dead body, four men in harness. The girl and a man were on the ground—the others—— Geraint sloped his spear and rode in.

Quick work—while it lasted, a scramble of surprised cut-throats caught like a fire by the wind. Geraint ran one man through; his dog pulled down another. He left his spear in the first scoundrel, and fell to with his sword. Three of the fellows were down before Geraint's men rushed in. Caradoc cut down the last of them.

Geraint rolled out of the saddle and stood over the fellow. The man was lying on his side, propped on one arm. Blood ran from him.

Geraint spoke. He was a big man, dark, quiet as death.

"Pia—Fidelis—men of the Second Legion—turned wolves!—That badge——"

The man lifted a bloody face.

"Pia—Fidelis—no pay for a year——! Pia—Fidelis!"

He let out a choked laugh, which ended in a wet moan. The tanned arm crumpled.—He fell on his face, and died.

Geraint looked at the girl. She was leaning against a tree, her arm over her eyes, her hair hanging in a cloud.

It was the colour of copper, and it hid her face. One hand, with fingers spread, held the clothes over her bosom. Her gown was of apple green, and below it a red shoe showed. The hound sniffed at the shoe.

She seemed to wrench herself round; she dropped the arm from her face; her dark eyes stared, for though her hair was bright and burnished her eyes were stag's eyes. She looked at the dead men, especially at the one who lay with arms spread and a red hole in his throat. She looked at Geraint.

"God have mercy——"

She seemed to shrink into herself, head down, her hands pressing against the front of her thighs, mute, dark, abject. There was blood on her shift. Geraint swept an arm at his men. He heard their feet brushing the dead leaves. He and the dog, the horse, the girl and the dead men were alone together. She was leaning back again against the tree, and her face was a white streak amid her hair.

He said—"God has pity."

She shuddered. She put her hair aside and looked at him for a moment like a frightened creature peering from a dark window. Her words came in a whisper.

"He is dead."

She let her hair fall over her face as though she could bear neither too much light nor too much looking, and then she fell a-sobbing. The dog nosed her leg, and his eyes were the eyes of a dog. One of her hands came to rest upon his head. As for Geraint he turned away, and walked to where the man in the black cloak lay spread like a cross. He was not a young man; he had a paunch on him and a little greyish beard. His eyes stared up through the beech boughs. He had the look of a rich man's steward or freedman. Geraint's horse followed him, stepping between the bodies. His white nozzle rested against his master's arm.

For a minute there was silence. He would have said that she needed it, the stillness and the half light of this

beech wood.   Her young shame had its anguish to cover.
She had sobbed it out amid her burning hair.

With an arm over the neck of his horse he turned and
looked.   She was bending down with her face pressed to
the dog's head.   He was smothered by her hair.   And
suddenly she straightened; her two hands put her hair back
over her shoulders, and for a moment she stood rigid.   Her
eyes had a blind look.

She spoke.

"I—would—go."

Geraint did not utter a word.   He went and lifted her
and placed her upon his horse, and taking the bridle, led
the beast out of the wood.   At the edge of the grass
Geraint's men were leaning upon their spears.   They
looked at their master and not at the girl.   He pointed into
the wood.

"Get the spades from the wagon.   Bury—the one in
the black cloak.   Take the arms and the harness from the
others.   Hasten."

He looked up at the girl.   Had she heard; had she any
orders for him?   She was mute.   He saw her cross herself.
So—she was a Christian.   He was not.

He led on across the grass, walking between the horse
and the hound.   His sword was bloody in its scabbard,
but for its cleansing it would have to wait.   But there were
questions to be asked, questions to be answered.

"How—this thing happened—you may tell me when you
please.   I am Geraint of the White Tower.   In two hours
we shall be in Calleva.   What is your wish?"

She looked at her two red shoes.

"I—lord—was for Calleva———"

"And whence?"

Her right hand was gripping the pommel of the saddle.

"Londinium.—My uncle—is dead.—I lived with my
uncle.   Justus—his freedman—yes—he who lies there—
was taking me to friends at Calleva."

They had reached the road.   The three men left with

the wagon stood and stared, but they ceased to stare when Geraint looked at them. He waved them to the wood.

"Spades. Work to do. Help Caradoc and the others."

They went. He put a hand under the girl's feet, and let her slip to earth. Her hair clouded his shoulder for an instant. She did not look at him, but sat down on the grass, and Bran the hound lay at her feet.

"I have not thanked you, lord."

He had slung his bridle over one of the horns of the wagon. She was caressing the dog. Her face was mysterious.

"Thanks come from the heart, child.—Tell me your name."

She seemed to murmur amid her hair.

"I am named Guinevra, lord."

2

Her seat in the wagon was a wine cask covered with a horse cloth. There was other merchandise in the wagon covered with dry fern, bars and pigs of iron from a furnace in the forest country beyond the White Hills. Geraint rode beside the wagon. A man walked beside the team; the rest slogged along behind it, spears over shoulders. Caradoc the smith, a bow-legged, oak butt of a man, had rude things to say of the world's affairs. As a smith he was feeling self-important.

"How does the law run, my lads? The emperor, God bless him, is neither here nor there. No man shall carry arms; no, not so much as a bodkin—unless he be a soldier.—I ask you—when soldiers turn cut-throats—should we good citizens get our throats cut without waiting for the sea-wolves or the Welsh?"

A tall yeoman spat.

"Ploughshares into swords—O—smith."

Caradoc jerked a thumb at the wagon.

"The stuff's there, my John. Our lord has a long head. My forge will be busy. A man who can hammer a sword——"

A little, black-eyed fellow who was the clown of the party, drew the back of a hand across his mouth.

"Our lord comforts outraged virtue. Puella yesterday, to-day—a . . ." and he laughed.

The smith swung a hand and clouted him.

"Be silent, and you—a Christian!—That was devil's work. I have girls of my own."

It was Caradoc who set the pace, and he shortened his step until the bunch of marching men were some thirty yards behind the wagon. For my lord Geraint and the girl were talking, and if Caradoc loved any man he loved his lord. Should a man be merciful, should he be able to say nay—not only to others but to himself? And did not Geraint love things that were good, men with straight eyes, hounds, horses, a boar-spear that would not break, the trees of the forest, wine and wheat. The chattering crowd in Calleva might call him Stoic—but they were twitterers, gabblers, men who hung about the market-place and chattered; shopkeepers, clerks, fellows who sweated in the public baths. When death came riding his black horse these little people might run to kiss the feet of the man on the white one.

Geraint, close to the front near wheel of the wagon, looked straight ahead down that Roman road. He did not glance at the girl, but she—out of the cloudings of her hair, had begun to glance at him. A dark-eyed bird in a burning bush, a bruised bird, crouching a little. Life had let her out of a cage, and then let loose wildness upon her. She still trembled; she still clasped her breasts. If she shuddered over the shame of it as no wanton shudders, but like a clean creature compounded more of dreams than of clay, she looked at the man who had saved her and was mute. "Unclean" was the cry of her heart—"Christ—Lord—I am unclean."

Should a man understand these things? My Lord Geraint had a wife of his own, one—Placida, a cold convention of a woman whose face was like her name. Placida! And here in this wagon was iron for swords, for, now that Rome was breaking, the Golden Age was a whirl of dying leaves. The barbarians were at the Wall, and on the sea, and the little dark men were watching from their mountains a world of scented fools and bishops, eunuchs and women who had got religion. Roman legionaires turning footpads, whole centuries deserting, the roads unsafe, country houses shut up and barred at night against—fear of the night. For nearly three hundred years Britain had known peace. Rome had kept the frontiers, and Rome was failing.

He looked at the girl. Loot? She, like the cities, was golden loot, a beautiful thing to be torn from its pedestal, a casket of jewels to be rifled. What would she be in this wild new world—no more than a little flame burning for a moment? So, she had friends at Calleva, Calleva with its great flint walls. Calleva might need those walls.

He had given her silence, but behind the plodding horses her silence was wearing thin. It began to burn her instead of to assuage. Her hands grew restless. She tried to put up her barbaric hair, rolling it into two ropes, but since she had nothing with which to master it, the cloud came loose.—What did it matter? So thought the man.— But these friends of hers?—He questioned her.

She seemed glad now of the chance to talk. She told him that she was an orphan. Her father had been an imperial official at Verulam, an assessor; when she had been left alone in the world her uncle had given her a home in London; yes, she had lived over a goldsmith's shop in the Via Augusta—off the Forum. The goldsmith, good man, had gone out to a burial in a March wind, and the wind had blown him to God. She crossed herself. Might his soul be where it should be. As for the Calleva folk, they were good people, silver refiners; one of the women had been the goldsmith's wife. Their names? Did not my lord know the name of Vetorix? Geraint knew it, but did not say what else he knew.

She ceased to trouble with her hair. She let it stream behind her shoulders over her apple-green tunic. Her hands lay in her lap—beautiful hands, yet strong. She looked at him less like a scared creature who had been saved from the claws of a hawk. Her glances went more levelly at him from under her straight, low forehead.

No—she was no mere suppliant, a poor creature who would be suffered in someone's house, and be put to weave and spin and keep the pet dog free from fleas. With a kind of quaint innocence she spoke of herself as an heiress. When the lawyers had finished with their parchments—she would have money—O—yes, quite a little fortune.—What would she do? She looked serious—serious as night. Dream dreams, attend Mass, grow flowers, pity the poor? But her world was so much like a window in which the glass had been shattered. She looked out of it and sought to see the same, familiar, friendly things.

Again, she shuddered a little and was mute.

Meanwhile, the country had become more gentle. They saw cows grazing, and a husbandman harrowing his young wheat. Two children stood by the roadside with handfuls of bluebells. They came to a broad valley white with thorn trees in blossom, and beyond the thorns were oaks all in golden leaf. The grass was full of buttercups. Two laughing girls with baskets on their shoulders showed to them linen fresh from a brook. The girls looked at the man on the white horse, but Geraint was thinking of other things, and their giggles and glances were left for his men. And suddenly, crowning a low plateau, Calleva broke the brim of the sky.

Geraint pointed.

"Calleva."

They could see the city wall, and the two black arches of the east gate, and the watch-tower on the wall above the amphitheatre. The high, oblique roof of the basilica caught the sunlight on its chequer of stone shingles, and near it the gilded statue of the city's Genius stretched out a little golden and benedictory arm. Windows glimmered. There were the red roofs of the Hospitium and the Baths. Some of the richer houses showed their upper stories, plaster work coloured red and blue, yellow and cream. Here and there a green tree spired up.

Guinevra looked at the city. It was very beautiful; it had a mystery. The little statue on the column seemed to stretch out a welcoming hand. She sat very still—gazing.

Her lips moved.

"Does my lord lodge in Calleva?"

He smiled at her rapt face.

"No—I pass through. But not before I have given you to friends."

Her face fell a little.

"Does my lord go far?"

"Fifteen miles on the road to Sarum.'

"And what is the name of my lord's house?"

"They call it Turris Alba."

B

CHAPTER II

Bishop Balthasar

¶ WHEN they came to the east gate of Calleva, they found both gates open and the guard-rooms empty. Two little black tunnels led from sunlight to sunlight. The street within was deserted, save for a dog scratching himself by a wall. Geraint looked grim. So, they kept no watch here, the fools! Moreover, he saw other things besides that flea-bitten dog: a choked drain and the black ooze of a puddle, offal, an old shoe lying in a gutter, oyster-shells thrown from a doorway. Calleva was forgetting both its guards and its scavengers. Had the city fathers abdicated, and the curia gone to sleep?

The emptiness of the streets challenged him, and finding Caradoc trotting beside his horse, he looked down into the smith's face.

"The place might be dead."

"It is May Day, lord."

May Day! And he had forgotten! Had all Calleva gone a'maying, leaving the place to Fortune and the dogs? The beat of his horse's hoofs seemed to echo from house to house; the wagon rumbled behind. When they came towards the centre of the town they saw that the shutters were up; even the wine-shops were shut.

"Strange virtue, Caradoc."

The smith growled in his beard.

Geraint was turning his horse into the Via Flavia when the silent town came to life like a pan of fat on a fire. A sudden shouting; the clamour of a crowd both shrill and deep. At the end of the Via Flavia the gateway of the

Forum was so packed with people that it looked like a fruit-stall. The crowd was set solidly round the Doric pillars of the portico, but as Geraint rode up the street that mass of coloured backs and black heads surged forward. The high wall of the basilica resounded like a cliff to all that clamour. Geraint reined in, and sat listening, looking. Those mob voices were shouting in unison.

"Balthasar, Balthasar, Bishop Balthasar."

Geraint rode on, but at the corner of the butter-market he turned in the saddle and spoke to the smith.

"Stop the wagon. Keep the dog with you."

He walked his horse to the gate of the Forum. The road continued through the pillared vestibule, and here in the shadow Geraint reined in his horse. The court of the Forum was so thick with people that a cat could have walked upon their heads, but Geraint was concerned with a particular face and not with Calleva's caputs. At the foot of the column in the centre of the Forum a man was standing on a tub, haranguing the people, a long, lean man in a purple cloak. His face was very pale. One arm was thrust out, fingers and thumb spread, and in the stillness his voice cut like a sword.

Balthasar the Bishop.

Geraint sat his horse in the shadow and watched him. Balthasar might stand on a tub in the thick of a May Day mob, but he was no huckster bawling tripe or conies. The crowd were the conies. This lean man with a face like the edge of the moon, both suave and ferocious, with the oblique glitter of his eyes and a voice that both caressed and cut, held the crowd. Moreover, Balthasar was a handsome man, a little flashy perhaps, and too ready with pontifical insolence, but he was clever, quick as sin when it sets out to convert virtue.

Balthasar spread his arms.

"My children, if Emperors and Councillors desert us, shall we be downcast?—I have dreamed a dream and beheld a vision. Are we not all the servants of

Christ—and citizens of this city?—Shall I tell you my dream?"

There were cries of—"Yes, yes, the dream," and Balthasar smiled about him.

"I dreamed that St. Peter stood by my bed and said unto me—'Balthasar, arise. Take thy staff and go to the people and say unto them—"Cast out the heathen from your midst——"'"

Again there were cries from the crowd, but Balthasar's right arm was up.

"Patience, my children—let me interpret my dream.— This city of ours—Calleva—shall we not make it a city of Christ—yea—and a city of faith and of love? Men have called it a Free City, but is there freedom when pride and privilege and riches rule? Listen, my people, in these days of darkness and destruction let us dare to be strong in the strength of our Lord. Let us take this city and rule it. Let us make it ours. Let us make of ourselves soldiers of Christ.—Need we a sign and a standard? Holy Cross —the People, a city and a state in which all men shall be equal——"

Thus spake Balthasar, and the Forum became a confusion of hands and sticks and caps. The crowd lapped up the rhetoric—for were not the children of the Holy Church poor? Geraint looked thoughtful, and he looked at Balthasar. This May Day mob might be silly or dangerous, for in Calleva, as in many cities, there had been battles of the gods. Had not the children of Christ, growing arrogant, chased Mars and Minerva from their temples? Balthasar had splashed oil and water about those temples and exorcised Olympus, but Balthasar and his mob had been a little previous. A new Emperor had taken the throne, Julian, philosopher and pagan, and the old world had recaptured courage and its own. The Bishop and his flock had been extruded from the temples. The old die-hards had restored Venus, Minerva and Mars. All this had happened less than five years ago, but Julian was dead, last hope of Rome, and the new world had its teeth in opportunity.

Geraint was about to turn his horse and ride back to the wagon when the eyes of the man on the tub were raised above the crowd. Balthasar saw Geraint on his white horse, and Geraint stood fast. He saw the other man smile a little, secret smile. For some seconds these two gazed steadfastly at each other—Balthasar in the sunlight, Geraint in the shadow. Heads were turned. Was my Lord Bishop beholding other visions? The crowd saw what Balthasar had seen, Geraint on his white horse like some symbol of old Rome.

Those hundreds of faces seemed to veer like wind vanes. Geraint had been looking at the backs of heads, but now he saw a mosaic of faces, unfriendly faces, mouths, eyes, noses, beards. The crowd gazed at Geraint, and Geraint, still as death, gazed at the crowd, and for the moment the crowd was as silent as he was. Calleva knew him, Lord of the White Tower, Stoic, Roman, uncompromising neighbour. His boundaries marched with those of Calleva, and Calleva had been made to respect them.

Then, someone in that silent crowd, shouted.

"Anti-Christ—heathen, spy!"

A woman shrilled.

"Are we dogs——?"

In an instant the brave crowd boiled up, a crowd of bawling mouths and teeth and fists. Love seemed to take flight and refuge above with the little gold Genius on the pillar. Half a dozen lewd fellows made a rush, but the white horse was not of their temper. He struck out with a foreleg, and showed his teeth. Geraint sat still, and looked at the crowd.

He spoke to the horse—"Quiet, Victor."

The lewd fellows thought better of it, and recoiled.

Meanwhile Balthasar had come down from his tub. A couple of deacons were shouting—"Make way for the Bishop." The crowd made a lane for him. Balthasar knew how to walk and how to handle his robes. He came with two fingers of his right hand erect—crying—"Peace, peace." His eyes were on Geraint, and Geraint's eyes were on Balthasar. This man was more dangerous than any mob.

"My lord—would be one of us?"

The face of the priest was suavely ironic. Geraint sat still in the saddle.

"I salute the Genius of Calleva."

He too could be ironic, but the silly crowd knew not whether to cheer or to howl.

Geraint raised an arm.

"*Salve—vale.*—Remember your gates, my friends.— Lock them when I go, and give the keys to your Bishop."

He turned his horse slowly, and rode for the sunlight, but directly his back was turned, the crowd scuttled after him. It hooted and mocked, but kept clear of the heels of his horse. One or two urchins threw stones. But a crowd such as this had to be mastered. It filled the street from house to house, and when Geraint reached the wagon team his men were handling their spears.

He turned on the crowd; it was an unarmed crowd, save for its fists and its sticks, and more ready to howl than to fight, and Geraint sat his white horse and said never a word. His men had closed upon him behind. The tail of the crowd was braver than its head; its impulse was forward, but the head hung back, not liking those levelled spears. Caradoc's teeth showed white in his beard. This city scrum would not come to be spitted. As for the girl, she sat on her wine cask looking just a little frightened, her hair shining in the sunlight. This May Day was not a day of flowers and perfume and singing birds. It had the temper of a harsh and blustering March, save that the morning was hot and the crowd could be savoured.

So, Geraint sat on his white horse and waited. If a man looked a beast in the eyes, the creatures would flinch and, swinging a stupid head from side to side, retreat, and the crowd, conscious of its own cowardice, sought to save its

face by making a mock of the thing it feared.   Clowns were
in favour.   They said lewd things about Geraint, and he sat
and looked at them without the flicker of an eyelash.

Then, a red-headed fellow, a fish porter, cut a caper in
front of the chorus, and pointed at the girl.

"See, gossips, he has his harlot with him."

The white horse, quivering with excitement between
his lord's thighs, felt the sudden pressure, and moved
forward.   Geraint's sword was out, but he struck with the
flat.   Red-head went down on his back, but Geraint's
horse ploughed on.   The wagoner started his team; the
spearmen closed up behind their lord.   The great hound
was loose and leaping.   The crowd ran.   It fell over itself.
It scuttled into doorways and scrambled over walls.
Geraint, his sword resting across his saddle-bow, called the
dog in.   Bran had fleshed his teeth in one fat rump.

Geraint and his party passed on.   A few stones and
potsherds were flung.   From the pillars of the Forum gate
the remnant of the crowd howled at him.   He spoke to
Caradoc who marched at his side.

"Any news of Vetorix?"

"Vetorix and his ingots have gone west, lord."

"Wise Vetorix.   We will try the house of Cornelia."

Caradoc grinned.

"That's an old lady with some spunk in her."

And Caradoc was thinking—"It is the girl—I wager.
Now, if it were my May Day—I would not leave such a
pretty thing to Calleva.   But when a man has a wife, and a
wife like the Lady Placida, sweet—sweet and—so suspicious!
The gods defend us from good women."

2

The house of Cornelia lay between the Forum and
the west gate, in a street beyond the dye-works, one of a
group of mansions amid gardens surrounded by high walls.

Geraint had brought his horse level with the wagon.   He had bad news for Guinevra.   The day was a day of black pebbles.

"Child—the house of Vetorix is empty."

She looked poignant.

"Empty!"

What a May Day was this!   Less than six hours ago she and the good Justus had left the mansio at Pontes in a carpentium behind two mules.   It had promised to be a day of great weather; there had been rain in the night, and a dawn of washed gold.   Now, Justus was dead, the mules and the carriage and her travelling trunk lost somewhere in the woods; Calleva had the face of a red-headed fish-porter, a head that was bloody from the flat of Geraint's sword.

She looked at Geraint like a child whose cup of woe is full, and behind the child glided the woman.   A branch might blossom quickly in such passionate weather.

"What shall I do?"

Her voice was as poignant as her eyes; there was a blackbird note in it, and her eyes showed dark and swimming pupils.

He said—"Leave this to me."

They had turned into a quiet street where flowering apple trees showed above a high, grey wall.   There was a greenness of other trees, old trees in young leaf.   The windows and white walls of a house were visible among the trees.   They came to a gate in the wall, a double gate between stone pillars.   The gates were shut, but the chain of a bell hung down one pillar.   Geraint leaned forward in the saddle and rang the janitor's bell.   The wagoner had stopped his horses, and unslung a leather bucket from the wagon pole.   The beasts wanted water.

A grille opened in the gate, and a face showed behind the lattice.

"Friends, Simon."

The janitor unbarred the gate.   He was a little, fat, oily man who smiled like Silenus.

"Enter, lord."

"Is your lady in, Simon?"

"She has just dined, lord."

Geraint rode in and beckoned to his men.

"Bring the wagon through. Better close the gates, Simon. A mad dog seems to have bitten Calleva."

Simon genuflected.

"Two mad dogs, lord. We live with our gates shut, and the hounds loose at night."

Geraint sat his horse and watched the wagon pull into the courtyard. He met the eyes of the girl, so strangely dark under the sweep of her burning hair. She was rather white, poor child. Her hands lay clasped together in her lap. He smiled at her, and dismounted. He patted the neck of the white horse and passed the bridle to Caradoc.

"Go and warn your lady, Simon, though she should have heard us."

Bran the hound was looking up into his face. He pointed, and the dog lay down on the courtyard stones. The girl saw all this, the way men and beasts obeyed him, and something in her consented and was glad.

Dame Cornelia met Geraint in the atrium. She was a stout and formidable old lady with a high colour, an out-jutting lower lip, and eyes that were uncompromisingly blue. Her grey hair towered piled up in front like a battle-mented gate. Unregenerate Calleva spoke of the lady as The Empress or Old Gorgon, but Cornelia liked where she liked and hated where she hated. Geraint was of her world, and her fierce old eyes were friendly.

Had he dined? Geraint kissed her hand, the clean kiss of a man who was well shaved. Cornelia did not favour hair on a face, perhaps because she had too many hairs on her own chin. And what brought him to Calleva? Geraint smiled at her. Her jocund, high-coloured vigour had to be humoured. Wine and meat were excellent things, and he remembered that the girl might be hungry.

He said—"I am here for a favour.—This morning on

the Londinium road we fell in with footpads. The scoundrels had taken a girl and her servant. The man was dead.—I have the girl here in the wagon. She was coming to Vetorix, Silver Vetorix, but they tell me Vetorix was not feeling safe in Calleva.—I can understand that. We had words—a little affair with a mob near the Forum.—Your bishop, Balthasar, had been blowing on live coals."

"He is not—my bishop, my friend. A slimy fellow. So—this girl——?"

She looked hard at Geraint, and Geraint smiled at her.

"I could have put her in a hostel."

Her answering smile was shrewd.

"Or presented her to Placida! But, your wife, my dear——"

Geraint did not smile. He was curt.

"The child's alone—her people dead.—She was to find a home here.—She's a gentle thing. When I heard that Vetorix had gone——"

"Others have gone, as well as Vetorix.—But, my lord—I am no Martha—but a tough old pagan."

He nodded and turned to the window.

"She is there.—Look.—The child has been through enough this morning.—I brought her here—because——"

She wagged a finger at him.

"No oil, sir, no oil. Leave the oil to the priests."

She walked to the window and, opening the lattice, stood at gaze, head up, her lower lip thrust out. Geraint stood and waited upon her mood, for Cornelia was a lady who was best left to make her own decisions. That formidable lip of hers seemed to jut out like the lip of a jug; her blue eyes stared; her sight was as sharp as ever. Guinevra, sitting on her wine cask, was not conscious of being observed; her hair was like a cowl in which she hid herself; she drooped a little in the sunlight as though the green stalk of her had wilted. Dame Cornelia stared. She was not a woman to put herself out for a slip of a girl, especially some tax-monger's daughter, but though Cornelia might

scold, she liked things to happen. The world might be
going to the dogs, but Cornelia would be in at the death.

She fingered her fat chin.

"You say her uncle was a goldsmith?—It's a pretty
creature, Geraint.   She's like a burning bush."

She gave him a wicked look.

"I'm an inquisitive old woman."

He met her mordant eyes.

"I have known you do kind things."

She flapped a hand at him.

"Moonshine—I am going to Aquæ Sulis next month.
—Meanwhile—— Well, bring her in."

When Cornelia gave you a yea you took her yea at its
value and did not turn it over in your palm.   Geraint went
out into the courtyard.   The girl had been watching the
doorway, and when he came down the three steps, she
straightened her young back.   Her eyes watched him.   He
came to the tail of the wagon and held out a hand.

"I've found you a friend.   Come."

But for some reason she was shy of his hands.   She
sat down on the tail-board and let herself slip to the ground.
She closed her eyes for a moment, and seemed to sway back
against the board.   Her eyes opened again; but they were
blind eyes.   Geraint caught her and carried her in.

He said—"She has fainted," which should have been
obvious—"The child's had no food since the early morning."
He stood there in the atrium, looking at the white face and
hanging hair.   Cornelia had taken one of the limp hands,
and to satisfy herself and without Geraint seeing what she
did, she pressed a thumb-nail into a soft finger.   There was
no flinching, no flicker of the eyelashes.   This was an honest
faint, not a wench's trick.

Cornelia rang a hand-bell.—Old cynic that she was she
allowed that Geraint and the girl made a pretty picture,
but not the kind of picture that Dame Placida would wish
to hang in her pinecotheca.   My Lord Geraint was looking
at the girl.   He seemed to forget a stout old lady in gazing

at that pale face in its cloud of hair. And then two women appeared between the folds of the curtain that separated the atrium from the vestibule, and Cornelia gave orders. Geraint was bespoiled of his burden. One of the women, a stout Frisian, took the girl in her arms, and waddling after her mistress, disappeared behind another curtain. Geraint stood and watched its purple folds fall back. He heard the voice of Cornelia sharp and decisive.

"Lay her there.—Fetch some wine and water. The child has been frightened, and has had no food. No, don't stick her head up in the air like that.—Pull that cushion away.—That's better. Bathe her face and hands, and give her a little wine.—Then food, bread soaked in wine—but not too much.—You understand?"

She reappeared from behind the curtain, and her blue eyes were less hard.

"I do not believe in a crowd round a couch, my friend. Come into the diætra and break your fast. I can give you wine and cold meat."

She clapped her hands, and one of the women looked out from behind the curtain.

"Tell Pompey to serve Spanish wine, and olives.— And bring me word when the girl has her colour back."

3

Cornelia did not use her dining-room and its couches save on Roman and state occasions, and in Calleva such occasions were becoming rare. Geraint was given her chair at a table, and meat and wine and bread were set before him, but he and the old autocrat of the battlemented hair had other matters to speak of. It was Cornelia who remembered his men; she stood at a window, clapping her hands until the janitor appeared.

"Tell Pompey to feed my lord's men."

"There are ten of them," said Geraint.

But Cornelia would have her way, and it was a large way, in spite of earthquakes and barbarians and bishops she was not yet a beggar. She arranged herself on a couch and put up her feet. She had questions to ask Geraint, and many things to say to him.

"Footpads on the London road! What next?"

Geraint dipped bread into his wine.

"Deserters from the Sixth Legion."

The old lady looked fierce.

"Ye gods!—Why do they not cut off a few heads?— We are growing weak, Geraint, silly and sentimental. They tell me those savages in the north are swarming near the Wall.—Why does not Duke Fullofandes do something? A weak fellow—that."

"They say his men won't fight."

"Ye gods!—I'll get into my chariot and go north."

Geraint smiled at her.

"We have trouble nearer home. The Cymri, ready to loot.—Do you know what I heard in the forest country? Nectarides has let Saxons settle in the woods not ten miles from Anderida."

Her lower lip was thrust out.

"The fool! A Saxon is a savage, Geraint. He is not a Frank or a Goth.—But as you said, my friend, the trouble is nearer home. Just when the strong hand is needed we have swollen heads here. That gouty old dotard Benedict —our vicar—is having his paunch kneaded at Bath—when he should be suppressing a man like Balthasar. These Christians are becoming impossible.—A slimy upstart like this bishop!—Do you know what the fellow is planning?"

"I can guess."

"The world's confusion—is—his opportunity. A little Priest-King, my dear—Calleva a City of God—with the scum squalling canticles, and Balthasar throned in the curia. Go round the city—see—the empty houses, the very people who should have stood up to the fellow— running away."

Geraint raised his cup to her.

"You have not run away."

Her old blue eyes stared.

"I am too fat to run.—Do you know, Geraint, that we have only three senators left in the place—and they shake at the knees. Shops are shutting; the council does not meet. Balthasar presides in the curia. Last week I was stoned in my litter. Go—not I.—I suppose—some day—the Emperor will remember this island and send us a man, and Balthasar will be put back in his kennel."

Geraint's face was grave.

"Or—the barbarians will break in. Guess what I have in my wagon?"

"You had—a pretty wench."

"Iron.—When gold becomes yellow dirt, iron is king; iron for swords.—If our soldiers will not fight, we must help ourselves."

She nodded at him.

"If I had my way I would give you the purple, my dear. —But a few words about this girl. Is she penniless?"

Geraint had finished eating. He wiped his hands on a napkin.

"I will tell you what she told me."

Cornelia listened. She managed her own estate, and was a woman of affairs. Yes—her lawyer had not run away; she would put the girl's business in his hands. Next week she was sending her freedman Felix to Londinium; the lawyer could go with him in the carriage and consult with the advocates who were dealing with the girl's inheritance. A goldsmith's shop in the Via Augusta—and money in the mortgages on property in Verulam? Well, the shop would have to be sold. Rhadamanthus the banker had transferred himself and his strong-boxes to Corinium, because Balthasar had sticky fingers. The girl's money could be banked at Corinium.

She said—"I like young things when they do not talk too much, and let me do the talking."

And then the Frisian woman appeared.
"The girl is sitting up—Dame?"
"Has she eaten?"
"Yes, Dame."
"Well, let us see her with her colour back."

Geraint had risen and was buckling on his sword, for the road should be his if he and his men were to see the White Tower before sunset. He went to the window and spoke to Caradoc who was sitting in the wagon with ale froth on his beard. The horses had been fed and watered.

"Get the men together. I am coming."

The hound, who had been lying in the sun, rose and loped across the courtyard, put his forepaws against the wall, and barked at his master.

"Coming, Bran, coming."

He turned and saw Guinevra in the doorway. Her hair was coiled and pinned over her ears and the nape of her neck; she looked taller, older, standing there in the green sheath of her young dignity. Cornelia, sitting squarely on the couch, stared the girl over, nodded, smiled.

"Well, my dear, my Lord Geraint is leaving me something pretty to look at. You can make your home here until you know what you wish to do."

Guinevra's eyes were for Geraint. Was it his wish—? —He smiled at her—with an air of consent she crossed the room, took Cornelia's fat right hand and kissed it. Her head was meek with its sleeked hair and downcast eyes. Cornelia patted her cheek.

"We shall be very good friends, my dear.—And now, my Lord Geraint is for the road."

The girl stood back from them both. She had a hushed look, but Cornelia saw the trembling of her knees. Her colour came and went, and with a little air of breathlessness she ran to Geraint, and knelt.

"O, my lord—I shall not forget."

She was confused, red, voiceless. Geraint raised her. He looked at her face, and then slowly kissed her forehead.

"The gods be good to you—Guinevra."

Then, he put her quickly away from him with the air of a man who had touched a thing that was strange and mysterious. He walked to the window, and stood looking out.

"My men wait."

When he had kissed Cornelia's hands, he had no more words for either of them. Head in air he walked to the door, turned, stood erect—raised an arm. Guinevra, hands hanging, did not dare to look at him. He saw the coils of her hair, the curve of a cheek. Her knees were trembling.

"*Vale.*"

He went out. They heard the barking of the dog, and the voices of the men. The wheels of the wagon rolled over the stones. But as Geraint's white horse swung out through the gate, he turned in the saddle and looked at the window.

CHAPTER III

Geraint Comes to The White Tower

¶ NEAR the fifth milestone from Calleva on the road to Vindomis, Geraint met a tribune riding at the head of three squadrons of Spanish horse. The tribune, sword-arm raised, halted his men, and putting his beast across the road, barred the way.

"Who are you that go armed?"

He was a high and mighty gentleman with a polished chin and waxed mustachios, his body armour very bright, his red cavalry cloak fastened at the throat with a gold chain. And Geraint smiled at him, that quiet, inward smile.

"We go armed, sir, because the roads are not safe."

"Ha," said the cavalryman, "say you so.—You look like a man who should know the law. Your name."

But, for the moment, Geraint gave no name. He pulled out his sword with the dried smears of blood on it and held it so that the sunlight shone upon the blade. This fellow on the high horse was altogether too lofty.

"My witness, tribune.—You see—the blood."

"I would have you explain it, sir."

Geraint put up his sword.

"You ride with ninety troopers, tribune—I—with a wagon and ten men. Had you been on the Calleva–Pontes road this morning—you could have used your troopers.— We had to fight, yes—Roman soldiers turned cut-throats. —What would you have us do?"

The tribune twirled a moustache.

"This is serious, sir."

Geraint looked grim.

"Serious—I should say so.—And you for one, my friend, should know how serious matters are.—My name is Geraint of the White Tower."

The tribune became polite.

"That name passes, my lord.—I grant you the news is —not pleasant.   The Cymri are restless."

"Yet you ride east."

"There is trouble in the north.   Isca can deal with the Cymri.   We go north—I turn left at Calleva.   Pass, my lord."

He drew his horse out of the way, and Geraint gave him a parting message.

"The gates may be shut against you, tribune."

"No gates are shut against me, sir."

"Then good luck to you."

Geraint sat his horse and watched the cavalry go by, dark little men on wiry chargers—but the fellows looked sullen and their horses were in poor condition.   "Too much garrison work," thought Geraint, "too much wine-shop and women.   And, our friend the tribune—is too waxed and polished.—The savage world is a hairy world and does not cry—'Pardon—by your leave.'"   He touched the white horse with his heels, and rode on.

Rolling country and a spacious sky, blue distances and dim mysterious hills, country that Geraint loved.   So had the first Gerontius loved it, who, coming to Britain as a prefect in the days of the Antonines, had stayed to found a family, and an estate.   The road descended to a brook and a stone bridge and beyond the bridge stood the eastern boundary stone of the Lords of The White Tower.   Geraint saluted it.   From the bridge for fifteen miles the land was his, downland and beech woods, forest, meadows, streams, red deer and fallow, boars, wild cattle, birds.

The high road cut the edge of the forest of Spinæ and struck open country, and from it a by-road turned south where a shrine to Sylvanus stood in the midst of a thicket of flowering thorns.   Horses and wagon went up a hill.

Here were beech woods, magnificent and still, dome on dome and brilliant in the slanting sunlight. From the ridge the ground fell away into a deep green valley, and letting the wagon go on, Geraint pulled his horse on to the grass and sat at gaze. The hound remained with him.

Looking down into the valley he saw all that was his—this green and beautiful spot begotten of three hundred years of peace. He saw the red roofs and white walls of the great house, the pillars of the ambulatory, the gate-house with its gilded wind-vane, the courtyard and garden. Behind it rose the thatched roofs of stables, barns, mews, kennels. The great orchard was still in flower within its wattle fences. Below it sloped the vineyard, vines all a-row. Beyond the orchard were more thorn trees, and below the vineyard the grove in which stood an altar to Sylvanus. High beech woods shut in the valley, and in the lap of it lay the Great Pool with its island and white tower.

Geraint looked down at the water and the island. Lilies and water-flags grew there, and the island was a smother of fruit-blossom. The white tower rose strong and straight from its green and white cushion. The evening sunlight made it brilliant, and played upon the still water. The black barge lay at the mooring-stage, and as Geraint gazed—he smiled.

Three hundred years of peace. The white tower on the island had become a whimsy of Gerontius the Prefect. In those days the Roman peace had been less sure and the tower of the first Geraint had given a name to the valley. Geraint of Turris Alba. Its glazed windows glimmered high up above the water and the fruit blossom. For three hundred years or so it had waited for war and for violent things when war was not. But—now? Savages in the west, in the north, and in the east, wild men running to loot the rich-ness of the great peace. Wolves, blood, fire, outrage and death, an Empire whose knees shook, an army that sulked and deserted.

Geraint rode on after the wagon with the dog beside

him, past the house of Mabon his *villicus*, and the cottages of his hinds. Could he make soldiers of ploughmen and cowherds and labourers? Would they stand steady and close with locked shields and stab with the short sword? He rode on past Caradoc's smithy to the great gate.

2

Rual, his major-domo, met him there, a bland and bald old man with a white beard. Rual held his lord's bridle. His white tunic was fresh from the wash, his forehead as peaceful as the sunset. Old Rual was of the ancient world. One might say that nothing untoward could happen in his presence.

"What news, Rual?"

According to Rual there was no news, and Geraint dismounted, and passed through the gate. The house was built round a courtyard which Geraint's mother had turned into a garden. Vines and roses were trained to the balusters of the ambulatory. Round the basin of a fountain wild flowers had been planted—bluebells and dog-violets, and wild musk.

Rual, who had left the horse with a groom, hurried with a haste that was decent to bow his lord into the vestibule.

"Where is my lady?"

Geraint had turned into the atrium where a worker in mosaic had laid a fair pavement, and in the centre of it—Venus was rising from the sea. Geraint, unbuckling his sword, stood upon the face of the goddess, which was ungallant, but the face of Venus had suffered from many feet, and her countenance was growing dim. Rual, waiting to take Geraint's sword—observed how his master's feet had come to rest upon the face of the goddess. Assuredly, it was an omen, and on occasions Rual could be a little deaf.

Geraint repeated his question.

"My lady?"

Rual took the sword.

"At her prayers, sir; they call them vespers, now—I understand."

"Have the sword cleaned. I had to use it."

Geraint passed through the atrium and the tablinum. There was a passage here running between the cloister walk and the herb garden, and Geraint took this passage. The oak door leading into the herb garden was open, and at the end of a grass walk Geraint saw his wife's chapel very white and new against the trees of the orchard. He had had the chapel built for Placida less than three years ago. As Cornelia would have phrased it, the wife of Gerantius had got religion rather badly, and was so busy saving her precious soul that nothing else was worth saving.—But Geraint was still in the passage when he saw the chapel door open, and a man wearing a brown cloak slip out. The man glanced sharply in the direction of the house, and then turned north along the orchard hedge, and with a certain sedulous and unseemly haste disappeared through the gate in the wattle fence.

Geraint's face darkened.—So that damned priest had been here again. These Christians seemed to be very careful in cultivating the women, and especially rich women. Geraint, standing in the doorway, saw the brown figure going hard up hill towards the woods; probably the mission-priest had left his horse up there—for he was a gentleman who rode from place to place and got his belly filled at most of them. But why—this secretiveness, this shirking of a confrontation? Neither a god nor his servant should flit by back ways.

Geraint crossed the garden. There was a hedge of Gallic roses on either side of the grass path, and in three weeks the first red buds would be bursting. The door of the chapel faced the west, and the evening sunlight shone in and showed to Geraint the feet and figure of a woman kneeling at the little altar table. The walls of the chapel were painted blue and gold, but Placida's gown was grey. She had her back to her husband, and with hands clasped and eyes closed she adored in a kind of ecstasy the sweet savour of her own soul.

Geraint stood in the doorway; his body cut off the sunlight, but since his wife's eyes were closed she was not aware of his shadow. Placida was so unaware of many things, and Geraint stood in the doorway and waited. Placida on her knees, adoring what? Herself, her new god, the poignant mystery of things? They had been man and wife ten years, and at the end of a year Geraint had realized the essential silliness of the woman he had married. He had been gentle with Placida, but silliness in the bud may become a little rank in the full flower.

His wife rose, turned and saw him. She was a short-legged, long-backed little woman, with a small Roman nose and a receding chin. She was growing plump, and plumpness did not become her. Like many silly women she was supremely sure of herself. Her smile came perilously near a smirk.

"My dear lord—welcome."

She stood like a little white candle before that smouldering torch of a man. She had given Geraint no children, and she was ceasing to give him her body—though Geraint no longer desired her. But Placida the Christian was concerned with her new prejudices and passions. She took her husband's hand.

"Will you not kneel with me, my dear?"

Her voice went tweet-tweet. She was so full of her saintliness—obstinately so, that she made love to her lord's soul. She—Placida—had seen the light, and it made her feel opulent and important. She exaggerated her meekness, but meek she was not. She lacked those secret prides; she gossiped. She let her small world know that through her—her lord—would turn to the new god. Besides, was not the new god now the respectable and official deity?

Geraint looked at his wife as he would have looked at an importunate, and unwise child.—But had she been the child he had married——! Behind her on the wall the Chi-Rho in gold caught a fragment of sunlight.—He was thinking of Guinevra. What did a man ask for, a piece of sanctified wax, or a creature who blew to him like fire?

He smiled at his wife. He neither refused nor explained but drew back from the doorway, and she, with an assumption of sweet patience, made the sign of the cross, and closed the chapel door.

"I pray for you daily, my lord."

And suddenly he looked weary.—Did she not know that there were other things? Of what use was a candle in wild and windy weather?

He said—"I am hungry."

O, carnal man; and she kept her fasts, and was becoming self-consciously prudish about things of the flesh! She walked with him mincingly to the house, hands together, eyes confronting the sunset, but within her burned a little, obstinate, pale flame. She would subdue the carnal man in Geraint, perhaps because the secret woman in her knew that the carnal man had ceased to care. She would instruct, convert—rule. Good women can fiddle at men and things with interfering fingers.

At supper he told her of the day's happenings, and of Guinevra. He did not tell her because he and Placida were of one mind in such matters, but because he knew that she would hear of the girl from the servants. He did not wish Placida to hear of her in that way. She listened brightly, her little nose in the air, complacently purblind. She asked questions.

"A goldsmith's daughter.—And soldiers—too! How—disgraceful! Poor thing.—And you left her with Cornelia."

"She is safe with Cornelia."

Placida twittered.

"You said the girl was of my faith?"

"I believe so."

"You should not have left her with that terrible old woman. You should have brought her here."

And Geraint looked strangely at his wife. Assuredly, Placida was a fool.

3

Moonlight, black water, the island with its tower and smother of fruit-blossom afloat in the profound stillness of the night. Restlessness possessed Geraint. He stood by the wooden stage and looked at the water. The moonlight made it mysterious, as mutable as life, a mirror and a masked face, a dial for the stars. Here it was black—there lambent silver. He was aware of reflections.

He had escaped from the candlelight and his wife's chatter. She had begun to talk to him of her religion like a woman shelling peas and throwing them into a basin.

Her religion—this thing that was both new and old, this new superstition that had sprung up when the old superstitions were dying?

And Geraint thought—"Am I a child? To whom do I pray or sacrifice—if I do either—not to Jove or Mithras, or Serapis or Jesus, but to the Unknown God. Are we children to whom old women tell stories?—Placida and her miracles, loaves and fishes, a man walking on the water, the dead rising. I have seen death, but never have I seen the dead come to life. I have seen no god walking, nor heard his voice. Ghosts? Illusions. The sun rises and sets, the seasons come and go.—I have seen no hand thrust out to stay the wheel. A man should be true to what he sees and does not see, but men are like frightened children in the dark, crying "Mother—mother."

The black barge lay at his feet. He stepped into it, cast off the chain, and taking the pole, thrust off for the island. Two faint ripples ran from the boat's bow, and diverging, died away behind it. Water dripped from the pole. Charon's ferry-boat? There was sudden strange laughter in him. Where did the dead go? Were the live any less blind? He looked at the tower as the barge drifted into its shadow, that strong, straight tower holding the moon like a shield. He eased the boat against the grass bank among the water-flags, and thrusting the pole into the mud to pin it there, climbed out.

Apple blossom, the smell of the night, a strange listening silence. He was wearing sandals, and he felt the grass wet with dew brushing his feet. It was as though a great net had been thrown over the trees and its pattern lay upon the grass. Was the Unknown God a fowler? Did he catch men in nets? Geraint came to the tower. It rose up straight and stark and white, and to Geraint its starkness had a beauty. Man should stand like a tower.

Somewhere he heard a bird singing, a night bird, and he stood still and listened.

And the voice of the bird sang—"Guinevra—Guinevra."

CHAPTER IV

Guinevra

❡ GUINEVRA was fresh from the bath. She put aside the curtains of the parlour and stood before Cornelia, and Cornelia on her couch by the window rolled up the scroll she was reading, and looked at the girl. She saw the burning hair coiled round the shapely head, the very still dark eyes, the poignant mouth. Guinevra was slim at the hips, less slim as to bosom and shoulders. "Assuredly," thought Cornelia, "a man should have something upon which to lay his head." Guinevra had height and straightness. You would not call her—"My pretty" or "My lamb." She did not simper or fall into attitudes. There was fine metal in the child. She was not the drooping, frightened thing of yesterday.

Cornelia nodded.

"Well, my dear, nobody has anything to be ashamed of. I have ordered my litter at ten. We still have shops in Calleva, and I shop—in spite of everything. For, no doubt you saw yesterday—that this city—is a little mad."

She pointed to a cushion on the floor.

"Sit down, my dear.—I say what I think. Youth says what it pleases.—I hear they threw stones at my Lord Geraint."

She watched the girl's face, and all that she saw was a darkening of those very dark eyes. Guinevra might be deep water. She did not break into easy ripples when an old woman dabbled with a mischievous hand.

"I will come with you—if I may."

"And chance the stones?"

34

"Do they throw stones at women?"

Cornelia chuckled.

"At ugly old women. They call me the Gorgon, my dear, but they are still a little afraid of looking me straight in the face. I'm a heathen—because I read Plato, and think Lucretius rather a fine fellow.—Well, shall we say that religion is a private affair? No doubt, as a Christian maiden——"

Guinevra looked up through the window. She was seeing the world in flower, and not a figure on a cross.

"You have been merciful to me."

"My dear, old things are mellow and merciful, wine, books, even some old women. Your religion preaches mercy—but then—it is so very young.—It is like a young man out for the first time with his sacred spouse. It is rather afraid of being laughed at.—But, tut-tut—I grow garrulous.—Well, come and shop with me.—No doubt you need a few things."

The girl looked at her red shoes.

"I have no money.—You see—poor Justus——"

She grew dark and seemed to shake off a shudder. My Lord Geraint who did things so swiftly and with the silence of death, had buried Justus with the money. Her wardrobe had gone crashing into the green wood at the heels of two frightened mules, and those men—content with the immediate plunder, had stood and laughed and shouted.

Cornelia tied up the scroll.

"You can share my purse, my dear.—I have sent for my lawyer to come and see you. Felix my freedman goes to Londinium next week, and the lawyer can go with him. Yes, if I say so—he goes.—Your affairs can be settled. The will is in the London Record Office—yes? Money is a useful thing, my dear, and only those who lack it—abuse it.—Even our dear Bishop here is discovering the virtue of property."

She thrust out her lower lip.

"Well, let us go.—You will have a Gorgon to guard you—instead of my Lord Geraint.—Yes, he has a wife who is a Christian, and a most pious creature."

Her glance was oblique.   She saw the girl's eyes flicker for a moment.   Then she sat very still, staring at her shoes. She seemed to be clasping something within herself.   Her face was secret.   And Cornelia, having rent a veil, felt that things might have been ordered more like the month of May.   This deep, dark, elvish thing with her bright head, and Placida, Placida with the eyes of a goat, a tallow candle of a woman who dribbled piety like grease! Cornelia disliked Placida, and when Cornelia disliked a person she did not spare her symbols.

Cornelia's shopping was a ceremonious affair—the procession of a goddess crowned with a mural crown. To the lions with all dogs and demagogues!   She had her high colour and a wicked eye, and more courage than most men.   Had she been Cæsar's wife, Cæsar could have gone campaigning and left the Seven Hills and the Senate and the Plebs—and especially the Plebs—to her.   Two German slaves carried her litter.   Her steward walked before it, bearing my lady's purse.   Two women came behind. Guinevra was made to hold the old lady's hand.—"Beauty and the Beast, my dear."

The courtyard gates were flung open.   The steward, a pompous person, a little uneasy, and therefore all the more pompous, marched forward with his staff of office.   They came to the centre of the city and its shops, the steward heading for the outer north ambulatory of the forum, where a goldsmith, a jeweller, money-changers and a silk-and linen-merchant traded.   Half a dozen lewd fellows were sitting at tables outside the wine-shop at the north-east corner, butcher's porters, for the shops of the butchers were in the east wing.   One of these fellows jumped up, and raising his mug, was witty.

"Hail—old dear!   Have a drop with me."

Cornelia stopped the litter.

"Carus—bring that fellow here."

Carus went—but delicately so.

"My friend—the lady would speak with you."

The fellow, swaggering and putting a finger to his nose, crossed over to the litter. And Cornelia looked at him— Cornelia smiled. She asked for her purse, and picking out a copper coin she tossed it to demos.

"Take a bath, my friend. There is the price of a bath."

The litter went on, and the casual crowd under the colonnade made way for it, for the Germans were big men. The face of Calleva was sullen. Hands made rude gestures behind the great lady's back. Cornelia, at ease on her cushions, pressed Guinevra's hand.

"See—how the people love me!"

But the shopkeepers were more urbane. They hurried out to the litter. What did my lady desire? Cornelia fanned herself. Her niece's desires—for why should not Guinevra pass as her niece?—were the desires of the moment. Cornelia looked at jewellery, while Guinevra bought slippers, night-gear, a comb, a mirror, linen, a green cloak, shoes. Her purchases were piled at the foot of Cornelia's litter. Carus, leaning with dignity upon his staff, hoped that the morning's business was over.

"Home—my lady?"

Cornelia grimaced.

"We have been nowhere. Carry me into the forum."

Carus looked worried.

"It is—very full—ahem—of the city."

"Am I not of the city?"

"Shall we go in by the north passage, my lady?"

"You are very modest, Carus, this morning. No, we will go in by the Great Gate."

And in by the main gate she went. The litter swung down the street between the butchers' shops and the Butter Market. Half a dozen women had stopped to gossip in the vestibule, and Carus, putting a solemn face to the adventure, swung his staff and gave tongue:—"Room for the Lady Cornelia." The little procession passed through to the tune of "Hoity-toity, what's she—after all? An old hag and an old heathen." The forum was crowded. People were buying meat, groceries, oysters, fish. The seats of the inner ambulatory were full. Calleva, Bishop Balthasar's Calleva, had become a city of tongues, more eager to talk than to labour. Here was demos in its best clothes; masons, carpenters, plasterers, painters, tilers, smiths, wheelwrights, basket-makers, coopers, farriers, cobblers, all waiting for oratory. The bishop and his new City Council were assembled in the Curia with the members of the guilds and brotherhoods.

Cornelia with her litter and her women, Roma Rediviva defying the new world, was a challenge to the crowd. It suffered her to pass, but not with respect. The two Germans strode stolidly; Carus tried to look more imposing and inviolable than he felt. Guinevra held fast to the imperial hand. She shrank from all these unfriendly faces, but she did not show it. Cornelia, grim and smiling, ordered the slaves to set her down at the foot of the column in the centre of the court. Calleva might growl, but it would not bite. She lay and fanned herself and talked to Guinevra.

"Above you, my dear, you will see the Genius of the City. I forget how much it cost to gild him.—The basilica, as you see, is rather new. Its predecessor was burnt when Allectus and his rebels made a last stand here. Yes, the Emperor still rules—though you might not think it. Over there you can see the offices of the Decemvirs, the Aedile, the Questor. That is the Collegium Sacerdotum, and the Taxation and Tribute Office. Yes, I understand—that most of our officials have taken a holiday. Officials are never very popular. Up above are the terraces—beloved of nursemaids and children."

She fanned herself and the crowd glared and made impolite remarks. Carus stood and perspired; the women

looked frightened, but they were more afraid of their mistress
than the crowd. It was a problem in poise, one formidable
old lady *contra mundum*. And then, one of the world's
clowns dropped from the skies, though he was by no means
a clown in his own estimation. He dashed in through the
vestibule with wild cries.

"Woe, woe—woe unto this island."

He was a hairy man and looking still more hairy in his
sheepskin. He brandished a small wooden cross. His little
mad eyes flared in a mask of hair. His legs were like
the legs of Pan, his toe-nails like barnacles, lumps of
horn. He rushed through the crowd, shouting and
sweating.

"Woe, woe.—Repent.—Anti-Christ is here.—Woe, woe,
blood and death.—Repent—repent.—I see fire—I smell
smoke. Woe, woe—to this city."

It was Hylas the Hermit hot from the woods—a very
holy man and a very dirty one. He ran around, slapping
people with his piece of wood.

"Ha," said Cornelia—"the mad dog!"

Then Hylas saw her. He came running on his horny
feet. He gathered the poison in his mouth and spat.

"Herodias—Babylonian—anathema——"

The drabble of saliva missed its mark and streaked
itself down Guinevra's gown. The crowd roared.

"The old heathen."

"Cast her out."

"Put her among the oyster-shells."

But the crowd was not to have its way, or to play
Alexandria to an elderly Hypatia. The centre door of the
basilica had opened and Bishop Balthasar appeared at the
head of a procession of priests, deacons, acolytes, consecrated virgins, catechumens, penitents, city councillors.
He stood, he saw. He raised a hand.

"Peace—peace."

His voice carried. He came sailing through the crowd
towards the litter and the saintly and hirsute hermit. Hylas,

like the Devil, was a useful grotesque with which to frighten and persuade froward people, but Hylas could make a nuisance of himself on occasions. Like a mad dog he might flesh his teeth in the wrong body. Balthasar, a stately and debonair Balthasar, came with hand raised.

"Peace, peace, Brother Hylas.—Let us not be harsh with women. Gentleness—gentleness."

Balthasar was suave, the courtier. The voice of demos might set the welkin ringing, but so often it was the voice of an ass. Balthasar chose to show his power, and especially so in the presence of the great. He stood beside the litter, two fingers of his right hand raised, sacerdos in silk. He looked at Cornelia, and he looked at the girl, and having looked at Guinevra he looked again.

"Matrona, we are simple people. We are devout people. Let not the simple be offended."

Balthasar simple! But the old lady understood him. The Church might not blink an eyelid, but it could deliver a significant and caressing gesture. She was an offence to the crowd, and deliberately so, and if Balthasar was one of those who could walk on the heads of the crowd, he was ready to let her join him in the promenade if she would walk somewhat to his liking. She smiled at Balthasar.

"I am but a poor old woman, bishop, a silly old woman. I come out to stare."

The crowd pressed close. Hylas was gnawing the end of his cross. The crowd had to be humoured as well as the lady.

"Matrona, only those are rich who give to the poor."

Applause from the crowd. Cornelia, demure as a virgin, drew her veil over her face.

"My lord bishop—is wise. One should grow old in virtue. I would not offend—dear—little children.—Carus, we go home."

She raised the hem of her palla and kissed it. Almost, she ogled the bishop. The Germans bent to the poles; Carus, rather white about the chops, made haste to profit by his mistress's humour. Balthasar stood stiff and stark, hand raised, observing Guinevra out of the slant of his eyes. The crowd exulted. Obviously, Balthasar had humbled the gorgon.

"Go in peace."

Cornelia murmured to her veil.

"But not—in pieces."

Hylas, who had been rather out of the show, let out a yell, and brandished his symbol.

"Woe—woe—to the proud, woe to the heathen——"

But Balthasar turned on him gently.

"Brother Hylas, we have planted the seed. Birds are not won with curses.—Did you not see how she covered her face?—Even the proud can be humbled."

Cornelia, holding the girl's hand, was carried past the shops of the butchers. She put back her veil. Her old eyes were grim.

"Woe to the heathen, my dear.—Your dear people— may be a little short-sighted.—The woe may be in other —stomachs if the heathen should come over the Wall."

2

Caradoc was in his smithy beating out a sword blade on the anvil when Malgo rode down the hill on his horse. Malgo came to the White Tower twice a week to fence with Geraint, for Malgo, ex-centurion of the First Cohort of the Second Legion, had been a famous player with the sword. A little, lean, quiet man with quick eyes and a grey head, he had bought with his gratuity and his savings a small estate at Vicus Flavus, a village between Turris Alba and Vindomis.

Malgo, hearing the cry of the steel between hammer and anvil, turned his horse towards the smithy. Through the doorway he could see the glow of the furnace and Caradoc's thick, hairy legs. Malgo knew when steel was

D

being hammered, and when the blade was neither sickle nor scythe.

Caradoc, stripped to the waist, was girt with nothing but a leather apron. The muscles showed in his back. One hand held the pincers while the other wielded the hammer. A big crock full of water stood beside the anvil. The clangour of Caradoc's blows filled the smithy, and he did not hear the padding of Malgo's horse.

The centurion watched him, smiling in his eyes. He waited until a pause came before he spoke.

"Who gave you the licence to forge swords?"

Caradoc swung his head like a boar's. He laughed; he showed his teeth.

"None of your little perfumed gentlemen who sit in chairs. We do what needs be.—One might say"—and he plunged the blade into the water pot—"that you will be back in harness, Malgo, or I'm no prophet."

This was a long speech for Caradoc. He ran a thumb along the edge of the blade.

"My lord was asking for you."

"I am here."

"We want your village smith. Can he do anything but hammer nails?"

Malgo reached out for the sword blade.

"Give it here.—Our fellow was an armourer in the Sixth. Yes, not bad, Caradoc. A little heavy."

"Not for my fist."

"Oh, it's to be yours, is it?—Stabbing's better than slashing, let me tell you.—Look over the top of your shield and jab a man's throat.—I could show you."

Caradoc rolled his big head.

"You'll be showing us, brother, or again—I'm no prophet. Hallo, here's my lord coming. You should have seen him spitting pigs on the Pontes road the other morning."

Malgo passed the sword blade back to the smith and turned his horse. Geraint, with a boar-spear in his hand,

and the hound beside him, was coming over the grass to
the smithy.   Malgo rode down to meet him; swung out of
the saddle, stood straight and saluted.

Geraint and the old soldier looked into each other's
eyes.   There was more than goodwill between them, more
than the game of leather coats and wooden swords.

"I wanted you, Malgo."

"It is—our—day, sir."

"In other ways—than that."

Geraint called a groom who was standing in the gateway of the stable court—"Take the captain's horse."   He
went with Malgo through the main gate into the forecourt
and garden, and clapped his hands for the house servants.
Wine was brought to them, and when Malgo had drunk,
Geraint looked at the windows, and laid a hand on the
centurion's shoulder.

"What I have to say—is not for the ears of servants."

Nor was it for the ears of Placida.   With the boar-
spear under his arm, and the dog still at his side he went
down with Malgo to the grove below the vineyard which
held the altar of Sylvanus.   The altar stood in a little glade,
and at full noon in summer the sunlight fell upon it, but
at this hour it was in the shade.   A semicircular stone seat
had been built above and behind the altar, and from this
seat the pool, the island, the White Tower and the hollow
of the valley were visible.

Geraint paused in front of the altar.   Upon its face
someone had daubed the Chi-Rho in red paint, and the
name of the woodland god had been cut away with a chisel.
Placida's orders.   In the hollow of the focus lay a little
bronze fish, not as an offering, but as a triumphant symbol.
Geraint said nothing.   His Unknown God was still veiled
and secret in spite of the officious meddling of a woman.

He sat down on the seat with Malgo beside him, and
the hound lay at his feet.   He looked long and steadily at
the valley with its island and pool and tower.

"Well, what news, Malgo?"

The centurion, leaning forward, elbows on knees, saw all that Geraint saw.

"Trouble in the north."

He began to tell Geraint all that he had been able to learn from Victorinus—the optio at Vindomis. The station at Vindomis held three men and a boy, twenty sets of arms and little else. The Second Legion at Isca was a thousand men below its fighting strength, and in poor fettle. Its Legate might be called an old lady. The Cymri were restless. At Deva, the Twentieth Legion, Victoria Victrix, was not much stronger than the Second, and was training a thousand young recruits. Moreover, the Second had two cohorts at Rhutupiæ, reinforcing the sailors and marines. The auxiliaries who held the Great Wall were—contrary to all tradition—considered to be more reliable than the legions.

Malgo did not like the look of the weather.

"Discipline is not what it was. They tell me that officers are afraid to use their sticks."

"You used your vine-staff, Malgo?"

"Sometimes it was more persuasive than my sword, sir—especially when men faltered."

"Did you have deserters in your day?"

"A few—but not by the score."

If Malgo had things to tell Geraint, Geraint had things to tell to Malgo. What of Calleva, its bishop, and its mob? There were the Saxons on the sea, and what was far more serious, the Saxon settlement in the forest country, on the south coast between Regnum and Anderida. Certainly, Rome had taken to herself barbarians, and she had made them Romans, but a Saxon was not a Gaul or a Spaniard or a Rhinelander. He was a savage. And that fool mob at Calleva was talking of turning cobblers into kings, and of transforming the old territory of the Attrebates into a sort of toy republic with Balthasar as its president.

"The curia full of noisy fools, Malgo. They are forgetting how to keep their streets clean. They leave the

gates unguarded. They crowd in the forum and talk.—
When the gods wish to destroy——"

He traced a line on the turf with the point of his boar-
spear.

"Let that be the Wall. Let us suppose that the men
from the north have broken through, and that the frontier
cohorts are either cut up or pinned in their forts. They
send up the legions from Isca and Deva and Rhutupiæ."

He drove his spear into the turf to mark Isca and Deva
and the Kentish station.

"You see—as well as I do—how the map would shape.
All the troops gone north, the west unguarded, nothing
but the ships between us and the sea-wolves. The whole
south defenceless, its forests full of broken men.—Supposing
the Cymri were to rush in, and the Saxons to land the
crews of a dozen ships.—What have we to count on?"

And Malgo answered—"Nothing."

Geraint was silent for a while.

"You know—and I know, Malgo, what that would
mean. Fire, outrage, plunder, farms and country houses
going up in flames. Cattle driven off or killed. Women——
Yes, Calleva and other cities might be saved by their walls,
and yet—I doubt it. The whole south overrun, burnt
out, raped, looted."

He pointed with his spear.

"That white tower.—How many years is it since the
first Gerontius built it?—And now, it is smothered up in
fruit trees.—This place is good to me, Malgo—this green
valley and the fields and the woods—and my home.—I
love it. And shall I sit still—and wait—for the—thing to
happen?—Are you—going to sit still in your farm-house,
with your wife and your three girls——?"

He lowered his spear and looked at the old soldier;
Malgo's lips were thin and his nose pinched at the nostrils.

"I shall fight, Malgo—to keep death and worse out
of this valley. And you——?"

Malgo nodded.

"I am with you, lord."

"Malgo—you shall help me to make soldiers—as well as swords. If the emperor cannot help us——"

"Will the emperor quarrel with us for saving what is ours?—I could raise fifteen men in the village, and six of them are old soldiers."

"And I—a score or so. We should need harness, arms."

Malgo laughed grimly.

"Soldiers are not made in a month, my lord—but there is good stuff here. As for arms and harness—we can borrow twenty sets from Vindomis."

Geraint smiled at him.

"What will Victorinus say—if we plunder his armoury?"

"Make Victorinus a tribune, my lord.—We old dogs still have our harness.—But what are fifty men?—We should cast our net wider."

Geraint stood up.

"There are the Aquilas at Fontes, Gawaine of the Black Valley. We might get another fifty men with them."

Malgo looked even more grim.

"Just one cohort—of country bumpkins—begging your pardon, sir."

Said Geraint: "Country bumpkins might fight, Malgo, rather than see their women—— And if they run—you and I shall be left—to the wolves."

CHAPTER V

The Bishop and the Lady

¶ It was very early, and mist lay in the valley when Geraint rode out. The tops of the fruit trees on the island showed above the mist, and the white vapour spread as far as the grove of Sylvanus, but the domes of the high woods on the hills were beginning to flash and to glitter. The valley was full of the singing of birds, and as Geraint rode up the farther slope rabbits scurried for cover. He was alone with the stealth of the morning.

The beech woods were dim and silent as death. A narrow ride with its grass all dew ran south between the great trees. Here the world still seemed asleep. Not a dead leaf stirred in the forest floor, not a live leaf on the branches. The ground rose and fell, and before him Geraint saw other woods towering like misty cliffs. He rode armed, in lorica and steel casque, his sword at his side, a spear over his shoulder. The lorica had been his grandfather's, and the metal plates were gilded. His helmet carried cheek-pieces. The white horse's harness was of red leather.

The beech woods extended for two miles. The last wooded ridge rose ahead of him, beyond it lay downland, and as he topped the slope, the trees became full of broken light. It splashed the grey trunks, and suddenly he saw a great yellow sun hanging above a world of hills and valleys. The landscape was silver, the sky pale blue. And a little sound came to him out of the high silence, a sound that was both plaintive and joyous, the notes of a shepherd's pipe.

47

Clear of the trees Geraint saw the shepherd and his sheep, and the little hut of skins and branches in a grassy hollow. The shepherd wore a sheepskin and leggings of leather. He was sitting on another sheepskin, with his dog at his feet, the fingers of his right hand stopping and unstopping the vents of the pipe. The yellow sunlight fell full upon the flock. Lambs were sucking, or nosing their mother's dugs. Two youngsters were frisking and leaping. The grass, still glistening with dew, was stippled with blue and yellow flowers. In the valley below the white vapour was wearing thin.

It was the dog who discovered Geraint. He was up, barking and growling, and the ewes, lifting meek heads, gazed at the man on the white horse, and did not seem to fear him. One or two called to their lambs. The shepherd was on his feet, and telling the dog to lie down. Both the sheep and the shepherd were Geraint's.

He walked his horse forward.

"The pride of the morning to you, Coel."

The shepherd was quite a young man with a mop of wheat-coloured hair and blue eyes.

"And to you, lord."

"Is all well?"

"All is well, lord.—I have not lost another lamb since that snow in April."

He stood holding his pipe in his right hand, and looking up at Geraint. His life was a very peaceful life. There were no wolves in these parts, and marauding dogs and men were rare. This lad had never seen blood spilt in anger. The great grey hills and the beech woods were serene. His blue eyes looked at Geraint. Why did his lord ride armed?

Geraint felt that look. But why trouble the lad, or put fear into his yellow head? On such a morning as this violence and fear seemed far away.

"Your lambs look well, Coel."

The lad smiled.

"Good weather, lord, great weather."

"May it stay so.—One word, Coel; up here you can see the hills at night."

"I can see miles and miles, lord."

"Watch.—If you should see fire on the hills, come down and tell us."

"Yes, lord."

Geraint smiled at him.

"The fire will be far away.—I am for Fontes.—You can play me on with your pipe."

Geraint rode eastward along the ridge before turning down into the valley. He came to a high and grassy bluff with banks and ditches encircling it, an old grass fort. The view from the fort was vast, hill upon hill, with the valley clefts all shadow. Geraint sat his horse there and looked east. He saw water flashing as the sun climbed, glittering woods, a dim horizon. Over there lay Calleva, and in Calleva Guinevra would be putting up her shining hair.

2

It was so.—Guinevra's window looked towards the east, and her room was an upper room and in a little wing apart. It had a staircase of its own and two doors, a floor of polished oak, walls coloured yellow and painted with swags and garlands of vine leaves. Below her upper window lay Cornelia's privy garden: grass, paths of pebbles, clipped box trees and yews, four parterres spread like mosaic round a fountain, all shut in by a high flint wall.

Guinevra looked out of her window at the sun and across the roofs of Calleva. She could see the pediments of temples, the roof of the basilica, the little golden Genius on his pillar. She let her hair lie over her shoulders, and the sunlight creep into her bosom.

Another day, and what should she do with it? Say
her prayers, go to the bath, sit sewing or reading to Cornelia,
walk in the garden? What did she dream of and desire?
She sat down at her dressing-table, took her mirror in her
hand and gazed. Was she comely? Vanity of vanities!—
But in the spring of the year a blood-red flower had sprung
up in a night, and her to-days were not yesterday.—What
was he doing now? Would she see him again? What was
his wife like?

She shook her hair as though shaking off certain
thoughts. He was a great lord—and she—— Yes, and
certain thoughts were sinful.—But could she help that?
Yet—dignity! And with an air of young severity she
began to dress her hair, plaiting it and rolling it about her
head. Cornelia had offered her a woman, but somehow
she did not want to be touched and watched by a slave.
Strange moods.—Why did she blow hot and cold, and go
red within whenever Cornelia spoke of Geraint? Foolishness.—Cornelia was a tease. She spoke much and often
of Geraint, and Guinevra—trying to appear casual—listened
with both her ears.

Yes, Cornelia was mischievous.

"Don't you want to go to church, my dear?—They
will not throw stones at you for going to church."

Cornelia burned incense and poured a libation daily to
tradition in her own lararium. It was rather difficult to
salute Divus Imperator when the emperor was a Christian,
but, like Geraint, Cornelia thought for herself. She read
the philosophers; she belonged to a world that was old,
and shrugged shrewd shoulders, and washed itself well and
smiled gently at the shadowy shapes of dead gods. To
Cornelia Christ was but another god, and already his servants were making him one of many. Saints, virgins,
martyrs, Saint This—Saint That. The Christians had pur-
loined temples and some of the pomps and ceremonies
of paganism. God grew out of god. Christ might
last a hundred years, or a thousand—and vanish like

Mithras. Faith! What was faith but wishing what you wished?

Cornelia was shrewd. She saw the girl's quick colour, her slanting and mysterious glances, the way she looked down under her lashes at her knees. Guinevra was growing deep.—But what a pity! For Cornelia would have said to her—"Love, burn, exult, my child, for there is nothing like love in the world," but in the middle of the magic mirror stood Placida; fussy, complacent, goat-eyed, short-legged Placida with her egg-like face and eggy voice. Drat Placida!—Certainly, ten years ago she had been quite a likeable girl, if a little smug—but now—she was just Placida, a good woman who went sniffling through the world telling people what they should do —according to Placida—and seeing that they did it.— Placida ought to join the choir of Balthasar's consecrated virgins, Caritas, Pia and Fidelis, three mewking cats who went about looking as though they had missed the cream.

But Cornelia was empress in her own house. Every morning after breaking fast the household assembled in the corridor outside the lararium for the daily ritual. Guinevra was spared that.—Then, Cornelia went the round of the house and gardens; she inspected the kitchen, the servants' quarters, the still room, the store.—Discipline, my dear, cleanliness and order; such virtues can be sustained without crying for the stars. Cornelia was as severe with herself as with any of her servants. She walked for an hour, morning and evening, in her garden. She even disciplined her chin.

Long ago it had threatened to double itself, but that was not its principal sin.—It was proposing to grow a beard, straggling grey hairs. Such insolence was not to be tolerated. Cornelia had a prejudice against being fussed and pawed by her woman. She sat on her couch, with a mirror and a pair of tweezers.

She poked fun at herself and at the operation.

"Age has to suffer many things—but I will not humour a beard."

Watching her benefactress peering in a mirror and groping for hairs, Guinevra was moved to secret laughter —and an impulse of affection.

"Let me—serve."

"You, my dear?—Beauty plucking the Beast!"

"You have done many things for me."

"Tut-tut. But you have soft hands. That's a fad of mine. I can't stomach common hands."

So, Guinevra sat on a stool, and with the bronze tweezers extracted hairs. She was a little too hesitant about it to begin with, for each tweak hurt. Cornelia, with her chin set, and her blue eyes closed, admonished her.

"Don't be afraid, my dear.—It is kinder to be stern."

But the morning was to provide other ministrations. The bell rang in the janitor's lodge, and they heard the sound of the great gate opening.

"Visitors.—Look out of the window, my dear."

Guinevra, tweezers in hand, ran to the window.—Someone from the White Tower, perhaps?—She looked, and her little dream was dashed.

"The bishop."

"Balthasar?"

"Yes, and alone."

Cornelia looked grim. Also, she looked in her mirror, and swung her feet off the couch.

"This should be a solemn occasion, my dear.—This is an honour that I have not sought."

Balthasar was received in the atrium, and with all the politeness due to a dignitary, for Cornelia held that a man of much self-importance cannot be accorded too much importance. Let silk meet silk. She smiled upon him.

"You honour me—unexpectedly, my lord."

Balthasar bowed to her. In those earlier days the Christian cleric had not evolved a multitude of vestments.

Balthasar wore a white tunic, a violet pænula, and sandals. He was a handsome man and he knew it, and believed that the outside of the pot is not to be despised. You might talk homespun to the poor, but in society you were with your equals, and you put on silk.

"May this house be blessed."

He looked at Cornelia, and he looked at Guinevra, but obliquely so as though it was not seemly that he should look at the girl too closely. In fact he turned his face a little from the fire. It was wise to assume coldness.

"Peace to you, my daughter."

Cornelia was jocund, bland. She did not miss much on a face or in a pair of eyes, and Balthasar was like a man looking out of a window and pretending not to see that which was well worth seeing. But how much did he wish to see, and what was his eminence's business? She gave Guinevra a glance, and Guinevra, eyes lowered, made her obeisance, and left them together.

Cornelia looked straight at Balthasar.

"Is it peace—or the sword, my lord?"

Her abruptness was not unexpected, and Balthasar gave her look for look.

"I am a man of peace."

"May I clap my hands for wine?"

He chose to be austere.

"I do not touch it—save as a priest."

He turned at his leisure and looked at the curtains of the atrium, and Cornelia understood him. Balthasar came as an ambassador, if as a self-appointed one, and vulgar ears should not listen behind curtains to the voices of authority. She led the way along the corridor to her parlour, and closed both door and window.

"Be seated, Balthasar."

She pointed to a cushioned stool, and arranged herself on her couch, covering her ankles carefully. That was a symbolic gesture. And what had Balthasar to uncover?

"Now, my lord bishop."

Balthasar sat erect, as though occupying the praeses chair in the centre of a church's apse. Circumlocutions did not count with Cornelia. She was like an old centurion in a brazen helmet. She looked him straight in the face.

The priest's mouth was sharp, like a line cut in stone.

"These are difficult days, matrona."

Difficult! How obvious! And who was making them difficult in Calleva but this turbulent priest and his people? The houses of the more wealthy citizens were shut up, and their owners had passed to their country villas or to towns that were less turbulent. Taxation might be an abomination and very ruthless, but it was a less disturbing neighbour than a fanatical mob.

"Difficult—indeed, bishop."

Balthasar had the air of committing a body to the grave.

"The empire is dying."

"You speak as a prophet?"

He spread his hands, palms upward.

"A new world, matrona, new ways.—I have seen the darkness spreading—but we—who serve Christ—carry a lantern. My light is not your light, matrona, and yet—are we not both—Romans?"

"You speak as a Roman?"

"May I speak—as one on the edge of a dark sea? I offer you the truth—as I see it."

"Say what you will.—I do not tattle."

His face had a narrow sheen, a stark edge.

"Men—deified.—No—I will not blaspheme against your faith. Yes, and you will answer me—'To-day—the Emperor is a Christian.'—But, matrona—behind the emperor—is Christ. The heathen swarm. Can man prevail? —I doubt it.—But God can prevail.—I believe in God the Father, God the Son, and God—the Holy Spirit."

She looked at the man, and the handsome adventurer was lost in the seer. Yes, there was more in Balthasar than she had allowed. The priest's face could shine like a sword.

"Your god—is—emperor, bishop?"

He looked at her searchingly.

"When storms come—men seek a light and a rock.—
I do not blaspheme. Emperors and kings become dust.
But if we found our kingdom, our temporal state upon—
God, it shall endure.—At night—I sit and think and hear
the wind moaning. Souls have to be saved, and not souls
alone.—I am a compassionate man, matrona. Do I wish to
see this island given to blood and death?—You may think
of the world as a slave world; I think of it as a world of
children—in Christ."

She thrust out her lip.

"Your children can be—very unruly children, bishop."

He spread his hands.

"What would you? — Confusion — everywhere, old
things breaking up—those who were rulers—ceasing to
rule.—Your mob, matrona, is a crowd of children, ignorant
children, rough children. If I seek to school them—is that
easy?—Patience, subtlety, faith. Are not children—envious
and quarrelsome?—Should not we who are wiser work for
other ends?"

She began to understand him.

"You offer me a seat on the curia?"

He smiled. He became suave.

"You are one of the few of the old world, matrona,
whose hands are strong enough to help in shaping the new.
—In these days of confusion—those who build—build for
God.—I am a bigot, but I am a bigot—with ideas.—Possibly
—I ask less of you than you would ask of me."

She sat thinking, that lip of hers thrust out.

"Just—what—is it that you need, bishop—my soul—
or my money?"

His face darkened.

"Matrona——!"

She looked at him slantwise.

"Let us not be too—delicate, Balthasar.—I know something—of mobs.—They must be fed, kept in a good temper.

—You will think me a scurrilous old woman—but is not—a crowd's god its belly?"

His face grew still more dark. He made a sign with his right hand.

"Behind me—Satan."

Cornelia gave him her grim smile.

"I think I am too old, Bishop, to change my clothes, and to put on new fashions.—Rome was made great by the centurion's vine-stick.—Will your staff—serve?"

He rose. He looked at her meaningly.

"Think—well—of these things, matrona.—I have said what—I have said.—I have come to you as a man of peace."

She gave him a blue stare.

"Am I to buy peace, Balthasar?"

He walked to the door, faced about, saluted her.

"Matrona, those who are not with us are against us."

3

At Fontes, Geraint found old Aquila in the meadow above the mill watching a young horse being broken in by a groom. The young Aquilas—Constantine and Chlorus—had gone hawking. The Fontes folk were great hawk-trainers, horse-masters and hunters, and the old man could still stand to his boar. He was a fierce old gentleman with a face like an eagle's, a patch of bright colour on either cheek, his eyes brittle and bright under bristling eyebrows.

"Ha, my friend—are you going to the wars?"

Geraint dismounted.

"I will ask you another question. Should war come to us, or should we meet it—over the hill?"

Old Aquila watched the young horse going round the grass. The groom had him in hand; his wildness was chastened.

"War—and rumour of war, Geraint.—My youngsters are out with their hawks."

"I want you and your young men, Aquila."

"The devil you do!"

"And I think you know it. Is any man wiser in telling the weather—than you?"

The lord of Fontes nodded.

"Those hunters of men and wenches beyond the Wall, what! And those damned cousins of ours, the Cymri.—Well, what's in the wind?"

"It blows—or may blow from every quarter, Aquila.—Shall we talk here—or?"

"No, come to the house. Ten miles is worth a drink."

Fontes was a rugged place, all thatch and timber, and as Geraint looked at it he thought how the house and its out-buildings would burn. It had no defences, not even a stockade. It was the house of a man who had ridden and hunted where he pleased, and neither man nor beast had said him nay. But he did not talk velvet to Aquila. He gave him the bearskin, the lore of the wolf-pack, and old Aquila understood such language.

"How many men could I raise?—Twenty.—Six of them can use the bow. Yes, we are horse-people.—My lads."

He looked fierce.

"Seventeen and nineteen, Geraint.—Mere whelps.—But if I told them to stay at home—they would fly in my face like a couple of hawks."

"We may not need the lads."

"What needs be—needs be.—They're not soft."

"Have you arms?"

"Boar-spears, bows, an old sword or two."

"You have a smith."

"And no metal."

"I can give you metal.—I have my smith at work, and Malgo is sending me an old armourer from his village.—I go on to see Gawaine. He has men who can ride."

Old Aquila looked hard at Geraint.

E

"It will come, you think?"

Geraint was slow to answer.

"I feel it in the wind."

"And when——?"

"It might come—to-morrow.—In the spring of the year, my friend, when men make love."

"Hot blood."

"And the spilling of blood.—Man lusts after three things, Aquila."

"I'll name them.   Women, plunder, god."

Geraint nodded.

"And the gods of the wild men are bloody gods."

From Fontes Geraint rode north-west into the Black Valley.   It was called the Black Valley because there was much moorland here, heather and pines and gorse, with scattered birch trees and dwarf oaks.   He found Gawaine and his people keeping the festival of Mel, a country goddess who was worshipped in the valley.   Mel dealt with the Bees, and the setting of fruit, and betrothals, for in the country men clung to the old gods.   In the cities they crowded to the new.   Geraint's horse was taken from him, and he sat in an arbour of green boughs with Gawaine and his lady, and drank honey-ale and ate new bread and venison.   The valley danced round the Pole of Mel, a young pine tree topped with a bee-skep and hung with flowers.   And to Geraint it seemed to him graceless to speak of violent and unhappy things on such a day, but when he mounted his horse, Gawaine walked with him up the hill. Geraint spoke to Gawaine of what was in his heart, and Gawaine listened.   He was wiser than Geraint knew.

Gawaine said—"Had you not come to me I should have come to you.   My men know what I know.   They may dance to-day, but they will stand and fight to-morrow—if needs be."

It was agreed between them that if bad news should come from the north or the west, Geraint, Gawaine and the Aquilas would get their men together and join forces, and if any warning reached Geraint he would light a fire on the hill where the old earth fort stood. They would rally there.

Geraint rode home, and entering the White Valley from the west he saw it with the sun behind him—very sweet and peaceful. Cattle were grazing. A girl was driving cows home to be milked. Three hinds were hoeing wheat in a field.—Well, to-morrow Malgo was to ride over and begin drilling these fellows.—He found himself listening for the sound of Caradoc's hammer, and presently he heard it, but Malgo could have told him that Caradoc was not hammering sword blades.

Geraint came to the smithy, and dismounting, he left the white horse standing, and went in. The smith was at his furnace, heating a bar of iron, and on the bench lay two iron candlesticks and a cross.

"What is this, Caradoc?"

The smith looked glum.

"The lady's orders, lord.—I obey."

With the tongs Caradoc withdrew the red metal from the forge.

"Four candlesticks for my lady's chapel, and a cross for the gable. She came—lord—soon after you had ridden out."

Geraint was angry.

"And you put the swords aside?"

"I did what I was bid."

Geraint went straight to the house, for a servant had run out to take his horse, but Placida was not in the house. He found her in the chapel. She was kneeling, but he was in no temper to humour a woman on her knees.

"My orders to Caradoc are my orders.—Leave well alone."

Placida was pert with him.

"I must have lights here.—And why does the man make swords?"

"By my orders—wife."

"Swords! How silly!—What do we need with swords?"

He looked at her darkly.

"You do not understand.—Let that suffice.   No more orders to Caradoc or any other of my men.—Remember."

She got to her feet and flounced past him out of the chapel.

"Am I a child or a fool, my lord?"

Geraint let her go in silence.   She was most certainly a fool, and that worst sort of fool, a pious one.

CHAPTER VI

In the Night

¶ CORNELIA did not trust her letter to the post. She tied up the tablet in its box with stout thread, sealed it, and calling in the boy who was to carry it, she told him to hide the tablet under his tunic.

"Ask my lord Geraint for a seal from his ring, Lud, and if you come back safely with it you shall have a silver penny."

The letter was safer with the boy than it would have been with one of Cornelia's house-servants, and for other reasons than she knew, and the boy, dodging out of the west gate with a party of charcoal burners and their asses, came to the White Valley soon after noon. The child was dusty, and had covered the last two miles bare footed, having broken the latchet of one of his shoes.

He was brought to Geraint, a bright lad with a snub nose and freckles, and somewhat primed with self-importance.

"The Lady Cornelia salutes you, lord."

He produced his letter-case, and before breaking the seal, Geraint looked the lad over. He was holding his shoes in his left hand.

"Fifteen miles on foot?"

"Yes, lord."

"Hungry?"

"Yes, lord.—And may I have my lord's seal to take back with me?"

Geraint smiled at him.

"You are hot for the road, my lad, but enough for to-day.   Go and eat and sleep.   See that he is well looked to, Rual."

Geraint went apart to read Cornelia's letter.   He took it with him to the Grove of Sylvanus.   This thing had come from the house where Guinevra breathed and moved.   Had she touched it?—He broke the seal, opened the leaves of the box, and looked at the tablet upon which Cornelia's firm hand had stabbed her message with characteristic firmness.

"My lord—greetings.
"I will begin with what is pleasant."

And Geraint smiled.   She wrote of Guinevra.   Guinevra was this, Guinevra was that.—But more froward things were to follow.

"I am somewhat shut up here, my friend, like an old sorceress on an island.   Alarms and excursions, new worlds and new fashions.   If I am shrewd, and I am— I do not write all that might be written.   A certain holy man waxeth big.   At Calleva—we are recruiting a Christian legion—butchers, shop-boys and what not, with staves and hammers and old iron on their shoulders, parading on the pomerium.   We have a standard; we drill.   An old pot of a sergeant bellows orders.—Almost, we propose to march on Rome.

"If you could ride hither in safety—your proud face would be welcome—but—we—do not welcome patricians and pagans.—I stay on.—They can carry me out in the washing basket if they choose, but I will not run.

"Guinevra salutes you.   She goes with me to Aquæ Sulis—when I choose to go."

Geraint was in the shadow of the trees, and this letter of Cornelia's seemed part of the shadows.   Calleva arming and drilling its mob!—The fools!   And yet Balthasar the Bishop was doing only what he and his friends were doing, with their eyes turned to the Cymric Marches and the sea.

But this priest leading his flock to battle? Was it against the wild men that Balthasar proposed to raise a shield, or was this to be war of another spirit, the city crowd against the country?

Geraint stood thinking.

He would go to Calleva before the week was out, and see things for himself.

But things fell out otherwise. Guinevra's bedroom on the upper floor with its little private staircase and double doors was shut away from the rest of the house. She was a deep sleeper, as youth should be, and when she woke on that May morning and saw the sun shining at her window, she could suppose that the day would be like all other days. She was happy in this house, and perhaps a little proud of being in it, and growing fond of its mistress, for the old Gorgon had a warm and most understanding heart.—Moreover, had not my lord Geraint placed her here, and had not Cornelia written him a letter, and might not that letter bring him to Calleva?

The house was very quiet, but then Cornelia loved silence and order, and held that idle noise was stupidity. Guinevra rose, washed and dressed. The garden below her window was as quiet as the house. She went down the stairs, expecting to find a servant cleaning the mosaic floor of the vestibule. She saw no servant, nor did she hear any sound of life. Strange! She went quickly along the corridor, but all the rooms were empty; nothing had been touched. She was perplexed; a little frightened. Had she left her bed an hour too early? Returning to the stairs she ascended to the corridor of the upper floor. The same silence, the same stillness, and suddenly her eyes grew big, for she could see the door of Cornelia's room standing open, a post of the bed, and bed-clothes trailing on the floor.

Her impulse was to cry out.

"Cornelia—Cornelia!"

The silence held, and she went swiftly to that doorway and looked in. The room was empty, but beyond those trailing bed-clothes she could see no sign of violence.   A cupboard door hung open.   Cornelia's slippers lay where she had left them under a chair.

And Guinevra was afraid.   What had happened here in the night while she was sleeping?   She ran down the stairs and out through the open door into the courtyard.   She saw that the courtyard gate was open, and a man in a white smock was at work on one of the gates.

She went down to the gate.   The man, brush in one hand, an earthenware pot of paint in the other, turned and smiled at her.   Dame Cornelia had been constrained to leave many things behind in Calleva, and this comely piece was one of them.—But did not the girl know?

"Good morning, sister."

He was a black-chinned, broad-faced wag of a fellow. He could wink.

"Painting you a new sign, my dear.   How do you like it?"

She saw that he was painting a white cross on the gate. He stood back and eyed it, head on one side.

"The mansion is a little quiet this morning.   Yes, the old lady left in the night.   They tell me that the property has been taken over for the benefit of our good women. Hence—this sacred symbol."

She stood very still, looking at him.

"I was asleep.—But, tell me——"

"The lady has gone on a holiday.   Her physician ordered it for the good of her health."

"Cornelia is not dead?"

The man laughed.

"Dead, my dear! No, very much alive—I should say, and kicking. Ambrosius the Deacon and the gentleman of the Fish Porters' Guild conducted her to the west gate of the city and wished her a happy journey.—But, listen, the saints arrive."

He poked his head round a gate pillar, and straightway became ostentatiously busy with paint pot and brush.

Guinevra heard the sound of singing, the voices of men and of women chanting as they came towards the house of Cornelia. She drew back from the gate. Her whole world had changed in a night, and what should she do with this new world? Cornelia bundled out of Calleva like a woman of ill-fame! But why had they not wakened her, and let her go with Cornelia? Had Calleva become a cage? She went quickly to the house; she had not broken her fast—but her hunger could wait. She would slip up to her room, gather a few things together in a basket, and escape.—But whither?

The chanting came nearer. She had reached the portico, and she paused there and turned to look back. She saw the man who was painting the gate put his pot and brush down, and stand in an attitude of careful reverence, hands together, head bowed. The figure of Bishop Balthasar appeared in the gateway. In his right hand he carried a basin of consecrated oil. The whole procession trailed behind him, deacons, acolytes, Pia, Fidelis and Caritas and sundry other good women. Balthasar held up a hand and the singing ceased.

Dipping a finger in the oil he marked the gates. "*In nomine Patris et Filii et Spiritus Sancti.*"

Guinevra stood still. The procession had moved forward again. Balthasar's eyes were fixed upon her; they seemed to hold her there on the steps of the portico. Balthasar was master here. She felt suddenly afraid of the priest, but move she could not. Balthasar was a pair of eyes in which she divined deep, dark, mysterious things.

He stopped at the first step, between the red pillars of the portico.

"My daughter, have no fear. The powers of darkness have been cast out."

"Alleluia," bleated Pia, Fidelis and Caritas in chorus.

Balthasar dipped a finger in the oil.

"Kneel, my daughter."

Her legs surrendered. She knelt on the stones at his feet.

"Thou—who art a Christian, my daughter, shall be signed with the sign, even as this heathen house is consecrated.—That which hath dwelt in the house of darkness— needeth the light."

With his oily finger he traced a cross on Guinevra's forehead. The holy women looked on with approving disapproval.

"Virgin, orphan—we claim thee once more as a child of the Church.—In thine innocence thou didst accept communion with the unbeliever.—We lay upon thee seven days of penitence. Thou shalt abide here with these good women. Go to thy chamber, my child, and pray."

Pia, Fidelis and Caritas raised their faces to heaven. "Alleluia—alleluia."

2

Dame Cornelia with her skirts tucked up, perspiring, dusty, but indomitable, used no such saintly language to her own soul. To be taken from your bed at midnight and bundled out of your house and through the streets and out of the city by gentlemen of the baser sort were matters to be met with dreadful silence. Her escort had made fun of the old lady.

"How far is it to Aquæ Sulis—Jack?"

"It will be a long walk for the old broomstick, brother."

"And she'll need a bath—at the end of it.—You will have lost some fat, Mother Cornelia, by the time you get to Aquæ Sulis."

There had been guards at the west gate, and Cornelia's gentlemen had swapped jokes with them.

"The lady is going to the bath—soldiers. Got your strigil, old dear?"

"And the bottle of ointment?"

"And clean clothes?—You will be a bit sweaty by the time you get there."

With laughter and ironic loutings they had thrust her and her one faithful servant out into the night. The rest of the household had been in the conspiracy, and in losing their mistress, such as were slaves had embraced freedom. Which, after all, was human. The gate had thundered to, muffling more laughter, and not till then had Cornelia uttered a word.

"We will walk, Martha."

Walk indeed, and whither? The scared Martha had been feeling more like fainting.

"But where do we walk to, matrona?"

"Where?—To Corinium, to Gleva, to Isca—to Rome —if necessary."

The woman had put her hands to her head and begun to whimper.

"But in the dead of night, in the dark, matrona."

"Shall we be devoured by lions?"

"But I was never good at walking, lady, and I have corns."

Cornelia had set her jaw at the night.

"Corns!—Much better have courage.—Forward."

The night march along the south-west road to Vindomis had been an affair of halts and exhortations. Cornelia had paraded her garden, but not for twenty years had she walked a mile along a road. But she was as grim as Cæsar, and as silent. Martha had flopped on the grass beside the road; Martha had asserted that she could not take another step, and Cornelia had assured her—that corns or no corns— she would go on walking.

"Get up, woman—or I shall leave you."

That had proved a sufficient persuasion, though Martha had complained and creaked.

"O, my poor feet!—Do they call that a Christian's act, turning us out of house and home in the middle of the night? —What's the world coming to?"

Cornelia had consoled her by asserting that by persisting in the business of walking they would come to my Lord

Geraint's place. Fifteen miles or so. What were fifteen miles to a determined and angry old woman? As for Master Balthasar and his flock, let them bleat canticles in Calleva until such a day—— But she shut her mouth and trudged.

Seven miles along the road—Martha and her infirmities —both physical and spiritual—had fallen by the wayside. Cornelia, sitting like some outraged Dea Mater under a thorn tree, had allowed Martha to sleep. After all, the good creature had been faithful, even if she lacked spirit. Cornelia, with her cloak over her head, had watched the dawn come up. The brightness of its brow had made her think of a girl's head. Guinevra? What had happened to Guinevra? Had the girl known?—But—of course not. And why had they refused to let her have the girl? Authority had stepped in and sundered them. Authority? Balthasar.—Ha—there might be more here than showed on the surface. The girl was an heiress. The girl was very comely. And Balthasar's face looking out of a window, and both seeing and not seeing? Was Guinevra a hostage to fate and to the sacerdotal fancy?

Cornelia had got to her feet, and nudged Martha with one of them.

"Up—woman.—We will break our fast and wash our feet in the White Valley. You have been snoring for two hours."

Geraint had ridden out very early to meet Malgo when he encountered the two old women hobbling down the hill. Martha was bent nearly double, but her mistress confronted the day with a fiery face and uncompromising eyes.

"Good morning, my lord.—You see two pilgrims."

Geraint was off his horse. He saw Martha flop on the grass, and sit moaning, but Cornelia stood like Rome.

"Well, here we are, my friend, early birds.—We have been on our feet most of the night."

Geraint asked no questions. He waited for her to tell him the why and the wherefore.

"Calleva had no further use for me, my dear. Yes, we were pulled out of our beds in the middle of the night and conducted to the town gate. And here I am, very ready for a bath and breakfast."

Abruptly she sat down on the grass like a large infant whose legs had failed it. Her face wore a look of surprise, and then she laughed.

"Tut-tut—I seem to be tired! Yes, apparently my house was needed, and my household had joined the new Calleva. Babylon has fallen.—Babylon needs a bath."

Geraint stood close to her.

"Balthasar?"

"Very much Balthasar, my dear."

"And Guinevra?"

She fanned herself with a fold of her cloak.

"Still in Calleva.—They would not let me take the girl. A couple of rude fellows had me by the arms, and out I went."

Geraint looked grim.

"The dogs!—I'll go and send a litter for you, and warn Placida."

But Cornelia was again on her feet.

"Give me an arm, my dear. I can manage. But what about your horse?"

"I'll put your woman on him."

"She will most certainly fall off. Martha—forget your poor feet, and walk."

She held on to Geraint's arm. Her old face had gone grey and old, but she endured. The white horse followed like a dog, and behind the horse Martha hobbled as though the road was hot metal.

"I am troubled about the girl, my friend."

Geraint was silent.

"Have they shut their gates?"

"There were guards at the gate last night."

And then she chuckled in spite of her dragging feet.

"I sent all my gold and plate and jewels to Corinium

a month ago.—Not much loot, my dear.—But I am troubled about the girl."

And still Geraint was silent.

3

Placida was at matins in her chapel by the orchard, and when Geraint had helped Cornelia into the house and sent women to serve her, he went for his wife. Placida on her knees was of no use to anyone save Placida, and Geraint was for the road.

"Cornelia is here."

Cornelia!—And what was the old pagan doing at Turris Alba at this hour when a woman should be on her knees or seeing that her servants were on their feet? Placida was not pleased.

"Cornelia?"

Geraint did not waste words.

"She has been on the road all night.—Trouble at Calleva. Go to her, wife.—They have turned her out of the city."

Placida rose from her knees. She had no liking for Cornelia, and such sympathy as she could command marched with Calleva.

"Well—I am not surprised.—She and her idols!"

"She is an old woman, Placida, and she has been on her feet all night."

Geraint remounted his horse. He met Malgo and two old soldiers from the vicus just beyond the bailiff's house, and he gave Malgo the news. Calleva had shut its gates and declared itself a free and rebel city. Malgo was not surprised. Calleva looked like becoming an uncomfortable neighbour. And were my lord's men ready for the day's work? Yes, Mabon was calling them together in the stable court, and Malgo could put them through their paces. There were spears, and Malgo could use the wooden fencing-swords to teach them the elements of sword-play. Malgo had brought half a dozen light javelins with him.

"I may be able to teach them to throw by hand. They will be too raw for the throwing thong."

The white horse was feeling his master's impatience.

"Teach them to stand shoulder to shoulder, Malgo."

"I can teach them that, lord, but a man must teach himself not to run away."

Geraint gave his horse the reins and Malgo watched him go. My Lord Geraint had the face of a man who had some business that would not wait. He rode up the hill to the beechwoods, and the valley's farewell to him was the sound of Caradoc's hammer in the smithy.

Geraint rode fast. He did not follow the road but took an old grass track along the hills. His way lay through wild country. Deer went trotting from him to cover in the valleys. He saw hawks overhead, and at one place where the track went down to a brook he put up a boar who was rooting in the boggy ground. Geraint had no eyes for any of these things. He followed the rise and fall of that ribbon of turf with its rabbit-nibbled grass, a track hardened by the coming and going of men and beasts in the days when Rome was not.

An hour's hard riding brought him to less rolling country. The sky had a more level rim. There were farmsteads here; he was in the Calleva country. He slackened to a trot. Oak trees replaced the beeches; grassland in the valleys became heather on the low hills. He came to a birch wood on some rising ground, and by a round barrow and a clump of yew trees he reined in and sat at gaze.

Roofs—a little golden finger pointing skywards, a tower, a faint haze of smoke—Calleva.

Riding on another hundred paces he was able to see the city wall, and the west gate with its two black arches. There were figures on the wall, little dark dots. He rode on still farther and again he paused, for out of the west gate of Calleva a thing like a coloured snake came gliding. Geraint watched it. A procession? No, men marching out to the level space outside the gate, a column of men two or three hundred strong. It halted on the pomerium and then broke into half a dozen sections; some marched this way and some that. Other little figures distinct from the companies, gestured and shouted.—Geraint sat and watched the men of Calleva being drilled.

He touched the white horse with his heels and, turning south, rode towards the woods that came within a furlong of the southern gate. The west gate was closed to him —yes—obviously so. He rode on and round to the eastern face and, striking the main road, walked his horse towards the east gate.

He saw men on the walls, men on the watch tower near the amphitheatre. Moreover, he saw that the gates were closed.

Geraint walked his horse to the east gate. There were men on the wall watching him, and the fellows were armed, though their spears were scythe blades set upon poles. Geraint reined in his horse, and sat waiting as though he expected the gate to be opened, but one of the men on the wall knew him. He shouted to the guards in the guard-room below.

A stone came flying from the battlements. It was followed by a javelin that passed over the back of Geraint's horse, and buried its head in the grass beside the road. Geraint heard the bolts being drawn. These bold citizens, seeing but one man on a horse, and remembering the occasion when this same gentleman had chased some of them up the street, were preparing to rush out in strength and engage him.

Geraint turned his horse and rode off just as one of the gates opened, and a dozen men tumbled out with much noise and valour. Their weapons were the arms of a mob, hammers, knives, and scythe blades on staves, clubs, an old

sword or two. Their courage was very much the courage
of a crowd when a chase is on and the game seems safe.
But Geraint had other and greater devoirs to do than to get
himself bludgeoned by a city mob. He put his horse
at a canter, and his pursuers—outdistanced—stood and
mocked him.

"Ha—ha—the gentleman runs away."

"Coward."

"Ya—ya—poltroon."

Geraint swung back into the woods and, striking the
Venta road, cantered along it for a mile before turning west
into a field track. Calleva was shut to him; he had been
chased away from it by those fellows of the baser sort.
And Geraint's face was not gentle. About half a mile from
the city he reined in and looked back. He saw the little
golden figure on its column shining like a torch.

He turned his horse again and rode westwards and life's
face was the face of a woman.

F

CHAPTER VII

The House of the Good Women

¶ IN Calleva some six patrician houses with their furniture, fabrics, linen, vessels and ornaments were dedicated to God—that is—to the poor. All Calleva swarmed in and took what it pleased or what it could get. Women from the alleys fought over the contents of chests and cupboards; silk robes were torn in twain, curtains pulled down and carried off. Men loaded up hand-carts with the loot. There was much noise, but no violence, for the wealthy had fled, and their slaves had joined the mob.

All that day Balthasar sat in the curia with his priests and councillors, while the people brought to him the things that he had charged them to bring. Balthasar had put hundreds of simple souls upon their honour.

"My children, that which is precious—all gold and silver and jewels—must be given to God and our City."

The people brought to their bishop the gods from the lararia, and they were thrown in a heap on the floor of the basilica. All metal was precious. They brought one hoard of coins in an earthenware crock, some silver dishes, but on the whole the plunder was scanty. Not till late in the day did Fidelis and Caritas appear with two stout fellows carrying a wooden box bound with iron. In the house dedicated to Good Women searchers had found Cornelia's strong-box hidden in a hypocaust chamber under one of the winter rooms.

Smiths were called for. The crowd pressed close. Here should be pay for Calleva's poor soldiers. The smiths forced the iron hasps that were fastened by two padlocks.

74

The lid was raised. The expected treasure within was covered by a red silk robe.

Balthasar rose to his feet.

"My children—let us will this treasure to God."

He made a sign to Fidelis to uncover the treasure, and when Fidelis drew the red robe aside, the jest of a wicked old woman betrayed itself. The strong-box was full of stones.

The crowd groaned, or was silent, but their bishop was a man of resource.

"Cornelia and her corruption have flown. Put the chest in the treasury, smiths. It shall stand there as a symbol."

Meanwhile, the house of Cornelia, unravished by the mob, but searched and put in such order as pleased them by Fidelis, Pia and Caritas and other good women, became for Guinevra a peaceful prison. She remained in her room, like a bird in a cage, listening to voices and the sounds of much activity.—What should she do? She had been caught up in Calleva's communion. She had knelt to Balthasar, but not in the spirit. She had been told that the gates were shut, and that she—a Christian—was to accept the community of saints. But Guinevra was no saint.

And then her upper room was invaded. Pia came into it with a bundle of belongings and deposited her bundle on Guinevra's bed. Pia was a woman with no eyebrows, and such thin lips that she looked lipless. Pia dead and wrapped in a cerecloth would not have differed greatly from Pia alive, and when Guinevra understood that she was to share her room with this living corpse, she began to pack her own belongings into a small trunk that Cornelia had given her.

"I will find room elsewhere."

Pia said nothing, but was silent with the air of a woman who could have said much. She let Guinevra and her baggage go down the stairs and into the garden court. Yes, the "Baggage" would find that the house of Cornelia had ceased to be a painted palace for idle young women with too much beauty. In the garden court Guinevra found

Fidelis, Caritas and three others sitting by the fountain and holding discourse after a crowded day. Fidelis was a big, raw-boned creature with a mouth like a hole in a wall; Caritas was meagre, pale and shrill.

Guinevra smiled at them and walked towards the gate. The gates were shut, but gates could be opened.

Said Fidelis—"And—where—are you going, young woman?"

"To the post-house, for horses and a carriage."

"Indeed!—Her ladyship would order a carriage?"

Fidelis rose and clapped her large hands and from the janitor's lodge appeared two other women.

"Marcia, Honestas, stand by the gates."

She turned on Guinevra.

"Go back to your room, wench."

Guinevra went white.

"I go where I please."

In a flash Fidelis had her by the arm, and Fidelis' big fingers pinched the flesh.

"Shall we have to teach you—to be humble?—You are to serve your penance here. A girl who consorts with old Jezebels.—Go to your room."

Guinevra shook her off.

"Don't dare to touch me."

Her hot youth flared; she stood still, realizing that the other women had drawn in to support Fidelis.—So, she was a prisoner here.—But—why? And what was she to do? Struggle with these formidable matrons, beat the wings of her youth in their faces, and be hustled into some dark cupboard like a passionate and defiant child?

She looked at Fidelis.

"By what right——?"

"By the right of souls to be saved."

Guinevra nodded at her.—She had heard such language before, but not from a righteous termagant like Fidelis.—This—indeed—was virtue—laid on with a whip. She grew deep—calm, silent. She walked to the fountain, and putting her hands into the basin, she took water into her palm, and drank. Then, she went towards the portico like a young tree walking.

Caritas tittered, and the sound she made was that of a rusty hinge creaking.

"Mercy—what a head in air!"

Said Fidelis—"We will make her bend."

Guinevra climbed the stairs very slowly, pausing at each step, and with each step she asked herself a silent question. —Why? What had these women against her? Had Cornelia's house become a sort of penitentiary?—By whose orders?—What did it mean? What should she do?—She had reached the last step when the secret word came to her. Balthasar? She stood a moment, staring. Then she crossed the passage, opened the door of her room, and saw Pia putting clean bed-clothes on the bed.

Pia smiled at her like a corpse come to life.

"Back again, sister?"

Guinevra stood with a hand laid to her cheek. The bed-clothes that had been hers were piled on the floor.

Said Pia—"Perhaps Fidelis will give you a mattress. I suffer from rheumatics, so I will take the bed. You had better go and ask Fidelis. She is matron here."

Guinevra put down the little leather trunk, and went to the window. She leaned out.—How high was the window from the ground? No, she was not going to ask Fidelis for anything.

2

Night and a full moon.

Guinevra would have gone to bed supperless had not Pia, who was less bitter against beauty than her fellows, brought to the upper room bread, honey and half a bowl of milk. A little earthenware lamp was burning, and Guinevra drank and ate. She was hungry. Pia, sitting on the bed,

began to loose her hair.   It was not like Guinevra's, but
the colour of pale sand.   Life and her heritage had not
been kind to Pia.

And suddenly, Guinevra spoke.

"Why do they keep me here?"

"For your good."

Guinevra dipped a spoon in the honey.

"Is it—because Cornelia was kind to me?"

Pia nodded.

"That—old harlot.—She used to dye her hair red."

"O," said Guinevra, "I never saw it.—You women seem
fond of hard names."

Pia pulled off her stockings.

"Make the most of the honey, my dear, you won't get
it to-morrow.—You are to be—disciplined."

Guinevra dissembled.

"But—I do not understand.—I am a free woman, not
a slave.   No one can say to me—'Stay here' or 'Go.'"

"This is a new world, my dear, a new city."

"Indeed?"

"And God rules it—through his vicar."

"Ah," said Guinevra, "is that so?"

She was to sleep on the floor, Pia in the bed, and it
was Pia who put the light out, but before she quenched it
Guinevra saw Pia pull her bed across the door.   So, Pia
had been put here as her keeper.   Guinevra said nothing.
She lay down and gathered the clothes round her and pretended to go to sleep.   She listened to Pia's breathing, and
when she thought that Pia was asleep, she sat up, put the
clothes from her, and crept to the window.

She saw the face of the full moon and glimmering
roofs, and Cornelia's privy garden below with its grass
and paths and clipped trees.   The shadows were as sharp
as the shadows cast by a gnomon.   How high was the
window from the ground?   She was young and supple—
should she dare the drop?—She leaned out, and then
suddenly she drew back.

Someone was walking in the garden.—One of the women on guard there? She peered. No, the thing in the garden was a man, robed, hooded, stalking up and down the grass. It was a strangely noiseless figure: it went to and fro, to and fro—striding, turning, striding—like some creature to whom the night was anguish, hunger and unrest.—Once the figure paused and seemed to look up at her window, but its face was hidden by the hood. And again it went on walking.

Guinevra turned sharply. She had heard a sound from Pia's bed. Was Pia awake? She was soon to learn that Pia was.

"You are wasting your time, my dear.—I sleep too lightly. Much better come away from the window."

Guinevra fell back into the shadow.

"There is a man in the garden, Pia."

"Nonsense."

"Can't you hear his footsteps on the grass?"

Pia turned over in bed.

"One of the vigilants, girl. Go to sleep. And remember, the garden walls are ten feet high, and all the city gates are shut."

Guinevra lay down on the hard floor and covered herself up. She lay and listened.—Whatever Pia might say she was sure that the thing walking in the garden was a man.

3

Balthasar took a key that was fastened to his girdle by a stout thread, and standing by the little gate in the garden wall, he looked up at that window.

"Fool!"

And suddenly he beat his fist against his mouth, and struck again so fiercely that there was blood on his knuckles. He slipped the key into the lock, opened the gate, passed out into the passage between the gardens, and relocked the gate.

Balthasar walked fast. Under his hood the moonlight shone on a pale chin and a lip that was bloody. In the lane the Spring night smelt of gardens, the green foam of the young year. Balthasar burned. But if a man can flame like a torch, Balthasar carried his own torch, and was moved to dash it against a wall. This sweet, terrible anguish of the flesh!

The streets were empty of everything save the moonlight, and when Balthasar reached the Forum he passed down between its shops and the Butter Market to the open space where the little church stood, Calleva's first offering to Christ. Calleva's temples had been reconsecrated to the true faith, but this little building near the Forum was the mother church. A white wooden railing marked off the courtyard. Balthasar paused at the labrum, and dipping his hand, washed the blood from his lip. He passed in between the pillars of the narthex and through the open door. Two candles were burning in the apse, and just within the door a man lay asleep. He slept heavily, and Balthasar stepped past him.

His leather shoes swept over the red tessarae of the pavement to where the wooden altar table stood between the apse and the chancel. Balthasar knelt. He spread his arms on the table like a man crucified; he let his face lie upon the wood. The flames of the two candles burned straight, but they were not more still than the man.

Balthasar was not praying. It was man who knelt—and in the spirit—gripped the throat of his manhood. Fool!—Balthasar, the butcher's son: Balthasar who, as a boy, had run away to Rome, tramped a thousand miles in search of god and fortune. Twenty years of sedulous sanctity, of serving men who were far less shrewd than he was—the soft voice, the suave smile, the silent progress. Until—! Power, reputation, sanctity; a man on a throne to whom other men listened. He held the crowd. But how did he hold them? As a flaming zealot; as a man whose justice and virtue were not of this world. As a man who spoke to the poor, and stood for the poor.

His hands clenched themselves.

Dreams—visions! Was not a new world being born, and had he not planned to be one of the masters of this new world? The empire was dying, but new life could be snatched from its death. The priest should replace the soldier, or rather—the soldier should serve the priest. Ruin, confusion, violence, and out of them emerging a new master—Christ's man, the king-bishop. And this Britain? What Carausius the pagan had done, could not he Balthasar do, differently and more triumphantly? Calleva was his. Venta, Regnum, Sarum might be his. He would go from strength to strength until he held the whole island in the hollow of his hand.

And was he to jeopardize all this—for a pot of honey? Why was he what he was? Balthasar the Bishop, the voice of the plain man, the saviour of slaves; saint, prophet, rhetorician. Even slaves will not forgive an idol which betrays feet of clay.—Should ice burn and melt?

His hands grasped the edge of the table. He jerked his head sharply, and the hood of his cloak fell back. He prayed to his God, for Balthasar's God was both a strange and familiar god, a god that was both god and Balthasar. He preached Christ crucified, but he preached him with the soul of a Hebrew prophet. He believed, but he believed as Balthasar. There was no meekness in the man, no self-effacement. If God was God, Balthasar was his Bishop, and Balthasar was—Balthasar.

He raised his arms, and his face had the exultation of a man to whom some inspiration has come. His cry was an inward cry. "O, God, I burn—but there shall be no outward flame. That which has tempted me shall be dedicated to thy service. The flesh shall be chastened."

He stood up; he bowed himself before the altar-table, and out of the night came a little sound. Balthasar heard

it, and stood listening. His chin looked as sharp as the
chin of a new moon. In the silence of the night someone
came running. Balthasar knelt again, and as the light of a
swinging lantern jerked in the doorway.

"Simon——"

The sleeping janitor scrambled to his feet.

"Who calls?"

"Is Balthasar here?"

"There is no one here."

But the man with the lantern had seen the kneeling
figure at the altar. His mouth opened as though to speak,
and then fell to. The saint was praying, and Melchior the
Deacon stood holding his lantern in devout impatience.
He was a little, round, hairy man with a bright colour;
somewhat out of breath. He was known among the faithful as Melchior the Zealot, but zeal might be unseemly when
the great man knelt before God. Melchior waited for his
breath to recover itself and for the communion with other
worlds to cease.

Balthasar rose slowly from his knees.

"Melchior."

"Father."

A wonderful man—Bishop Balthasar—he knew who was
there without turning his head to look!

"What of the night, Melchior?"

"News."

Balthasar bowed to the altar, and putting his hood forward, came with arms folded down the nave.

"Messengers—Melchior?"

Melchior's small eyes were very bright above his
beard.

"From Venta—from Londinium."

"Two?—That is—almost miraculous, Melchior.—
Where are they?"

"They came to my house, father."

The house of the deacon was in the court of the old
temple of Jupiter near the east gate, though the temple had

been cleansed and rededicated to St. Joseph, and Melchior served this church. Balthasar did not hurry, or seem to hurry, but Melchior's stocky little legs took three steps to the Bishop's two. His lantern was still alight—though the moon made of it less than a farthing candle.

"Did you need a lantern to find me, Melchior?"

"I had it in my hand, father, when the men came to the door."

Yes, that was Melchior's way, the urge of the zealot. He ran with his loins girded or ungirded when the cause called.

Balthasar put his hood back.

"What says the night, Melchior?"

"The men carry sealed letters in the hollows of their staves."

And Balthasar smiled.

"Did you learn nothing from them, Melchior?"

"Terrible news from the north, father."

Balthasar's chin rose sharply.

"Terrible—?— But that is God's news. That—is what we need."

Melchior's house stood in what had been the enclosure of the temple of Jupiter, and the spread of the temple roof showed black against the moon. Melchior opened a door in the wall, and raised his lantern to light Balthasar into a passage. The deacon closed the outer door and scuttled past Balthasar to open a second door.

"The men were hungry, and I sat them down at my table."

"Good servants should be fed."

Melchior opened the second door, and Balthasar saw two men seated at a table with bread and cheese and a bowl of milk between them. From the spout of a lamp rose a little yellow flame. The men were dressed like labourers. One of them had a slice of bread in his hand, but he put the bread down on the table, and looked round-eyed on Balthasar. Then, both of them fell on their knees at the bishop's feet.

"Welcome, my children.   You bring letters?"

"Yes, lord," said they, in chorus.

Each man had a staff under his stool.   Balthasar sat
down in the chair of the deacon, and watched each messenger untwist the end of his staff and draw out a roll of
parchment.   Balthasar stretched out a hand.

"Venta—first.   Hold the light, Melchior."

Balthasar broke the seal and unwound the thread of the
letter from Venta.   The parchment crackled as he unrolled
it.   Melchior, holding the lamp, tried to read over the
bishop's shoulder what was written in the letter, but the
writing was small, and the light too feeble.   Balthasar's
hands seemed to tremble.   He read the letter, rolled it up,
and put it in his bosom.

"Our brother from London."

When Balthasar had read the second letter, he sat a
moment, staring.   And suddenly the light went out, for
Melchior had let the lamp tilt, and the oil had flooded the
wick and put out the flame.   In the darkness Balthasar's
voice was heard.

"Almost—that was a sign from God, Melchior.—So are
man's pride and power quenched."

Melchior was groping his way to the window.   He
opened it and let the moonlight in, and Balthasar's figure
seemed to turn to silver.

"Finish your meal—my brothers," he said as he rose.
"You have done well.—Let us go out into the night,
Melchior."

The deacon opened the door for his bishop, and followed
him into the moonlight.   Balthasar walked as far as the
podium of the church of St. Joseph, with Melchior beside
him, looking up into his face like a dog eager for a bone.

"Great news, Melchior, terrible news."

Melchior's mouth was open.   Almost he seemed to
slaver.

"The faithful in Venta will join with us.—Regnum too
—is for our city."

"And the news from Londinium, father?"

"Londinium shakes like an aspen.—Duke Fullofandes has been slain in the north. The heathen are over the wall."

Melchior threw up his hands.

"Is not the news too terrible, father?"

"Do you fear?"

"If the heathen come south—before the Emperor can send us help."

Balthasar looked at the moon.

"Have you no faith, Melchior? When carnal men fail, Christ's man rises up. Ruin rushing from the north.— But—we—gather—soldiers of the Cross. Up, Melchior, up. I will put a sword into your hand. I will put a sword or a spear into the hand of every workman and slave.— Christ—and his Bishop—shall save Britain."

Melchior flopped down on his knees.

"Give me a sword, father."

Balthasar signed him with the cross.

"You shall have your sword, Melchior. Come. There is much to do. We must send out our letters."

CHAPTER VIII

The Two Men from Calleva

¶ GERAINT had ridden out to see Cornelia safely on the road
to Corinium, for Cornelia needed clothes, money, and—as
she put it—a new temper. Her money and valuables lay
with Rhadamanthus the banker, who had had the sense to
transfer himself and his affairs from Calleva to Corinium.
Cornelia and Placida had not fallen upon each other's necks,
and if Placida had put her house and her wardrobe at
Cornelia's service, she had done it with the air of extending
a long spoon to Satan.

Placida said the wrong thing—and always with the air
of being sure that it was the right one. She had presumed
to assert that she had much sympathy with Calleva and its
bishop. People should move with the times; if Calleva
was founded in Christ—which it was—could it be blamed
for assuming that Calleva should be for the Christians?

"Assuredly," said Placida with her nose in the air, "we
should accept the light when it is revealed to us."

Cornelia had asked the lady a question.

"Calleva is a near neighbour of yours, my dear.—Supposing Calleva should show a liking for this house and
estate, and propose to turn you out."

And Placida had replied—"I am a Christian. One
should give to the poor."

Two days of Placida had satisfied Cornelia; Placida was
a fool, Placida argued, and never for a moment did Placida
fail in her faith in the rightness of Placida. Geraint might
be out and away from dawn to dusk, and at supper his wife
would peck at the dark silence of her man. What was all

this nonsense, this playing at soldiers, grooms, hawksmen, huntsmen, house-servants, farm-labourers sloping spears and shouting "Ha"? Joseph the gardener had had his head cut open with a wooden sword. Was this a Christian country, or proposing to be a Christian country? Were there not plenty of soldiers in Britain and the emperor across the sea? The thing was silly. A few poor, misguided savages dancing and shaking spears, and what of it? There had always been trouble at the Wall. There always would be trouble there until a Christian mission was sent to the heathen and the poor creatures were baptized.

Cornelia, getting into the light carriage at Geraint's gate, had blown out her old cheeks—Poof! Good-bye to Placida! Geraint had ridden his white horse beside her, and a couple of armed and mounted men had followed behind. Much that might have been said had not been said because of Martha and the driver, but before parting Cornelia had left the carriage, and Geraint had dismounted and passed his horse to one of the men.

Geraint and Cornelia had walked up a little hill together.

"Strange days, my dear, and your wife sees nothing."

Geraint had had nothing to say of Placida.

"Where shall we all be this day year?—I am an old woman, my lord, and I have a feeling that our world is passing. I can remember Calleva when half the excellencies and dignitaries in the island had houses there. I can remember the last fight of gladiators in the arena. Yes, that was a brutal business, and better done with.—But the brute is slow to die, my dear. He gets into a new and less shaggy skin—perhaps.—One last word—I am troubled about—the girl."

Geraint had looked at a little wood on the sky-line above them.

"I have not forgotten.—One may think too much, matrona, of a person who does not think of us at all."

Cornelia had given him a shrewd look.

"Can one think in a cage?—I would not be at the mercy

of any man or crowd.—Try to find out, my dear, if the bird likes the cage."

Geraint had nodded.

"I will try and get a message to her."

"I would have her with me at Corinium or Aquæ. She has beauty, my dear. I like to look at beauty. It is a cup of wine."

Geraint sent his men forward with the old lady and rode back by the way of Vindomis. Vindomis lay in a valley where the road crossed a stream, a little place with a mansio and a small garrison station which had ceased to be of any importance. Vindomis showed its roofs among the trees, and as Geraint rode down the hill he could look into the market square. There seemed to be some stir and excitement in the village. Men were running to and fro loading a wagon, and the sunlight, glinting on these little figures, marked them as men in armour. There was a crowd round the wagon, women, children, dogs. An officer on a black horse appeared to be speaking to the people. Geraint saw him raise an arm and point. Yes, that was Victorinus the optio. Were Victorinus and his handful of men on the march somewhere?

Geraint rode into the market-place as the men were falling in. There numbered a dozen or so, mostly oldish men who were near the end of their service. They were to march light, for spears, shields and javelins were piled in the baggage-wagon. The crowd was a silent crowd; it stood and stared glumly. One or two women were weeping.

Geraint saluted the optio, and rode round the fringe of the crowd.

"Marching orders, Victorinus?"

The optio looked worried. He made a sign to Geraint, and they walked their horses across the market-place away from the crowd.

"Bad news, lord. We had our orders less than an hour ago. Every man is to march. No, the people do not know how bad the news is."

"So—it is as bad as that," said Geraint.

Victorinus tightened his belt.

"The orders run that every station is to send every man who can walk. The rallying point is at Ratae. Forced marching."

"Do you know what has happened?"

"They give us orders, lord, not explanations, but the messenger watered his horse here and had a cup of wine."

"And he talked. What did he tell you?"

"The Duke has been slain. The barbarians came over the Wall in the night. Fullofandes, marching too hastily to reinforce the Wall—was ambushed. They say that half a legion was cut to pieces. Most of the forts and mile-castles have been stormed or cut off. Fullofandes had part of the Twentieth and two cohorts of the Second with him. Every man is to go north."

Geraint looked grim.

"And what are they leaving us?"

Victorinus shrugged.

"How should I know. A century or two at Isca—perhaps, and the same at Rhutupiae. If they are calling on police posts—such as ours—the business must be ugly."

"Who is in command?"

"They say—the Tribune of the Twentieth."

"He's a poor thing, Victorinus, a fat old man who goes red—and screams."

Victorinus flapped his bridle.

"It is to be one of those bloody scrambles—I suppose. Fighting savages who appear from nowhere. Well, we will keep them from coming south, sir, if we can."

They shook hands, saluted each other, and optio rode off to get his men moving. Geraint never saw him again, for Victorinus was killed in a skirmish near Isurium where the remnants of a legion and a composite force made up of the auxiliaries who had retreated from the Wall were fighting to hold back the barbarians.

Geraint sat his horse in the market-place until the soldiers had marched off. The crowd gave them a feeble

G

cheer. Most of the men were in the fields, and the women and a few old gaffers gossiped at doorways. One woman, who had been weeping, came and stood beside Geraint's horse.

"My man has gone, lord. What does it mean?"

Geraint looked at her kindly.

"You, a soldier's wife—should know."

"Will they come back, lord?"

And Geraint was silent for a moment.

"Pray to the gods, woman," but the emptiness of the words reproached him.

2

It so happened that Caradoc was working late that night in his smithy by the light of two torches. He had left the door wide because of the heat, and he stood stripped to the waist. The forge was a fading flower, for Caradoc had sent the bellows-boy to bed. He had but three spear-heads to hammer into shape, and the day's work would be done.

He was sweaty and his shoulders glistened. Through the open doorway the blue night showed marked here and there with stars as though the sky had been shot through with silver arrows. Between his hammerings Caradoc would pause with the hammer at rest on his shoulder, and look at the night, for Caradoc loved the stars. They might have been made by some celestial smith, bright studs in a vast shield.

He threw a spear-head into the sandbox, and took the last one from the forge. He beat it with his hammer. Sparks flew. Letting the head of the hammer lie on the anvil, he spat, shook his big head, stared. A moment ago the doorway of the smithy held nothing but the night; now, two figures were standing there.

"Hallo," said Caradoc; "looking for work?"

He could not see the men very clearly, for they were in the shadow. They leaned on their staves and looked at him.

"Hail—brother!" said the taller of the two.

Caradoc spat.

"Ale, brother, would be more to my fancy. But who may you be?"

"Friends."

"Come into the light and let us look at you."

But the men remained leaning upon their staves. Said the taller of the two: "Why do you make weapons of war, brother?"

Meanwhile, the spear head had grown cold upon the anvil, and Caradoc thrust it back into the forge, laid down his hammer, and put on his shirt. The glistening and knotty bulk of him disappeared under the garment. He took one of the torches and went to the door of the smithy.

"Since you are shy of the light, let me look at you."

He held the torch shoulder high. One of the men had a red beard and sly eyes; the other was a mere lad with a face that hardly needed the razor. They were strangers to Caradoc, and the smith saw that their shoes were dusty.

"Travellers, hey?"

He of the red beard looked cunningly at the smith.

"We travel on God's service."

"Ha," said Caradoc, growing wary, but showing his teeth in a smile. "What could be better?—And what does God want with me?"

Master Red Beard went a little closer.

"I have good news for such as you, smith.—I have God for my master, and God is a better master than man."

Caradoc seemed to ponder that saying.

"Maybe—maybe.—Whence come you?"

"Calleva."

"Ah," said Caradoc, "Calleva is a goodly city. And you have good news.—I'd like to hear it."

The man stood close to Caradoc, looked over his shoulder into the darkness, and then into the smith's face.

"It is very precious news, brother—and secret.—Let us come in and shut the door."

"By all means, brother."

They entered the smithy, and Caradoc closed the door. He put the torch back into the holder; there were only a few inches of the brand left. A four-legged oak settle stood against the wall.

"Be seated, brothers——"

Red Beard sat down, but the lad remained on his feet. Caradoc stood with arms folded, watching the face of the seated man. He did not like the look of the fellow—but Caradoc could play dog to his fox.

"I am a poor man, brother. Have you good news for the poor?"

"I speak to the poor."

"I am your man, brother. I sweat and toil."

Red Beard looked at him carefully. Then he began to speak, and Caradoc, arms folded, listened as though the stranger offered him wine and honey. He grunted; he let out gruff commendations; he spat.—"These—are—words, brother."—"Better and better."—"Why do I toil and sweat?"—Red Beard became more eloquent and brotherly. He got up and clapped Caradoc on the shoulder.

"You are the man for us, smith."

"No doubt about it, brother."

Red Beard fawned on him.

"Are there any more good fellows in this place who might like to hear the news?"

"Assuredly," said Caradoc, "I could soon find you a dozen. Our master is a hard man.—Why should we serve him when we could serve ourselves?"

Red Beard kissed him, and Caradoc took the kiss, and bided his time.

"I salute you, brother, with the kiss of peace.—Now, for the good work——"

"Stay you here," said Caradoc; "it is a safe place. I will go and gather the men together.—Our master is a heavy sleeper. Let him sleep."

Caradoc went to the door, opened it, nodded his big

black head, and disappeared into the night. He did not run, but walked solidly, smiling into his beard. It was late, and when he came to the gate of the great house he found it shut. The windows were dark, save the windows of the summer parlour. Caradoc rubbed his beard as he stood with his face close to the open grille of the gate. He could hear someone walking in the courtyard. A figure came down towards the gate, and even by the starlight Caradoc knew his lord.

"Master."

Geraint came to the gate.

"You, Caradoc?—What brings you here?"

Caradoc's face was close to the grille.

"Strange visitors, master. Two gentlemen from Calleva. I was working late at the forge, and suddenly—two fellows were in the doorway. 'Hail, brother,' said they. Now, when a stranger with a red beard calls me brother, lord, I begin to smell a fox."

Geraint had drawn back the bolt of the gate, and he stood with Caradoc in the entry.

"What has Calleva to offer to you, Caradoc?"

"It would seem," said the smith, "that we are to have a new heaven and a new earth. Every lewd fellow in Calleva is to become as good as his neighbour—and better. You, master, and such gentlemen—are to be sent on a journey and your house and your lands given to the poor."

"Did not that tempt you, Caradoc?"

"Am I a fool, lord?—Do I hold myself to be no better man than a city scullion?—Feel my arm, lord. I would wager that there is no such arm as mine in Calleva, and they think that I—a smith—the man of the hammer—should be their fool."

"Is that all, Caradoc?"

"No, lord.—There are captains and councillors in the world, and always will be, and I—a free man—choose whom I follow. A dog is a wise and a faithful beast, and should not a man be wiser than a dog? I am your man, lord. I ask to serve no better."

Geraint put his hand on the smith's shoulder.

"I would have no better man at my back.—Where are these fellows?"

"In the smithy, lord.—I did pretend to them that I would go and gather them more disciples.—What shall we do with the rogues? Hang them?"

Geraint stood thinking.

"I will come with you, Caradoc. Are the fellows armed?"

"One is only a lad, sir—and I could break the other's back for a penny."

"We may find a use for these fellows. Let's to the smithy."

Caradoc chuckled. He claimed his jest.

"Let me go first, lord, and prepare the way.—I want to see Red Beard's face when you stand in the doorway."

"Have your jest, Caradoc."

Caradoc ran. He opened the door of the smithy, and drew deep breaths like a man who had come fast up hill. He picked up another torch and lit it. His teeth showed in his black beard.

"They are coming—brother, to hear the good news."

He stood holding the torch. Red Beard smirked at him. The lad, leaning on his staff, watched the doorway with eyes that were like the eyes of a hare.

"The night is ours, smith," said Red Beard.

"And the stars and the moon, brother," said Caradoc.

Then, Geraint came to the doorway and stood there, a big, dark, silent man in lorica and purple tunic. His head was within two inches of the beam, and the eyes of Caradoc looked at him like the eyes of a dog.

"These—are—the men, lord."

Geraint, arms folded, was silent as death. The lad shrank back against the wall. Red Beard's hand disappeared like a snake's head under his cloak.

Geraint spoke.

"I am not—it seems—so hard a master—that those

whom I trust—can be taught treachery by men who come to them in the night.—Stand up, you with the red beard."

The man leaned forward, the toes of his shoes pressed against the earthen floor like an animal crouching to spring.

"I stand where I please."

And suddenly he sprang, knife in hand, his eyes mere slits, mouth awry, the flaming, red-headed fanatic. But Caradoc had been watching him. The smith jabbed the lighted torch in the man's face, caught him as he went back singed and howling, and with one twist of his smith's arm, wrenched the shoulder-head from its socket. The knife fell to the floor, and Caradoc, flinging the fellow in a corner, stooped and picked up the knife. The lad stood with his mouth open, flinching against the wall.

Geraint had not moved.

"We will put these two in the stable for to-night, Caradoc. In the morning I will say what shall be done with them."

The smithy smelt of singed hair. Caradoc held his torch aloft, and stood over the man on the floor.

"Come up, you fox, trot."

The man moved a little, and got up, supporting his useless right arm.

"You heathen shall pay for this."

"Heathen," said Caradoc, "heathen! You keep a civil tongue in your head. My mother chose my god for me, and I'll swear that my mother was a better woman than yours."

3

In the morning Geraint let the men go. He had them fed and sent his barber to bind up Red Beard's arm, but before Calleva's messengers took to the road, Geraint wrote a letter and called Morgan to him in the orchard.

Morgan was a motherless and fatherless lad whom Geraint had brought up on the estate and trained as a hawksman. Morgan was dark and slim, a lad with a quick smile, and the best runner in the valley, and to Morgan Geraint was god, a man to be loved and served.

"Can you keep a secret, Morgan?"

"I can keep any secret of my lord's."

Morgan had been with Geraint on that day when he had left Guinevra at the house of Cornelia. Geraint showed Morgan the letter hidden in the hollow of a quill. He gave Morgan no orders; the lad could choose for himself, but he looked into the lad's eyes and trusted him. Someone was a prisoner in Calleva, and Calleva was a closed city, but if Morgan followed Red Beard and the lad, and made them believe that he had fled the valley and wished to be one of them, Morgan might enter Calleva with those two. Yes—this letter—if possible—was to be delivered to Guinevra; the Lady Cornelia had desired him to write it. Morgan would have to find things out for himself, and if he could bring a message back from Calleva, so much the better. He would need to use his wits to get out of the city.

Morgan smiled, but his eyes were steady.

"Give me the letter, lord."

"There may be danger, lad."

And Morgan laughed.

"Am I not young?"

Red Beard and his fellow had taken the valley track to the west road, and Morgan hid the quill in the hem of his tunic, filled a wallet and ran. He overtook the two about ten miles from Calleva, and came up to them breathless, looking back over his shoulder as though he had been running for his life. He threw himself down on the grass beside the road, and panted.

"Take me with you, brothers."

Red Beard looked at him suspiciously from under singed eyebrows.

"Who are you?"

Morgan sat up, breathing hard.

"I have run away from the White Valley.—Shall I live for nothing but kicks and blows? Geraint shall pay—some day.—I wish to come with you, master, and serve your God.—In Calleva I shall not be a slave."

"So—you hate—Geraint?"

"Have I not cause to hate him?—Take me with you, master. In Calleva I shall be free."

He embraced Red Beard's knees.

"There were others who would have come, had they dared.—They sent me up to drive in some cattle, and I took my chance and fled. Do not turn me away, master. You are a good man and have suffered at Geraint's hands."

Red Beard smiled into his scorched beard.

"You may be useful to the good cause—my child.—What is your name?"

"Morgan."

"You shall come to Calleva with us, Morgan."

CHAPTER IX

Fidelis Uses the Shears

¶ PIA woke very early.

"Matins, girl."

The women assembled in the courtyard and in the grey of the morning they went greyly to church. Guinevra walked beside Pia. She had Caritas in front of her, and one of the portresses behind. Fidelis led, stalking at the head of the procession with her great gaunt chin showing under her hood. Guinevra soon discovered that no one was allowed to speak, for when she spoke to Pia, Fidelis called for silence, and the woman behind her trod on Guinevra's heels.

The Consecrated Virgins and Sacred Widows, being of a particular holiness, attended at the Mother Church. Balthasar himself served here. Fidelis paused at the labrum, took water into her palm, and all those who followed her did the same. She went in by the left door of the narthex, hands together, head bowed. The nave and aisles of the little church were crowded, but room was made for the Good Women.

A deacon stood by the altar table.

"Alleluia! *Benedictus qui venit in nomine Domini.*"

The people cried—"Alleluia."

Balthasar strode up the nave with two acolytes behind him. The deacon gave place to his bishop, calling to the people.

"*Silentium facite.*"

Balthasar turned at the altar table. The little church

was very grey, but through the gable window above the porch the rising sun shot in a sudden shaft of light. It fell full upon Balthasar's face, leaving the rest of him in the shadow. To the people it was as though heaven had laid a finger of light upon the face of their priest.

Balthasar saluted the congregation. While the canticles were being sung, the sunlight crept down Balthasar's figure and made a golden blur over his heart. Guinevra, ranged with the women, looked under the droop of her hood at Balthasar. He stood there at his full height, a handsome and stately man before God. His eyes looked up at the sunlit window, and yet to Guinevra it seemed that those eyes saw every face in the church.

She could not say why the eyes of Balthasar made her mute while the others were singing. She had a feeling that those eyes saw her, and that that which was man behind them gave her other glances that burned their way under her hood. If she was a little afraid, she was conscious of more than fear. She lowered her head, but not as a penitent. Her young dignity might dissemble, but it would not kneel. If there was hot blood in her—it was not for Balthasar.

There followed the lections, psalms, gospel. Balthasar, standing in the apse, with the Chi Rho painted in gold on the wall behind him, gave the homily. He was both rhetorician and priest; his voice had a mordant solemnity. The times were dark—the world full of war and the rumours of war, but let not the faithful be discouraged. God was to try the souls of the faithful in this island. Let empires go—but Christ remained. His face was very pale. He stretched out an arm almost like a man thrusting with a spear.

"I charge you—have faith.—In these dreadful days let no man or woman think of self.—Let all pride and prejudice be surrendered.—We are all servants together, soldiers together. Let us humble ourselves and be proud—only— in service. Yes, I charge you, if violence and confusion come—we shall stand together about the Cross, not as men and women, but as those dedicated to God."

He knelt and all the church was on its knees. He prayed.

"Young men and old, matrons and virgins, we consecrate ourselves to the true faith.—I am bishop but I am servant, so shall you all be servants and soldiers sanctified in the faith. Let us put from our hearts all little things.— Let us dare greatly and humbly.—In this sign we shall conquer."

Rising from her knees with the rest Guinevra heard the whole church draw its breath with a sound like a rustling of leaves. The sacrament was to begin. The deacon, standing by the altar table, dismissed the catechumens and the penitents. Guinevra felt fingers on her arm.

"Come."

She looked into the woman's face. She did not understand that she was not to share in the sacrament. The woman's arm drew her.

"Penitents—must go."

She went, but the woman accompanied her, and in the morning sunlight Guinevra put back her hood. The woman reproved her.

"Cover your head, girl."

In fact, she tweaked the hood over Guinevra's head, and walked beside her with folded hands.

"You have much to learn, girl."

"So—it would seem."

"And one thing—is to lower the eyes and not to answer back. Did no one ever teach you what is expected of penitents?"

Said Guinevra—"Tell me my sin."

The woman grunted. "Did you not pick at the pot with that old heathen? We—who save souls—serve God."

The city was stirring. A bell clanged in the basilica, and in the street of the Forum men were hurrying. They had arms in their hands, or on their shoulders, hammers, rude spears, clubs, bills or scythe blades fastened to poles. A few carried shields made of painted wood. One fellow had a great maul on his shoulder. They hurried in twos and threes through the gate of the Forum, shouting to each other. "Hail, brother." "God's morning." "Any news from the country?"—One little, imprudent fellow saluted the two women.

"Sisters, be proud of the men of Calleva. Britain for the British, say I, and down with all the gentlemen and tyrants."

Guinevra and her guardian came to the house of Cornelia. The gate was shut, and while they waited for it to be opened, Guinevra asked a question.

"Does Calleva make war?"

The woman sniffed.

"They will go to take what is theirs, my dear, the land that should be theirs. The rich thieves shall be cast out; and are not—most of them—heathen?"

"Rich thieves?"

"Assuredly.—The whole tribe of tyrants, the Aquilas, the Gawaines, the Geraints, the Vortimers, the Aurelians. This city of God shall overthrow them and rule."

Guinevra went to her upper room, not because the woman bade her go to it, but because she wished to be alone. The grey morning had become a golden day, and a blackbird was singing in Cornelia's garden. "Peace—peace"—and peace was not. She stood at the window with a hand at her cheek. She seemed to listen, watch, and from the distance came to her the sound of many voices. Calleva was cheering its bishop.

She sat on Pia's bed—which had been her bed.—Did my Lord Geraint know of the things that threatened him?—What could she do?—How could she warn him? Was the whole world mad?—Why was she kept here?—She bit a finger and frowned. She looked at the door and at the window. Humble?—obedient?—Not she!

Presently, she heard Pia's footsteps on the stairs, and Pia was climbing in haste. She called to Guinevra even before she had opened the door.

"Come. You are wanted."

Guinevra sat where she was, and Pia's pale face was urgent in the doorway.

"Did you not hear?—Come."

"Who wants me?"

"Ask no questions, but obey."

Guinevra rose and followed Pia with her head high and her eyes steady.—What—now? Her heart might be beating against these scolds, but its tumult was secret. She walked softly, but her youth was in arms. They came to the vestibule and Pia paused here and signed to Guinevra to pass on into the atrium. Her feet glided over the mosaic floor. Someone was watching behind curtains, and suddenly a curtain was plucked back. Guinevra saw Balthasar seated in the chamber of honour, his staff across his knees, his eyes like the eyes of some figure painted upon a wall.

She stood still. She was aware of Fidelis holding back the curtain, a red paw clutching folds of purple cloth. Fidelis mouthed at her.

"Come.—Kneel. Have you not wits?"

But Guinevra did not kneel. She passed through the curtains and stood before Balthasar, and Balthasar gazed at her steadily.

"Daughter—I have certain things to say to you."

Fidelis dropped the curtain, but remained behind it, for Balthasar had given her his orders.

"Proud flesh must be chastened."

His eyes devoured her, but he spoke like a man who—standing amid burning faggots—exults in the martydom of the flesh.

"They tell me you are froward and worldly, daughter. —Such sins must be subdued."

She looked at the hands which held the staff.

"By what right am I held here?"

"Souls must be saved, daughter, and God has given me authority to save them. Shall I shirk?—I warn you, daughter, you are God's prisoner—for your good.— I would find you—humble—devout—ashamed of the garment of the flesh."

She dissembled.

"Am I to be ashamed, father, of my body?"

Balthasar's face was white.

"Do you speak to me of the body?—It is corruption, a stench, a bag of worms.—Beauty! Beauty is an abomination, a curse, a snare. Let it be cast out upon a dunghill. I would save you, my daughter.—You shall dwell here with these good women—until the body has ceased to flaunt itself.—Beauty—Satanas!—I can be ruthless for the Lord.—Cast beauty from you."

He rose. He beat on the floor with his staff, and Fidelis came through the curtains.

"Sister—let her hair be cut off. Teach her—chasten her."

When Balthasar had gone they fell upon her like crows upon carrion. She was taken into the dressing-room of the women's bath. It was a small room, and they crowded about her. Fidelis took charge. They tore the clothes from her body.

"The old harlot gave you these—I guess."

They held her, though there was no need for such clawings, for she did not struggle. Struggling would have made the business more shameful. They stripped her naked. Fidelis brought out an old shift and robe left behind by one of Cornelia's women, and flung them at her feet.

"Get into those, my beauty."

Her naked body was beautiful, and it added to their rage.

"Cover—your nakedness, girl. It is an offence to God."

Their hands had left red marks on her arms. She put on the old clothes, and her young dignity stood in the midst of them. She was very white and still.—So, she was to be allowed no shoes or stockings.

Caritas brought a stool, and Fidelis thrust her down upon it.

"Bend those stiff knees, young woman."

It was Fidelis who handled the shears, and as she snipped she spoke pious words.

"Vanity.—A woman's glory is her hair! Be not deceived.—Flies come to the honey-pot. In ugly bodies dwell beautiful souls."

Guinevra sat and smiled.

"Then—my soul never shall be as beautiful as yours, Fidelis."

"Slut!"

Fidelis gave a tug to a strand, and Guinevra winced. The shears did their work and as each lock fell something seemed to fall from Guinevra—illusions, the gentleness of other days, childish faith in the beneficence of things. She sat rigid, and as the locks fell her youth seemed to snatch at them with secret passion. She was no longer a child, but a woman whose treasure had been reft from her. She understood certain things as she had never understood them before: the ripe kindness of Cornelia, the charity of that jocund old pagan, the bitterness of these pious shrews. They hated her; they exulted in spoiling her; they stood around and watched Fidelis and her shears, and with sour joy acclaimed the goodly outrage.

The thing was done. Fidelis pushed the plunder away with a foot.

"Burn it, Caritas."

Guinevra stood up.

"Have you finished?"

Fidelis looked ugly.

"Still—head in air, shameless one. Go to your room. Stay there.—Go."

She went, with her boy's head unbowed. She looked at none of them. She climbed the stairs, shut the door of the upper room, and sat down on Pia's bed. She stared at the red marks on her arms, stigmata left by those holy hands. She was very still, but the spirit of her was ablaze. —She had been a child—but now!

2

Geraint was riding back from Malgo's village, a red and windy sunset behind him, when a man came running from the high woods, waving his arms and shouting "Lord, lord—I bring news."

The man did not belong to the White Valley, but as he came loping down the hillside between the old yews and thorns, Geraint knew him for a cattle-drover named Balan who travelled the roads between the country of the Somersetae and Londinium. Balan had driven cattle for Geraint, and sometimes in hard seasons Geraint's steward had given him work as a herdsman.

The man was a tall, long-legged rascal with a face bitten by every sort of weather. He was sweaty and dusty, and spent with running, and when he spoke to Geraint his voice was hoarse.

"Danger, lord."

"Whence came you, Balan?"

"From Calleva."

So spent was he that he leaned against Geraint's horse, his hands clasping Geraint's knee.

"Calleva?—Has the war come to Calleva?"

Balan's dusty, sweaty face looked up at him.

"I lodged last night in Calleva, lord. Wine shops are still open in Calleva, in spite of the bishop. I got the news from men who were drinking. They had drunk too much—and they talked.—You are to have the Calleva crowd at your throat to-morrow."

H

Geraint laid his hand on Balan's head.

"Man—are you mad?"

"Honest truth, lord.—I am not so mad as that city. And it is a mad dog, lord, that will bite.—It took me till noon before I could get out of the place, and then I had to take the east gate and swear I was bound for Pontes.—I know not what all this madness means, save that Master Balthasar is at the top and the bottom of it. The fellows were boasting that they would set your house alight to-morrow."

Geraint held Balan by the hair and looked into his eyes.

"You are a true man to me, Balan?"

"Lord—I swear.—You have done good things to me."

"To-morrow, you say?"

"Yes, lord."

"How many will there be of them?"

"They boast that they can send out three hundred men. They have arms—of a sort. They are out for fire and plunder. They talk of taking for Calleva all the country between the river and the sea."

"And they will begin with me, Balan?"

"Yes, lord.—Get out your wagons, round up your beasts. Put your women and gear into the wagons. You have till to-morrow."

Geraint sat and looked at the quiet country.

"Shrewd words, man, but shall I run away and leave all this—to Calleva?—We are not women."

Balan pulled a handful of grass and wiped his face.

"It is no time for talking, lord, and I am as dry as an old shoe.—I can drive your cattle for you and cheat those lousy townsmen. I know all the ways."

Geraint put his horse forward, and rode down into the valley at a canter with Balan running beside him.

In the porter's lodge of Geraint's house hung an old Roman long trumpet which was used only when the janitor put his lips to the mouthpiece and blew a few blasts for practice. At the sound of the tuba blown continuously the valley knew that something unusual was afoot, and that men, women and children should hurry to the manor house. When Geraint came to the gate he found the porter eating his supper in the doorway, the bowl of pottage between his knees.

Geraint left Balan to take his horse to the stables, and the porter's wooden spoon scooping up the last of the pottage. The empty bowl was set aside on the step, and Simon, wiping his mouth on the back of his hand, ran in for the trumpet. Blow, Simon, blow! Never before had he blown a blast that was to send a shiver through the valley, and make men look at each other and at their women.

Rual, coming out to meet his lord, saw the porter putting the brazen tuba to his lips. The trumpet screamed, and Rual, who was an old man, looked suddenly bewildered. Geraint was speaking to him, and each word seemed to sing like an arrow.

"Get the women together, Rual. Send a man for Mabon. Every wagon we have is to take the road."

Rual's mouth and eyes were three circles.

"The heathen—lord?"

"Ask me no questions. Hasten.—You will go with the wagons in charge of the women and children."

"And whither, lord?"

"To Corinium. Go, man, go.—Where is my lady?"

"In the chapel, lord."

So Placida, was at her prayers! Geraint went quickly through the house and into the garden. Behind him the sunset blazed like a beacon, and the sound of the trumpet made the twilight tremble. The orchard looked dark and strange. Through the open doorway of the chapel he saw two candles burning, and his wife kneeling before the altar-table.

"Placida."

She turned on her knees.

"Can I not pray in peace?"

Geraint stood by the door, looking in at her.

"It is not—peace, Placida.—You and all the women are to go to-night.—I have ordered the wagons."

But Placida could not be Placida without picking threads from a garment.—Go?—Leave the valley?—And why—and whither?—Geraint had much on his soul, and he was gently curt with her.   He gave her the news, and she would not believe it.—The thing was monstrous, fantastic.   A Christian city like Calleva do violence to its neighbours!   But she did not know the man who was her husband save as a rather silent stranger who had suffered her to go her way when their little world breathed quietly.

"I have no time to waste words, wife.—Every woman in the valley is to go.—I stay with the men."

She looked as though she would remain there on her knees, and he went in and blew out the candles.

"This may be no place for women.—Pack all the chests and coffers that you can fill.   We will save what we can."

She rose from her knees, and mouthed at him.

"You are mad, my lord.   Do Christians thieve and burn?"

Geraint's arm swept her out.

"Some day, my dear, Christians will burn men, even as Rome crucified them."

She went sullenly into the house, and an hour later Geraint found her sitting in the atrium watching half a dozen frightened women making confusion everywhere. Almost, her face suggested that her husband was a coward and a fool.   He had let some ridiculous rumour scare him. —Well, she would go to Corinium, but with a disapproving face, convinced that she would return in a week to ask him to show her the ashes.

Both courtyards were full of men and horses.   Geraint stood by the gate with a servant holding a torch to light the tablets in his hands.   He called men to him and gave them orders.

"Gareth.—Go to the hills at once and warn Coel. Help him to drive his sheep down here. Hasten."

Caradoc was fitting a new lynch-pin to a wheel. He came to his master.

"Do we men run, lord?"

"No, Caradoc."

Caradoc spat.

"Shall we send word to Malgo?"

"I have sent him word.—Where is Mabon."

Caradoc brought the vilicus, and the steward was hot and fluetered.

"Mabon—mount two good men. Here are letters to Aquila and the Black Valley.—They must be delivered before dawn. Understand me?"

"Yes, lord."

"Are the cattle in?"

"Balan has gone with the herdsmen.—Some are lying out on the upper pastures."

"Number the women and children, Mabon. The wagons must not leave till—all—are with us."

There was to be a moon, and Geraint wanted the women and children away, for he had other and grimmer tools to handle. But, for the moment he could do no more, and leaving that little world of shouting men and distraught women, he went down to the quiet water in the valley. He saw the rising moon hanging in the beech trees. The valley was still, utterly still, save for all that stress and stir up yonder. The island and the water were deep in the shadow, but the top of the white tower caught the moonlight.

He stood thinking, listening, watching. What a strange world! Three hundred years of peace in this valley, sunrise and sunset, dew, rain, wind, and snow. The seed sown, crops gathered in, the hay falling to the scythe. And in the north—blood and confusion, and over there beyond those hills Calleva, drunk with new wine.

And Guinevra? He had sent that lad to Calleva,

perhaps to his death.—But death himself might come steal-
ing through those woods.

A sound drifted to him, and he stood listening. He
heard the bleating of many sheep, and the wailing of lambs,
a plaintive, confused chorus. There was the barking of
a dog, and a lad's voice calling. Coel was coming down
from the hills with his flock.

CHAPTER X

Guinevra Lands on the Island

¶ MORGAN was a lad of parts. With Red Beard in bed nursing a scorched face and an aching shoulder-joint, Morgan was commended to God and Melchior the Deacon. Morgan found neither the deity nor the priest; his concern was the house of Cornelia, and with a straw in his mouth and looking as stupid as sin, he loafed and stared. Morgan could produce a squint in a crisis, and drop his lower lip, and make intelligent noises.—"Aw—but I be oop from the country."

The house of Cornelia had a gate that was opened and shut by a woman with a formidable frown, and Morgan did not waste his wits on the lady. Also, the wall was unclimbable in broad daylight, nor did Morgan know whether the house held the person to whom he was to deliver his letter. Only fools asked questions. Morgan discovered the door in the lane, and the door had a hole in it where a knot had dropped out of the wood. Morgan's eye, applied to that peephole, saw Fate at her window, and Morgan whistled softly, slapped a thigh, and wondered what had happened to the creature's hair.

He was in luck.—But one should not ride one's luck to death in broad daylight.—Would he know that particular window by moonlight?—He was sure that he would.— So, Morgan went off to play bumpkin to Calleva, and sat on a seat on the sunny side of the Forum and stared and scratched himself.—Calleva itself was as restless as a dog afflicted with fleas.

Guinevra was given bread and water for her supper.

Pia pushed them in at her, a Pia who was kinder than her sisters.

"You can sleep on my bed if you like."

Guinevra thanked Pia, and Pia prepared to close the door.

"I am keeping a vigil—till sunrise."

Guinevra sat very still until Pia's footsteps had shuffled into silence.   She ate the bread and drank some of the water, but her mood was not bread and water.   She was ready to dare anything that could be dared.   Two sheets knotted together and fastened to the bed-post would make her a a rope.   She would have to climb that wall, but she felt in a temper to climb anything.

Calleva was strangely quiet.   Balthasar had bidden men sleep and women pray, for to-morrow Calleva would cross its Rubicon.   Guinevra, leaning out of the upper window —savoured the silence.   She saw the moon huge on the horizon.

"Ssst."

Someone was below her window.   She saw a dim face close to the wall, looking up at her.

"Is it Guinevra?"

She whispered back at the face below.

"What do you want with me?"

"A letter.—I come from the White Valley."

"For me?—Wait."

She went to the door, opened it, listened.   There was not a sound.   She returned to the window.

"Whose man are you?"

"My Lord Geraint's," said Morgan, feeling very much a man.

Guinevra spoke between hollowed hands.

"I am coming down.—I have a rope."

She knotted the end of a sheet to the bed, lowered the other end and, climbing on to the sill, let herself down. Morgan saw a pair of very shapely legs in the moonlight, and being a discreet lad he turned away.   There was that quill with its letter to be slipped from under the hem of his tunic. But the adventure was not shaping as he had ex-pected it to shape. He found himself looking into the face of a crop-headed girl who was taller than he was, and whose eyes were two dark circles. Her face was very close to his.

"You are my Lord Geraint's man? Swear it."

"I swear," said Morgan, "and I have his letter to prove it."

"What is your name?"

"Morgan."

She laid a hand on his shoulder.

"Morgan, you must help me. I have been a prisoner here. I must escape from Calleva."

Morgan braced his shoulders.—The thing was not so easy, but he was feeling very much a man.

"There is that wall.—And then—there is the city wall."

She was in a swift, whispering passion.

"That wall—first.—If anyone should come to the room and find it empty."

Morgan looked at her and then at the wall.

"If I get on the top of it, I can give you an arm."

"Quick."

Youth was not balked by that wall. She was almost as active as he was. She dropped into the dark lane, and Morgan, letting himself down, became the child of an in-spiration. That cropped head of hers, and her long legs? What—if they changed clothes? As a country lad she might be able to slip through one of the gates when the labourers went out to the city fields. He said—"You will never get out of the city in those clothes, lady."

She stood listening, hugging the shadow of the wall.

"But I must, Morgan—I must."

"Take my clothes and let me have yours. With your hair like it is, you could pass."

Shocked?—not she.—But what would happen to Morgan? He swaggered.

"A man can find ways.—Will you do it?"

"But where———?"

"Here. The lane goes nowhere. I'll leave my clothes up there, and hide in a doorway, until———"

She nodded.

"But the letter?"

"You'll have the letter in my tunic. It is in a quill tucked under the hem."

She gave him her hand and he kissed it.

"You are clever and brave, Morgan."

He felt both clever and brave.

"Wait here.—I'll put the clothes in the right-hand corner where the lane ends, close to the wall. Count a hundred."

He slipped away. She counted her hundred and added twenty and then went up the lane, looking straight ahead of her. Morgan, standing slim and naked in a doorway, felt her pass. She was very quick. She came back and past him, and he darted for the dark end of the lane. She had taken his wallet, but forgotten the staff. The boy in him chuckled. This was an adventure.

He found her thirty yards down the lane in the shadow of a wall. She looked a tall lad—but her bare legs were too white. Morgan eyed her critically.

"You forgot the staff. Better take it."

"And your wallet?"

"I can do without it.—I think you had better rub some dust—on your—legs."

She looked at her legs, and her act proved that she agreed with Morgan. She bent down, dabbled her hands in the dust of the lane, and rubbed her legs until their whiteness was dim. And for the sake of thoroughness she dusted her face and neck. Morgan nodded approval.

"Look silly—if anyone speaks to you. Can you look silly?"

"Show me."

In the moonlight he let his lower lip drop, and turning his face sideways, played the idiot.

"I'm oop from the country, master."

She had to laugh.

"I'll try and look like that, Morgan."

Morgan took charge of the adventure. The city was strangely still, and Morgan made for the wall near the west gate. There were some penthouses along the wall where masons kept stone and tools. Morgan explored. He found some straw in a corner of an open shed.

"There's a bed—of sorts."

"And you, Morgan?"

He put his shoulders back. He might be wearing women's clothes, but he felt vaingloriously man.

"Oh—I—keep awake—I am going to prowl down to the gate and see what I can see."

He disappeared, and Guinevra sat down on the straw, but sleep was very far away. She ran her fingers along the hem of Morgan's tunic, and felt the quill that held the letter. She pressed it against her body. To-morrow, when it was light, she would read his letter. To-morrow— perhaps——?

Morgan, returning, reported the gates closed and a strong watch set on them. He sat himself down with his back to the wooden side-wall of the penthouse. He had had a long and desperate day—but he was determined to keep awake, and his comrade in the adventure was more poignantly wakeful than he was. Morgan, in a whisper, began to tell her of the visit of Red Beard and the lad to the White Valley, and how my Lord Geraint had set him to fool the men of Calleva. Yes, and had he not fooled them quite prettily? As for my Lord Geraint there was no other man on earth to match him for all the things that go to the making of a man.

Guinevra listened.

"We are all in danger, Morgan."

"By the gods, lady, that's true.—If I were the Emperor I would make my master General of Britain."

Morgan was full of news, and he imparted it with

authority to the lady. The heathen were over the Wall, and likely to come south unless the soldiers could stop them, and Calleva was braying like an ass full of oats. Stirring times—indeed! Men were needed, men like Geraint—and Morgan.

But Morgan fell a-yawning. He pressed his shoulder-blades against the wood to admonish the flesh, but the body had its way. He fell suddenly asleep like a tired young dog, his head sagging, and Guinevra let him sleep. The short, summer night would soon be over.

She sat and watched the greyness of the dawn make that which had been vague and dim gradually distinct. She heard the singing of birds in a garden, the footsteps of a watchman passing along the wall above. The man let out a yawn just above their hiding-place. She saw Morgan huddled against the wall in the dirty old clothes the good woman had given her, and she looked curiously at the lad's face. He seemed to be smiling; he had eyelashes which would have graced a girl, and crisp hair that curled.

She decided that she ought to wake Morgan, and she touched his foot with the staff. He seemed to unwind like a spring, jerking his head back and shooting out his feet. Who——? Where? His face was comic in its gravity; no, he had not been asleep, just dozing. He crawled to the open face of the pent-house, and peered round a corner-post. There was no one to be seen.

"All quiet—lady."

He came back and squatted. He looked at Guinevra like a lad who wanted to laugh, but who held that laughter would not be seemly, for Guinevra had dusted her face more thoroughly than she knew. She had a streak of dirt down one cheek.—Morgan took the adventure in hand.—There was some bread and cheese in the wallet, and if Guinevra was a wise girl, she would put food inside her before the day's work.

She was wise. They shared the bread and cheese, and Morgan talked in a whisper.

"Do you know how to reach the White Valley?"

She did not, and he told her.

"Follow the great road for twelve miles or so, and you will come to an altar among some thorn trees. Take the lane on the left. That will bring you to my lord's place. —But, to begin with—I should keep off the road. It is open country, and you can follow the road—by your eyes. —Now, as soon as the city wakes up—I'll go and scout near the gate. There are cattle and crops to be seen to outside the wall, and you can slip out with some of the hinds.—Put a bold face on it, lady, but not too bold. If anyone should question you—remember to look silly.—A farmer sent you to Calleva with a sucking pig to sell. You sold it, and you are going back to your master."

Guinevra nodded at him.

"I'll remember to look silly, Morgan."

"Just grin. Can you make your voice sound—like a lad's?"

She tried it, and the attempt was not very convincing

"Humph," said Morgan—"I'd grin and say nothing, or just make noises. The world is full of idiots."

She laughed, though the affair was serious as death. By now, someone might have discovered that empty room, for Pia's vigil ended at dawn.

"Go and see if the gate is open yet, Morgan."

He went, but in two minutes he was back.

"Here's luck. Cattle and drovers waiting to come in and quite a little crowd going to the fields."

She stood up with staff and wallet. She looked anxiously at Morgan.

"Do I look like a lad?"

"Not so bad," said he; "but don't walk too nicely Turn your toes in and slouch. And grin, lady, don't be solemn."

He went with her to the street opening in the gate, they stood in the shadow of a house, and the luck of the day was theirs, for the gate was opened and the cattle were

driven in. The beasts were frightened, and two steers
tried to bolt. Men shouted, dogs barked. The people
who were waiting to go out to the fields crowded beside
the gate.

Morgan gave her a push.

"Now, lady—I stay. There are things to be watched
here."

Toes in, and trying to look as oafish as she could, she
slouched across the open space to the gate. The last of
the cattle and the drovers were through, and those within
were in a hurry to get out. Guinevra escaped with the
old men and women who carried hoes and baskets. No
one spoke to her. Two men on guard had taken toll from
the drovers and were counting the money, and finding it
short. One of them ran shouting after the drovers.

Guinevra saw the open space of the pomerium before
her, and the road leaving it like a white thread. She
walked a little way, sat down on the kerb like a lad who was
in no hurry. The workers went on towards the fields.
Guinevra pretended to search her wallet; she found a crust,
stuck it in her mouth, got up and idled on, gnawing the
crust. When she reached the road, she turned and looked
back—saw that the gates were shut. Ahead of her stood a
little grove of birch trees. She walked towards it until
she reached the trees, and slipping in among them, ran.

2

Guinevra, following Morgan's advice too closely, lost
the highroad and her way three times that morning. Moreover, she was very shy of the open road and of what might
come along it, and whenever she saw anything moving,
she hid herself. About five miles from Calleva she had a
fright. Two mounted men sighted her, and came riding
down, waving and shouting, and she bolted for cover.
The country was all gorse here, and though the men did

not find Guinevra, the spines of the gorse did.   She had a scratched face as well as a dirty one.

She heard the men calling to her.

"Come out, you fool.   We are not robbers."

Had she known that they were two of Geraint's men scouting towards Calleva, she would have saved herself time and scratches, but she lay hid there for the best part of an hour, and crawled out at last like a rabbit ready to bolt back to cover.   After this fright she was very careful. When there was open country she would skirt round it, using what cover she could find, and sometimes at the end of such a digression she discovered that she had lost touch with the highroad.   Woodland offered her secret passage, but it might conceal other perils.   She had not forgotten the beech wood that morning in May.   She glided between trees—sometimes standing very still beside some tall trunk, imagining sounds—movement.   What was that over there? Surely, a man had slipped behind a trunk?   The green glooms seemed more sinister than the sunlight.   The white road became a welcoming, friendly presence.   The farther she travelled, the more she trusted it.   Moreover, she had had no food since dawn, and her legs were not the legs of Morgan.

At last, daring the road completely, and meeting neither man, woman, nor child, she came quite late in the afternoon to the altar among the thorn trees.   She knew it at once. She saw a little pool in a green hollow; it was half covered with water-crowfoot—but the whiteness of the bloom had gone.   She was thirsty.   She went and knelt by the pool, and took water in her hands and drank.

She had disturbed the mirror, but when the surface had become glass, she looked at herself in it.   Ye gods!   She had a scratch across her forehead, and another down one cheek, and a smear of dirt on the other.   Again she took water in her hands, and washed her face.   Then she sat down to rest among the thorn trees, picked that quill from the hem of the tunic, extracted the letter with a grass-stem, and read.

It said—"The friends of Guinevra are troubled.   If she would send news to her friends, the messenger is to be trusted."

She put the letter in her wallet and dreamed. So few words, and yet how like him. Friends. Would she see his wife? Was Cornelia at Turris Alba? What would he say, how would he look? She went to the pool, kneeled down and scanned herself again. Her hair was a sort of ragged halo. She would never forgive those women. But she was up and swinging along the track that climbed a grassy swell towards a beech wood. She was not afraid of the woods now, and presently she came out upon a hillside and saw below her Geraint's valley, the house, out-buildings and cottages, the parkland and fields, the great pool with its tower and island. She saw more than these: a group of men and horses on the grassy space below the great house. The sunlight made play upon points of metal. A man was leading a white horse up and down, Geraint's horse. And suddenly a strange confusion possessed her. She sat down under a tree. With bare legs and a cropped head was she to appear before all those men?

3

The great house was shut up, gates, doors and windows closed. Geraint and Malgo stood apart, watching the woods on the farther side of the valley. Malgo had come in from Vicus Flavus with two men; the rest had refused to meddle in a business that was not theirs, for if neighbours quarrelled that was their concern. Let my Lord Geraint and the city of Calleva fight out their feud or compose it.

Geraint was growing restless. An hour ago his scouts had ridden back with the news that the men of Calleva were on the march. These fellows of Geraint's had ventured within sight of the walls of Calleva and had seen

Balthasar's people pouring out and taking the road to the
west. The sun had been well past noon when the gates
had opened.—Geraint had looked grim. So, it was to
be a night attack, timed so that this armed crowd might
expect to break in and cut throats in the darkness.

He looked at the sun.

"They are late, Malgo."

For Aquila and Gawaine of the Black Valley had sent
word that they would join him at Turris Alba. If the
White Valley were over-run and plundered, the same fate
might overtake other countrysides. Geraint had no more
than twenty men, and even if old Aquilla and Gawaine
rallied to him, they would muster together less than fifty.
He had his plan. It was to wait for the Calleva crowd in the
woods between the high road and the White Valley, for
if Calleva came south it would mean that Calleva had marked
down its prey. He would attack them at dusk. Fifty
men charging out of the woods, and keeping well together
might rout three hundred.

Caradoc was at the forge, putting in a few last blows
before letting out the fire and donning his lorica and helmet,
when a lad appeared in the doorway. Caradoc stared, for
the lad was a stranger, and somehow strange at that. He
said that he had a message for my Lord Geraint, a most
urgent message.

Caradoc jerked a thumb.

"You will find him—over yonder."

The lad walked into the smithy and sat down on the
settle in the shadow.

"It is a very secret message, smith."

Caradoc stared.

"So! Where do you hail from?"

"Calleva."

"Ha! And what's your name?"

"Thomas."

Caradoc looked hard at the lad. Where had he seen
him before? But if the lad came from Calleva——

I

"You would speak with my master here?"

The lad nodded. He seemed rather shy of using his voice. Caradoc looked at him again, spat, walked out of the smithy, and went towards the house. He found Geraint standing with folded arms, his face dark and watchful under his brazen helmet.

"A lad has just come into my smithy, master. He says he has news from Calleva."

"Bring him here, Caradoc."

"There is something strange about the whelp. He seems to like the shadow. He asks to see you alone."

Geraint dropped his arms and turned towards the smithy.

"Remember Red Beard, master," said Caradoc.

And Geraint smiled.

"It would take a good knife to get through this metal, Caradoc."

He walked up the hill to the smithy. Caradoc followed him to within fifty yards of it and stood at a gaze like a dog. He saw Geraint disappear under the thatch.

Guinevra was on her feet, hands folded over her bosom, eyes downcast. Those bare legs of hers trembled a litttle.

"Guinevra!"

His eyes were not the eyes of Caradoc. She raised her head and looked at him, and then—suddenly—she fell on her knees.

"Have I sinned—in coming, lord?"

He stood a moment—gazing at her as a man gazes at something deep and strange. He took her by the arms, and raised her, held her.

"Child—Morgan found you?"

"Yes."

She was all red, and unable to hide it. Her eyes looked at the plates of his lorica.

"But—your hair? Was that——?"

"They cut it off in Calleva."

"Who?"

"Balthasar, and the women who had charge of me.—
They held me a prisoner."

"You?"

"Because of Cornelia—because——"

Geraint's eyes never left her face.   He saw the scratches
—the wild, slanting loveliness of chin and cheek, the half
hidden eyes, the glowing, poignant confusion.   And she
was here.   He was touching her, and she did not flinch
from him.   But at what a moment, when there was not
a woman in the valley, and the woods were waiting for
the men!

"You have come at a strange hour, my dear."

She looked at him slantwise, faintly smiling.

"And in strange clothes.   If one of your women can
spare me a frock."

He stood back.

"There is not a woman in the place, but I doubt not that
I can find you something."

"Not a woman here?"

He turned to the door of the smithy, and his eyes bade her
stand there beside him.

"See.   Men in harness.   Your good friends in Calleva
are on the march against us.   You cannot have been
very much ahead of them.   We have sent our women
away."

She looked very serious over this.

"What am I to do with you, Guinevra?—Give you
a horse and a man, and send you into the west?   And time
is short."

She stole a glance at him.

"I am tired—Geraint—I have not eaten since dawn."

"Child——"

"And the road—at night—I would feel safer here.   But
I will do what you bid me do."

"You are too precious, Guinevra."

She stood with downcast eyes—Precious?—Could there be any safer place than where he was?—Why could she not ride with him?

"Let me stay, lord."

"But, child, we go up to the woods to wait for our enemies. We fight."

Her voice was like a little golden thread.

"Could I not hide here?"

Did he want her to go?—No, by the gods!—As for the mob from Calleva—not a man of them should reach the valley. And below him he saw the pool and its island and the white tower, a casket for such treasure. She would be safe there for the night, with the barge moored at the island. She should have food and clothing and a bed.

"Guinevra."

"Yes, lord."

"Do you see the water and the island and the tower—would you be afraid there?"

She looked at him with full, deep eyes.

"No, lord."

"Come.—Time is short. Go down to the water, Guinevra. I'll follow."

With one look at him she went, and Geraint called Caradoc to him.

"The lad is frightened, Caradoc. I have told him he can spend the night on the island."

He looked hard at the smith.

"Have you seen that lad before, Caradoc?"

"Somewhere, master—but I can't remember."

"Then do not remember—till I tell you."

He took Caradoc with him to the house, and unlocking the door opening from the stable court, he bade Caradoc go into the kitchen quarters and find what food he could. Geraint passed into the summer-room, tore down a purple curtain, and tossing three cushions and a rug on to it— tied the corners of the curtain together. He heard Caradoc in the vestibule, and Caradoc had possessed himself of some bread and a pot of honey. That should be good enough for the lad.

"He can fill his belly with bread, lord."

They passed out, Geraint carrying his bundle, locked the door after him. He went by way of the orchard and along the vineyard fence, and over the grass towards the Grove of Sylvanus. Caradoc followed. His master was taking a very roundabout road. Why all this trouble for a yellow-haired whelp?

They came to the pool.—Guinevra was sitting on the bank, legs drawn up, arms wrapped round them. She was a lad of understanding, and she gathered that she would have to serve as her own ferryman. Caradoc put his platter and pot in the bottom of the barge, and Geraint threw in the bundle.

He looked steadily at Guinevra.

"That's your supper, my lad.—You'll find the door of the tower open."

Guinevra got on her feet, and Caradoc unfastened the chain.

"In with you, whelp."

She stepped on the gunwale, and sprang down, and picking up the pole, gave Geraint one mysterious glimmer of the eyes. Neither of them spoke. Caradoc thrust the barge from the bank, and Guinevra dipped her pole. The two men stood to watch her, but with very different eyes and feelings.

Said Caradoc—"A most unhandy lad—that. It might be a girl. He'll fall in—if he's not careful."

Geraint said nothing.—He was wondering if the girl could swim. But Guinevra, like a wise virgin, was using the pole as a paddle, first on one side and then on the other, and the barge moved slowly over the water. There was no wind or current to trouble it.

"He'll do, master. A most unhandy lad—though."

Suddenly, they heard the winding of a horn, and looking

up towards the high woods in the south they saw men on horses and on foot streaming into the sunlight.

Geraint's eyes flashed.

"Aquila!"

Caradoc spat.

"Ha, the old eagle!"

There was a smile on Geraint's face.   He looked across the water and saw that the boat had reached the island.

CHAPTER XI

The Island

¶ THE tower held two rooms; wooden stairs led from the lower room to the upper, and from the upper room to the leads, and Guinevra, having made fast the boat and carried her gear to the tower, climbed the stairs. A trap-door had to be opened at the top of the second flight of stairs; spiders had spun webs here, and dust fell as she raised the trap.

She stood against the parapet, and the island was like a green ship becalmed in still water. There were water-lilies floating on the lake. The blue of the sky was a canopy supported by the towering woods, and to her drifted the smell of hay. A man had been scything the grass among the fruit trees, and the pale swathes had dried in the sun.

But, for the moment, the tower was a vantage-point from which she watched other happenings. She saw Geraint on his white horse riding down to meet Gawaine and his men who had followed close on the wings of Aquila. She saw Geraint and the Gawaine reach out and clasp hands. They rode up the hill together, Gawaine's black horse beside Geraint's white one. They joined old Aquila, and the three of them rode slowly up and down while their men stood in little groups or lay on the grass. Gawaine's men—there were but ten of them—brought their horses to the lake for water. Guinevra was trying to count the men who would follow Geraint against the rabble from Calleva, and they seemed so few, not more than fifteen mounted men and a score and a half on foot.

She looked very serious over her numbering of the company. But had she not seen Geraint deal with the mob at Calleva? Her faith in him was miraculous and a thing of the heart. He had but to show himself on his white horse and the rabble would run.

But they were moving up yonder. A trumpet blew. She saw the riders mounting their horses, and the footmen falling in. Geraint led, with old Aquila and Gawaine on either side of him. The horse followed next, with the footmen in the rear. She saw the coloured shields and the sloped spears go up the hill, and the sunlight playing upon the war-harness. Where the tall woods began Geraint drew aside as though to watch the men go by. He was still there when the last file had marched in among the trees. The white horse and the figure in the gilded lorica showed vividly against the dark trunks. Geraint was looking at his valley empty and still in the late sunlight. She saw him raise an arm.

She waved, and his arm fell and rose again. He turned his horse and disappeared.

She put her hands over her face.

"O, my dear lord, God keep you."

That was all her prayer, and there she stood still and straight, her face burning. O, my lord, my love! She clasped herself and her secret. What a wonderful world was this with its blue sky and its burning sun, and the great woods and this deep valley! The tower was a pinnacle, and the water-lilies fallen stars floating at her feet. The smell of the hay was like a song. She put her arms behind her head and closed her eyes.

"O, my lord, my love—why should I be so happy?"

She drew a deep breath and stepping on the stairs, she closed the trap-door. Sudden darkness, diffused light below. She stood a moment, mysteriously still, touching the mortar between two stones. She had things to do, and every little thing was mysterious.—She descended to the lower room and looked about her. She

saw an oak bedstead like a box on legs, a stool, some pots
on the window-sill, an old black cloak hanging on a nail.
There was a rough cupboard in a corner, and going to
open it she found a cup, two plates, and an old knife that
was rusty.—She looked again at the bed, and then at her
slim long legs.—How should she use that curtain, as a
robe or as a blanket?—She remembered the hay, and running out among the trees, she took an armful and found
that it was dry; and it smelt like heaven. This would
make her a bed. She carried in several loads of the hay
and spread it on the boards of the bed.—She discovered
the cushions. He had remembered to find her a pillow!

And she was hungry. She took one of the pots from
the window-sill, and carrying it to the water, washed and
filled it. Bread and honey, what could be sweeter? She
made herself a seat among the hay where the sun shone,
and took her supper there. The sky flamed. The water
was as still as death, with the colours of sky and cloud
reflected in it. The white lilies dreamed. The world
smelt of mown hay.

With the coming of the twilight and the falling of the
dew her mood put on another dress to meet the night.
Two black bats had emerged from the tower and were
fluttering noiselessly against the afterglow. The woods
grew more high and dark, the valley more deep. Green
grass and leaves became grey. Gold was transmuted into
silver. The silence was supreme, every leaf and grass-
blade motionless, the water like steel.

Guinevra grew restless in the midst of this great stillness. She walked up and down, or stood listening. She
remembered that she would have no light but the light of
the moon. A few stars pricked the sky. She went in and
climbed the dark stairs, and let herself out on to the plat-
form, and looking up towards the black wall of the woodland, she felt her heart like some goblin-pick striking
muffled blows in a hollow place deep in the earth. What
did the night hide? What violent things had happened

beyond those woods? But this was mere foolishness, fear fluttering around in the twilight like those bats. She said to herself "Dear God—why am I a coward? Is not my love well able to guard his head?"

She stood there for a while, straining her ears and her eyes until the night and the profound peace of the valley made her accept that which could not be questioned. She closed the trap and looking down felt that the dark tower had become like a wall. And suddenly her knees shook; she was afraid of falling; she went down step by step with her body and hands pressing against the wall. When she reached the floor of the lower room she drew one long deep breath. Her world seemed to have grown dim and cold and ghostly. The window was a mere patch of greyness in the wall; she could smell the hay, but she could not see the bed.

She groped for it, found it, and felt her hands touching the dry grass. Could she lie down and sleep?—Impossible. This was to be a vigil in which her heart would go to and fro on restless feet. The room chilled her, shut her in. She went out and down to the bank where the barge lay, hands stretched out like the hands of a blind girl feeling her way.—When would the moon rise? Stooping, she touched the grass and found it wet with dew. The boat lay close to her feet, and somehow the craft offered itself as a cradle to her fears. She stepped into the hollow of the black shell, and groping—found a seat.

Presently, the moon rose. She saw it first as a pale splendour tangled in the trees, while the shadow of the high woods still covered the valley. She sat and watched the moon climb above the tree tops. Could anything look more peaceful than that moon? Even the sleeping water became alive, and dabbling a hand in it she watched the tremulous ripples of light. She said to herself that these soft splendours were beautiful and solacing. She was still dabbling her hand in the water when she heard that cry.

It seemed to shoot up suddenly out of the stillness like

an arrow, hold a high note of anguish and then falter and fall back into the night's silence. She sat rigid, her right hand trailing in the water. Once more the silence was profound, but the mute mouth of the night was a circle of fear. Would that cry be repeated?—It seemed to her that it had come from the woods in the north, the woods into which Geraint and his men had marched. She stood up, and her face was as white as the moon.

Had the night no other message for her? And then she heard a faint sound, or rather a confusion of sounds which was no more defined than wind in a wood heard far away on a quiet night. She climbed out of the boat and stood on the bank, listening and gazing. The sound grew, and from a murmur became like a cluster of voices, or a fire made up of many little flames. The shouting of men! It seemed to spill over the lip of the valley and come nearer, but as yet she could see nothing.

The white house and its outbuildings were no more than a vague patch of light upon the hillside, but presently she got the impression of movement, something dark like a cloud shadow drifting over the slope. Men; a crowd of men, running, shouting, howling. Was it Geraint returning?—But would Geraint ride back at the head of a screaming mob? A sudden, great chill struck her; she shuddered. Something seemed to dim the white wall of the courtyard, blotches of hurrying figures. She heard blows struck as though a gate was being beaten in. She stood rigid, fascinated. All that was happening over yonder was a shadow play, save that the voices were the voices of wild and exultant men.

She drew back under the trees, shivering both in soul and body. What had happened? Had Geraint and Calleva met, or had they missed each other in the woods? Had the crowd poured unhindered into an empty valley?— But that cry?—Disaster? Wounds and death in those dark woods. She shivered. And then she saw a sudden brightness over yonder. A torch flared. Windows became light.

She saw a little tuft of flame rise like a red flower from a roof. The thing wavered and spread. It seemed to leap, and gather strength from the howls and shouts of the little dark figures that were running hither and thither.

Geraint's house was burning.

2

With her face between her hands she sat under an apple tree and watched the house go up in flames. Its glow lit the valley. She could see the men of Calleva leaping and shouting like madmen.—She felt cold with fear, not because Geraint's house was burning, and that mob was shouting and exulting, but because the night hid things from her. Had Geraint and his men met disaster in the woods up yonder, or was the fighting yet to be? She would not believe in disaster. The Calleva mob had come by some other way, and Geraint would ride back to find his house alight and that fool crowd waiting to be slaughtered.

But a voice came over the water, and the night uttered her name.

"Guinevra."

She started to her feet.—Who had called her?—And again the voice came to her over the water—like a voice smothering in blood and anguish.

"Guinevra."

She peered under a hand.—There was something over there on the farther bank; the moonlight touched metal. —She rushed to the barge, threw off the chain, and poled out, and to her passionate hands the clumsy black shell seemed glued to the water. The moonlight made a sheen upon it, and upon the thing she gazed at.—It was a man, and the sheen was the sheen of his armour. He was kneeling, and supporting himself on his arms, his head hanging low and showing her the crown of its helmet.

Geraint!

The nose of the barge ran in among the water-weeds
and flags. She put down the pole, stooped for the chain
and jumped. The heavy chain was itself a sufficient
anchor, and she let it sink into the green growth.

"O, my lord!"

She was down on her knees beside him and suddenly
he raised himself and she saw his face. There was no blood
upon it, but his lorica was all one dark stain.

"I bleed—Guinevra—I bleed."

And suddenly her love was fierce in her. She looked
over a shoulder at the burning house and those little figures.
—That way lay death.

Her hands held him.

"The island.—Have you strength?"

He knelt, hollow-eyed, like a man praying. She could
hear the pain and labour of his breathing.

"I might——"

She lifted his left arm and laid it across her shoulders,
and clasped him with her right. She felt the warm wetness
of him.

"Now——"

Her young body rose with him. He took three steps,
tottered, and leaned upon her, groaning. She stiffened herself, and held him.

"O—my lord—three more steps."

He straightened.

"I'll do it.—Now.—Steady."

Somehow she got him into the boat, and he sank down
with his head against the gunwale. She pulled in the chain,
poled the nose of the boat out, and set it for the island.—
Would they be seen?—She could have torn that moon
down out of the sky. As she panted, bending to the pole,
she expected to hear shouts, and the sound of men running
towards the water, but the crowd up yonder was too busy
about its blaze of victory. She brought the barge to the
farther bank and into the shadow of an overhanging
tree.

And here began her second anguish.   He lay there like a man who was dying.   As she bent over him his lips moved.

"Guinevra—water."

She took water in her hand, twice—thrice, and let it run into his mouth and over his face.   He looked up at her and seemed to smile.

"That's—better—child.—They were too many for us. Some of our men—ran.—I got a spear under the ribs."

She put her hand on his mouth.

"Yes—yes.—Save your strength—lord.—Could you reach the tower?"

"I'll try."

"Could—I carry you?"

"My dear—I can crawl."

It was slow agony getting him out of the boat and across the grass to the tower, but get him there she did.   The bed would serve.   He fell into the hay, and lay panting, one leg hanging outside.

"Guinevra."

"Lord."

"Go—now.   Leave me.   Take the boat across and make for the woods on the west.—Go."

She lifted that helpless leg.

"Never."

"But—child——"

She found a cushion and put it under his head.   She was blessing the moon now, for it was shining in at the window.

"I stay.   Do not speak to me again of going."

She thought of nothing now but how she could save him.   Was he to die?   Dear God, no.   She drew aside to let the moon do what it could, and bending, looked. She saw the rent in his harness where the spear had stabbed him, and a dark ooze still spreading from it.   Should she let him lie there in his harness, and trust to nature, or use her hands?—She had no linen, no oil, no wine with which to wash the wound.—He was lying very still, gazing at her.

"Lord—could you bear me to loosen your harness?"

"Try—child."

His lorica was fastened at the back with straps—but first she unbuckled his sword belt.   Then slipping her hands beneath him and into the hay, she groped for the buckles and managed to release them.   Then, very gently, she drew the harness from him and laying it aside, looked at him. His tunic was all blood.   She turned it up and saw the wound under the ribs, a red slit from which blood still oozed.—Would she be wise not to meddle, but to let him lie there and pray for the bleeding to cease?

"I have no clean linen," she said.

"Do I bleed?"

"But little, now."

"Leave well alone, child.—It is good to lie still.   If my body is quiet——"

She nodded.

"I have some honey and bread——"

"No.   Give me water."

She brought her crock and held it to his mouth, and let the water dribble into it.

"Ah, that's good."

"I'll fetch more water."

She went to the lake, and in the moonlight she saw the blood upon her hands.   She washed them, and filling the crock, hurried back.   She heard his voice.

"Guinevra."

"Dear lord."

"I'm cold—so cold."

He was shivering, and her heart shivered with him. She remembered the purple curtain, and she covered him with it.   There was that old cloak on the wall.   She plucked it down, went out and shook the dust from it, and laid it over the curtain.

"Shall I rub your hands, Geraint."

She was kneeling beside the bed, and he turned his head on the cushion.

"Let me lie still and look at you."

For a little while there was silence between them, and she listened to his breathing and to the distant voices of Calleva. The mob was growing less noisy. And what did that signify?—Would they be content for the night with their victory and the burning of the manor, and eat and drink and lie down to sleep? And to-morrow? They might see the barge lying by the island, and guess that someone had passed over. The floor was of stone, and hard to her knees, and she slipped into a sitting position, her shoulder resting against the bed. She was frowning, and biting at her lower lip, and wondering how she could hide the barge.

"Guinevra."

She turned her head swiftly.

"Yes, lord."

"I have two quarrels with Calleva. They have burnt my house, and cut off your hair, and yet——"

"Yes, lord?"

"You are as—fair—without it——"

She looked slantwise at him.

"I am what my lord—pleases.—But should my lord waste his breath on me?"

"I cannot waste my eyes, child."

"Is my lord less cold?"

"Guinevra—I have a feeling that I do not bleed."

She rose swiftly and softly, and turning back the cloak and the curtain, she peered, her face close to his body. Had the lips of his wound sealed themselves? She could not be sure by the light of the moon, and very delicately she put a little finger against the wound and saw that no blood flowed over it.

"It has ceased, lord."

There was sudden strength and passion in his voice.

"Ye gods—I'll not die from the bite of a dog.—There shall be——"

She put her hand on his mouth.

"O—be still—be wise, or it may break—again. You frighten me."

He kissed her fingers.

"Guinevra—pardon—have no fear."

Her hand came away from him slowly.

"I want my lord to live."

And suddenly she fled, and out there in the moonlight she flung her arms across her face and stood quivering. She wanted to laugh and to weep and to pray—and to cry to God and her own heart—"I love I love. There is no sin—no shame. Dear God, save him—not for me—but for the loveliness of life, for pity." She swayed a little, and then stretched out her arms to the moon. She was happy, so happy that she wanted to run wild, and sing. She burned to do things for him, and remembering the barge, she went instantly and soft-footed over the grass and searched the southern bank for shelter. She found another overhanging tree, and going back to the boat she slipped into it and taking the pole brought the barge round the island keeping close to the shadow of the bank. She moored it under the branches of the tree, and crossing to the other side of the island, looked up at the ruined house. It was a mere glow now, blackened and flameless, and Balthasar's people were growing quiet. They had lit watch-fires, and she could see figures round them. The night was claiming its own.

Women can be very wise when they love, and Guinevra was wise for Geraint's sake. Returning to the tower, she stood in the doorway, listening. Wounds and the heart are eased by sleep, and if he were asleep it would be witless to wake him. But Geraint was not sleeping. He saw the dim shape of her in the doorway.

"Guinevra."

"Lord."

"I thought I had lost you, child."

"I have brought the barge to the other side of the island and hidden it under a tree."

J

"You are very wise, Guinevra."

"One is wise—perhaps.—But, lord—I would have you sleep."

"Sleep?—But you must be very weary, Guinevra.—And I have stolen the bed."

"There is hay under the trees.   I can make a bed."

"Here, Guinevra?"

"Yes, lord.—For, in the night you may need me."

She went out and gathered hay from under the trees where the dew had not wetted it, and spread it a foot deep upon the floor, going and returning five times.   The smell of the dried grass filled the room, and Geraint watched her moving against the moon.

"Have you eaten, child?"

"Yes, lord.   And there is bread left for the morning."

"Lie down, Guinevra, and sleep."

"If my lord will sleep, so will I."

She stretched herself on the hay with Morgan's wallet stuffed with hay under her head, and lay and listened to Geraint's breathing.   The valley was as quiet as death, and she snuggled down into the deep hay and let it cover her legs and body.   She told herself that she would not suffer herself to fall asleep until she was sure that Geraint had no more need of her, but his quiet breathing was like drugged wine.   She might be in love, but she was very weary, and presently she fell asleep like a leaf falling into deep water.

CHAPTER XII

The Red Flower

¶ GUINEVRA woke soon after dawn to find the room filling with light, and the hay smothering her like a spider's web. A great stillness covered the valley, and so still was everything that she sat up in a panic and looked and listened.—Was he breathing?—Geraint's right arm hung over the side of the bed, and rising on her knees, she peered, round-eyed and anxious. No; he was breathing; he was asleep, and his face was profoundly still. She knelt in the hay and crossed her hands over her bosom. She gave thanks—"O, God—I kneel. Be merciful."

But the dawn was her call to compassion. There would be peril in the day—great peril, and her hair was full of hay, and her heart calling. She crept out among the trees as full of guile as some wild thing, and lying down in the shadow behind a cock of grass, she scanned the valley. The house up yonder was a blackened shell sending up a smudge of ghostly smoke. The bailiff's house and the smithy and the cottages had not been fired, and she saw a few figures moving. Other men were asleep on the hillside about the vapoury watchfires, and they looked like the dead.

Very cautiously she crept down to the southern bank, and saw that the boat was there among the water weeds under the tree. The water was dark under the branches, and the black flanks of the boat seemed part of the water. That side of the valley was empty, and she knelt and washed, and with her fingers combed the hay out of her hair. Then, she filled the pitcher that she had brought with her, and crouching, stealthed her way back to the tower.

Geraint was awake.   His eyes looked at her from the bed, and she stood, finger on lip, her eyes—mysterious.

"Some of them are awake.—Voices carry."

He smiled at her, and she put down her pitcher and bent over him.

"How is my lord——?"

She whispered, and he whispered back at her.

"Alive, Guinevra, and the better for sleeping."

Very gently she turned the clothes aside, and looked at his wound.   The blood had clotted about it.   She mused a moment, faintly frowning, and while her eyes were on his wound, Geraint's eyes were on her face.

"What news, Guinevra?"

Her beautiful, mute seriousness held for a moment.

"It does not bleed.—If I had clean linen——"

"I am a foul creature, child—all blood——"

She looked at him wide-eyed.

"Is—blood—unclean—lord?—There are things that I would do, and yet—there may be—less peril—in your lying still."

"Is my face——?"

"No."

"But, my hands, my dear."

She looked at his hands.

"I'll tear a strip from the curtain and wash your hands, lord."

"And my mouth, Guinevra.   I could drink."

She supported his head with one hand and gave him water in a little bowl.

"Could you eat—lord?"

"A few mouthfuls."

She broke bread with her fingers and dropping a little honey on each piece, she slipped the bread between his lips, and watched him while he ate.—But he could not eat much. He shook his head over the fifth morsel, and smiled faintly.

"Enough, my dear.—Now, you eat."

She looked shrewdly at the bread.

"I am not hungry, lord."

"Eat—Guinevra."

"Lord—we must be—thrifty."

"I bid you eat, child. The gods have been kind as yet.
Your strength is my strength, Guinevra. Be bold—and eat."

She smiled at him slantwise, and broke herself a piece
of bread, but denied herself the honey.

"If they go, lord—I may find food in the valley—or
friends may come."

He watched her with deep eyes. He did not tell her
what he thought, that Balthasar's people would leave the
valley picked to the bone. But he was both too weak to
feel bitter, and too much a man in the force of his years
to look on yesterday as final. If fate spared him he would
be even with Balthasar. He had lost friends; how many
he did not know. He had seen Malgo with his back to a
tree, holding off four fellows; he had had a glimpse of
Gawaine with his face all blood. There had been confusion in the twilight, the few struggling with the many,
and but for his white horse, Geraint would have been
left there in the woods. He had turned the good beast
loose in the valley and managed to reach the water.—
Could he blame those men of his for running, hinds who
had never carried arms before? His foresters, huntsmen,
and household servants had fought well, and paid the
penalty—poor devils.

But Guinevra was up and at the door. She had heard
some sound that he had not caught; she leaned against the
doorpost listening. Voices, the splash of water. And
suddenly she turned, and ran to the stairs, and climbing
to the upper room, crouched down below a window. She
raised her eyes to the level of the sill, and then let out a little
sob of relief. The horses had been brought down to the
pool to be watered; another fellow had a wooden bucket
at the end of a rope and was casting it in and drawing water
and filling casks. There was much stir and movement
on the hillside as though Balthasar's people had other work

in hand. Two wagons were being loaded. The men across the water showed no interest in the tower or island, for Balthasar had had spies in the woods who could swear that the tower held neither goods nor women.

Guinevra sped below.

"They are watering horses, and loading wagons, lord."

Geraint raised his head.

"Then—the gods are with us. There are other places to be plundered. It is the turn of Aquila."

"I will go and watch."

"Yes—watch."

She knelt at the upper window. Could the good thing be true? Hardly did she dare to believe it, and yet before the sun had topped the trees Calleva's little army had formed up on the hillside. She saw a man in a white cloak come riding on a black horse from the bailiff's house.—Balthasar. He carried a staff with a gold cross mounted on it. He raised his staff on high and spoke to the men of Calleva. They fell on their knees and shouted.

Balthasar turned his horse and rode down into the valley, and the men of Calleva followed him. Guinevra ran to another window. She held her breath. Were they leaving the island unsearched? She saw Balthasar and his captains and men, horses and wagons cross the valley and take the track that climbed to the woods on the southern ridge. They marched like men for whom the day had other and grim work. She watched until the last man had disappeared among the trees.

She went down the stairs, flushed, glowing.

"They have gone. Dear God, they have gone."

2

Ten of the clock, and the valley full of sunlight and silence, and no live thing to be seen.

For the best part of half an hour Guinevra had watched

the valley, until she was sure that Balthasar had left no
men behind him, and then without a word to Geraint she
unchained the boat and ferried over. She wanted food,
linen, wine, and perhaps a skirt to cover her bare legs,
but she had not much hope of finding any of these things
in the smouldering house. But her luck and Balthasar's
orders gave her what she had not hoped for. Balthasar
had suffered his men to plunder and burn the rich man's
house, but he had bade them leave the bailiff's house and
the cottages of the labourers untouched.

"Take from the rich, my children, but pity the poor."

In the house of Mabon the vilicus she found linen and
coverlets in a press, a loaf of bread and a flask of oil, cheese,
and some honey ale in an earthenware jar. In a cupboard
she discovered a green kirtle hanging, and though the thing
was old and worn, it would serve. A box of salt, an iron
spoon, a bowl of beech, and two platters of hollywood
were added to her plunder. Twice she went to and fro
between the bailiff's house and the pool, and with the gear
loaded, she crossed over to the island.

She appeared before Geraint, carrying her bundles.

"Food—lord."

His eyes looked at her dully. His face was flushed,
and his breathing uneasy, and each breath stabbed him.
And the joy of her exploit went out of her. She bent over
the bed and laid a hand on his forehead. He had fever.

"Pain—lord?"

He moved his head.

"The wound catches me."

She had her fear, and did what heart and head advised.
She tore up linen, and brought her bowl and clean water
and washed him, but she did not touch the wound. She
poured oil on a pad of linen and laid it upon the wound,
and with a knife cut away the bloody tunic. She bathed
his hands and his face, and her eyes were as gentle as her
hands.

"Would you drink, lord?"

"A little water, Guinevra."

She gave him water, but food he would not touch.

"Do you lie easy, Geraint, or shall I fetch more hay?"

"Turn me a little, Guinevra."

"Put your arms about my neck, lord."

She helped him to turn so that he lay a-new. She took away the curtain and the cloak, and covered him with a sheet and the coverlet. The sun was pouring in upon the bed, and she managed to fasten the curtain across the window so that too much light should not vex him. Then she stood, and with hands hanging, knew that she could do no more, save hope and pray, and minister to his body's needs. She was conscious of no shame in all that she did, nor did the simple realities of her service shock her.

He put out a hand.

"Guinevra, does a man—forget?"

She held his hand a moment, her face poignant and mysterious.

"Do I not owe my lord much?"

"Guinevra."

"Sleep—Geraint—try to sleep.—I shall be near."

She went out and sitting under an apple tree she watched the valley. Perhaps some of his men would return? She would give herself to the last heartbeat, but she was greatly troubled and fearful for his sake. In Verulam, Londinium or Calleva one could call a physician, and here—she a mere girl—had nothing but her love and her eyes and hands.—What if he were to die? Could she find help?— But could she leave him? She watched the dark woods, and nothing came from them. The trees seemed to stand and stare. The great house smoked a little.

Presently, she rose and going to the door of the tower, she listened. She heard his breathing, but the rhythm of it was not even. It seemed to catch like silk drawn over a splinter of wood. Moreover, she heard him making a kind of pitiful muttering. The fever had increased.

She crept in and stood close to the bed. His face

looked dusky. He had thrown off the coverlet. His eyes stared straight at the beams of the floor above. A spider hung there by a thread—but his eyes were not looking at anything.

She touched his forehead, and his head gave a jerk. He muttered at her.

"Someone—here—— Who?"

"Only—Guinevra, lord."

He stared at her.

"Hair. They have cut off her hair."

Again, she bathed his forehead and hands, and he lay staring, and breathing as though something in him was broken. Her love yearned in her and was mute.

He was very restless and his restlessness quickened her suspense. She would sit by him for a while, and then climb to the top of the tower and watch the valley. The day was serene and still, a few white clouds floating, not a ripple on the water to rock the lilies. She moved round the trees. The high woods seemed asleep. If man could not help her, what of God? Her faith had been a very simple thing, an affair almost of the nursery, sheltered in illusions. She served Christ—but so did Balthasar and the men who had wrought this ruin, and Geraint was not of their faith. What did men make of their God? A minister to their prides and passions, an idol who should nod consent when they so pleased, a fellow-plotter in their pursuit of power? It seemed to her that some men served God in order that their god might serve them. They moulded a mask of clay, and with it covered the face of their deity. He should frown when they pleased, and into the mouth of the idol they put a tongue that was but the tongue of a priest.

Christ crucified—Christ the Saviour, the Christ of her childhood, not the Christ of Balthasar and of Fidelis and her women. She knelt and prayed to the Christ of her young heart, the God of love and of compassion. And kneeling there in the sunlight she felt comforted. Had not God been smitten with a spear, even as her love had been wounded?—Moreover, other thoughts came to her. If Geraint and Cornelia were not of Christ, was it not because they had been shown the priest and not the God? Balthasar might cry—"Christ is God and I—am His servant," but the shrewd old eyes of Cornelia had seen only Balthasar.

In truth Cornelia would have said to her—"My child, your God is indeed a God—but I like not his people. They are vulgar, ignorant, arrogant and noisy. I could live with your God, but not with His bishop."

The day drew on. She sat beside Geraint and listened to his mutterings. She moistened his lips, and spoke to him as though he understood. Sometimes he seemed to know and to understand; sometimes he did not. She washed his poor face, and was not shocked by the frailties of the flesh. Her love, during that anguished day, ceased to be the fancy of a girl, and became the love of woman. She endured, and towards the evening it seemed to her that the fret and the fierceness of his fever grew less. He lay very still with eyes closed; he slept.

Was this life or death, a steadying of the flame or a failing of it? Did he bleed inwardly? Very gently she raised the clothes and looked at his wound, and saw that no blood showed. She knelt beside the bed and prayed, and knew that she could do no more.

In the dusk he opened his eyes, and his hands moved on the coverlet.

"Guinevra."

"Dear lord."

"You are there?"

"Yes—I am here, Geraint."

"Is it growing dark?"

"Yes, lord."

"Then—I have slept.—Give me a little water, child."

She gave him water, and he looked at her in the dusk.

"Your hands are very gentle, Guinevra.—I will sleep again. The pain has passed."

She sat by him till he was asleep. There was gladness in her, exaltation, for she had a feeling that he would live. Had the prayer of her heart been answered?—She went out into the night, and looked at the stars, and they were like kind eyes. She knelt in the grass and poured out her soul.

"O, God—Lord Christ, let him live.—Can there be any sin in compassion?"

3

That night Guinevra slept heavily, for she was very weary, and death seemed less near, and in the morning she found Geraint awake, his head turned upon the pillow so that he could see her.

She was up instantly, remorseful and confused.

"How shameful of me."

He was so weak that he smiled only with his eyes. Had ever a man won a more blessed wound? As she stooped to the bed he felt the beautiful young dignity of her hallowing him.

"My lord has slept?"

"Better than I deserve."

She touched his forehead.

"Less fever.—Would you drink, Geraint?"

"Yes."

"And eat?"

"A few mouthfuls, Guinevra."

She could not hide her joy, nor did she seek to hide it.

"My lord—I must wash."

She slipped away out into the dew and the soft dazzle of the dawn, and going to the water she washed, and prayed while she washed. Her heart gave thanks. She looked at herself in the water. Was she fair—fair to him, and would any God who had made this beautiful day condemn her beauty? She ran her fingers through her hair, and sitting on her heels, looked at the morning. What would the day bring?—Nothing but good things, surely?

She returned to the tower, and taking water and linen she washed his face and lips. He felt himself an unclean thing, but her eyes saw no uncleanness. She gave him drink, and a little bread and honey, sitting on the stool, each morsel held between finger and thumb.

"Eat—lord. It will give you strength."

He managed six small pieces of bread and honey, and smiled a shadow of a smile.

"That's all I dare. Eat—Guinevra."

"I am too happy to be hungry, lord."

"One should be happy because one is hungry. Eat."

She rose and stood in the doorway with bread in her hands.

"When you are hungry—I shall be hungry, Geraint."

And in the heart of each those words seemed to burn like little flames on a secret altar.

CHAPTER XIII

Balthasar

¶ IT was a little before noon, when, Guinevra, climbing to the top of the tower to scan the valley, saw a sight that made her go cold. She crouched, and keeping her head below the parapet, crept to the stairs. The upper room had a narrow window facing south, and Guinevra, standing close to the wall, looked round the stone of the window.

Balthasar!

She saw him on his black horse riding down from the woods with the men of Calleva behind him. Two soldiers in harness walked beside his horse. Calleva was marching as it pleased, for it had taken its pleasure in the Black Valley and burnt the eyrie of the Eagle. More plunder— more wagons. Balthasar was returning to Calleva to share in the city's little triumph, and to lay upon the altar the title deeds of three estates. The patrimony of Calleva had enlarged itself. From the city, parties of colonists were to be sent out to hold and possess the lands of Geraint and his friends. The League of the Four Cities was in being. Venta and Regnum had thrust out their rich men and their councillors and officials, taxmongers, assessors, and what not, and had elected Balthasar as their praeses.

But Guinevra trembled at that upper window. Had they seen her on the tower? Was Balthasar passing by, or had he returned to establish his men here? She drew back from the window into the deeps of the room, and that panel of sunlight and of green grass was like a picture hung before her. It framed Balthasar, the marching

149

crowd and the wagons. She could only press her hands to her breasts and pray that the enemy might pass.

And then she saw one of the men beside Balthasar stand and point. Balthasar stopped his horse. O, horror, had they discovered the boat lying by the island under the shade of the tree? She stood rigid. Balthasar was bending in the saddle and speaking to the man. She saw the fellow turn, and raise an arm. He shouted to those behind. Could any man among them swim?

She went down the stairs with her knees shaking under her. Geraint lay asleep. Should she wake him and tell him they were trapped? She crossed the room swiftly and closed the door; it could be fastened by heavy bolts, and she shot them.

She faced about. Geraint's eyes were open. He had seen her thrust home the bolts.

"Guinevra——"

Her eyes were two dark circles, her voice a whisper.

"Balthasar."

"Ye gods——!"

He tried to rise on one elbow, and she ran to him.

"No—no.—Lie still. There is hope—yet."

He lay back, groaning a little.

"Are they on this side?"

"No—but they have seen the boat."

"They will come over.—Hide, child.—Quick.—There is some fern at the west end of the island."

She knelt by the bed.

"The door is fast, lord.—They may think that there is no one here."

He put a hand on her shoulder.

"What?—With the door bolted?—Open it—child, keep under the bank and hide. They can find me. I'll tell them two of my men brought me here and went for help."

She knelt with eyes lowered.

"I will stay, lord."

"Guinevra——!"

"Hsst!"

They looked into each others eyes and were silent, for there were voices on the island. Three men had swum across and were sniffing like dogs round the tower. They came to the door, tried it, and found it bolted.

"Hallo—there!"

Guinevra laid her face against the bed, and held Geraint's hands. She would be with him—yet—for a few moments, alone with her love and her anguish. The men were whispering at the door.

"There are some rats in this old place."

"Take the boat over, Noddie, and bring help. Rats can bite."

"Let's try a window."

"And get a knife in one's throat! The more—the merrier—and the safer, say I."

Guinevra felt Geraint's hand on her head; his fingers sank into her hair.

"I would look at you, child."

She raised her face from the bed, and his hand dropped to her shoulder. They gazed into each other's eyes, and in that look the soul of each was stripped of all secrets. Guinevra's face seemed to dream. She let her head droop until it was close to the face of Geraint. Not a word did either of them utter. Geraint kissed her hair, and then let his hand cover her head.

So, close together and in silence they waited for the coming of Balthasar.

2

Balthasar was ferried over with half a dozen of his men. The sun was at full noon, and so was his fortune, and he walked between the apple trees to Geraint's tower with the large and deliberate air of a man whose yea and nay

carried.   When he came to the tower he bade one of the
men knock on the door, and the fellow beat upon the
boards with the butt of a spear.

"Open—open in the name of God and Balthasar."

Balthasar stood and smiled.   Such a summons suited
both the occasion and his temper.   God and Balthasar!—
But within the tower there was silence.   Geraint and
Guinevra were looking into each other's eyes.

"Break down the door" said the Bishop.

Geraint drew Guinevra's face to him and kissed it,
and very gently thrust her away.

"Open to them.—It will save time."

She rose to her feet, and going to the door she shot
back the upper bolt, just as a man with a smith's hammer
was measuring his distance for a blow.   Balthasar heard
the sound, and held up a hand.

"Peace.—All doors open to us."

Guinevra slipped the second bolt, and drawing back,
she stood beside the bed.   Balthasar's men were cautious;
there might be a trap here.   They handled their weapons
while one of them thrust the door open with the point of
a spear, and crowding in the entry they saw a man lying
on a bed, and a girl standing beside him.   Balthasar was
taller than any of his men, and looking over their heads,
he saw what they saw.

The face of Balthasar had been sleek and unctuous,
but suddenly it seemed to narrow to a bleak edge.   He saw
the girl, and knew her, and his eyes grew cruel.   The
face of the man on the bed was in the shadow.   Balthasar
stood a moment—very still—but within something gnawed
at his vitals.

He bade his man stand aside.   He walked through the
doorway with arms folded—like a priest entering a church.
His face had a strange starved look, as though his secret
lust devoured him.   So, the wine-cup that he had put
aside had been held to the lips of another.

He stood, half ice, half fire.   He looked at Guinevra,

and at the man on the bed. He knew him now. He spoke sharply to the fellows behind him.

"I have other sins to shrive—my friends. Shut the door and leave us."

They obeyed him. Calleva had come to know that their bishop was master, and Balthasar waited until the door was shut, and he heard the footsteps of his men departing. His eyes were like two pieces of glass. He smiled, and his smile was the edge of a sword.

"God has sent me here—it seems—to save one soul.— You ran away from us so fast, my lord—that we could not find you, and thought—you lost. But God is wise— blessed be God."

He crossed himself.

"How did this woman come here?"

He looked at Guinevra standing with her eyes hidden from him—but it was Geraint who answered.

"Of her own free will—bishop—and by chance.—Let her go. I am your—enemy."

Balthasar smiled at him cunningly.

"You are wounded—my lord."

"Should I be lying here?"

"Truth—my lord, truth.—We will let wounded men lie—and pray—to their gods.—But as for this—harlot——"

Geraint rose on one elbow.

"That is a foul word—bishop, and as false as it is foul. But for her pity—I should be a dead man."

"Is that so—my lord."

Geraint struggled for breath, and Balthasar, watching him, knew that death still stood beside the bed.

"Let her go—where she pleases.—You can do with me what you will."

Geraint sank back in the hay, for his strength was like wax, and with a little cry Guinevra ran to him.

"O, my lord, do not vex yourself for me."

She took the bowl of water and, supporting Geraint's head, she gave him drink, and Balthasar watched her, arms

K

folded, his finger-nails clawing his arm-pits. So, all the urge of her youth was towards Geraint. The flower of her virginity was his. Balthasar's face looked ravaged.

He spoke.

"The girl shall go where God pleases.—Come, you wanton——"

He flung open the door, and his voice cut like a whip.

"Out—out into God's light.—Leave—this man—to his gods."

Guinevra stood holding the bowl. There still was water in it, and some of the water spilled itself on her feet. She looked at Balthasar as though she did not yet divine the thing he meant to do.

"He is very weak.—Let—someone——"

Balthasar pointed.

"Out.—Did you hear me—girl."

And, suddenly, she understood. Her eyes grew big with horror, horror of the thing and of him. Her lips moved—but for a moment no words came.

"Out.—I have certain things to say to this man.—Out with you, wanton."

She was shaking. She dropped the bowl amid the hay, and going to Balthasar, she fell at his feet.

"You will not leave him here.—He will die."

Balthasar stared down at her upturned face. Its beauty was strange, agonized, wounded. So, should her face be —lying below him—when he was master. And suddenly he struck her on the mouth with his open hand.

"Get you behind me—harlot.—Shall I call my men? Out with you."

Her hands dropped. She knelt and looked up at him, and her face seemed to go grey. Then, very slowly she rose to her feet, and with eyes that looked blind, she went to the door. She turned there, hands hanging, throat showing white and clear. She looked at Geraint. Her lips moved, but nothing but a little soundless anguish came from them.

She passed out into the sunlight, and Balthasar standing

in the doorway, watched her, his teeth showing in the white
glare of his face.   He called to his men.

"Take the woman.—Tie her hands behind her back,
and put her in a wagon.—I follow."

Balthasar waited until he could see the boat moving
beyond the trees, and then, turning about he stood in the
doorway and looked at the man on the bed.   There was
no sound save the sound of Geraint's breathing.   His eyes
looked at Balthasar.   No word was spoken by either of
them, for Balthasar's mercy was death, and Geraint would
not ask for mercy.—But the eyes of Balthasar saw other
things, the bread and the jar of water.   He went in and
emptied the jar upon the floor, and taking the bread he
tossed it out of the window.

For some seconds he stood in the doorway looking at
Geraint, then—with two fingers of one hand raised—he
slowly closed the door.

CHAPTER XIV

Guinevra Among the Good Women

¶ AFTER a night of thunder and of rain Leo the Prefect rode out of Corinium to meet his Excellency, Boniface—Comes Britanorum. His Excellency had been bathing and taking the waters at Aquae Sulis when the beacons had begun to blaze, and to begin with he had not hurried, for Count Boniface was fat, and the colour of raw meat, a little, angry man with purple cheeks who sat in a chair and screamed.

Dame Cornelia, lodged at the house of Rhadamanthus her banker, and feeling the whole house and her host shaking in their shoes, had said caustic things about his Excellency and the world in general. She had said them to the Prefect at his dinner table, and Leo had smiled down his long white nose at her.

"While that fat old fool sweats in his bath—the whole island will go up in flames."

Leo had caressed his chin, while reminding her that in a world of Vicars, Counts, Prefects and Legates, no dog could bark until some bigger dog had given tongue. The defence of the island was Count Boniface's affair, until such a time as the Emperor might choose to intervene.

And Cornelia had rapped on the table.

"The Emperor—yes, the Emperor—My lord, some day there may be no Emperor to help us. He may be too busy with the Germans or the Goths.—Let us count heads. In this island the Emperor is served by a Vicar, a Comes, five Prefects, and two soldier Legates, the Duke of Britain is dead and we will leave him out of the story—while the Count of the Saxon Shore is on the water—nine eminent and elderly gentlemen, my lord, who sit and dictate letters to each other—while the barbarians use the sword.—Let someone put on a helmet and call the island to arms."

Leo had looked at her slantingly under white eyebrows. He was a genial cynic, and something of a wag.

"I could name no better man than yourself—matrona, Britannia in arms."

"And I could find you a man to-morrow, my lord—but you would provide him with six secretaries and twenty clerks.—Rome is dying of a surfeit of scribblers."

It was a day when men sweated easily, but could not rid themselves of their sweat. Two rows of tall poplars, moving never a leaf, seemed to make the road more breathless. People panted along it from the west, countryfolk who were flying for fear of the Welsh. Cattle trod up the dust as the road dried, and gentry in their carriages, peasants riding upon donkeys or mules, and those who trudged, pushing their belongings in hand carts. Some fussy frontier-warden had started beacons blazing.

Leo, lean, long and sixtyish, with a skin like vellum, reined in his horse, and spoke to some of the people.

"Why this haste, my children?"

"The Cymri, lord, the Cymri."

"They tell us Glevum is in flames."

"That is strange, my children, for I—the Prefect—have not heard the news."

He smiled his dry smile when the fugitives pressed on towards the walls of Corinium. Sheep! But could one blame them when a world of officials had taught the common folk to behave like sheep? When the sheep-dog barked they obeyed him, and when there was no sheep-dog they were stampeded by the imagined howling of a wolf.

He rode on with his retinue, one eye half shut, the other very wide to the world. Leo Gallicus had found one drooping eyelid very useful; turned, on occasions, towards loquacity, it had persuaded a brother rhetorician to conclude that Leo was somnolent either in the spirit or the flesh.

Those delicate long fingers would support a drooping head. Meanwhile, his eminence's smile would trickle down his nose.

It was at Pontis Nigra that Leo saw the plumes of his Excellency's horse-guards shimmering through dust and sunlight. They came on at a walk, for Count Boniface was travelling in a litter. The flesh forbade him to hurry, but inside the litter a fretful, fat and perspiring soul made haste to meet disaster. Boniface had kept his secretary walking beside the litter recording the great man's whims, which passed for ordered wisdom. The poor fellow with the tablets was wishing the great man in Hades, and himself elsewhere. He had walked ten miles, trying to sift his chief's petulances from remarks that were official. What were all these damned people doing on the road, cluttering it with their wagons, sheep and cattle?—Flying from the Cymri? What?—Besotted boors! Not a Welshman had crossed the Severn.—And there was too much dust. Boniface had squealed for the captain of his guards.—"Must you smother me, sir. Take your squadron on, sir, take them on, or let 'em follow behind. Am I to travel in a dust-cloud?" Moreover, flies had become attentive. His Excellency was a succulent morsel, and flies do not pass through the school for sycophants.

When Comes and Prefect met on that white road between the poplars, Leo dismounted, and Boniface's litter was set down by its bearers. Leo saw a bald head and a fringe of hair, and a halo of buzzing flies, and a black switch made of the tail of a horse contending with the insects. Leo was bland and debonair.

"I trust your excellency has travelled well?"

For the moment the Count's face was as pathetic as the face of a fat and indignant baby.

"As you see, sir—like a tub of butter.—I'll get out; I'll get out."

He would not be assisted. Leo watched two huge legs roll themselves out of the litter, and one of those legs had a bandage upon it. His excellency got on his feet, and flourishing the switch, toddled heavily to the side of the road to humour nature.

"Well—what news—what news?"

Leo's open eye looked down its sagacious nose.

"Much news.—May I suggest to your excellency that we share it—in private."

The Count faced about and stared at him.

"More trouble—more trouble   The fates are like these flies, and the world like my bladder.—I'll walk—yes—I'll walk a little way.—There's no air to-day."

He waved a pudgy hand at his people, soldiers, officials, clerks, servants.

"Get on, get on with you.   Don't leave me your dust. And give me my sunhat, you fellow."

The litter and its escort passed on, and the Count and the Prefect took the road, Boniface walking as though his immense legs were made of wood.   His straw hat with its down-turned brim made him look even more like a large and petulant baby.   He kept his horse-tail moving.

"Well—well, my friend—your news is fresher than mine. Let us have it like olives in oil.   Begin—begin."

Leo looked cool as marble.

"I had a dispatch this morning from Verulam.   Magnus is shut up in Eboracum; Aurelian is holding the country round Deva.   Our friends the Picts can walk south at their leisure. There is nothing to stop them but the walls of our cities, your Excellency's valour, or the sea."

It was said so sweetly that Boniface did not catch the sardonic note.   He stumped along on his huge legs, swatting the flies that sought the shade and the juices under his hat.

"Ha—strategy, perhaps."

"How so?"

"My Legates will let the scoundrels come south, and then fall upon and annihilate them.   Magnus shall march from Eboracum, Aurelian from Chester.   I shall send orders

to Isca and muster the last man.   Rhutupiæ can spare its
garrison.   I'll call on Nectarides for men from his ships."

"But—that—is not all the news, your excellency."

"What, more?"

"My spies tell me that the Cymri have come down from
their mountains."

"Those damned Silures."

"Yes, those damned Silures, and others.   We hear that
some Irish ships have crossed over."

Boniface smote peevishly at the flies.

"Tell me some more—my friend.   Have you any more
Pelions to pile?"

Leo caressed his chin.

"Unfortunately, yes.—We have it from Rhutupiæ that
Saxon ships have been sighted in the Channel."

"Well—that is Nectarides' affair—not mine."

"It may prevent him lending us men."

"Granted—granted.   A fellow like Nectarides will
think only of his own reputation.—So—that—is all."

"Not quite—all."

The face of the little fat man seemed to flare under his
hat.

"Ye gods!—What else?"

"His Excellency has heard of the affair at Calleva?
Shall we call it a new Christian republic."

"That fellow Balthasar.   A farcical fellow.—Surely,
Prefect, you don't take that riot seriously?"

"The Bishop has levied troops."

"Without my authority.—I'll levy him, sir."

"I hear that Regnum and Venta have joined him."

"They shall regret it.—Well, is that all?"

He looked up with an air of pathetic truculence at the
face of the man who walked so coolly beside him.   Leo's
blind eye was towards him, upper lid subtly drooping.

Said Leo—"Can one make confusion worse con-
founded?   Words are useful things, like soldiers, when
they serve, but when words fail and soldiers desert——"

Almost, he knew what his poor comrade in chaos would blurt at him.

"Desert!—Roman soldiers never desert, sir.—A man who has taken the oath to the Emperor——"

And Leo sighed. Boniface buzzed like a blowfly.

"Forgive me, but they—do.—They are even deserting to the barbarians.—Ought we not to remind ourselves that some of them were born—barbarians?—They are forming robber bands, and taking a hand in the business—of plunder."

He said no more, for he began to be afraid that Boniface would dissolve into tears or grease. Was not the poor, gouty old pagod to be pitied?

His Excellency took off his hat and fanned himself.

"I think I will get back into my litter—friend. This heat is very trying."

And suddenly he stood still in the middle of the road, his face convulsed like that of a child about to weep.

"But—what shall we do?—Ye gods, what shall we do?"

Leo caressed his chin.

"Sit in our cities, hold what we can, and wait for the Emperor. Let the wild men wear themselves out."

2

Calleva went out with alleluias and green branches to meet its bishop, though the routing of three country squires could not be recorded in the city's annals as an epic victory. But Calleva had become a city of new men led by a new man, and if two or three rich men had been tumbled in the dust, that was a sign in the heavens. *In hoc signo-vinces!* Balthasar's men marched in through the city gate, shouting and tossing their weapons. Melchior the Deacon, leading a choir of the faithful, sang roundly before his lord. Hylas the Hermit, leaping out of the crowd, danced like David before the people.

And, in a wagon, seated on a coffer that had been looted from the House of Aquila, the very symbol of a world's salvation was carried along above the heads of demos. Balthasar's plunder, beauty saved from the beast.—Her face was pearl grey, her eyelids lowered, her cropped head bowed down. The noise and the dust were but part of her martyrdom, love reft from its compassion and carried like a severed head dripping secret blood. Guinevra did not look at the faces of the people, but at her knees and the hands that rested on them. Behind her a summer sunset blazed above a world of flowering grasses. It lit up Calleva's walls and roofs and coloured plaster, and flashed upon the little gilded genius high upon its column.

She felt the wagon stop, and came out of her love stupor. Someone was speaking to her. She was aware of faces: the familiar faces of Fidelis, Caritas and Pia, like masks nailed to a wall. The wagon had stopped before the gate of the house of Cornelia. Balthasar, high on his horse, stretched out a hand and pointed. The crowd was silent. Balthasar's voice was a scourge.

"Get thee down, harlot. Behold those who shall save you."

For a moment she did not move. Why should this man throw a foul word in the face of her love, this man who had left her love to die?—And then—she rose. She stood very pale and straight, looking at the faces below her. She was no more to them than a strumpet sentenced to be whipped. They gloated. Some lewd fellow shouted—"We have brought back Geraint's whore." She looked full at the man like a child, eyes wide, lips slightly apart as though about to speak. Then, she put a foot on a wheel, and holding to the side of the wagon, let herself down.

Instantly, Fidelis had her by the arm.

"Go in, shameless one."

She shook Fidelis off, and the crowd laughed.

"The girl's some sauce left in her."

"Give her the whip, dame."

The women, crowding round, hustled her in through the gateway, and Fidelis, beckoned by Balthasar, went and stood with folded hands beside the bishop's horse. Balthasar rode demos as he straddled his horse. He had to flatter the crowd and his own virtue. Calleva had ears and eyes—and tongues, and for the moment Balthasar was its prophet. He spoke to Fidelis so that the people should hear.

"A brand plucked from the burning, my sister.—Let it be quenched. I give her into your hands."

The return of the prodigal was the occasion for no love feast. The Sisterhood of the Consecrated Virgins of Calleva had a ritual of its own, which, without being bland, could be applied to most blemishes. Guinevra suffered these humiliations in the cause of holiness. Her love had tried to staunch a wound, and was accounted sin.

They took her to the common bath and set about stripping her. Fidelis saw the bloodstains on her shift. These stigmata were strange and exciting, and Fidelis poked a yellow finger at them.

"What's this—what's this?"

They peered like witches, and then, Fidelis, pulling up the garment, uncovered a skin that was virginal and without a wound.

"How did you come by this blood, girl?"

It was Geraint's blood which had stained her when she had lent him the strength of her young body. She had forgotten those stains, but they were sacred.

"The blood of a man."

She spoke with an air of innocent insolence. Caritas made a clucking noise; Pia crossed herself. Fidelis, with a jerk of the hand, rent the garment from her and left her naked.

"Disgusting."

"You shall be washed," said Fidelis.—"We can make clean the outside of the cup, and please God—we will save your soul."

She was pushed into the sunk cistern which formed the bath, and with a crock Fidelis poured water over her head. Fidelis was the symbolist, but heavy-handed. Love had made the body of Guinevra unclean, and they scrubbed it until the skin was red, and rubbed in oil which had been blessed by the church. Guinevra was made to kneel naked on the red tiles of the floor, and with solemn faces, they prayed over her.—She watched Pia's pale lips moving. How strange was all this. And more strange still was her own humility, a mood of incredulous, wounded pity. For, in that valley her lover lay dying, and she could do nothing, while hiding in her heart hatred of the man who had left him to die.

They brought an old linen smock that had been washed, and put it over her head.

"Stand up."

She rose to her feet. Caritas was holding a grey frock with a hempen girdle. Caritas' hands were so like claws. The frock was dropped over her shoulders, and Fidelis tied the girdle, pulling it so tight that the cord sunk into the flesh.

"That's as it should be."

Then, they took her to a narrow cell that had been a store-room in Cornelia's time. It had a slit of a window and a tiled floor. It contained a stool and a wooden bedstead, a basin and ewer. They pushed her in.

"Think of your sins," said Fidelis as she shut and locked the door.

3

Geraint lay and watched the sunlight from the window move across the floor. At full noon it had rested upon the bed of hay where Guinevra had slept, but now it was slanting towards the door. The yellow edge began to climb the brown wood and Geraint's body cried out—"I thirst —I thirst."

The sunlight crept up the door. The fever had blazed

in him again, and made his thirst even more bitter. He had fallen into profundities of rage and helplessness listening to voices that were the voices of an illusion. Had he seen Balthasar empty the water-pot upon the floor, and Balthasar standing there in the shadow looking at him with eyes of infinite meaning? Had these things happened, or was this the fog of his fever in which figures came and went like the particles of dust drifting in and out of a sunray?

And suddenly he cried out—"Guinevra—Guinevra."

Silence, and that yellow edge of light creeping up the door. He lay for a while in a kind of stupor, and then the fierce craving of his body for water seemed to subdue the very phantasies of his fever, and to become a wild and passionate mouth shouting at him as at one who must be made to hear. "Fool—you have been left here to die. Give me water, or I shall perish. There is no help on earth for us—save in water.—It is there, so near, just under the green bank. Water, water, cool, deep, wet."

The voice of his body roused him. His consciousness seemed to clear, and to take on the likeness of the water that he burned for. Ye gods, he had been left here to die, but die—he—would not. He had matters to settle with Balthasar whose lean face had slipped through that doorway like a white and malignant half-moon. Water—life, love, blood! Even that red hole in his side was another mouth parched and calling for water. The sanity of struggle came to him. He drew up his legs and rolled off the bed, but when he tried to stand, his legs would not carry him, and his head spun like a wheel. He went down on his hands and knees and crawled to the door. He put his hands against it, clawed himself up, and fumbled with his right hand at the latch. But there was no strength or cunning in his fingers; they were like the fingers of a glove stuffed with wool. He pushed the latch up with the ball of his thumb only to realize that the door opened inwards, and that his fool body was leaning against it. And then he fell sideways like a drunken man, and the latch dropped to.

For some moments he lay with his mouth against the cold stones. His lips sucked at them.—He would try again, supporting himself against the wall, so that the door would not be cumbered by his body. He got on his knees, and resting one shoulder against the wall, reached for the latch. His hand went up and down like the hand of a sot trying to light a candle, but he managed to raise the latch and open the door six inches. He put his head in the gap, and like a dog—enlarged it, and burrowing through with his shoulders, he crawled out on to the grass, and there—he fainted.

It was there that Morgan found him, a Morgan who had swum the pool just when Geraint's thirst and anguish had clawed their way into the air. The lad came up long-legged and dripping. He went down on his knees beside his lord, and his wet hands touched him.

Geraint moved, groaned, and rolling sideways, looked up into Morgan's face. His eyes were sunk in his head like dead coals in a brazier.

"Water—water."

As Morgan bent over him some drops from his wet hair fell on Geraint's face, and one drop lighted on his mouth. Geraint's tongue came out like a little hungry flame and licked it up.—But Morgan had seen enough. He was up and running to the tower, and finding the empty crock, he went to the pool and filled it.

Geraint had drunk, and a great peace seemed to come to him. He lay on the grass with an armful of hay under his head and looked at Morgan, who squatted on his heels beside him. There was something strange about Morgan. His face was no longer the face of a lad: it looked pinched and old, for Morgan had seen dead men, old Malgo lying with a spear sticking through him, his face the colour of clay.

"My life—was in that water-pot, Morgan.—Who sent you here?"

The lad looked at him intently.

"God's chance or my own wits.—I have been lying out in the woods, lord—watching."

"And you saw——?"

Morgan nodded.

"I waited—to be sure, lord—that none of them were left behind.—I have seen things that make one cautious. Calleva breeds strange Christians."

"Dead men, Morgan?"

The lad's arms hugged his knees.   He shivered.

"Yes, dead men, lord, lying up there in the woods.—It is not good to be like that, all yellow and starved, with a nose like a beak and the eyes of a dead fish.—Have you eaten, lord?"

Geraint turned his head on the hay.

"Go and look on the south side of the tower and you may find half a loaf of bread.—Our friend Balthasar threw it out of the window when he emptied my water-pot."

Morgan's eyes stared.

"He left you—to die—lord, without bread or water?"

Geraint smiled at the sky.

"But—death—may come to Balthasar."

That night, just when dusk was falling, Morgan saw a ghost across the water, but a solid and helpful ghost: Geraint's white horse, who had found his way back to the valley and come to the pool to drink.   Morgan ran into the tower and told Geraint.

"The beasts are merciful, lord.   Victor—is there, drinking."

"My horse?"

Sudden strength came to Geraint.   He rose from the bed, and leaning upon Morgan, went down to the pool. He could see the grey shape across the water, and he called to his horse.   The beast threw up his head and answered him, and man and beast were one across the water.

Said Geraint—"If there be a God, lad, He has not deserted us.   Go over and tie Victor to a tree.   Be gentle with him—tell him from me—to-morrow—with help—I could get upon his back.—This is no place for us—for our friend Balthasar will send to see—whether I am ripe for the worms."

Morgan nodded.

"The forest, lord.—I know a place."

"You seem to know, much, Morgan."

The lad laughed.

"I have had quick feet, lord, and much curiosity."

CHAPTER XV

The Forest

¶ THE way went north. It began as a grassy lane leading from the Calleva highroad, and after passing a farmhouse and a ruined shrine, it glided into the forest like a snake. Morgan, having put a cheek to the wind and looked at the sun, led on, holding the white horse by the bridle. Before sallying they had unsaddled Victor, and Geraint lay along the good beast's back, his head against the horse's neck. They had less than five miles to cover, but five miles in the forest were worth six leagues of open country.

It began with a smother of birch trees whose silver pipes broke into green sprays, hummocks of bramble, old thorns, bracken, and patches of heather and rabbit nibbled grass. A light breeze blew through the birches. Geraint could see no track. The green earth slid under the white horse's belly, and Geraint, weak as a woman after labour, left the adventure to Morgan. The lad seemed very sure. He had bright eyes, bread in a wallet, and a water-pot in the crook of his left arm.

The birch woods dwindled, and the ground became more heathy and open, with a great sky overhead, and a wooded ridge shutting out the north. Morgan held straight for this ridge, but the going was slow and heavy through heather that was knee-deep. Gradually the ridge ahead of them ceased to be a green and hazy curtain, and became a wall of beeches, old trees with vast trunks, the branches sweeping the ground. The sun was hot on Geraint's back, and so weak was he that he felt faint with it, but when they reached the trees, a large cool hand seemed to lie gently on his head. The ground sloped upwards, all brown with dead leaves. In the deeps of the wood the trunks rose straight and tall, with hardly a crevice of sky showing in the canopy above. The silence was utter, save for the horse's plodding hoofs, and the rustling of Morgan's feet amid the leaves.

But on the crest of the hill the view opened out, and Geraint raised his head to look. He saw the forest like the sea, or some immense city in which every roof was a green dome. In the distance dim hills seemed to float across the sky. Morgan had paused in the shade of a tree. He held the water-pot to his lord's lips, tilting it sideways, but Geraint, lying on the horse's back, found drinking difficult. He had to turn his head and let Morgan dribble the water into his mouth.

"The gods gave us no better gift than water."

Morgan stood at gaze, his eyes like a young hawk's.

"It is not so far, lord," and he drank.

"I feel stronger," said Geraint.

Morgan's eyes were searching for a high green hill in that rolling landscape. He saw it, stared hard at it for half a minute, and made sure how the shadows fell. The wind, such as it was, still blew on his left cheek, but there would be no wind in those deep woods. The way lay straight ahead, and his task was to keep it when the sky was blotted out.

They went down and on, with Morgan turning now and again to glance at the sun-blur above and behind him. The silence was profound, but presently Morgan heard a little sound, and holding the horse in, stood to listen. His eyes lit up, and moving on they came to a forest stream. The white horse had its drink here, and near by Morgan found a place where the crossing was easy, and then went uphill again through the trees.

"That is Alban's stream, lord. It runs round the hill, and when we see it again, we shall be there."

Geraint had faith in the lad.—It was easier for him when the horse climbed a hill, and he lay and watched last year's leaves and the green pads of moss going by past Victor's flanks.

Beyond the hill they came to a little secret valley shaped like a wheat seed, strung upon the forest stream, and shut in by the crowded trunks of the trees. The sunlight lay along it and the scalloped curves of the water. Geraint saw a cottage built of wattle and clay and thatched with heather, with one or two huts standing behind it. Someone had been scything the grass in a little meadow, and the swathes had been cocked. A fence of wattles enclosed a garden, and the wattles were over-run with wild roses. On a patch of grass in front of the cottage stood a wooden cross some ten cubits high, made of the trunk of a pine, and on the arms of the cross four ringdoves were perched.

Morgan pointed.

"See, lord, there is Alban, at his prayers."

Geraint saw a strange sight, an old man with a long white beard and a halo of hair, and mustachios that were as large as sickles. He was on his knees by the cross, and about him were gathered a most strange company, a roebuck and his mate, a hare, two magpies, a doe rabbit and her young, two black rats, and a company of small birds who hopped and fluttered and chattered. And to crown that quaint picture a thrush had perched himself on the old man's head, and with a water-snail in his beak was using Alban's skull as a cracking-block, a most unsaintly piece of work which did not seem to disturb the old gentleman's devotions.

Morgan laughed. He and Geraint saw all this in miniature, the beast and the birds and Alban spread on that little green carpet.

"A man may have mice in his beard, lord, and yet be very holy."

Geraint would have chided the lad had he had the strength for it.

"We will wait here till he has finished his praying."

"He has heard our voices, lord.   He looks up."

"Shall we frighten his friends in a place where no fear is?"

"I have been here before, lord, and had the deer licking my toes."

Alban had risen from his knees, and was looking up at the white horse and the man and the lad, and Morgan hailed him.

"You know me, father.   Here is one who needs healing."

Morgan raised his right arm.   The thrush had dropped to the earth to eat his snail.

"Welcome.   Come in peace."

And Morgan led the white horse down to Alban's hermitage.

Seen at a little distance the hair and mustachios of Alban made him look as fierce as some wild man of the woods, but Alban had the gentlest of eyes, brown as a birds and as soft.   He was meticulously clean, like his birds and his beasts.   He came and stood by the white horse, and he and Geraint looked into each other's eyes.

Said Geraint—"The boy brought me here, father. I have a wound, and enemies, and I am not of your faith."

Alban looked wise.   Geraint was a sick and a wounded man, and that was sufficient.

"All may come to me who can."

"Even—we men of blood."

"Blood washed away the sins of the world, my son. But let us get you off your horse."

There was a sweet and simple sanity about this old man; nor were the birds and the beasts troubled by the coming of these strangers.   Mother Rabbit took her youngsters nearer the wattle fence.   The crows hopped away a few steps.   The doe came close and gazed with curiosity at

Geraint, and her eyes were like the eyes of a woman. Moreover, Alban could use his hands. He was not a creature who sat all day digesting his own soul. He grew his own corn and ground it in a quern, and cut his timber, and laboured in his garden. No man was more wise in the ways of the wild, or in the wisdom of God.

He led the white horse to the door of his cottage, and between them he and Morgan carried Geraint in and laid him upon a bed of fern.

"In the forest we use what the forest gives."

There was only one bed in the room, and the bed was Alban's.

"I come as a robber, father."

Alban smiled at him.

"There is fern for us all. The lad can sleep in one of the sheds. Now, let us look at this wound of yours."

He knelt down beside the bed, and Geraint was moved to ask him a question.

"You do not ask who I am, or how I came by my wound."

"It is a wound, and that is sufficient."

"You help and heal and ask no questions."

Alban was silent as though Geraint spoke foolishly, or like a man who had not hung with Christ upon the Cross. He uncovered the wound, and moved aside to let the light fall upon it.

"If a beast is lame, or a bird has a broken wing do we ask it to sing a credo before we are merciful?"

"Your faith is a good faith."

"It teaches me all manner of wisdom, my son.—This was a spear thrust—and it went deep. And it is angry.— Have you had fever?"

"I was light in the head, father, and dying of thirst."

"Were you left lying?"

Geraint closed his eyes.

"Yes, but that is another story."

Alban was wise as to herbs and their uses, and he grew them in his garden. He went out and gathered what he needed, and made a compress and placed it on the wound, and from a phial in a cupboard he gave Geraint as much of a brown liquid as would lie in a man's palm. Then he half closed the door, and stood looking at Geraint.

"You will sleep. Sleep your fill.—I have work to do and the lad shall help me."

Morgan was given a fork, and he and Alban went to uncover the haycocks and to spread grass to dry in the sun, and while they worked Morgan told the old man all that he knew. Alban, leaning on his fork, and twisting one of his white mustachios, looked both gentle and fierce. Thirty years ago he had been a soldier, a centurion of a picked hundred, and he had seen violent things done, and himself had done them.

"You say Balthasar burned Geraint's house and left him to die?"

Morgan nodded. This was rather a poser for Alban. And how would the old gentleman escape from it?

Alban whirled his fork and tossed hay right and left.

"Then—Calleva—is not Christ's, my lad, nor Balthasar its bishop. Death and wounds—and proud flesh.—There is a peril in priests."

All the rest of the morning Alban was silent, spreading hay and turning it as though exposing souls and shames to the sun. But Geraint slept; he slept till sundown, and when he woke he found a hare beside his bed, sitting up and washing its face with its paws.

2

By the seventh day Geraint's wound was healing so happily that Alban let him get on his feet and sit in the sun. Geraint might be a stranger, but Alban's birds and beasts did not grudge him sanctuary, nor did they fear him.

Doubtless, in due season, the cracker of snails would have used Geraint's pate as he used that of Alban, but as yet Geraint was a guest.

Youth had gone upon adventure and to get the news, for Morgan loved running wild, and about the time when the shadows began to spread across the little valley Alban came back from milking his cow. He carried the pail into the cottage, filled a cup with milk, and added a raw egg to it, and stood looking at Geraint who was sitting on a fern-cock close to the cross. Here was a man, thought Alban, whose body could mend itself, but whose spirit chafed incessantly. But that was understandable. The wisdom of thirty is not that of sixty, nor would life have it so, or the rhythm of life would be out of measure. A man in the force of his years may love many things, and know bitterness because of them, himself, a woman, power, conflict, the temporal things which are his.

Alban carried the cup to Geraint, and giving it into his hand, sat down beside him. He had some wheat grains in the pocket of his smock, and two ringdoves fluttered down from the cross and perched upon Alban's shoulders.

Geraint drank the warm milk, and he drank it slowly. He looked across the valley at the old yews and the glittering hollies and the beech trees with the sun upon them. The shadows were behind his back, and he was conscious of them as a man is conscious of the dark things within himself.

"When shall I be fit for the saddle, my friend?"

Alban was feeding his pigeons.

"When the sparks can fly upwards.—There were days when nothing came better to me than buckling on my sword."

Geraint turned to look at him. Alban was holding out his hands, palms upward, and the birds were picking the seed from them.

"Did you ever kill a man—father?"

And Alban nodded.

"I used to boast that I could make the point of my sword stick out behind a man's shoulders."

"You loved killing?"

"No—strength and skill.   A butcher can kill."

"And now—nothing dies here, nothing is afraid."

Alban smiled like a man who laughs gently at inward things.

"Why should one kill?—It is foolishness.—Is not beauty better than blood?   Man does not live by killing but by loving.   These creatures are beautiful and beautiful to watch and to live with."

"And men——?"

Again, Alban smiled at that dark and cunning question. Had not men asked that question through all the ages, and would they not go on asking it?

"You would say, my son, that there is no peace among men.   Man goes out to conquer the world; he is a trampler, a slayer, and because of it all the world fears him.   But until man has conquered the world and has come to that—pass—when there is nothing left to conquer but—himself?"

"And then——?"

"All men will live as I do.—That wooden cross of mine will have rotted, and thousands of crosses like it—but my God will live, and the brother—that is—I."

Geraint sat thinking.   He too had loved the beautiful, sweet, simple things of life, and if all men were like Alban, living would be easy.   But what of the wolf and the fox in Arcady, and the wolf and the fox in man?   The Roman Peace had endured, but now it was breaking, and no man could say, what the world would be like.   Even Alban and his happy family could not endure without peace.

"Were you ever on the Wall, father?"

"Was I not!—I got this on the Wall."

Alban pulled up his smock and displayed an old wound in his thigh.

"The Picts are over the Wall. The Cymri are restless. There are the Saxons on the sea.—Should one sit still and wait for them to come?"

It was Alban's turn to sit and think.

"God is wise."

"Would you fight if the heathen came to this valley?"

Alban smiled at him.

"That would be foolish.—I should stand by my cross and die—if needs be.—I am not afraid of death, my son. It comes to us all. It is but the darkness before that other dawn."

Geraint was silent for a while. Then, he asked Alban another question.

"Is not a man justified in fighting for that which is his, or to recover things that he loves?—I had a house, woods, fields. If my neighbour comes and spoils me, am I to sit still and do nothing?"

Alban was slow in answering.

"All things are God's.—But you will do—that which your strength wishes to do. I will not gainsay it. Maybe, we fight and struggle—that we may learn. I am an old man, my son, and you are a young one. Blood is hot. My blood is not your blood. I would bind no man. He must choose and learn."

The buck and his mate were grazing just beyond the stream, and Alban saw the buck's head go up.

"Someone comes."

It was Morgan. He came running out from the beech wood, a lad full of himself and the news. He leapt the stream, and laughing, threw himself on the grass before Geraint and the old man. He had something in his right hand, wrapped up in half an old grey riding cloak.

Geraint smiled at him, but his eyes were dark.

"Well—lad?"

Morgan was very pleased with himself. He had been to Vindomis and the White Valley. Yes, Calleva was busy in the White Valley, establishing itself upon the lands of Geraint.   They were clearing the ruins of the burnt house, and cutting down trees, and working in Geraint's fields. Morgan had seen Balthasar there, sitting on a horse and watching the work.

"They are making themselves at home, lord.   They are there to stay."

"What else?"

"At Vindomis they say that the Cymri are up."

Geraint looked meaningly at Alban.

"The wind blows from every quarter.—And what have you got there—Morgan?"

The lad hugged his knees.

"I went to the place in the woods where the dead lay. The Christians have buried their own dead.—But Malgo and our others were still there."

"They have left them—lying?"

"What is left of them, lord.—Wild beasts, and carrion-crows—and flies," and Morgan held his nose.

Geraint looked grim.

"What think you of that, father?"

Alban pulled a mustachio.

"I think little of it, and less of this brother Christian. It is not God's work to leave the poor dead unburied.— But the lad has something——"

Morgan uncovered his trophy.   It was a naked sword, and Geraint knew it at once by the pommel.

"Malgo's sword!"

"They had left it lying by him—which—to me—seems bad business, lord.   Perhaps old Malgo had used it too well, and they held it—accursed."

Old Alban stretched out his hand and took the sword, and a light came into his eyes.

"It is a good blade and well balanced.   And who was Malgo?"

"A centurion of the Sixth before he took his discharge."

"Ha," said Alban, and made two or three cuts and passes with the sword—"she's sweet, she's sweet. The man who——"

And suddenly he laid the sword on the grass between himself and Geraint, and looked coy and ashamed.

"Get thee behind me, Satan."

Geraint smiled a little, dark smile. He reached out and took Malgo's sword into his hand, and Alban saw how his fingers tightened themselves round the handle.

"Thanks—Morgan. This may serve."

He sat with the sword across his knees, looking at the woods. The shadows were covering the valley, and Geraint thought—"This old man may be wise, but first I will kill my enemy," and Morgan, gazing up into his lord's face, saw death there.

3

Guinevra heard footsteps in the passage. Shut up in that narrow cell she had learnt to distinguish the footsteps of those who came and went. Caritas shuffled; Pia's austere feet went pit-a-pat, but Fidelis walked like a man. And these were the footsteps of Fidelis; they paused outside the door, and Guinevra heard the key turning in the lock.

She sat on her stool and waited for Fidelis. They had given her seven days of semi-darkness and bread and water, thinking to quench life by starving it, or to bleach it white like a plant under a stone. Pia and Caritas might fear life and the flesh, but Fidelis feared nothing save to be disobeyed. She was the pious shrew, and so set in her shrewishness that it was a crown of thorns. She did not open a door as Caritas or Pia opened it, with affected humility, but flung it open as though sending some froward child about its duty.

"God's grace to you, girl."

Fidelis had her hood drawn, and her bony chin stuck

out.   She was gaunt in all that she did and said and wore,
a woman who took her pleasure in forbidding things that
were pleasant, but if Fidelis loved one thing it was authority.
She loved it as Balthasar loved power, and Balthasar knew
what he knew.

Moreover, in an age of chaos and confusion, Balthasar
promised with a little good fortune, to be a great man.   In
a world that was falling to pieces he might gather up some
of the fragments and work them into a new pattern.   He
could flatter the poor, but while flattering he knew that he
must feed them.   The plain man loves a show in which he
can carry a banner and feel the women's eyes on him, and
Balthasar would call him brother.   As for the barbarians
were they not but new meat for God's mouth?   Was not
Rome a patchwork of Frank, Vandal and Goth?   Balthasar's
brain and long fingers were busy.   The legions and the
heathen might destroy each other in the north, the Cymri
raid Isca and Glevum, the Saxons keep the Count of the
Shore busy.   Rumour had it that the Emperor was in love,
and discreetly concealing the adventure on the Rhine.   And
while all these powers confused and effaced each other and
tore at each other like dogs, Balthasar would gather strength.
He had other cities with him.   Londinium still hesitated,
but Londinium was a city of merchants and shopkeepers.
Let him remit taxation and Londinium would listen.   The
peasants should be given their land, the poor coloni freed
from their bond-work.   Calleva should be the heart of a
priest-state, and Britain establish itself about God and
Balthasar.

Meanwhile, Fidelis stood in the doorway.

"Have you a heart of grace, girl?"

Guinevra had a heart, but it was hidden, and for seven
days she had lived alone with it.   She had waited for some
gleam of news, as a bird may wait for the dawn.

"I am here, Fidelis."

Which was obvious, and Fidelis never caught a toe in
an occasion that was obvious.

"Get up. Cover your head, and come with me."

Fidelis strode and Guinevra followed her. She was led to the summer-room, and there on a chair sat Balthasar looking like a god on a throne. He wore gloves of white kid-skin, and on the whiteness of one finger a red stone shone.

"Greeting, my daughter."

Fidelis gave her a push.

"Kneel—fool."

Balthasar's face was almost as white as his glove.

"Gently—gently, my sister.—Leave the child to me."

Fidelis went out and closed the door, but she remained there to listen, and Balthasar knew his Fidelis. That was the very place for the woman when he was to speak with sleek severity to this girl alone. The red stone on his finger was a symbol of that which Balthasar hid. Saintliness had to be served.

Guinevra was on her knees, not because she reverenced Balthasar, but because her legs shook under her, and she felt less like betraying it when kneeling. She had come to fear Balthasar, and his eyes of black glass, and that face, like a piece of iron white from the furnace. Her hate and her dread of him knelt hand in hand, but Balthasar spoke gently, looking into Guinevra's bosom and wishing his hand there.

"It is well.—Have you put carnal things away from you, my daughter?"

She raised sudden eyes and caught that glance of his deep in her bosom.

"What are carnal things, lord?"

She was as white as Balthasar's gloved hand, and far more cold, for she had begun to understand why this man was bitter against her. He was bitter because he burned; he was bitter against that which he desired. And she guessed that he had bitter words to utter.

"Still—blind of soul? Was there no shame in you,

girl, when you fled to your paramour—a wedded man?"

She felt the scourge, and was mute. She waited, and the words came.

"The man is dead, and we have buried him."

She said never a word. A man could not lie about death, and she knelt with hands hanging, unable to hide her horror of the thing and its anguish. Her lips fell apart; her eyes stared. So, he had come to tell her this, he who had left Geraint to die!—And Balthasar, watching her, and seeing how she was stricken by the news, felt his lust rage in him. She should pay, she should pay.

"Such—is your shame."

He stood up and over her.

"Weep adulteress, pray to your God, pray that your sin may be washed away in the blood of repentance."

He laid his gloved hand upon her head, and instantly something was loosed in her, anger, scorn, the tumult of her young splendour. She was on her feet, and no longer afraid of him, or too fiercely moved to feel her fear. She drew back and stood with arms spread and pressing against the wall, her bosom rising and falling, her face aflame. She did not utter a word, but stood there panting, and looking at him with a beautiful fierceness that he could not misconstrue.

Balthasar licked thin lips.

"So—we are shameless."

He looked at her, walked to the door, turned and looked again. He seemed to hesitate, his desire like a flame licking her young body. And then, without a word, he went out, but Guinevra had guessed all that was in his heart.

The hands of God and his good women hustled her back into her cell. She had been insolent to that good and patient man! She was deaf to their scoldings, and when they had locked the door, she threw herself face downwards on the wooden bed. She did not weep, but lay stiff and still, yet her heart cried out—"Geraint—O—my dear lord. Dead!"

The world was like this little, narrow cell with its slit of a window, and her young anguish lay stretched on the bed and found no hope in anything. She was both child and woman, locked in a dark cupboard.—And Balthasar and his bitter, burning eyes! She seemed to see his lips red with blood in a bloodless and hungry face.

CHAPTER XVI

Balthasar's Dream

¶ CORINIUM sunned itself, and Cornelia, sitting on a seat in the city gardens over against the church of St. Simon, read a letter. It was a long and sententious letter, and it had come all the way from Gaul. The garden was planted with lime trees, and Cornelia, with the letter on her knees and the sunlight and shadow flecking the earth about her, was moved to wonder why news came from far away when you listened for news that was near. No post had travelled from Calleva, nor had she had tidings of Geraint. As for the Cymri they had vanished into the mountains like the rumour of their ravagings.

But the letter. It had been penned by a cousin of Cornelia's, a senator and eminent publicist who owned an estate near Arles. Sidonius' ink was very black and so were his prognostications. He wrote gloomily and at length and like a prophet whose head was bald, and he marshalled his facts as though he had prepared a statement of accounts.

Taxation was crushing. The currency had gone to the dogs. The country was being bled to maintain the Imperial Court and a vast bureaucracy, and to feed the idle mob in the towns. Farms were derelict. Too few children were being born, and labour could not be got for the land. The army was full of Germans, and so was the Court. The caste system was smothering society. Men ran away from obligations that were penal, and hid themselves. It was better to be a slave than a sponge. Moreover, the whole social scheme was dissolving in sentiment, sapped by

184

a religion that spoke of nothing but souls. The universal and selfish individualism of Christianity was wrecking the universality of Rome.—Finally, Sidonius was completing the last lines of his poem upon the Emperor Julian. He would send his dear cousin a copy. It contained the quintessence of the Plotinian philosophy.

Cornelia smiled.

Yes, she would show this letter to Leo, and she would watch Leo's face while he read it. And Leo would rub his delicate hands together and say—"Excellent, dear lady, excellent. A most perspicacious document, but this tottering world will last our time. I have had a crock of fresh oysters from Clausentium, and a parcel of books from Rome."

Cornelia, happening to look in the direction of the portico of St. Simon's, saw someone whom she knew, and misliked, for Cornelia had a quick eye for people who were displeasing to her. She was prejudiced against being bored, and became blind and deaf when the bore had been spotted, but in this case she saw Placida and her women descending the steps of the portico. Not so many years ago St. Simon's church had been the temple of Venus, and most certainly Geraint's wife did not sacrifice to Venus.

Placida in Corinium! Placida might be a boiled turnip, but she would have the news. Cornelia got on her feet, and holding Sidonius' letter like a poet's scroll, set off to intercept Placida. Geraint's wife, with her women following two and two behind her, had reached the end of the avenue of limes when she heard herself shouted at.

"Placida—hallo—what news?"

Now, even her friends had to allow that Cornelia misused her voice, that she shouted after you and at you on occasions. Leo Gallicus had described her as an old pirate. To Placida she was a red-faced, loud, and objectionable old woman who called a smell a smell, and was quite unshameable. Therefore, when Placida heard the

M

voice, she walked on as though she had not heard it.   She
had been avoiding Cornelia.

"Hallo—Placida——"

One of Placida's women lacked discretion.

"There is someone calling you, lady."

Geraint's wife snubbed her.

"Remember—Nona, that one is not shouted at in
public places, and especially—after kneeling in church."

But her sedate procedure was not proof against Cornelia's
rolling stride.   Cornelia loomed up, an old pirate who
would not be outsailed.

"Why so deaf, my dear?   Is it wax in the ears?"

Vulgar person!   Placida, with her face properly
arranged, discovered the inevitable.

"Why—Cornelia——!   I was thinking of other—
things."

Cornelia laughed.

"I'm a loud old woman, and most people hear me.—
Since when have you been in Corinium?"

Placida was precise.

"Six days."

"Dear, dear—a pilgrimage?"

"You may call it so.—I humour my husband."

"You don't say so—Placida!   Is my lord Geraint——?"

"My dear lord was most absurdly informed that the
citizens of Calleva proposed to rob us."

"They robbed me, my dear.   So Geraint sent away his
most cherished possession."

"Such were his commands.   He drove away his sheep
and cattle.   I wait here for news before returning."

"Then you have had no news?"

Placida made sheep's eyes.

"Obviously.—Because—there can be no news.   Men
get so absurdly excited.   Yes—I am lodged at the hospitium.   Meanwhile, I shall make the pilgrimage to St.
Honoria's Well and keep a vigil there."

Cornelia wrinkled up her nose.

"You are very much Placida.—I must say that I am just a little curious as to what those dear Christians of yours have been doing."

"Doing?—What would they do?—Do you think we are savages?—Really, Cornelia—the world seems full of absurd rumours."

"It is so, my dear. But I would not define a Pict as an absurd rumour.—A few days ago we expected the Cymri. May those other absurd rumours remain in the mountains. —Meanwhile, you are completely unworried.—Your faith —I suppose."

Placida tilted her nose.

"Yes, my faith, Cornelia. God guards His own."

She gave Cornelia a prim little salute with two fingers, and prepared to pass on, and Cornelia, having assured herself that there was nothing to be learnt from Placida, returned to her seat in the sun.

She thought—"What a mate for a man! And what a mate there might be. Boiled mutton and the golden fleece! I would like to show—Placida——"

And Cornelia laughed, for at that moment she did not see Placida as a figure of tragedy.

2

During those summer days Bishop Balthasar was a man of many affairs. He rode out, he wrote letters, he received deputations, he preached to the people. So well was his little world shaping that he had made a pact with certain in Londinium which he had christened the League of Peace, but to ensure that peace he was enlisting soldiers and promoting veterans to be captains. Almost, he had frightened the official world into accepting him as a power and a portent.

For Balthasar understood the virtue of insolence. The bold man accuses without waiting to be accused, and his insolence should be inspired, his eloquence that of the Servant of God. Balthasar, greatly daring, rode in some state to Verulam and delivered himself of a homily. He scolded those whose prerogative it was to scold.

"My friends, see what a mess you are making of government. Will our reverend Emperor be pleased when he hears of this ruin and confusion? Ha—and you will tell me that I am without authority, that I have no official position.—Well—I tell you—gentlemen—that I stand forward as God's shepherd, and that my prerogative is— zeal. Can a man sit still when ruin threatens? Does he stand upon ceremony and say—"With your Excellency's permission, I will shut and bar my door and wait upon disaster?"—I am the servant of God, the Emperor, and the people. Forbid me, at your peril—to do what I can."

The official world looked askance at Balthasar. This interfering, rhetorical priest! But the official world was shaking in its shoes. Emperors were not kind to servants who failed them, and the island was on the edge of chaos. The soldiers were making no headway against the heathen; the Cymri threatened in the west. The country was full of broken men and deserters who saw in the confusion a chance to live the life of loot and licence. This fellow Balthasar might be unorthodox and an interloper, but as dignitary of the official church he might be recognized as a coadjutant in the crisis. Verulam decided not to suppress the bishop. The times were abnormal, and Balthasar might be of use.

But Balthasar did a more audacious thing than admonish the men who sat in chairs. He sent churchmen, two priests and a deacon, across the sea into Gaul, and with them he despatched a letter. "To my most Serene and Noble Master—the Emperor—whom God preserve, from his humble servant—Balthasar." The bishop wrote of the state of Britain. He excused his boldness in writing. He justified his humble efforts in the cause of Christ and the

Empire.   What he might do was not for himself.   The times were terrible, the Church itself in danger, and he—Balthasar—was the Emperor's humble and devoted servant.

So much for diplomacy and the public weal, but Balthasar had affairs of his own.   If it was necessary to walk delicately before Emperors, it was even more necessary to wear soft shoes when treading the passionate earth.   Balthasar sent for Hylas the Hermit.   Hylas might be very hairy and afflicted of God, but whisper a few words to him concerning the lusts of the flesh, and he became mad.   He scourged himself daily.   "If thine eye offend thee, pluck it out."   Hylas was eternally offended.   He was like a ram to whom all other rams are filthy and abominable.

Balthasar whispered to Hylas.

"Go, search for the adulterer.   He should be dead—this corruptor of virgins.—Perhaps, someone took away the body.   But shall sin—live?"

This was red meat to Hylas.   He girded up his loins and took his staff and ran.   Hylas always leapt or ran; you never caught him strolling.   He would shout in people's faces, and run past without waiting for an answer. —"Woe—woe—to the world."—"I see sin in thee, brother.   Cast it out."   Hylas could live on a handful of nuts and a crust, and people said that like Samson he lived on his hair.

Hylas ran.   He ran through Vindomis and Vicus Flavus, dodging into cottages, brandishing his wooden cross.   He tore the bedclothes from an old hag who was bedridden, as though uncovering adultery.   He fell upon men working in the fields.   As for the White Valley where the bishop's people were restoring Geraint's house, he searched it like a dog following an interesting smell.   He found the altar of Sylvanus still standing, and knotting himself into a hairy ball he rolled it over; but of that child of sin—Geraint—he found no trace.

Then, one morning, in the woods he came upon a lad

standing by a little mound.   There was dew on the grass, and rabbits had been scratching at the earth of the grave. Alban and Morgan had come and buried Malgo here, and when the thing had been finished Morgan had gone behind a tree and vomited.

Hylas leapt upon the lad and held him by the hair.

"Hast thou seen sin?"

Morgan was cunning.   He knew Hylas; he had seen the hairy one in Calleva.

"How should I know sin when I see him?   Does he wear breeches or a smock?"

"Has thou seen Satan?"

Morgan was meek.

"I am but a lad, holy one."

Hylas breathed in Morgan's face.

"I seek a filthy fellow named Geraint."

Morgan grew still more meek.

"He is dead, sir.   You cannot find him."

"Dead?"

"He lies there in that grave.—I saw two men bury him.   Indeed, they told me that they found him dead in the White Tower.   They put the body on an ass and brought it here."

"Why—here?" shouted Hylas.

He twisted Morgan's hair, and Morgan was longing to kick Hylas' holy shins.

"Because, holy one, other of his men were slain here, and the two good fellows thought Geraint might like company.—I can show you the graves."

Hylas still held him.

"Who are you?"

"I am a poor lad from the forest.   I come this way sometimes, holy one, to snare rabbits."

Hylas let him go.   He spat upon Malgo's grave.

"Lust begets worms.   Be warned, boy, by the fate of this carnal man."

Morgan looked much impressed.

"Indeed—I will be warned, holy one.   Is it sin for the worms to feed upon a fellow like Geraint?"

"Corruption—corruption," shouted Hylas, and set off at a run, and Morgan, shaking his head, put a thumb to his nose and spread his fingers.

3

The news that Hylas brought was very welcome to Balthasar, for Balthasar had dreamed a dream of a green valley in which birds sang, and the sun rose and set above old trees. In this valley the moon would look down upon water-lilies and the face of a woman. The valley had been Geraint's, and so—in measure—had been the woman, but now that Geraint was dead, both the valley and the woman might be Balthasar's.

Balthasar erred in not setting men to dig into that grave, but he did not err in the rendering of his dream. His conception was catholic, in that it accorded with the spirit of the times when fastidious and sensitive souls, despairing of the world of men, withdrew themselves into the wilderness to live apart and wait for death and translation into paradise. In fact, Balthasar, inspired by love, was born before St. Benedict. Already, the west was beginning—as ever—to copy the east in its holy fashions. The cenobites in Egypt were a sign of the times, brown men burning themselves into consecrated crusts in the desert. There were holy houses into which those who would read and meditate upon the priesthood might retreat. There were women willed to God. But Balthasar was perhaps the first to dream of a community of holy sisters in Britain living apart in a sheltered world of their own, hallowed and haloed.

Guinevra's golden head inspired the halo, but what of that? She should be planted in a green valley with good women to guard her, a valley into which Balthasar might

sometimes descend in the likeness of god, a holy man minis-
tered to by devoted hands.   Did not a consecrated virgin
sometimes serve in the house of a priest?   The Church
allowed it, and held such service to be right and reasonable.
The dream might prove other than a dream.   It might
contain an ultimate reality.   Meanwhile, Guinevra of the
Golden Head would be withdrawn from the world of men,
and lie hidden like some precious thing in a casket.   Mys-
tically, she would be his, a hoard to be gloated over,
a light burning in secret, both saint and woman.   Balthasar
could be very subtle with himself.   He could begin with
the saint and leave the future to find the woman.

He spoke to Fidelis.   He knew his Fidelis and how to
humour her.   These good women might be very comfortable in Calleva, thank you, and sufficiently human to
like to walk the streets to church, and look out of windows
and into windows.   Fidelis loved interfering, visiting,
lecturing, managing other people's morals.   No door could
keep her out.—So, Fidelis would have to be supplied with
authority.   She must be in a position to give orders, to
admonish and regulate.   Fidelis was the fore-doomed
matron of Balthasar's dream-house in the valley.

The Sisterhood of the Bleeding Heart!   And though
Fidelis's heart was leather and did not exude blood, she
listened to Balthasar.   Balthasar was both circumspect and
eloquent.

"While kneeling at the altar, sister—I heard a voice say
to me—'Balthasar, build me a house for my doves in some
secret and gentle place.'—Now—I confess, Fidelis, that I
was perplexed by the message, but presently the meaning
of it came to me.   I saw a noble house and buildings and
orchards and fields in a green valley where gentle souls could
live apart.—I saw the valley that was Geraint's, its house
restored and full of the splendour and sweetness of good
women."

Fidelis was neither a dove nor splendid, and the picture
seemed to please her, but so did Calleva.

"A community of women, father.—But in this city we care for the cause."

Balthasar smiled.

"This house could remain sacred to the sisterhood.—But, if I understand the voice, Fidelis, it spoke of a sanctuary where women could be trained and sanctified to good works. You would have fields, orchards, servants to labour, women to teach.—It would be a task for a wise and capable mistress. She would be the Matrona. She would rule. She would be the mistress of wood and water, fields and pastures.—That woman is very near to me, Fidelis."

Fidelis held her head on one side, and seemed to guess who that woman was.

"A great work—holy father."

"It is yours, Fidelis. You are marked out by God for it. I said to myself—'Fidelis is the woman. No other is as wise and good as she.'—So, my sister, what do you say? You would rule both houses.—You would train your women in that other place, and when you had put your spirit into them, they could labour in this city."

Fidelis bowed her head.

"It is a great honour, holy father."

"Embrace it.—Already the house of Geraint is being put in repair. The houses of the villicus and the cottages stand. And there is a tower which could be used for such as need solitude. Take this task on you, Fidelis."

"And furniture and food?"

"Everything shall be provided."

Fidelis kissed his hands.

"It shall be my pride to serve."

That same morning, Geraint, helped on to the back of the white horse by Alban and Morgan, set out to ride gently in the open beech woods for the good of his body. The lad had laughed up at him—"Remember that you are dead and buried, lord, and beware of Balthasar."

But there was no death in Geraint's heart, save death to his enemy. He rode in among the great trees where the ground was steady, and keeping the flicker of the forest stream in sight, he let the white horse walk. It was deeply green here, and cool and still, but Geraint, like Balthasar, had the face of a woman before him, though Geraint saw it more clearly than did Balthasar. For, to Geraint, Guinevra was compassionate eyes, and tenderly passionate hands, a woman to be desired like no other creature. She was neither hot metal nor honey, but something out of heaven, and Geraint, riding among the trees, saw love like a white light in the green glooms.

He rode a mile or more through the woods, a dark man as silent as those green aisles. The white horse, seeming to understand his master's need, went gently over the dead leaves and the moss. He carried Geraint up a little hill where there was a break in the sea of foliage, and Geraint reined in there and sat looking over the tree tops. The sun was near full noon, and Geraint's eyes were turned to the east. There was nothing on the horizon save the trees, but his inward eyes saw the walls and roofs and temples of Calleva.

4

Placida had ordered her carriage for the morning. The Well of St. Honoria lay some fifteen miles from Corinium in a valley among the hills. The shrine was served by a holy woman, who provided in a small mansion accommodation for pilgrims and those who came to keep a vigil. St. Honoria was much revered by women who were barren and who desired children, but that was not the provocation of Placida's pilgrimage. She desired—perhaps—to be a little singular in her holiness, and as travellers boast—"I have seen Treves, Milan, Rome," so Placida would say— "I have prayed at this shrine and at that."

Just before dawn on that particular morning a sleepy

watcher on a turret saw a little red blaze break upon a far hill in the dark west. The man stared at it awhile, and then ran down to warn the "watch," but when these others joined him on the tower, day was breaking, and the beacon was hardly visible.

One fellow scoffed.

"Tom has wind-up about the Welsh."

"Do you know what that is, lad?"

"A beacon—if ever I saw one."

"Go and tell it to Mithras.—That was a farmer burning rough old grass."

"Would he do it at night?" asked Thomas.

"He was up with the dawn, my son, and he put a brand to the hillside—to start the day well.—Haven't you ever seen furze or fern burning?—Well, that's what it looks like. My eyes are older than yours."

Certainly, that spurt of flame upon the hills was reported to the captain of the city guard, but not as a signal that was to be taken seriously. Moreover, Corinium was a little mistrustful of false alarms, and the city went about its business on that summer day as though nothing untoward was to be feared. Placida, with a maid and a manservant, drove out of the west gate three hours before noon. Fortune was not kind to Geraint's wife, for the way to the Well of St. Honoria left the highway as a grass road about five miles from Corinium, and had Placida's carriage been later in starting she would have met two men galloping to warn Corinium that the Cymri were out. As it was she took the grass road through wild country into which news came late, and it came too late for Placida.

5

That night hundreds of little, dark men on ponies and on foot poured down upon Corinium. It was a raid in force, shrewdly planned, for the Cymri had marched by night and remained hidden in the woods by day. But Corinium had been warned, and the gates were shut, the walls manned, and the rush was foiled. The Cymri had no ladders with them, and though they cut down trees and piling them here and there against the walls, tried to storm the city, those on the battlements beat them off. Repulsed, they attacked at the western gate; they beat down the gate, but found the great grid lowered and archers behind it, and from the tower boiling water and oil and stones were poured upon the wolf-pack below.

Corinium proved too strong for the wild men. A week's work with sap, ram, testudo and catapult might have shaken the place, but against it a sea of spears could do little. Moreover, these tribesmen had not the patience for such a siege. They had come to spoil and to plunder, and finding the city a rock, they broke away for easier game: the villas and country houses and villages that were scattered about the land. Corinium was saved, but the countryside knew terror, death and flame, for the little dark men were passionate and cruel.

CHAPTER XVII

Geraint Finds His Wife

¶ FIDELIS, having seen the White Valley, became even more zealous in the fulfilling of Balthasar's dream. Caritas grumbled a little, for Caritas hankered after the streets, but Pia, who was a country woman and had a passion for poultry, began to count her eggs. Half a score other women would be added to the community, and to it were to be attached six manumitted slaves to work in the fields, draw water and cut wood. Fidelis had the choosing of these male servants, and Fidelis chose six strong men, and shrewdly so, for Fidelis was to be a hard and unsentimental taskmistress.

Fidelis had a sense of property. Already she saw herself as matrona and great lady, administrator of an estate, and her large hands began to reach out and possess those woods, and fields and pastures. Geraint's harvest was there for the gathering, and so was the fruit in the orchard, and the white grapes in the vineyard. Men were putting a thatched roof on the great house, but Fidelis did not wait for the thatchers. This world was to be hers before the frosts came.

Calleva accepted the order. In fact Calleva gave the good women gear and a public blessing, for Calleva did not regret the passing of Fidelis. Three wagons were loaded with much of the furniture and stuff from the house of Cornelia, and with the gifts of the faithful, they set off for the White Valley. Fidelis had collected two cows, six sheep and a ram, a couple of goats and a reliable housedog. The procession was blessed at the West Gate by

Balthasar, and Hylas, who was always available on such occasions, leapt and ran for five miles before Fidelis and her company, giving praise to God.

"Bless ye the Lord, ye holy virgins, bless ye the Lord, ye sheep and cows," for Hylas was not always happy in assembling his phrases.

Guinevra rode in the second wagon, with Pia, two other women, and piles of household gear. Fidelis had very definite ideas as to what was to be done with Guinevra. This strong girl should be put to work with rake and hoe, her skirts turned up for those pretty legs of hers to be burnt by the sun. Guinevra should wash and scrub; Guinevra should pray; Guinevra should fast. Beauty, indeed! What was beauty but proud flesh? Fidelis took life and Balthasar literally, and beheld nothing mystical in a golden head.

As for Guinevra, she saw the world as a strange place in which that which had seemed right to yourself, was wrong to others. She was in deep water, and she wanted to struggle, but struggle seemed useless. It was as though her heart had given out for the moment and there was no hope in anything. The world was a grey world, full of grey women and bread and water, and in the shadow stalked Balthasar with his glassy eyes and hungry, wounded mouth. What could she do?—Even this ride in a wagon was mockery, life caricaturing a memory that was dead.

The White Valley, Geraint's valley, where love had bled and died. She would gather the fruit under the eyes of Fidelis, bitter fruit, for the blossom had fallen. Somewhere her love lay buried, and the earth lay over her heart.

She sat and watched Hylas leaping in the dust as though the hairy creature was the very soul of mockery. In fact, Hylas, before taking his leave, sprang upon the tail-board of the wagon and shouted at her.

"Woe to you, harlot.—Repent, repent."

Always that fool, foul word. She looked at Hylas with a little wincing smile, and was mute. But if the red badge was pinned upon her she wore it with secret passion, and with an inward, flaunting wildness. Let them think what they would. Yes, she would have given herself and gladly, if life had been otherwise. She would have chosen, not the lily, but the colour of the wild rose.

So, Fidelis and her women and her labourers, and her wagons and horses and cows and sheep came to the White Valley when the shadows were beginning to lengthen on the grass. Pia, who could go into prim ecstasies about nature, if she could not applaud nature in man, twittered like a bird.—"Isn't it lovely? Isn't it sweet? And look at that dear little island, and that dear old tower. So picturesque, so romantic!" And then Pia remembered that most unseemly things had happened in that tower, and that they had happened to Guinevra. Pia put her face in order. But how very exciting.

Fidelis had chosen for herself the bailiff's house. Caritas, Pia and the rest could be accommodated in the cottages until such a time as the great house was habitable. Already, Fidelis was becoming separative and stately. Two of the women should be detailed to wait on her. As for the men creatures—they could build themselves shelters made of the boughs of trees, or sleep in the barn. It was very necessary that these common males should be kept in their places. The horses were unharnessed, and the men set to unload the wagons. Caritas was to supervise the feeding of the community, Pia the details of the household, while Fidelis supervised everybody.

"Up, girl, and help."

For Guinevra was sitting on the grass and gazing at the island and its tower. Had they buried Geraint upon the island? Fidelis' voice cracked like a whip.

"Carry in the pots and pans. There are to be no idle painted vases here."

It was near sundown before the wagons were empty, and all the gear disposed of. Fidelis, who had carried nothing, called Guinevra to her.

"Get bread and some water, girl, and a blanket—and I will see you lodged."

Had Balthasar whispered in Fidelis' ear? Guinevra did as she was bid. Fidelis called one of the men, and the three of them went down towards the island. The man would have carried some of Guinevra's gear for her, partly because he was there to serve, and partly because the girl was comely, but Fidelis would have none of it. The fellow was to handle the boat. Fidelis stalked, with a face that suggested that she knew all that there was to be known about the happenings in that tower. Sacred irony! The very stones should preach, and the sinner be returned to the place of her sinning. Could anything be more just and apposite?

"Can you swim, girl?"

"No."

"Do not lie to me.—And remember, God's waters are deep."

The three of them got into the boat—Fidelis standing, Guinevra daring to sit, for she was suffering strange anguish. The man poled them across, and Fidelis bade him wait in the boat while she and Guinevra went to the tower. And Guinevra's love was in her mouth like a mouthful of warm blood. Her feet carried her as though they were the feet of fate. But Fidelis had no understanding of these things, nor did she care.

The door was shut and she flung it open, but Guinevra hung back, leaning against the wall.

"Have you no pity?"

Fidelis' eyebrows came together.

"Ha! Shame? You tremble. That is good."

Guinevra threw her head back, and clutched her blanket to her bosom.

"Enough, Fidelis.—What have I to fear?"

She passed in and saw the hay still on the floor, and the wooden bed, but someone had taken the bloody clothes from the bed and burned them. She put her waterpot and the bread on the window-sill, and stood holding her blanket. Her face had a strange white calm.

Said Fidelis—"This shall be your lodging until such a time as the spirit in you is chastened. Where you did sin, there you shall fast and pray."

Guinevra said never a word, and Fidelis, holding up two grim fingers, turned and left her, and was taken into the boat.

When Fidelis had gone Guinevra stood awhile in a kind of stupor. The day was passing, and the light beginning to fail. The room was growing grey, a room for ghosts to walk in, and suddenly, Guinevra shivered and looked about her as though she had been sleeping. So, her love had died in that bed, and Fidelis had put her to sleep in it. But her dead love was stronger than a live fear. She gathered up the hay and spread it on the bed.

Fidelis had left the oak door open, and Guinevra saw the last of the sunlight streaming under the apple trees and lighting up the grass. She went out, and with the courage of one upon whom life could press no more pain than that which she had suffered, she searched the island. The same black bats fluttered against the afterglow. The water-lilies waited for the moon. Surely, if Geraint had died in the tower, they would have buried him on the island? She searched everywhere, but nowhere could she find any sign of a grave.

Had they thrown his dear body into the water—and—oh—horror—would she see it floating——? She shut her eyes for a moment, and her soul rebelled against that thought.—No, that was not possible. She would not believe it.—They had taken the body away and buried it somewhere in the valley, and she would not rest until she had found the place where he lay.

She ceased to be afraid of that dark room in the tower. Why should she fear that which was beautiful and bitter? She clasped her sorrow and took it in with her, and sat with it while she broke bread and drank water.

N

She left the door open to the twilight and the stars.—But she thought also of the man who had left Geraint to die here, and her hatred was deep water and soundless. She would not forget; she would not forgive.

But presently she put this dark mood from her, and in spite of Balthasar and Fidelis she knelt down to pray. She prayed as old Alban would have had her pray, gently, passionately, poignantly.

"O, God, let me be forgiven if I have loved.—Need love be sin? He whom I loved is with Thee somewhere. Be gracious unto him, and help my heart."

Then, as though the place was holy and sweet, she lay down on the bed, and listened to a little night breeze moving in the apple trees.

2

Geraint was for the road. His wound had healed, and though his strength was not what it would be, a man's restlessness drove him. He had a wallet full of food, Malgo's sword, and no money, and though the world might be in confusion, and the heathen and bishops rage, innkeepers demanded money. Old Alban saw the face of his God, but never a gold aureus, and all that he could give Geraint was some food and his blessing.

Said Geraint to him—"Blessings can come back to roost, old friend—but what can a man give to one who is happy?"

He left Morgan at the hermitage, for Morgan was to be Geraint's eyes.—"Watch Balthasar, Morgan." Also, he bade Morgan put himself at the old man's service until such a time as his lord should return. Morgan ran and walked beside Geraint's horse as far as the Calleva road, and there Geraint left him.

He turned the white horse into the woods, for whatever Calleva might threaten he was minded to look down into the White Valley before he rode west, and keeping to the trees and riding cautiously he came to the green edge of the valley. He saw the pool, the island, and the tower, and men at work upon the roof of the great house. Also, he saw the figures of women moving near the main gate, and supposed them to be the wives of the workmen. A solitary figure in grey was raking grass in a meadow, and little did Geraint guess that he was looking at Guinevra, but he saw nothing but a little grey figure at work alone in a great field.

Geraint turned his horse and rode back into the woods, woods that were his, for he was no acceptor of the new dispensation in which a demagogue and a rabble could dispose of other men's goods. That might be part of the new philosophy as it was taught in the school for savages, and the Calleva mob might be closely related to the Caledonians, but yet there was a difference. The Law might codify itself but the verdict still lay with the sword. Roman Law could confound Balthasar in the courts, but Geraint was not moved to run to the lawyers. What had been taken from him by force, he would take back by force, despite Alban and his teaching, and when the times were in his favour. "Love thy friend, and hate thy enemy, and do not cease from hate till thou hast slain him or seen him in the dust." That was Geraint's text.—And then, there was Guinevra.

So, Geraint rode west with his horse's head towards Corinium. He could suppose that his strong-box and his sheep and cattle were safe, and that Placida was praying in the churches of Corinium. Yes—Placida! But he was not concerned with Placida and her religion, but with men and horses, and spears and swords. These rough times were to his temper. Peace could lie in his wife's lap while he threw himself like a strong swimmer into a turbulent sea. He would raise men and arm them and make war for Rome, or for his own hand against that city scum. Rome might fail, and in the confusion Briton and barbarian would be intermingled.　Men would follow a man who could lead.

Geraint was three days on the road, for he was not yet hardened to the saddle, but when he came within two leagues of Corinium he began to see strange sights.　There had been wild work here, and the country was as silent as death. Geraint passed a posting-house outside which a man lay dead, face downwards with a red hole in his back.　Geraint dismounted, and looking into the post-house, saw other dead, a woman with a child in her arms lying on the floor. An old crone was sitting in a chair as though asleep, but flies were thick about her, and the place smelt of death.

Geraint rode on.　He beheld smoke rising from behind a tuft of trees, and turning aside across a meadow he saw whence the smoke came.　A country house showed black against green trees, a mere shell from which vapour rose and drifted in the sunlight.　There were more dead here, and when Geraint had seen them he looked grim.

A mile farther along the road he met his first live man, sitting beside the road and sucking a grass stem.　The fellow had the dull, dumb face of a man who was alive in the flesh but dead in the spirit.　He did not hear Geraint till the white horse was close upon him, and then he sprang up with the snarl of a frightened animal.　He put a forearm across his forehead, and stared at Geraint from under it.

Geraint spoke to him quietly.

"There is no need to run, my friend.—What has happened here?"

The fellow's mouth hung open.　He was slow in speaking.

"The Cymri, lord."

"The Cymri?—As far as this.—And Corinium?"

The man's arm dropped.

"I know naught of Corinium.—I have seen enough— here.　They fell on us like wild beasts."

He showed Geraint a wound under his smock, and the smock itself was foul with soot.

"I hid in the furnace till they had gone, and the house was burning over me.—Have you any bread, lord?"

Geraint opened his wallet, broke off a crust and threw it to the fellow, and he put his teeth into it like a starved dog.

When Geraint came to Corinium he found it shut up like a fortress ready to withstand a siege. There were sentries patrolling the walls, and watchers on the watchtowers, and Geraint rode up a white and empty road to the east gate. The city was sacrificing nothing to fortune, and Geraint was questioned by men on the gate-turret before they would let him in.

"Who are you?—Whence come you?"

The gate was opened, but in the passage between the gate and the grid two men stopped him with crossed spears while the captain of the guard catechized him. These men were "regulars" belonging to a century from the garrison of Isca. They had marched in two days before the raid.

"You are taking no chances, captain."

The centurion was a bluff fellow.

"Orders, sir. We saved this place with no more margin than the wink of an eyelid.—And what is your business here?"

Said Geraint—"I sent my wife and goods and cattle here for safety. That was more than two months ago."

"I fear you will find no cattle, sir. The scoundrels have cleared the whole countryside.—But, your wife, of course."

"Do you know where she is lodged? The Lady Placida."

"No, sir—I do not."

"Or Dame Cornelia?"

"No, sir. Ask in the city."

The spears fell and Geraint passed on. At the corner of a street he met a postman with staff and satchel, and he reined in to question the man. The fellow knew Cornelia and where she was lodged, for he had carried letters to her.

"The house of Rhadamanthus the banker. Second street west of the forum. Turn left, and the gate is the second one. It has a brass hand nailed to it."

Geraint found the gate, and drawing his horse close he knocked with the pommel of Malgo's sword. A lame porter opened the gate, and there was no need for Geraint to ask questions. The courtyard contained a garden with a fountain and beds full of flowers, and sitting on a seat under the shade of a lime tree was Cornelia.

Geraint dismounted, and leaving the white horse with the porter he walked up a path paved with red tiles. Cornelia had risen. She was frowning; her blue eyes stared, searching Geraint's face to see how much he knew.

"Well—well, my friend, and where have you been all these weeks?"

"To tell you the truth, matrona, in bed."

"Wounded or sick?"

"Balthasar's people took the valley, and I took a spear under the ribs.—But that is a long story.—I have come here to find what is left to me, goods, cattle, and a wife."

He wondered why Cornelia's blue eyes stared.

"We have had the Cymri here.—But—Placida—is not here, my dear.—She went on a pilgrimage the very day before the wild men raided."

"Then, where is she?"

Cornelia nodded at him.

"No one has been out of the city.—No one knows.— We have had a few terrified country folk panting at the gates. The country is a—waste."

"Which way did she go?"

"West.—You know, my friend, poor Placida could not help falling on her knees wherever a place was supposed to be holy.—She went to the Well of St. Honoria to pray and keep a vigil. That is all we know."

Geraint looked strangely stricken, like a man whose heart accused him.

"How far, matrona?"

"Fifteen miles—or so."

"Is the place easily found?"

"No. It lies in wild country."

"I'll take a guide."

Cornelia looked sceptical.

"If you can find a man, my dear, who will risk his skin five miles outside these walls."

Geraint saluted her.

"Then—I'll go alone."

3

But Geraint found a guide, a man from an outlying farm who had come into Corinium with a tumbril full of young pigs a few hours ahead of the Cymri. His name was David of the Red Head, and his farm lay in the same valley as the Well of St. Honoria. David had but little hope of finding anything but death and ruin, but the man was eager to go with Geraint. He left the tumbril in Corinium and straddled his cart-horse, a lean, stark, silent man with dark eyes that smouldered. Geraint, looking him over, told himself that the farmer would be a good comrade in a tight corner, a fellow who would put his back to yours and fight silently and to the death. David had no weapon save an axe which he had bought in the city, and he carried it with the handle stuck through his leather belt.

They rode out of Corinium about sunset, for David had travelled the road scores of times and would not miss the way. The grass track turned off from the highway where three tall poplars grew, and the countryfolk called them the Three Grey Sisters, mysterious trees who kept up a whispering even when the night seemed windless. Geraint and the farmer rested their horses here, and ate, for haste would not help them, and they had five hours before dawn. David sat and listened to the flutter of the poplars' leaves and the sound they made was full of foreboding.

"Do not hope too much, lord."

"What do the trees say, David?"

"That which I fear."

Presently, they mounted and rode on. High woods shut them in, and between the high woods were the stars. The grass road climbed gradually, and about two hours before dawn they came to a level place in the valley where a pool gleamed black and faint. They watered their horses here, and in the deep silence Geraint heard David utter a sigh, as though all the breath had gone suddenly from his body.

"No need to go farther, lord, till the light comes."

David stood looking across the water and into the darkness beyond.

"My place lies over there.—When the darkness lifts——"

And suddenly he was silent, and Geraint understood.

They tethered their horses, and sat down under a tree, but the man was restless. He gnawed grass; he would get up and look at the east, and then sit down again, but during all that bitter waiting he said never a word. Then, when a faint greyness began to creep into the sky, he stood up, stark and still.

"Go, man," said Geraint—"I will wait for you here."

The world had changed from grey to green, and the first yellow rays of the sun were touching the water in the pool when David returned. There was no need for Geraint to ask questions; he had only to look at the man's face. David might not have slept or touched food for three days, so gaunt and grim and grey was he. His red hair seemed to flaunt itself strangely above the face of a corpse.

"I have seen—what—I have seen, lord."

He went to his horse and untethered him, and stood for a moment with his face pressed against the beast's neck. Then, his shoulders gave a shudder; he mounted, and

Geraint, knowing that his turn had come, unfastened the white horse. They did not speak, but David took the lead. About a mile up the valley where the woods began to thin, David drew in, and gave a jerk of the head.

"On such business—a man would go alone."

Geraint left him there, and a furlong up the valley he came to the pool and shrine of the saint. There was a great silence here, but Geraint saw a man tied to a tree with three spears sticking in his body. Geraint dismounted, and went to look at the man's face. The dead thing's chin was down upon its chest—but Geraint knew him, it was Hoel, the groom.

Geraint went to the shrine. It was like a baptistry built over the spring. There were three dead women here, one of them with her head in the water. Placida lay crouching against the altar, her face against the stone, and from her throat.—But Geraint felt sick. He went out into the sunlight, and covered his face with his arm. The dead woman was his wife; there had been no love between them of late, but for the dead Geraint felt pity.

He tightened his sword belt, for his belly had dropped, and there was other and ugly work to do, and mounting his horse, he rode back to the pool. David looked in his face, and asked him no questions, for there was death in the eyes of Geraint.

"We must bury our dead, David."

The man nodded and mounted his horse.

"I can find a mattock and a spade."

So, those two, in silence, and with set faces, laboured together for three hours. The graves were none too deep, but they would serve, and Geraint's muscles and heart were not yet hard, and the sun was hot. Moreover, such work was not to his stomach. The farmer was harder and grimmer than he. He stood by a woman's grave and gnawed his lip.

"So that's finished, lord. No more farming for me. I would—kill."

"Come with me, man."

"Assuredly—I will, lord. I should see ghosts here. Make me your man."

They rode back to the pool, and washed themselves there, and turning their faces towards Corinium, set out to master a new world. David was to be Geraint's man, and if death had brought them together, neither of them was to regret it.

CHAPTER XVIII

Geraint Takes the Road

¶ ABOUT this time the vicar and prefects of Britain received letters from the Imperial Court and though the official procedure was catholic in that it passed through the proper channels, from Gallic prefect to British vicar, and from vicar to the prefects of the provinces, other and confidential messages were distributed direct to the Imperial servants. Even to Balthasar was dispatched a gracious communication, and the bishop read it in the curia to Calleva. Leo Gallicus, one of the few men whom the Emperor trusted, received a sealed letter at Corinium, and when he had read it, and smiled down his long nose over it, he hid the thing away in his bosom. The document was not for the eyes of clerks and secretaries, for there was a subtlety in the epistle that needed cherishing. Britain had a reputation for producing tyrants. It had brought forth Carausius, and was —in days to come—to exhibit a second Constantine to the world. An episcopal dictator might be a new product, but not beyond the bounds of probability. The Donatists and the circumcellions in Africa—those gentle socialist fanatics who smote their brethren with clubs because the sword was forbidden—were setting an example that might prove troublesome. Moreover, in Britain the Germans were unpopular. There were men in the islands who said that Rome would never be Rome again until the Germanizing of the Empire in the West had been halted. But since the Emperor held the Rhine and the Danube with troops— more than half of whom were German—such talk was embarrassing and—perhaps—dangerous.

As to the military situation, Count Benedict reported that he was making headway against the heathen in the north. The Cymri were mere wolves, and should be dealt with as such. Nectarides, Count of the Saxon Shore, was sufficiently strong to keep the Saxons from the coasts. The condition of the Island might be a little disturbed, and its mood somewhat emotional, but the Emperor had other and grave matters absorbing his attention. Let his prefects confront the various problems with energy and resource, and all would be well.

Leo Gallicus took the imperial letter and laid it before the one person in Corinium whose tongue and shrewd sense could be trusted, even Cornelia. Though Leo held that most women were fools, the exception proved the rule. He found Cornelia sitting in an arbour in the garden of Rhadamanthus, for the day was hot.

"A confidential dispatch, matrona. I pass it to you."

He sat with eyes closed, caressing his chin, while Cornelia read the epistle. She licked her lips over it. She relished its delicate and suave cunning.

"The Emperor is no fool, my dear."

Leo opened one eye at her.

"You will appreciate the rather unusual suggestions, matrona. Men of quality are to be permitted to enlist their servants—and others—within reason—for the defence of their own districts. We, the civil side, are to bless them. The soldiers are not to be consulted. A dangerous precedent, but the Emperor—and his advisers are clever. In a multitude of captains there may be more safety than in one roaring Cæsar. Divide, rule—and wait.—Moreover, you may appreciate the reference to our friend the bishop."

Cornelia's blue eyes twinkled.

"The imperial finger has indicated Balthasar."

"Precisely so.—Balthasar is—perhaps—to be encouraged to climb a tree and hang himself. Read those sweetly ambiguous words again to me, matrona."

And Cornelia read, holding the letter firmly with both hands.

"We do not look with favour upon those who cause trouble in the state, and who—whatever inspiration they may plead, disturb or dispossess their neighbours. Ambitious persons should be watched. We do not countenance broils and private war, but if any man or men of substance—have suffered wrong, they should—of course—submit it to the Courts, but where the wrong has been flagrant and performed with violence, we shall not look too closely at individual acts of redress. We wish the order of the state to stand. Those of our servants who set out to recover order from confusion —will be upheld."

Leo chuckled.

"That it is a stick to shove between Balthasar's legs.— And you know the man, matrona, who could handle the stick."

Cornelia smiled at him.

"I have named him. You have dined with him."

"Geraint of the White Tower."

"And how does he strike you?"

"I would prefer not to be struck by him, matrona. A man who says little when he means much.—I think I shall send for Geraint."

A messenger from the prefecture called at the house where Geraint was lodged. Leo's summons was so un-officially friendly that it invited Geraint to supper, gave him oysters and Spanish wine, and took him by the arm into his excellency's garden. Leo was in a jocund mood. True, Geraint had lost his wife, a deplorable business, but Leo had never had a wife to lose. In the days when sexual self-expression had been necessary to him he had found mistresses more exciting and less like your daily dinner, blessed by God and wearing virtuous frills. Moreover it was a saying of Leo's that an old man might lose his whole family and survive, but that the loss of an estate or a fortune killed him.

Leo was discreet.

"I have heard of your—misfortunes, my friend.—Between gentlemen things may pass in a gentlemanly way. There is a certain person named Balthasar whom—I would describe as an enterprising cad.—It occurs to me that you may be moved to remove this person from a house and estate which does not belong to him.—If this should happen—I shall neither be aware of it—nor interfere."

Geraint was in no mood for subtleties.

"Balthasar has Calleva behind him. He can put three hundred men in the field."

"And you have no—following, my lord?"

"At the moment, your excellency, I can count on one man and a boy. And what is—the—inspiration?"

Almost, Leo winked at him.

"There are people whom I will not name, who are a little prejudiced against—this prelate. People in authority, my dear Geraint.—I may tell you in confidence that—gentlemen—understand me—will be permitted to use force to safeguard what is theirs—in these rather noisy days. It may be possible for a man of enterprise to raise men—for his own service."

"How would one pay them, your excellency?"

Leo stroked his nose.

"The bankers might think it good business. Other citizens who had been dispossessed might be willing to contribute to the pay-chest.—Then, there is Calleva."

"Calleva?"

"Your men might find—advantages—in reducing Calleva to order. A little looting—while—you were looking the other way. In confidence, my friend—I should not be sorry to see that city mob—chastened."

Geraint took thought.

"And—Balthasar?"

"If anything were to happen to the bishop, it would—of course—be regrettable, but not a calamity.—It might depend on the way it happened.   Or, our friend would be put back into his slippers and be dealt with by some obliging superior.   Do not let the sanctity of this holy bounder discourage you."

Geraint laughed, but half to himself.

"Are there limits to my—recruiting?"

"I should not take heed of two hundred men, my lord, foresters, huntsmen, old soldiers, stout vagabonds, what you please.   Two hundred such men ought to cut up and truss lewd demos.—Well, well—that is between gentlemen.—The stars are very bright to-night."

Geraint sat thinking.   He might be concerned with swords and a woman's eyes, but the stars were—in heaven, and he—needed men.

Yet, the very next morning a man came to Geraint's lodging when his barber was with him.   Geraint's visitor was as broad as a barn door, he had a fresh scar on his forehead, and much black hair.   Wearing a lorica and sword, and with a leather cap plated with iron on his head, he looked so formidable and rough a customer that the woman who opened the gate to him, wished it shut.

"What do you want?" said she.

"I want Geraint.   They say he is lodged here."

"But the barber is with him."

The man laughed, and chucking her under the chin, shouldered in.

"There's something pretty that doesn't need a razor. Go, tell my lord, that a friend is here."

The woman left him in the courtyard, and he ambled round it on his big, bowed legs.   Geraint, coming into the portico, and dabbing his chin with a napkin, for the barber had cut him, knew the man by his legs and the back of his massive neck.

"Caradoc!"

Caradoc it was, but not the Caradoc of the smithy.   He

had the burly air of a man who wielded authority in lieu of a hammer.

"Lord—this is a good day."

He saluted Geraint, and his eyes loved him.

"I did not know whether you were dead or alive, Caradoc."

"Alive and lusty, master, with a score to pay. I have a debt to settle with the man who cut me across the face. I am here to serve."

Geraint took Caradoc's hand.

"I was asking for men—and here is—a man.—Any news for me, Caradoc?"

"You need men, lord?"

"Two hundred."

"I have a dozen with me."

"You?"

"Yes, lord. I have been doing a little business of my own round about Calleva. Yes, taking toll from Calleva on the roads. My fellows do not stand on ceremony.— And there are more to be had—for pay—and adventure. Old Aquila is dead, but his lads are in the woods with a score of fellows waiting for their chance. Gawaine is in hiding, but I know where he is to be found. Is that news for you, lord? Come and lead us."

"Can we find the men, Caradoc?"

"Scores of them, lord."

2

Caradoc could do that which his lord could not do, sit and drink in the taverns of Corinium, and explore the thermae for likely men who fancied a little fighting. There were fellows like David Red Head whose blood was bitter in them, and who, though eager to be led against the Welsh to recover an eye for an eye, were willing to try their hands at the game in other quarters. Caradoc was a shrewd recruiting-sergeant. He had no use for weedy boys, or fellows who were thinking more of plunder than of hard knocks, and he made his men strip and show their muscles, and gripping a fellow by the shoulders would stare him in the eyes.

"Think you I could break your back?"

If the man said—"Try it," Caradoc was satisfied, and passed his man. He got seventeen in Corinium, three of them old soldiers, and eight who were riders. Caradoc's bow legs could straddle a horse, and Gawaine of the Black Valley had saved his horses. Geraint's company was to have half its men mounted, for he and Caradoc were agreed that if they could catch the men of Calleva in the open, a charge of a hundred horse would turn Calleva into a mob to be slaughtered.

As to the pay-chest its filling proved easy. Geraint had money with Rhadamanthus, and so had Cornelia, and the banker himself put a hundred gold pieces into the common fund. There were other contributors, people whom Balthasar had driven from Calleva, and who were ready to pay for the purging of communism. Geraint bought a dozen horses, six of them draft, and three light wagons. Arms proved less easy, for Corinium could boast only one armourer, but Caradoc stripped off his shirt, and for seven days became the smith. The regular officer in command of the small garrison, becoming aware of these preparations, attempted interference and appealed to the prefect.

Leo reassured him.

"Do not worry, captain; it is for the good of Britain."

So, Geraint and Caradoc marched out of Corinium with nearly forty men at their backs, and at their first halt a dozen of the legionaires joined them. The men had deserted to see some fun and to follow a leader who did not hide behind stone walls. Geraint stood not upon ceremony. He closed one eye and told the fellows to take off their badges, and sit down round the mess-pot.

o

But, if a man will not learn from life, then no school can save him from folly, and Geraint had learnt that to haft an axe-head on unseasoned wood was foolishness. This little war-machine of his was to be no reckless improvisation. It should be taught to fight as one man and to hold together in tight places, and never to panic or scatter. Moreover, there should be no licence and no looting, save on particular and triumphant occasions. He and Caradoc were of one mind in this matter. They chose their subordinates very carefully. They would march east to join the Aquilas and Gawaine, getting such men as they could, but there should be no tilting at windmills. They would drill their men, making them hard, and as Caradoc put it—"Give an edge to the axe that would not break or turn."

On the second day before marching Geraint called his men together and spoke to them. He was quiet and calm. He spoke of the larger issues, the simple realities that these fellows could understand. If there were men among them who loved this island and its woods and hills and fields, and who would save them from despair and ruin, let them remember what the Cymri had made of the country about Corinium. This war was against the wild men on the borders, and the rebels within. There was to be no raping and no robbing, and, at a sign from Geraint, Caradoc held up a rope.

"The first man who is caught at that game will end on a tree."

Men will accept mastery when the master is strong. Geraint was no frothmonger, and men asked to be led. A rabble will come to despise itself in the consciousness of rabbledom. Generation after generation sees an illusion shattered, and having listened to the men on tubs, turns again to the man who is not afraid to be master.

His men began to honour Geraint. He could look them in the eyes and show them authority, and a man may feel that authority is a good stout buckle to his belt.

So, Geraint and Caradoc and David of the Red Head marched east towards the forest and downland country that lay west of Calleva, gathering a man here and a man there, and seeing to it that their recruits held the road like soldiers. The men from the legions and the veterans drilled their fellows each day, and taught them spear and sword craft. Geraint avoided the villages, save when bread and meat were needed, and in this summer season his men lay at night under green leaves. He kept his marching as secret as possible, so that Calleva should get no news of it. And, on the fifth day they came to a glade in the forest country, where Gawaine and the young Aquilas lay harboured, thirty-five men with forty horses. Gawaine was still stiff with a wound that Calleva had given him, and the young eagles were wild to tear the city that had brought death to their father.

When Geraint and his men marched in, the Aquila lads rushed to him, and held him by the knees.

"Geraint——"

"Give us blood, lord.—Now, we shall be strong enough to whip those whelps."

But Geraint was not to be hurried. He had a secret of his own, precious things to be recovered, and he hid these things in his heart. He wanted to find Morgan and to hear what news the lad had to give him. There was a flame within him. Leaving Caradoc and David with Gawaine and the young Aquilas to drill and gather in more men, he rode out alone in the grey of the morning for those far beech woods where Alban had his cross.

CHAPTER XIX

Guinevra Washes a Man's Feet

¶ It might have been said of Fidelis that she never left an apple ungathered or an egg uncounted, and in the matter of discipline the community began to feel her hand. She had a bell brought from Calleva, and hung between two posts outside her porch, and at five o'clock in the morning Fidelis herself set that bell ringing. Her women had to be up and doing; her six men to tumble out of their huts and parade before the lady with the fierce eyebrows and the jutting chin.

Those grey, still mornings were both sweet and bitter to Guinevra. Sometimes it rained, sometimes the sun crept through the trees like a lover, and if the spirit of Guinevra was restless, her body was loth to leave the bed. Each night she lay down tired and aching, for Fidelis was ruthless. The boat was poled across the first thing in the morning by the oldest and gruffest of the men, with Guinevra's work-mate in it to safeguard the male creature from being suborned by youth and beauty.

Volumna, Guinevra's work-mate, was neither young nor beautiful. She had the face and the shape of a sow; her nostrils were two holes in a snout; her chin hung down. A great, big creature who waddled, a guzzler; she was good-natured provided her belly was filled. She had come from the lowest of the people, was very strong, and could carry a sack of corn like a man.

Guinevra and Volumna, or Lumna as she was called for short, were put to the roughest work. They emptied slops, cleaned dishes, scrubbed floors, and when the housework was finished, Fidelis sent them to work in the fields or garden. They were not allowed near the men. If there was mown grass to be raked up and cocked, or ground to be weeded, Volumna and the girl were put to it. Fidelis had given Volumna her orders.

"Let this strong young wench learn what work is. Never let her out of your sight—woman."

Volumna understood. She might be a good-natured and thick-skinned creature who took some pleasure in watching silk become sackcloth. Guinevra was strong and young, but her hands were soft, and her back unused to bending. She wasted her strength, and blistered her hands. She grew as brown as a man, after the first sun-burn had passed, and this nut-brown bloom became her. Volumna was all pig-skin and the colour of it.

But Volumna's big body sweated, and her juices attracted the flies. Guinevra would never have believed that there were so many flies in the world or that they could have found human bodies so tempting. Volumna was the bait, but the flies and Beelzebub discovered the sweetness of Guinevra. The flies swarmed, and buzzed and bit. Volumna did not appear to mind them; her skin and soul were less sensitive than the girl's. And when your hands were fouled with dirt from weeding, a dab at the cheek or forehead left a mark.

Sometimes, Guinevra would straighten her back and stand looking down into the valley at the island and the pool. Why did she endure this? Was she to go on enduring it? Was there no escape into the world which had once been hers?—though it was a world which to her young mind would never be the same. Everywhere she went about the valley she was always looking for a mound or strip of raw earth, the place where her love lay buried, but she had not found it.

Volumna would grunt.

"Now—then, don't stand and stare. What are you looking for? Ghosts?"

Volumna owned a coarse sense of humour.

"Or a lover?—How do you fancy old Thomas, tee-tee? Don't you let Fidelis catch you mooning. We're holy women, we are. And what's more, I don't want to be left with all the work. You know she'll be up here before dinner to see how much ground we have grubbed."

And Guinevra would bend her back again and toss weeds into the basket, and edge a little way from Volumna, her horde of flies and her odour. But Volumna was a sociable beast, and liked to work cheek by jowl with her mate. She would even gossip, and tell unseemly stories, and stop to quake.

"We're holy women, we are—but—bless you—one must make the bed shake sometimes."

In the middle of the month the craftsmen from Calleva had reroofed the great house, mended the pavements and replastered the walls, and when the workmen had gone Volumna and Guinevra were put to the cleaning of the place. It meant days of work on hands and knees with bucket and swab, and Guinevra's hands began to grow red and rough. Fidelis was in and out, seeing to it that there was no shirking. She intended the sisterhood to move into the great house before the summer passed. Volumna and Guinevra scrubbed and polished. The room which had been Placida's chamber, with a private door opening on the orchard and the chapel, appeared to have been chosen for some particular purpose. Fidelis gave it severe attention. The walls were white and spotless, the newly-tiled floor immaculate. Fidelis began to have furniture carried into this room, a bed, a press, a gilded chair from the house of Cornelia, an oak table. The room could be warmed in winter, for there was a hypocaust below it.

Guinevra, constrained to polish that floor, drew her own conclusions.

"Fidelis means to be comfortable."

Volumna, sitting on her heels, chuckled and quaked.

"You talk scandal, girl."

"I do not blame Fidelis——"

"Tut-tut! Will Fidelis sleep with the bishop?—This is to be his Eminence's chamber when he comes to withdraw himself from the world in meditation and prayer."

Guinevra's eyes looked startled.

"Balthasar coming here?"

"To be waited on by us holy women. What of Martha and Mary, and the Magdalene—my dear? There is his holiness's private door by which he can reach the chapel."

Guinevra went on with her scrubbing, but the news had roused her out of her stupor of consent. She had borne with Fidelis and hard work and humiliation because the joy had gone out of her life, and she had not had the spirit in her to rebel, but with Balthasar in the valley black spiders would spin webs. Something began to harden in her and to take shape, as though her heart hardened with her hands. She cherished her secret, and brooded over it like some precious and blood-stained relic in her bosom.

But she hid her young fierceness. She seemed to grow more meek and obedient. She answered Fidelis sweetly. She dissembled. And Fidelis, watching beauty on its knees with brown neck and feet and roughened hands sedulously scrubbing, began to assume that the spirit of Guinevra was broken.

"Blessed are the meek. You are learning wisdom, girl."

Guinevra dipped the cloth in the bucket, and wondered in what way Fidelis was blessed, but she answered submissively.

"When one is young, matrona, one thinks that the whole world should be a mirror to one's wishes. One is all self."

"Ha!" said Fidelis, looking pleased; "we shall make something of you yet," and she promulgated her approval by allowing Guinevra honey with her bread, and two cups of milk a day.

On Monday it happened that Guinevra and Volumna were sent up to the woods for faggots. The men were busy getting in Geraint's harvest, for the weather was set fair and the corn ripe for the sickles. A stack of faggots had been left on the edge of a coppice by Geraint's woodmen, and Guinevra and Volumna went up into the woods. Volumna had a couple of apples, summerlings, in her pocket, and being in a good temper she offered one of them to Guinevra.

Also, Volumna had to be allowed her bite at nature.

"Queer names they do give to fruit, my dear. What do you think this sweeting is called?"

Guinevra did not know, but the apple was pretty, all red and green.

"Virgin's Blush! That's as it should be, what? When I was young and hung a stocking out of my window to let the lad know I was blushing and willing, I wasn't as ripe as this."

Volumna bit into her apple. She had to be content with windfalls, since other fruit did not come her way.

"Fidelis is down in the cornfield making sure that those fellows are sweating. We need not hurry ourselves, my dear."

Volumna was in a jocund mood. They had the whole morning before them for the carrying of faggots. Yes, and maybe the dried sticks were to heat bath-water for the bishop—though Balthasar was not exactly a stick. "They say he was a devil of a lad, my dear, before he took religion." Volumna proposed that they should amuse themselves, ramble at their leisure.—"I'll show you something, girl." Volumna, like many women of her class, loved to enjoy herself gaping at things, weddings and funerals, betrothals, and the whipping of rogues. She liked to go and look at graves, as though the mouldering dead provoked her appreciation of good living. The poor corpses could not fill their bellies; Volumna could and did. Moreover, she was moved to play a prank on Guinevra, show her a mound of earth, and watch the girl's face. For Volumna, like many large, gross creatures, would suddenly conceive malice, and snap at her trough-mate.

Fidelis had come to know of the Grave of Geraint, as the Valley now called it, and she had told Caritas, and Caritas had told the others. Volumna knew the place. She led the way through the beech trees and over the brow of the hill into a broad glade running east and west. One great tree stood out in the open grassland like the king of the forest, and it was here that Malgo had fought his last fight and been buried. Green sods had been laid against the mound, but the dry summer weather had burned them brown.

But when they came to the place Volumna's jest turned sour in her mouth. She was not a bad-natured creature at the bottom, and after all—it was hard to lose a lover, and to think of him rotting under the sods. Volumna would have waddled on past the grave, but Guinevra had seen it. She stood still as stone.

"Is it—that—which you brought me to see?"

Volumna lied to her.

"O, no, my dear. One does not come to gape at such things, does one?"

But Guinevra knew that she lied.

"You can tell me.—It is Geraint's grave."

Volumna, suddenly contrite and full of flabby emotion, blurted out the truth.

"What a fool I am—yes—I forgot.—Now, don't you take on, my dear——"

But Guinevra was not listening to Volumna. She walked slowly towards the mound of brown earth and baked sods, and stood by it dry-eyed. The great tree threw a broad shadow, but the grave was in the sunlight, for when Alban and Morgan had dug it they had chosen a place where roots would not balk their spades. The stillness

and the silence of Guinevra were beyond Volumna's understanding, for to Volumna and her likes grief was shallow
and noisy water.   None the less, Volumna did flop on her
knees, and cover her face with her hands, but she watched
Guinevra through her fingers.

She saw Guinevra bend down and take something into
her hand, a small piece of sun-caked soil.   She put it to her
lips, and then, letting it lie for a moment in her palm, she
turned her hand sideways and let the thing drop back upon
the grave.

"Bless us," said Volumna to herself—"she's a cold piece
of goods.—If I'd been in Geraint's arms, and they say she
was there—I would have knelt down and let myself go on
his grave."

Guinevra had turned aside and was standing in the
shadow of the tree.   Her two hands were pressed hard
over her breasts, her face strangely calm.   She seemed to
be looking into the deeps of the wood where the great
trunks of the beech trees drew together like grey pillars
in the green gloom.   But to Guinevra the boles of the
beeches were a grey wall and hanging upon the wall was
the face of Balthasar.

2

They were making their third journey with faggots on
their shoulders when Caritas met them half-way up the
hill.

"Fidelis wants you both."

"Oh," said Volumna, "what have we done amiss?"

Caritas liked to be supercilious and superior when
Fidelis was not present.

"Ask your conscience, Volumna.   You will find Fidelis
in the great house.   There is work to do."

Volumna sniffed.

"I know what that means.   Fidelis has had news from

Calleva. We are to dust the bishop's chair, and put
lavender sprigs under his pillow."

Caritas snubbed her. A woman with a snout like
Volumna's needed ringing.

"That's as it may be. Fidelis will give you your
orders."

And give them orders Fidelis most certainly did. She
had brought two of the men away from the harvest to scythe
and sweep in the garden. Balthasar was coming to lodge
in the guest-chamber, and to consecrate both with his
presence and his public ritual the Mansio of the Sacred
Sisters. Fidelis fulminated. The chapel floor had to be
washed, and candles placed on the altar. The guest-
chamber was as sweet as a new spice-box, but Fidelis's
orders were that it was to be cleaned again. She would
strew fragrant herbs on the floor, and put flowers in the
vases. This coming of their lord and founder was a
sacred occasion, and Volumna and Guinevra were put
to work.

There was the bishop's bed to be made, and Fidelis would
have nothing on it but new linen over a feather mattress
that had been freshly stuffed. Fidelis was so full of zeal
and so ruthless in her attention to detail that Volumna
whispered to her mate—"Anyone would think that she
was going to bed with his holiness." Guinevra, on her
hands and knees, polished tiles with an air of dark diligence.
Almost, she could see faces looking up at her from the
shining floor, the face of Geraint pale and stricken, and the
face of the man who had left him to die.

Fidelis sent Guinevra out to gather herbs in the herb-
garden, mint and sage, marjoram, thyme and lavender.
Fidelis herself strewed the sprigs about the floor. It was
right and good that the chamber should smell sweet when
these herbs were crushed by holy feet. Guinevra, watching
Fidelis strewing her herbs, seemed to see strange shapes
moving over the polished floor.

3

Balthasar rode out of Calleva on a black horse about three hours after noon. He rode alone, like a man riding for his pleasure in the country when the sun is in the west, and the day beginning to cool. He wore a grey cloak fastened with a brooch on the left shoulder, but this drab colour hid finer feathers. His shoes were of red leather, and on his head was a Phrygian cap of red cloth.

Balthasar looked sleek and debonair, but his stateliness paraded with unction for the simple world's worship. He might be a handsome man, and proud to show no pride when labouring folk stood cap in the hand by the roadside. Balthasar blessed them, stretching out a fine white hand.

"Peace to you, my children."

Matters were going well for Balthasar, so well that God, the Emperor, and men had united in flattering him. Moreover, Balthasar could flatter himself, and with a little mocking backward glance at yesterday, promulgate the privileges of power. "Get thee behind me, Satan," might become—"Satan, my slave, thou shalt serve." So beautiful and smooth was life that Balthasar was persuaded to laugh at the disharmonies of sin and of saintliness, and prepare to reconcile them. A green valley, peace, obedient and ministering sisters, a little passion that might be preserved from profanity. Surely, life could allow so successful and singular a man tender relaxation? It might be christened fatherly playfulness. "One should learn," said Balthasar; "one should learn, even from love."

He chose to ride on the grass, in and out of the shadow of great trees. He saw cattle sheltering from the heat, and men enduring it in the harvest fields, catching the cut corn in the crooks of their brown arms. His power extended over all this countryside, over men and beasts, and the wild creatures, the woods and waters. All these little country communes looked to Calleva, and Calleva had become Balthasar. He sat in the curia with the city council, and men from other cities came to honour him. He administered justice according to the laws of the church, was followed about Calleva by deacons, acolytes, and a guard. The people saluted him as he passed. Children pushed through the crowd to look at the great man.

Balthasar came to Turris Alba in a slant of summer sunlight, and the valley was like a golden shell lying in the green lap of the woods. He saw the pool as a silver shield, the floating island with its tower, blue smoke rising, sheaves in stook in the cornfield. A man in a brown smock was driving red cows home to be milked. Trees cast long shadows. And on a little grassy knoll half-way down the slope a figure in grey stood at gaze, Caritas watching for the coming of the bishop.

Caritas ran, though Caritas running was not an act of grace. Fidelis was on her knees in Placida's chapel, the women gathered in the courtyard. Caritas's voice became shrill when she was excited.

"Balthasar."

Fidelis got on her feet.

"Our bishop, women, our bishop.—Has he people with him?"

Caritas's voice fell three notes.

"No.—His holiness is alone—and riding."

"Would he be walking?" said Fidelis, sharply. "Have some sense, woman, and put your veil straight."

Fidelis cherished the occasion. She strode through the herb garden with Caritas carried along by the draught of her like a blown leaf. Peremptorily the women were paraded and led forth, walking two by two. Fidelis admonished them like a drill-sergeant. "Hands folded—eyes on the ground.—Silence." She led the sisterhood out of the courtyard, and up the hill to meet Balthasar. Volumna and Guinevra were the last links in the grey chain, and Volumna, who had been eating an apple when Fidelis had appeared, and who had not dared to munch in public,

swallowed the secret mouthful and drew the back of a hand
across her lips.

She whispered to Guinevra.

"A cat may look at a king, and the man's only the son
of a butcher.—And if you ask me—Fidelis——"

But Guinevra was not listening to Volumna. She
walked darkly and devoutly, hands folded, eyes downcast,
like a woman alone with her secret self and listening to
inward voices. She saw nothing but the heels and the grey
skirt of the sister in front of her, but she knew that in a
little while she would see the face of Balthasar.

4

The women knelt on the grass, while Fidelis kissed the
gloved hand of the bishop. Fidelis was the formalist, and
mistress of the occasion.

"We welcome you, holy father and founder. In this
place may you find peace."

Balthasar, looking over the devout head of Fidelis saw
the women kneeling two by two, and his glances were
quick to discover Guinevra. Her eyes looked darker than
he remembered them, but Balthasar's glance was too shrewd
to loiter. He had Fidelis to remember, Fidelis—the formalist—who had to be flattered.

"I shall find peace here, matrona.—Surely, the place is
very beautiful.—I would see all that you good women have
done here."

"Will not your holiness take some rest and refreshment.
—Your chamber is prepared."

Balthasar's visitation was to be no formal affair, though
he saluted the formalist in Fidelis. He had come from
the city to the country to find life sweet and reflective among
friends. He would get off his horse and walk. Let the
good women be spared more kneeling. Balthasar's smile
was jocund. "Suffer me to be mere man, matrona, a man

among my friends. These rustic scenes are soothing. The patient beasts and the fruits of the earth.—Show me—all that you have to show." His gracious simplicity slipped subtly out of the saddle. He unbuckled his cloak, and let it fall open. He had the air of a man at his ease, and from whose shoulders the cares and confusions of life were loosed. He stood with the sunlight across his face, breathing the soft air.

"What peace—matrona! Woods, fields, and water.— I can draw deep breaths here."

A man came running to take Balthasar's horse. Fidelis dismissed the women.—"Go to your labours." It pleased her to think that she was mistress, that she could send those others away, while she remained to speak and walk with the great man. Almost, she felt herself Balthasar's equal. This little world was hers, and by right of authority and zeal she stood to display it to him, and the things she had done and yet would do She was full of the pride of accomplishment. "See—you chose me, and you were wise. I have not failed." Fidelis walked like the mistress that she was, erect, severe, confident, displaying her domain. Could a man have done things better, produced in these few weeks so much order and smoothness? She walked as though she were keeping step with god, a god who could not fail to be impressed.—"Nothing happens here that I do not know of. Nothing is done—but through my foresight and by my orders.—There—is my harvest—there my orchard. I say yea and nay—and I am obeyed."

Balthasar could walk delicately even with a woman so conscious of her capacity as Fidelis, for Fidelis was no fool. She came of farming stock and she strode like a man, and was more man than her men when she gave them orders. She could milk a cow and handle a sickle and help a calf into the world and mother a motherless sheep. And here was a stately property, enriched by centuries of good tillage and cattle-craft. Fidelis knew what she knew, the corn that could be grown, the sheep run on the upland pastures.

Almost she read Balthasar a lecture. She spoke of the herds of swine that could be fed on the beech mast. She led Balthasar to the byres and barns, and showed him the great orchard rich with fruit. She grew eloquent over her granary, her poultry, her still-room, her threshing floor, but Balthasar, though he applauded her enthusiasm, was thinking of other fruit.

"It was a fool mob that burnt the great house."

Balthasar humoured her. He confessed that a crowd was like muddy water. You had to allow it to spill itself on occasions before the sediment settled.

"But, mark you, matrona, we have rebuilt you the house, and Calleva has paid for it out of the public funds."

Fidelis led him to the vineyard on the sunny slope of the hill, and walking between the rows of vines, Balthasar began to persuade the tongue of Fidelis to speak of other things. No—there was no mildew on the grapes, but let viticulture pass for a moment. What of the inward life, spiritual values? Was the sisterhood growing in grace and harmony?

Fidelis took the bait.

"I have no trouble with my women. I work them hard, and do not encourage gossip. We rise at five in the morning, pray, sing a canticle, and then—to work."

"Excellent," said Balthasar—"excellent. Discipline, my dear Fidelis, discipline. Good sheep are happy as sheep with a wise shepherdess. And no one—is—contumacious?"

Fidelis held her head high. Let them dare!

"Even that young wench of Geraint's is becoming tractable."

"Ah," said Balthasar, "that pleases me. A brand snatched from the burning. So, she grows meek and chaste, matrona?"

Fidelis nodded.

"She is as milk."

"And honey, matrona. You can mother souls as well as fields.—When these grapes are ripe——"

"You shall have grapes at Calleva—my lord."

The sun was going down, and Fidelis was not Joshua. She remembered that she had walked the great man over much ground. His holiness should be cherished. She spoke of the chamber she had prepared, supper and bed, and his holiness's feet should be washed. She led the way up to the great house, and let Balthasar in by the privy door opening from the garden. "Your holiness will be undisturbed here. And there is the path to the chapel." Balthasar stood on the threshold and saw the evening sun shining in through the windows. The sweet herbs were under his feet. He raised a hand and blessed Fidelis and the room.

"I am a little weary, matrona."

"You shall be served, sir," said she—"I will see to it."

Let the gods witness that vanity prompted Fidelis to choose Guinevra to be the bishop's handmaid. She would show Balthasar that she could chasten and subdue souls as well as she could manage an estate. The girl's humility should be presented to the bishop like a bowl of milk. Fidelis sent for Guinevra, and gave her her orders.

"Get a basin and clean water, girl, and let the water be warmed, and go in and wash his holiness's feet."

Guinevra gave Fidelis a strange, dark look. Did the woman know?—But that was not possible.—Guinevra answered her softly.

"Yes, matrona. And who will give me a clean napkin?"

"Ask Caritas.—And remember, girl, speak only if you are spoken to."

"I will remember, matrona."

She went to the kitchen for her water, and saw something lying on a table. Martha the cook was busy at the fire, and Guinevra swept the knife from the table and hid it in her bosom. It lay between her breasts, and she felt the

P

point pressing against her skin.   It could slip no farther because of the girdle she wore tight about her loins.   She filled a ewer with warm water, set it in a braze basin, and went in search of Caritas.   Would Fidelis be with her, or would she kneel at Balthasar's feet alone?   She got her napkin from Caritas, and with it neatly folded over the rim of the basin she went to the guest-chamber.   For a moment she stood listening.—She heard no voices, and she knocked.

Balthasar's voice bade her enter.

He was standing at one of the windows in the full light of the setting sun, and the purple of his tunic seemed to flush.

"You—my daughter?"

Arms folded, he let his surprise and its pleasure sleek itself, but his eyes grew hot.   He saw her—meek as milk, standing there with her ewer and basin, deep-eyed and deep bosomed, gentle and consenting.

"I am to wash my lord's feet."

Sweet words with secret poison in them.   Balthasar's red lips seemed to twist.—Beautiful irony!   And he had said in his heart that Fidelis was no fool—She was exhibiting but another plant that was growing pliant to her will.

"Your hands are welcome, Guinevra."

He did not see the little sudden flame behind her lowered lashes.   Guinevra!   Lord!—So, she and Geraint had spoken to each other.   She felt him move towards the chair, and as she knelt the smell of the herbs was in her nostrils.   She placed the basin on the floor, and poured water into it, and the water seemed to laugh.

"Your shoes, lord."

He sat easily in the chair, bending forward slightly, one hand on his knee.

"You do me honour, Guinevra."

"Shall I unlace my lord's shoes?"

He was smiling.   He gave her a gracious movement of the head.

"Red shoes—and white hands, my dear.—Tell me, are you happy here?—For, it is my wish, child——"

Her hands were busy with his shoes. My lord's stockings were of green silk, and if a man can be proud of his ankles—Balthasar had cause to think well of them. God had not stinted his gifts. Guinevra's head was still like that of a boy, but as she bent over his feet he saw the brown of her neck melt into the white of her shoulders. That was no boy's neck, but swansdown, sensuous and soft, fruit to be bitten into.

Her voice breathed awe of him.

"My lord's stockings——?"

Plainly, she was shy of Balthasar and the intimate occasion. But how right and exquisite and provoking was this timidity, the slanting velvet of her eyes, her perplexed forehead and hesitant hands. Meddle with a man's garters—and that man so eminent and splendid. And Balthasar laughed within himself. His passion chose to be playful. There was less sense of sin when you sinned with a smile.

"My hands shall serve for that."

He was aware of the grave young stateliness of her as she knelt and waited. Her lips were firm and full; her eyelids gave never a flicker.—Balthasar put his feet in the basin. He had no need to excuse the shapeliness of his legs. Deliberately, and with the solemnity of one performing some sacred office, she poured the water over his feet.

Suddenly, Balthasar's hand was on her head.

"Is there—no goodness in me, Guinevra?"

She was utterly still, eyes lowered, her hands in the water.

"I am—my lord's—servant."

"No more than that, my dear?"

His eyes watched her. How still she was, how pale! His fingers stirred amid her hair.

"Is it—your shame and mine—that I would make

you forget—yesterday in to-morrow?—What say you, Guinevra?"

And suddenly she looked at him, and her face was soft and wanton. It glowed. It had all the glamour of a woman's face when desire is born in her, swiftly, like a window struck by the sun.

"My lord—I—am—your servant."

Balthasar bent over her. Was the thing true? Those consenting, wayward eyes, and that poignant—passionate mouth!—She would take him as her lover? Her coyness was a cloak to be dropped in the darkness.

He whispered over her head.

"Sweet things can happen to us.—Be wise—Guinevra, be very wise—and wash my feet."

She glowed with exquisite, warm confusion, and then —growing suddenly bold, she looked at him and smiled.

"I—am—wise."

Balthasar, burning, sat and watched her wash his feet. He was thinking of the darkness, and the night, and of how Fidelis had told him that their penitent slept in the tower upon the island. And Guinevra was thinking—"I will not strike him now. He will come to me in the night. He shall die where my love died."

CHAPTER XX

Balthasar Comes to the Island

¶About sunset a little wind sprang up, ruffling the trees and the water, and making curtains belly at open windows. Balthasar had supped, served by Caritas and Pia, who could but admire Balthasar's gracious conversation and the fine movements of his hands.

"A little wine, father?"

Balthasar had suffered himself to drink a cup of wine, for would not the night be purple wine? He had shown a stately playfulness in accepting the cup from the hands of Caritas.

"In the country and in such company, sister, cares fall from a man's shoulders."

At the end of the meal they had brought him a bowl of water and a napkin, and after washing those fine hands of his, he had stood at a window and watched Guinevra being ferried across the water to the island. He had seen the boat return, and the man moor it at the bank. How singular were the workings of passion and of providence! The white tower had caught the afterglow and shone white like a woman's bosom.

Just when dusk was falling Fidelis came in with two candles. She found Balthasar walking up and down the room over the fragrant herbs, hands folded, head bowed as in meditation. Fidelis set the candlesticks on the table, and would have gone out without speaking, but Balthasar turned as she reached the door.

"Matrona."

Fidelis waited upon his words.

"Matrona—I came for peace and I have found it. Let not your good women vex themselves further on my account. I shall sleep a little, but it is my habit to rise soon after midnight and keep watch and pray. Sometimes —I like to walk a little under the stars.—I would disturb none of you, nor be feared as a ghost."

Fidelis took all things literally.

"You have your own door, father, leading into the garden. I have had lamps lit in the chapel, and they will burn till dawn. The chapel is yours. I will see that no one trespasses upon your peace."

Balthasar raised a white hand.

"Bless you, my sister, and thank you. In the silence of the night one's thoughts are clarified. And the troubled state of this island concerns me. Peace to you, Fidelis, and to your house."

Fidelis bowed herself before him.

"Peace to your prayers, father," and with the air of a woman proud of the day's consummation she passed out and closed the door softly upon her saint.

A night wind was restless and wayward. It would blow suddenly through the valley, rousing the trees from their sleep, setting curtains swaying and candle flames aslant. There would be a complaining of doors and of windows, and then—quite suddenly—everything would be still. The sky held stars, but no moon, and the darkness and that little wayward wind with its flurries of fretfulness made the night more secret. When the house was asleep, Balthasar put on his cloak, and leaving the candles burning, went out by the door into the herb-garden. It was very dark and still here, but he could see the door of the chapel as a panel of light. A broad path of freshly scythed grass ran straight towards the light, and Balthasar, with arms folded, went towards the chapel. If the night had eyes they should see that which it was fit for them to see. The wind came again as he reached the tongue of light from the open door. There was a rustling of leaves, and a sound of apples falling on the orchard grass.   The chapel door creaked, and the little flames of the two Roman lamps wavered.

Balthasar stood still a moment.   The thing which was in him was whipped by the wind.   It answered the "Ah" of the woods above.   Shadows flickered across his face.   Then, he entered the chapel, and closed the door. No eyes could see him there, for the windows were high in the wall and narrow.   He did not kneel, or pray that this passion should pass from him, or dissemble before his God.   He walked up and down between the door and the altar, and whenever be turned, his eyes avoided the lamps and the altar, but looked steadily and consentingly at the door.

The night had grown still again, but when—at last—he opened the door, he stood waiting for the wind, and presently he heard it in the tree tops down the valley.   It came, breathing in the apple trees and swelling in the folds of his cloak, and the man in Balthasar exulted.   He went down into the darkness of the valley with the wind upon his face.

2

It was very dark on the island, but the water was less dark than the trees and the grass, and Guinevra was restless.

It seemed to her that she had waited half the night. She had watched the lights go out, all save the lights in those two windows.   Why did he loiter?   Had his lust failed him?   Should she have struck while she was kneeling at his feet?—But had he not said to her—"Be wise." He too was being wise, waiting for the world to be asleep before setting out upon his pilgrimage.—She walked up and down.   She sat in the grass and listened, and wished that the night was windless, for just when the night seemed to hold its breath and she fancied that she could hear sounds upon the water, the trees and water weeds would rustle and the water break into almost inaudible frettings among the flags and sedges. She felt cold from heart to head, with death tucked under her girdle. She would not let herself think. She was a creature coiled like a spring, waiting for the release and one swift movement. She did not think of to-morrow. This dark, wicked, inexorable night was sufficient.

And then she heard a faint sound, wood chafing against wood. Water and weeds and trees were still for the moment. She stood up, but could see nothing, but she could hear the pole rubbing against the side of the boat. He was coming. She seemed to hold her breath, and her hand went to her girdle.—Be wise.—Yes, she would be very wise. She could distinguish something that was darker than the water moving in towards the island. It was coming straight towards her, for the man in the boat could see the grey shape of the tower. She went three steps nearer to the water. Her feet and her hands felt cold.

The boat ran its nose among the weeds. He stood in it like a shadow of a man. She saw him put down the pole and move forward. There was the rattle of a chain, and her breath came sharply.—Should she——? But there was an inexorable guile in her that bade her wait. Let him show himself in all his nakedness of soul before she struck.

She gave a little laugh, and felt how incredibly false it was. Again, the chain rattled, but Balthasar had heard her, and to him the night shivered.

"Guinevra."

She answered him, and was astonished that she could make her voice so soft.

"I am here, lord."

He was on the solid earth now, and close to her, but his first touches were delicate.

"Guinevra—heart of desire."

She trembled, but stiffened herself against her trembling. His hands were on her shoulders. His face came closer and closer, and suddenly he was no sacred shadow, but man. He seemed to fall over the edge of his own soul. He held her body fiercely against his. He was like a man famished.

"Can I kiss—girl?"

He was beside himself, and his hot lips seemed to bite. He had her arms pinioned, and she dissembled.

"Never man kissed as you, lord."

She was smothering, breathless. She made herself laugh.

"Ha—you shall see—girl."

She lay in his arms.

"Let us go in, lord.—Hold my hand.—No, let me walk of my own will."

He humoured her, and she gave him her left hand. Woman's ways were woman's ways, and he exulted. He was very tender now. She should take him as she pleased.

They came to the door of the tower, and the wind was in the trees. And again she laughed.

"I will go in first, lord."

He kissed the hand he held.

"Is it not my lady's chamber."

She slipped within, and stood with her right hand free, the door half covering her body.

"Come, dear lord."

Balthasar put his arms up as though surrendering to the night, and to her. She struck twice, and then stood still, the edge of the door between her two breasts. She felt him jerking and choking at her feet.

3

She leaned against the door. It was as though she had let her own blood flow as well as his. She felt faint, sick, empty of all anger against him and against life. She shook at the knees; she heard him moaning and twitching there like an animal in a trap whose struggles grow less and less. Dear God, why didn't he lie still? And then, something warm touched her foot, and a horror of that wet, warm ooze possessed her. She was naked fear, shivering and unashamed looking backwards over her shoulder at a face of horror. She slipped past the thing on the floor, pressing herself close against the door, and even her feet seemed to shrink. She was on the clean, sweet grass, and it was wet with dew. The night had sunk into utter and absolute stillness.

She was no more than fear now on flurried feet, hurrying to be where that thing was not. She found herself by the water's edge with the nose of the boat at her feet. She stooped for the chain and felt metal touch metal. The knife was still in her hand. She straightened, flung it far out into the darkness, and heard it strike the water. Her fingers tore at the chain which was caught in the sedges. She slipped in, groped for the pole, drove it in and pressed her body against it. So blind and confused was her haste that she lost all sense of direction in the darkness. Once, she missed the bottom with the pole and fell sideways against the gunwale. She splashed her way over the dark water, not conscious of breathing in short jerks. That crossing seemed endless, for the boat ran in a half circle, and at last she touched ground where the water narrowed at the western end. She scrambled out and up through the water weeds wet to the knees, and ran, nor would her fear take thought and pause until she had reached the woods.

There, her hands touched the smooth bark of a beech tree. She spread her arms and leaned against it, her face against the cool grey skin. She shook at the knees, and made a little moaning.

"Dear God, would I were dead."

CHAPTER XXI

Guinevra and the Hermit

¶ MORGAN, who was making it his business in life to keep watch upon Balthasar's world at all hours of the day and night, came early in the morning to Malgo's grave. Morgan was for the valley and a spy's nest in a patch of fern, for Morgan had seen Balthasar ride down to the House of the Grey Sisters, and Morgan had thought— "Ye gods, does the fellow keep a house full of wives?" Patches of mist hung in the woods, and heavy dew lay on the grass, and the rabbits had left their tracks in the dew. Morgan would have passed across the glade where Geraint had fought the men from Calleva, leaving Malgo's grave fifty yards on his left, but Morgan had sharp eyes and he saw something that made him pause. There were footmarks on the dew-drenched turf.

They were like the links of a chain, and they led towards the grave near the big beech tree. The morning mist still hung in this open place after the heat of yesterday, and presaged fine weather. The light was pearled silver. Morgan, half crouching, followed the dew-track, and suddenly, he was down like a dog, his chin on his crossed wrists.

Someone was sitting on Malgo's grave, a woman, and Morgan lay flat and watched her. He saw her in profile, her elbows on her knees, her chin on her hands. She just sat and stared. She was so much part of the mist and blurred by it that Morgan saw her merely as a grey figure in a grey haze, one of those women from the valley. But her stillness made him wonder. Why did she sit

243

like a figure of stone set up on old Malgo's grave? And what was she doing here at this hour of the morning?

Morgan lay low and watched. She seemed utterly unaware of his presence. The lad would have said that she was utterly unaware of anything. Was she waiting for someone, a lover? But what a place to choose, and whatever her business was she did not look happy over it. He nibbled grass. Well, if the woman was a study in stone, he could lie like a stone and be patient, though the dew had soaked through his tunic.

Presently, into this vapoury cleft in the high woods the sun began to penetrate. The tops of the beech trees were burred with gold. The mist seemed miraculously to lift, and melt away in little ghostly drifts. A slanting sun-ray shining through an oylet hole in the high foliage touched the figure on the grave like a mysterious finger.

Morgan would have said that it startled the woman, and warmed her to life. She raised her head. She looked up at that yellow knot in the dark foliage; she put up her hands as though there was—for her—a kind of horror—in the eyes of the morning.—But if the light had disturbed her, Morgan was on his knees.

Guinevra!

God's luck indeed!—He was on his feet, and minded to steal in and play a trick upon the girl who had scrambled with him over Dame Cornelia's wall. He was within ten yards of her when some instinct made her turn her head. She saw him, and Morgan saw her face. It was so still and pitiful and strange that he stopped and stood staring, and so sobered was he by her stricken face that he could not get out a word.

It was she who spoke.

"Morgan——! Do not come near me, Morgan. I have blood on my hands."

Her voice was like a little moaning wind. He saw her look at her hands.—But he had to say something for her sake and his, and curiosity was quick in him. He went a few steps nearer.

"Blood—lady?—I see no blood."

"Keep away from me, Morgan."

Was she out of her senses?

"Whose blood—lady?"

She seemed to shiver.

"Balthasar's.—He would have forced me.—Yes—I must speak to someone, Morgan, even to you.—I have been in the woods all night—and there was—stillness, such a dreadful stillness. I have killed Balthasar."

Morgan was almost as white as she was.

"There was a reason.—I am not a child——"

Her voice broke like a snapped thread, and Morgan understood.

"I would have done it for you, Guinevra, had I been there.—But—why—do you sit on that grave?"

She looked at him suddenly with wide eyes.

"Why?—Where else could I go? For he—to whom —I was clean—and would be clean—for ever—lies here."

Morgan's mouth fell open.

"Geraint?"

She nodded, and Morgan could have leapt in the air.

"That is Malgo's grave."

Her eyes seemed to grow more wide.

"Malgo's?—Is it one of those other graves in the wood?"

Morgan's face was as bright as glass in the sunlight.

"Geraint is not under the sod; he lives.—Why—lady, he is on horseback somewhere—seeking me.—He left me here to watch."

She was on her feet, and Morgan saw her close her eyes and press her hands to her breasts. She stood in the ray of sunlight, her eyes turned blindly to it, and then—the strength seemed to go out of her knees, and she sank down on the grave.—Did good news kill? She looked like death for a moment.

"Is it the truth, Morgan?"

"Should I lie? I love my lord as you do."

She opened her eyes; almost, she smiled at him.

"Come to me, Morgan. I would kiss you for this news."

Morgan was very solemn over the kissing. It was her ritual, not his—but he knelt and was kissed on the forehead. He shut his eyes, and did not breathe in the lady's face. Meanwhile, he was burning to ask her a question, and he asked it.

"Who told you my lord was dead?"

"Balthasar."

"The holy liar!—Why, it was I who found Geraint on the island, dying of thirst. That filthy priest had emptied the water-pot and thrown the bread out of the window and left him to die."

Guinevra sat rigid, and her eyes were fierce.

"Now I know why he lied to me."

"You were right to put that knife in him, lady."

She looked at Morgan, and the fierceness went out of her eyes.

"There is blood on my hands.—O, Morgan—what will my lord say?"

Morgan sat on his heels and observed her. Surely, women were strange creatures. They seemed to blow hot and cold, use a knife one moment, and fall on their knees the next. He answered her in his rôle as a man.

"I should say that my lord will be glad and sorry."

"Sorry, Morgan?"

"Why, lady, look at it through Geraint's eyes.—I can promise you that my lord was cherishing a sword to send Balthasar's head spinning. And now—you have done the trick.—After all, it was a job for a man."

He saw that he had shocked her, but how and why? Squeamish things, women. She sat and shivered and was silent. She began to cast quick, wild glances into the woods.

"Morgan, I am afraid."

She looked it.

"Ssst—did you hear dead leaves rustling?"

He listened, but could hear nothing.

"Not a sound—lady."

She pressed her hands together.

"They must have found—him—by now.—They will search for me, Morgan. They will hunt me like a wild thing."

He sprang up.

"I know a safe place.—It was where Geraint lay when he was being healed of his wounds.—Come, lady—I know the ways."

2

The man who had served as Guinevra's ferryman came running up the hill. He was an oldish man and out of breath both with his news and his running, and the first person whom he met in the garden-court of the great house was Fidelis. He blurted at her.

"Blood—dame; he's lying there like a stuck pig, with blood all over the floor."

Fidelis, who had proposed to mark the day with a red letter, turned on the fellow tartly. What was he gabbling about?

"Don't shout, man. You will wake his holiness."

"It's of his holiness I'm telling you. He's lying down there on the island with a hole in his neck—stuck like a pig."

Fidelis's head seemed to go back and up with a jerk.

"What nonsense is this?"

The man became peevish.

"Well, if you don't believe me, go and see for yourself. That wench must have done it.—Stung him like a yaller wasp. And she's flitted."

Fidelis went grey.—"Wait there. Not a word." In six strides she was at one of the windows of the guest-chamber. She craned in, saw the gutted candles and the empty and untouched bed. Her face looked pinched. She went back to the man who was grinning and looking self-satisfied.

"Sleeping like a blessed babe, is he, dame?"

"Silence," said she. "Shut your mouth and come with me."

She strode, and the man followed her, rubbing his chin and grinning. This was a nice business. And what had Balthasar been doing on the island to get himself stuck? A wench, what!

Fidelis's voice rasped at him.

"Did you speak to—his holiness?"

"Speak to—he?—Why, he's a corpse."

"How do you know, fellow?"

"Well, he's lying there with his eyes shut, the colour of chalk, with blood all over the floor."

"In the tower?"

"Just inside the door, dame."

"And the girl's gone?"

"I saw no girl, dame. What I did find was the boat in the weeds right up tother end of the pool. Someone must have come across in a hurry, and that someone must have been she."

Fidelis froze. They had come to the pool, and she entered the boat, and the man took the pole and ferried her over. She scrambled out and stood on the bank. She bade him stay there. She went straight to the tower, and with a face like a grey flint, she looked in through the doorway.

Balthasar lay there on his back just as the man had said. He had a red wound in his throat, and another under the ribs to judge by the blood on his tunic. His face looked like white wax, and Fidelis stared at it. She was sure that Balthasar was dead.

"Mother of God——!"

Then, while she was staring at that waxy face Balthasar opened his eyes and looked at her. They were strange, glassy eyes, pale and very still, and for some seconds Fidelis and Balthasar looked at each other.

Fidelis fell on her knees. She saw Balthasar's eyelids flicker, and his lips move.

"Water."

"Who did this thing, father?"

"Give me water."

She looked about her, and seeing Guinevra's ewer, she took it and kneeling again and putting a hand under his head, she dribbled water into Balthasar's mouth. There was no compassion in her hands. She looked lean and fierce, and she was thinking—"What brought him here?— All this blood!—A damned, unholy mess! And if he dies —this little world of mine will be in the pot. One had better tread gently." She wiped Balthasar's chin and mouth with her apron, and watched his eyes as she bent over him.

"Can you bear to speak now, father?"

Balthasar closed his eyes, and but for the movements of his lips Fidelis would have thought him a corpse. It was like a dead man speaking.

"I will tell you, matrona. I was walking in the valley close to the water when I heard someone call me.—It was the girl. I spoke to her across the water. She besought me to come over to her, and thinking that the poor child had her sins to speak of—I entered the boat and crossed over."

His voice seemed to die away like the wind from an empty skin. He opened his eyes and looked at Fidelis. Fidelis was frowning, but she nodded. She did not ask Balthasar how the girl knew that he was walking near the pool.

"So, you crossed over, father."

"I found her on her knees.—She seemed in great grief. She besought me to come here and hear her confession. I went with her, and in the doorway——"

Q

Again, his voice died away, and he lay still, scarcely breathing. Fidelis was biting her lower lip.

"The young she-wolf—murderess! The little harlot struck for her dead paramour."

Balthasar opened his eyes.

"The guile of her—Fidelis.—Give me more water."

She held the jug to his lips.

"She shall pay."

But Balthasar was afraid of dying. A faint sweat showed on his forehead.

"Send to Calleva.—Send for a physician, Urbanus—for choice——"

Fidelis got to her feet, the fierce pragmatist.

"We will have you carried over and put to bed, father."

But Balthasar refused to be meddled with.

"No, no, matrona.—I fear to bleed again.—She struck me twice.—I will lie here till Urbanus comes.—Send quickly, Fidelis.—My work is not yet finished."

Fidelis placed the water-pot beside him and went back to the boat. She ignored the boatman's ironic grin. Well, what did she think of the news now that she had seen the dead man and the blood? Fidelis was thinking hard, but of other things. She sat herself down, and gnawed a crooked finger while the man poled the boat across. Had Balthasar's story convinced her? It had sounded very much like an improvisation, and there was one bad piece of work in the picture. How could Guinevra have divined the nearness of the holy presence across fifty yards of water on a moonless night?—Fidelis bit hard at her finger. What was she to do? Accept the portrait and assist in glozing over its inadequacies? Moreover, even if there had been some arranged meeting between Balthasar and the girl, might it not have had a godly significance? The boat touched the bank, and Fidelis stepped out, knowing that she would breathe fire and smoke in the cause of sanctity.

She gave the boatman his orders.

"Gather the men together. Tell Samson to have a horse ready."

She went straight to the house. She called the women together, and with an air of shocked and solemn grief she gave them the news. She spoke swiftly, fiercely. She added one or two convincing touches to the story.—In a moment of holy compassion and of kindness this good man had turned aside from his meditations to help a sinner who had assumed penitence and anguish. The women looked shocked, stupefied. Only Volumna allowed herself a secret snigger.

But Fidelis was for action.

"The murderess must be hunted and taken."

"God have pity on her," said Pia.

"Pity!—She has shed blood: the blood of a saint."

A man was sent galloping to Calleva for Urbanus the physician. The rest of the men, and six of the women, were to search the valley and the woods for the infamous creature who had raised her hand against God's saint.

§

When Morgan and Guinevra came to the edge of the woods above Alban's hermitage they saw the old man at work in his patch of corn. Stripped to the waist he was harvesting the wheat, the sickle flashing in the sunlight. Birds were thick about him in the stubble, and pecking at the wheat-ears where Alban had laid the cut corn.

Morgan and Guinevra looked at each other.

"Go down alone, Morgan.—Tell him that there is— one—here who has blood upon her hands."

She sat down under the shade of a tree, and Morgan went to speak with Alban. She watched the old man and the lad, and their voices came to her with the sound of running water. Alban was holding a bundle of yellow corn in his left arm; he stood and listened to Morgan. The lad was an eager advocate, and Guinevra saw Alban make a sign with his sickle and look up towards the woods.

Morgan waved to her. She went slowly down to the stream, and crossing the footbridge, saw that Alban was coming to meet her. Morgan had taken the sickle to save wastage of good weather; he and the birds were of one mind in the matter, save that Morgan called them feathered thieves. Guinevra stood by the wooden cross, waiting for Alban to come to her, and when she had looked into the old man's eyes, she fell on her knees.

"I have shed blood, father."

Alban had put on his tunic, and his brown arms and throat made the linen look as white as the breast of a gull.

"Morgan has told me, child."

His voice was as gentle as his eyes. He gazed steadily at the girl, and he who loved all beautiful things was wise as to the soul of Guinevra.

"He would have shamed me, father.—My shame is— if it is shame—that there was guile in my eyes, and hatred in my heart. He would have taken—that—which—I kept sacred, because——"

Alban nodded.

"I know this—Balthasar. I have heard how he left a man to die."

"He lied to me, father. He told me Geraint was dead."

Alban watched her face.

"And you love Geraint."

Her eyes met his.

"I have cause to love him, father, and cause to know— that my love cannot be spoken of. Yes—I love him, and my love is glad that he lives—though he and I may never come together."

Again, Alban nodded.

"He has a wife, child."

"I am of your faith, father, and though I have blood on my hands, there is no treachery in my heart."

Alban took her by the chin; looked steadfastly into her eyes, and spoke.

"It is a sacrament, my daughter. When a man has sworn faith to a woman—that faith must hold. Break faith and all life is tarnished and false and ugly. If you love this man—and love cannot be gainsaid—it should be a secret and hidden thing. Such is my judgment."

She looked up at him.

"My love is great enough for that."

"Swear it—on that cross, my daughter."

"I swear it."

He took his hand from her chin.

"Then—you shall remain here.—This place shall be a sanctuary until such a time as we can send you safely else-where. Stand up, my daughter."

But she moved forward on her knees, took his hand and kissed it.

"There is—weeping in mercy, father. Trust me—and I will keep my pledge. All—shall be hidden."

He raised her and kissed her forehead.

"Even evil blood must be prayed for. I do not judge —but—blood—is—blood, my daughter. To-night—you shall wash in the stream, and in the darkness—your heart. —We will build you a little booth of branches by the wood, and if enemies should come here—you shall sit and hold to that cross.—But this is a secret place, my dear, and few men know of it, and the lad shall watch."

She rose, and her eyes had lost their fear.

"I shall not forget, father. Maybe—that I shall find peace here."

The day was still young, and when Alban had given her food and drink he took a billhook and went to cut green branches for a booth. Morgan was busy with the sickle, and Alban called to him, but he had other orders for Guin-evra. "You will find some dry fern in that shed. Lie down and sleep, my dear. You look like a ghost." Alban cut a score of hazel poles in a thicket, and he and Morgan set them in the earth on the edge of the wood, and Alban showed the lad how to interlace them and fasten them as a woodman fastens a band round a faggot. They covered the framework with green boughs, and strewed fern on the floor.

"That will serve," said Alban, "as long as the fine weather holds. I will get back to my corn. But lie you down and sleep, boy, till the sun is past noon.—I have other work for you."

Morgan looked pert at being called boy.

"My legs are good for thirty miles, father."

"Well—cherish them, my dear.—I want news of what they are doing in the White Valley.—If the hunt is out for the girl, we must have warning of it."

"Leave that to me," said Morgan; "I wasn't born yesterday."

But he lay down to sleep in the shade, and Alban went back to his corn.

Guinevra was still sleeping when Morgan took to the woods. He trotted as far as the road to Calleva, and there he grew cautious, keeping in the shade and slipping from tree to tree. Two furlongs from the high road he came to a woodland ride, and poking his head round a thorn bush he saw two men in the ride. One of them was kneeling and tying the latchet of his shoe. They were two of Fidelis's fellows who had been scouring the woods.

Morgan leaped out into the ride and hailed them.

"Am I right for Vindomis, brothers?"

The men stared at him.

"Who are you?"

"A cattle drover from beyond the river. I tried a short cut and got lost."

The man who had been tying his shoelace, stood up and came over to Morgan.

"Seen a girl anywhere on the ways?"

"What sort of girl?"

"A handsome wench with a cropped head—about your height?"

"I did see a wench sitting in the grass not far from the high road. What do you want with her?"

The man spat.

"She's a whore, and she's wanted for sticking a priest."

Morgan looked shocked.

"Murder!—Ye gods——!"

"Well, as near as could be," said the man—"but the fellow's not dead. He's bled white—but he's alive.—How long is it since you saw the girl?"

"Why, it might be an hour, brother.—It was on the other side of the high road.—Which way do I turn for Vindomis."

The man pointed down the ride, and called to his mate.

"Come on, Jack.—We had better see if we can get a glimpse of the wench the boy saw."

And without troubling further about Morgan and his affairs they broke into the woods in the direction of the high road. Morgan grimaced after them.—"Boy indeed— you bullocks! Go and look for a clothes-peg in a hayfield.— And Satan go with you!"

Morgan ran, but away from the Calleva high road and the two men. This was news—indeed! No doubt a rogue like Balthasar was a black cat with nine lives, and Guinevra had bungled the business as a girl might be expected to bungle it. Morgan, feeling impudent, held on for the White Valley, and lying under an old thorn tree, saw a sight that was worth seeing—Balthasar being carried on a litter from the water's edge to the great house. Four of the grey women held the poles of the litter; Fidelis walked on one side of it, Urbanus the physician on the other. Morgan saw the litter come to a pause half-way up the hill, and Urbanus bending over the bishop as though to satisfy himself that Balthasar did not bleed. Morgan whistled softly to himself. So, the men had told him the truth. Balthasar was alive.

Guinevra slept till sundown. Looking out from her shelter she saw Alban on his knees by the wooden cross with a queer company of birds and beasts about him. A hind was licking the old man's feet as he knelt.   The little corn-field and its stooks were in the shadow.   Alban might love the beasts of the field, but they caused him much labour, in that his corn and his garden crops had to be stoutly fenced against them.   Guinevra stood watching.   And then she remembered that Alban had told her to wash in the stream, and with the coming of the twilight she went down to the water and finding a place where the stream had hollowed out a tiny pool she put off her clothes.   A shelf of sward served for their bestowal.   The stream had a gravel bottom here, and the water was some two feet deep, and she stood and took water into her hands and splashed it over her body.

She was washing her head when she heard a whistle, and Morgan came running out from the dark woods.

"Guinevra—Guinevra."

She went down on her knees, and let the water cover her bosom, and Morgan, as much surprised as she was, saw nothing but a head, a throat and a pair of white shoulders.   He looked, and laughed, and suddenly became sober and self-conscious.

"News—lady—Balthasar is not dead."

He turned left to the foot-bridge, and crossed it with the air of a man who knew how to behave with discretion when a woman had naught but the water and the dusk for her clothes.   A planet twinkled at him, and he went up in the twilight to where Alban still prayed by the cross.

Guinevra, arms crossed over her breasts, knelt in the water, and looked at the sky.

Balthasar lived!   The news was both merciful and perilous.

CHAPTER XXII

The Heart of Guinevra

¶ GERAINT was caught by the night on the hills north of Vindomis. It was shepherds' country and very solitary, rolling grasslands, with beech woods in the valleys, and Geraint, having watered the white horse at a stream, held on for the high ground. A clump of old thorns on a hill offered him some shelter, and he tethered his horse where he could crop grass, and spreading his cloak in the shelter of the thorns, he made a meal. The great hill seemed pushed up among the stars, and below him the earth was like a tumbled sea pocketed with shadows. The forest country lay close on the north, and by riding soon after dawn he knew that he would reach the hermitage before the sun was in strength.

Geraint slept, wrapped in his cloak, with his sword beside him, and his shield under his head. He had grown hard and strong, and as a bed the earth did not irk him. He was awake with the first grey of the dawn, and having eaten the last of his bread and drunk from his flask, he harnessed his horse and led the beast down in the valley to find him water.

The day was still young when Geraint, riding through the forest country, struck the stream flowing through Alban's glade. The morning was windless, the fern unruffled. In the distance Geraint heard a hart "belling," a bellowing which was early for the time of year, but even the beasts may be forward in love, and the stag may have had his Balthasar. Geraint was impatient for news. He promised himself that he would find Morgan at the hermitage, but he was to find much more than Morgan.

He came out of the woods with the sun behind him, and saw the glade spread below him. Old Alban was in the corn-field turning the sheaves to the sun; Morgan splashing in the stream at the place where Guinevra has washed herself in the dusk. The lad saw Geraint and the white horse, and with a shout, scrambled out of the water and ran naked to meet him.

"Lord—lord."

He kissed Geraint's foot, and his eyes grew knowing.

"There is Alban, and here am I, and the birds and the beasts. But yesterday we found a strange beast, lord."

Geraint smiled down at him.

"Had it two legs or four?"

"Two—and two other members, lord. A white doe with a gold crown on her head."

Geraint reached out and caught Morgan by the hair, and the man's eyes sobered the boy's.

"Who?"

"Guinevra, lord."

Geraint let Morgan go, and sat straight on his horse.

"Is she here?"

"In that little green booth, lord, under the woods."

"Whence did she come?"

"From the White Valley, lord. Balthasar had made the place a home for saints.—But she would tell you the story herself, I reckon."

Geraint swung off his horse and threw the bridle to Morgan, but as the lad caught it he looked solemn.

"She thought you were dead, lord.—She has had many things to bear from those good women—and——"

"Balthasar?"

Morgan nodded, and Geraint, with the look of a man in whom love was both deep and fierce, went by way of the wood's edge to where the green booth lay at the feet of the morning.

Guinevra was seated on her bed of fern, mending a rent in her gown with a thread and needle that Alban had

found for her, when she heard in the valley the voices of
Morgan and Geraint. Her eyes grew wide. Almost,
there was fear in them. She sat very still, with the morning
sun shining in and touching her bare feet. She had not
seen the face of Geraint since the day when Balthasar had
made her his prisoner and left Geraint to die, but she
knew his voice instantly.

She bent down and put on her shoes, and with her
hands in her lap, sat pale and listening. Dear God, how
her heart beat. The pupils of her eyes swam black and
big. She could hear his footsteps on the edge of the wood;
and the promise she had made to Alban lay like a cold
stone in her bosom.

"Guinevra."

She drew her breath deeply.

"Yes, lord."

Geraint did not come to the doorway of the green booth,
but stood to one side of it as though the shelter of boughs
was her secret chamber, and the mood of the morning
hers. And, for the moment, the woman in her knew
great fear. How would his eyes look at her?—For, so
many weeks had passed, and she had tragic things to tell
him. She would hide nothing. Her love was too dear
for lies.

"Stand there, while I speak to you, lord."

He answered her—"Am I not—Geraint—to you,
Guinevra?"

"Yes, lord, but I have blood on my hands."

Very simply she told him her story. She did not say
that she had suffered and been treated as a wanton and been
put to pick the threads of penitence. "They told me that
you were dead, lord." Of Balthasar she spoke sparingly
but with a simplicity that was stark in its innocence. "He
desired me, lord, but not as a woman such as I—would be
desired.—I know now that all that he planned in the
valley was deceit and treachery. He would have had me
in the very room where you had lain near to death. I let

him come to me in the night—because it was in my heart to take my revenge, and in the doorway—I struck him—as he entered.—I struck twice, lord, and fled. They say that Balthasar lives—but there is blood on my hands."

Geraint's eyes were deep. He could not see her sitting there, but his love saw more than his eyes.

"Guinevra."

"Lord?"

"The shame is with Balthasar. Leave that to me."

His voice made her tremble.

"Let there be no more blood spilt, lord. I shall have the stain of it—in my thoughts."

She saw his shadow on the grass. He came and knelt on one knee in the booth's doorway at the foot of her bed.

"Guinevra."

She looked and was afraid, for the face of Geraint was the face of a lover, proud and shining and unashamed. Her hands lay in her lap, and she sat and stared at her hands.

"Be merciful to me, lord."

He did not understand the whole cry of her heart, or that there may be deeps in a woman that are beyond the knowledge of man. He was her lover now, and there was to be no barrier between them, but as yet he was not minded to tell her of that other woman who lay dead in that valley beyond Corinium.

"Guinevra, why speak of mercy?"

"I need it, lord."

"My dear."

He took one of her hands, and bending it, kissed it and she saw a little blurred reflection of herself in the shining metal of his helmet.

"Mercy from me?—Shall I not see to it that not one hair of your head is harmed. Life shall be good for us, Guinevra."

She let her hand rest for a moment on his shoulder.— "Yes, lord." And then, she shut her eyes, because he was so near to her and her courage felt like fainting.

"Be patient with me, dear lord.—If I am weak, it is because—I was so dead—till yesterday."

And suddenly, she hid her face in her hands and sat very still. Her voice was hushed.

"There is no shame, lord, nor shall there be shame. There has been naught but beautiful and good things between you and me. I would ask but one favour. Let me be alone for a little while."

He looked at her dearly.

"Love is a secret and a sacred thing, Guinevra.—I do not come as Balthasar came. Even in man there may be a kind of trembling."

She put out a hand.

"Kiss my fingers again, Geraint, and I shall feel them clean."

Gently and devoutly he kissed her hands, and putting them back in her lap, he rose to his feet.

"You shall be alone, my dear. Shut the door of your dear self, but let it not be closed against me to-night.— And now—I have things to do.—I shall take Morgan with me."

She looked frightened.

"Where do you go—Geraint?"

"For news, and to look at what is mine."

"Lord, there is danger."

"Am I to fear anything on a day such as this?"

He smiled down at her.

"To-morrow—or the next day—I shall have men at my back. I can take what is mine."

She sat very still—inwardly stricken.

"Yes, lord, and God keep you."

He looked long at her, and in his heart he believed that he was wise as to her nature. She was deep; she was chaste. She had suffered, and shrank a little from the thing men call love; she would sit and think and not be hurried. She was not to be won at the first asking.— Such was Guinevra, and he loved her the more for it,

woman making a mystery of that which should be deep
and mysterious. Was he a wild, raw lad? Did he not
understand her and say in his heart—"My dear, I—too
—am deep.—I will come to you gently."

He spoke her name—"Guinevra," and turned away,
and going down to the cornfield, he held old Alban by
the shoulders and said his say.

"I owe you for many things, father—and not the
least of them is this—mercy and kindness—to her. I
have work to do. I am taking the lad with me."

Alban looked at him strangely.

"You come back to us, lord?"

And Geraint laughed.

"Am I to die?—To-night, old friend—I shall have
things to tell you of."

2

So, Geraint and Morgan rode for Turris Alba, and
Guinevra sat on her bed under the green branches, and
watched Alban at work in his corn-field.

She had given Alban her promise, and this promise
was in accord with her mood of the moment. Balthasar's
lust had persuaded her that her love would never be of
that raw redness. She was both wild and chaste. She
might make a mystery of giving that which was hers to
give, but to woman—if she is wise—love is a mystery.
No man for long desires a wanton when once he has had
her, but in Guinevra there were other prides and subtleties, and she would make a sacrament of surrender. So,
in the stillness of her sincerity she sat looking down into
that quiet valley, knowing that there would be anguish
in the thing she would do, but that it would be a beautiful
anguish. She would never blame herself because of it,
never feel shame.

She said to herself—"I am his—and I am not his.

There is that other woman between us. A man cannot swear two oaths and serve both."

She knew that she would have forgiven him had the thing happened, but herself—no. Also, she knew that she did not ask of life that she should have to forgive anything. She wanted the mystic fruit to have no blemish, no hidden wound at the core.

Presently, she rose and going out into the sunlight she went down to the wheat-field where Alban was busy with his sickle. Her feet made a dry crackling over the stubble. She was very pale but very sure.

"I would speak to you, father."

Alban straightened his back, turned and looked at her. She smiled at him, but her mouth was poignant.

"I shall keep faith, father."

Alban nodded, and taking the whetstone from his belt, he sharpened the sickle.

"If faith has no edge, my dear, labour is lost. This is a bitter business—I am thinking, but sin that is sweet may turn sour in the mouth."

She said—"There might come a day when he would hate me. I should be a secret clog upon him. Nor, if faith were broken could I give as a woman should. That is how I feel, father."

He answered her—"Child, you are wise."

She went back to her shelter of leaves, and Alban bent again to his work. He swung his sickle like a sword. Dear God, but it was not easy to throw hard words in the face of love. But he would speak to Geraint. So, he laboured at his reaping in the heat until the sun was at noon, and then he thrust the sickle into his belt, wiped the sweat from his forehead, and thought of meat and drink. The girl should eat with him in the shade.

Alban went up the hill and called her.

"Daughter, let us eat."

No answer came to him, and going to the green booth he found it empty. Guinevra had slipped away into the woods more than an hour ago, and Alban looked blank. He called her again—"Guinevra—Guinevra. Have I spoken too hardly, my daughter?"

No voice answered him, but a dove flew down from a tree, and settled on his shoulder.

3

Geraint saw less of the White Valley than he wished to see, for when he and Morgan, holding to the woods and bearing well to the south, came to a wooded hill from which they could overlook the valley, it was as populous as though the whole countryside was keeping a festival. Calleva had heard the news and Calleva had come in its hundreds to kiss the hands of its stricken saint. Not that Balthasar's hands could be kissed. He lay like wax in the guest chamber with the curtains drawn, and his breathing less than the rustling of a leaf. The whole house moved on careful feet. Urbanus, sleek and wise as a tom-cat, had ordered wine and water, the white of fresh eggs, and silence.

"He has bled inwardly, dame. I fear lest he should bleed again. Nothing must vex him."

When the Calleva pilgrims became a crowd outside the gates of the garden court, Fidelis went out and spoke to them. Their saint was invisible; they must trust to the mercy of God.—She would send Urbanus to give them the latest news. Meanwhile, let there be silence for the sake of this holy man who had been stricken by an evil hand when the world had most need of him. But gossip had got abroad, and the crowd—like all crowds —became restless and ugly; it wanted to express itself, to take its revenge, to howl and to hunt. The wench who had done the deed had not been captured.

The crowd was debating what should be done with the murderess, when Hylas arrived in the valley. Someone had breathed in his ear, and Hylas was hysterical. He ran up and down in front of the crowd, waving his little wooden cross, and howling.

"Death to the harlot.—Let her be smelt out.—Blood, blood, the blood of saints and martyrs.—I am the hound of God.—I will smell out the bitch.—Adulteress, murderess. —Let us find her."

That was what Geraint and Morgan saw, the hairy saint running up and down before the crowd, and leaping like a goat. They could hear him howling, if they could not catch the substance of his ravings. Morgan lay on his belly and laughed.

"Behold a mad dog, lord."

Geraint remembered Hylas, but he did not divine the sacred significance of Hylas. He was concerned with the crowd outside the gates of his house. Was Balthasar dead, and had Calleva come to mourn him? There was nothing to be done in the valley with all those dogs on the prowl, but to-morrow or the next day he would have a scourge for their backs. Meanwhile, he and the lad lay low and watched the valley. They saw Hylas with a little crowd trailing at his heels go up the green slope towards the northern woods.

Morgan rose on his elbows.

"The mad dog is leading the chase, lord.—Should he know of Alban's hermitage——"

That was enough for Geraint.

"Come, lad."

They had left the white horse in the thick wood, and with Morgan holding to the bridle they went north-west, moving fast until they were across the Calleva high road. They saw or heard nothing of Hylas and his crew, and a little before sundown they glimpsed the open sky over Alban's glade.

Alban was sitting by his cross, solemnly pulling one of his white mustachios. He did not rise, for he had bad news for Geraint and was troubled about it, and in a mood

R

to scourge his own self-righteousness.   But the lad was
superfluous.   Alban made a sign to Geraint, and Geraint,
leaving the horse with Morgan to be unharnessed, groomed
and watered, went forward towards the old man and his
cross.

Alban was looking fierce.   His eyebrows bristled.
He wanted to be rid of the news, and he blurted it out.

"The girl has gone, lord."

Geraint looked at Alban as though he did not understand him.

"Gone——?"

"Yes, my son.—And in some measure the fault was
mine.—I know what I know.—I laid a promise upon
her—and perhaps I was too hard with the child."

Geraint was in no mood for words.

"Be quick—man, tell me.—Whither has she gone?"

Alban looked rueful.

"Into the woods.—She was here—and she was not
here.   I went up to call her for dinner, and the booth
was empty."

"But, man, they are hunting her.   The Calleva rabble
is out.   Why did she go?"

Alban crossed hmself.

"My son—there is a wayward wisdom in women.
Listen.   Is there not love between you two, and might
not a woman fear such love, for your sake and her own?
The girl is no wanton.   There is a love that is not the
love of the beasts."

But Geraint's face was fierce.

"Ye gods—we are both of us fools—old man.   And
did she believe——?   My wife is dead, father.—She was
slain by the Cymri, poor soul.—I would have told her
to-night."

Alban got to his feet.

"Man—why did you not tell me this morning?—She
has taken her wound with her.   She——"

But Geraint had finished with words.

"If those dogs run her down.—Which way did she go? Man—can you tell me nothing?"

Alban looked at him with helpless eyes.

"How should I know?—She just slipped away——"

"She may be hiding. Take those woods, Alban.—I'll try the woods on the west.—Use your voice."

Morgan, rubbing down the white horse outside one of the thatched huts, heard the voice of Geraint and Alban sounding in the woods.

"Guinevra—Guinevra—all is well.—Guinevra."

Morgan stood listening with eyes aslant. Had the girl run away? And what—in the name of heaven—was her reason of it? Surely, there was no coping with women!

Geraint came back to the valley in the twilight, and the night was in his eyes. Alban was on his knees by the cross, but to Geraint in his passion—such a symbol seemed mere foolishness. Morgan sat on his heels by the cottage, watching and waiting for his lord.

Geraint called the lad.

"Go and sleep, for to-morrow you shall run as you have never run before."

He held Morgan by the shoulder.

"You know the way to the Black Valley?"

"Yes, lord."

"Ten miles west of the Black Valley is a place called the Wizard's Wood. Caradoc and Gawaine wait for me. You must find them, Morgan, and bring them here, and every man they can muster."

Morgan looked into his lord's eyes.

"I will find them."

"Go at daybreak, and run like the wind."

"Perhaps I can steal a horse, lord."

"Steal heaven, Morgan, if you will. Gawaine will give you a horse. Now, go and sleep."

"I sleep heavily, lord. Who will make sure——?"

"I will wake you."

There was still a little light in the valley when Geraint went up to the shelter of green boughs, and stood looking in. There, Guinevra had slept, Guinevra who had fled because love was too great a thing to be spread like honey upon bread. And Geraint's love was both fierce and tender in him. He went in, and kneeling down, he put his face to the fern where Guinevra's head had rested.

The stars had been out a long while, and Alban, who could neither pray nor sleep, heard footsteps going up and down on the grass outside his cottage. Alban arose and went out into the starlight, and his voice was gentle.

"Lie down and sleep, my son.—I will watch. The lad shall not miss the dawn."

Geraint was silent in the darkness, standing there like a ghost, and his heart was bitter because of the darkness.

"Does she sleep, think you, father?—I tell you I shall not sleep till I have found her."

Said Alban—"Does it help for a torch to burn itself out? Go in and sleep, man, and save your strength. She may need it—more than your burning."

CHAPTER XXIII

Guinevra Rides on an Ass

¶ GERAINT might hold his sword at the throat of the morning and charge it to deliver its secret, but the sun came up in splendour, and the great trees hid what they knew. Already, Morgan had the dew on his feet, and was running with the rising sun behind him in search of Caradoc and Gawaine. Geraint had been ready for the road before daybreak, and when the alleys of the woods grew grey, he left Alban standing by his cross, and rode out in search of Guinevra.

Geraint had nothing to guide him save conjecture. He could ask himself a very simple question and try to answer it.—"Of whom did she think, and whither did her feet carry her?" and he was moved to think of Cornelia. Had the girl remembered Cornelia and taken the road to the west and Corinium? He could try the road, and hope to pick up news of her upon the highway or at the posting-stations. But there were two roads to Corinium, the north road which would lie beyond her knowledge, and a country track which left the Vindomis-Sarum road some ten miles beyond Vindomis, and turned north-west over the hills to join the northern highway.

Geraint struck the road about two miles east of Vindomis. The day was still young, but travellers were few that tragic summer, and even the posts ran seldom. Geraint met an old farmer driving two cows, but the farmer had nothing to tell him, and was shy of a man in harness. The roads were not safe, and the woods becoming the haunt of sturdy robbers. Nearer Vindomis

Geraint fell in with a travelling priest riding on a grey ass, but the priest was no more helpful than the farmer.

He held on to Vindomis. The village had a sad and dusty look, with hens scratching on dunghills, and a few old women sitting spinning at their doors. The men had gone to the fields. Geraint rode into the market-place, and at the fountain he saw a woman drawing water. He remembered her face. She was the woman who had spoken to him on the day when Victorinus and his men had marched for the north.

Geraint hailed her.

"Peradventure you can help me, dame."

The woman stood holding her water-pot. She looked tired and sad.

"What would—my lord—of me?"

"I seek someone.—Have you seen a girl pass through this place, a tall girl with her hair cut short?"

The woman's eyes quickened.

"A girl in grey?"

"Yes, dame."

"There were strange happenings here last night, lord, just before sundown.—I had come out to draw water, and I found a girl sitting here on the seat by the fountain. —She looked as though she had walked far and had not much heart for the journey. I spoke to her, lord. She asked me for a drink from my water-pot, and how the road ran to Corinium. 'Corinium' said I—'that is a long trudge. You had better lodge here for the night." She looked at me strangely, and was giving me back my water-pot when a crowd came running like mad dogs into the village."

Geraint's face grew grim.

"What happened?"

"There was a hairy man with a cross—one—named Hylas. They came from Calleva.—The girl had no chance, lord. She just stood there and stared, and the men took her."

Geraint's horse was pawing the ground.

"God——! —and then?"

"They were very rough with the poor wench.—They shouted that she was a wanton and a murderess.—I thought they would tear the clothes from her.—I saw her face, lord, and it——"

But Geraint was turning his horse.

"They took her with them?"

"They stole an ass from a stable, and tied her to the beast's back, and went up the hill, lord."

"On the road to Calleva?"

"Yes, lord, to Calleva."

Geraint waited for no more news. He turned and rode out of Vindomis and steadying his white horse up the hill, he pulled aside on to the grass and put the beast at a gallop. The whole night lay between him and Hylas and his crowd, but there was a chance that he might come up with them before they reached Calleva. Geraint repassed the priest riding on his ass, and the farmer driving his two cows. In truth, when the farmer heard the galloping horse he drove his cows off the road towards a thicket, but Geraint went by without looking at him.

"Lord," said the farmer, "there goes Death on a White Horse."

For Geraint's face was the face of a man who would kill. Fool, not to have told her; fool not to have understood a love that was both wild and chaste! He had let her be thrown to the mob, mauled by dirty hands, and howled at by dirty mouths. What would they do with her? There were things of which he dared not think.— The woman had said—"I saw her face——" And Geraint rode, seeing the face of Guinevra and the faces of that cruel crowd, cursing himself and his blindness. God, if only he had Caradoc and his men! The white horse sweated, and his master did not spare him.

2

In the night Hylas and his crowd with the girl in their midst found their way back to the White Valley. The noise of their coming brought Fidelis and the women to the gate. Hylas and two of his fellows carried lighted torches, and the glare lit up the gateway.

The gate was closed and barred, and Hylas howled outside it like a dog.

"Open the gate, good women. We have the harlot here."

Fidelis reproved him.

"His holiness is asleep, and sleep is precious.—Be silent."

But Hylas kept up his howling.

"Here is the adulteress—the woman of blood—tied to the back of an ass.—God guided our steps.—Open the gate, women. Let our father Balthasar say what is to be done with the strumpet."

The crowd was as mad as Hylas, and talking of hangings and burnings; and Fidelis, realizing that Hylas was a dog who would go on howling until the gate was opened to him, she had it unbarred. Also, she was more than ready to share in the show, to look sin in the eyes and shame it. Beauty bound on the back of a beast!—But she stood in the gateway with her women about her, for she was not going to have this mob trampling her garden.

"Show me the shameful one, brother Hylas. Stand back, you men. And remember—our saint sleeps."

One of the fellows led the ass forward. Hylas held up his torch, and Fidelis saw the face of Guinevra. Her right cheek lay against the donkey's neck. They had lashed her face downwards on the beast's back; she was half naked, and bleeding, for the crowd had used its sticks.

The dumb beast stood still, and the eyes of Guinevra were dumb and blind.

Fidelis stared at her.

"So—murderess, wanton—your sin has found you out."

Guinevra said never a word; she was beyond words. She looked at Fidelis, and her lips trembled.

"Anathema—anathema.—There is blood on your hands."

Pia, who stood beside Fidelis, let out a little whimper, and the eyes of Guinevra looked at Pia.

"A little water.—I thirst."

Pia turned to go, but the hand of Fidelis plucked her back.

"Did not our Lord suffer, and shall not sin suffer?"

The crowd growled approval.

"Stuff the torch in her mouth—Brother Hylas."

But Pia found the courage of compassion. She went close, put an arm over Guinevra's neck, and shielded her face with her bosom.

"Is she not—a woman?"

Fidelis glared. Yes, there was too much of the woman showing. She spoke to Caritas.

"Get an old sheet—cover—the nakedness.—It is not seemly—even in sin."

Fidelis was the mistress of the moment.

"Stand there, all of you.—I will go and see if our saint sleeps. He is the one to judge what shall be done with the wench."

She strode, and there was some whispering among the women. It was Volumna who waddled to the fountain in the court, soaked a fold of her skirt, and joining Pia held the wet cloth to Guinevra's lips. She squeezed the water into Guinevra's mouth, while Pia shielded them both.

"She shall drink."

"Aye, so she shall," said Volumna; "keep off, you louts. I've got a clout in my hand. Keep off."

Guinevra's lips sucked up the moisture, and suddenly she kissed one of Volumna's coarse hands.

"Thanks, sister."

And Volumna kissed her face.

Two small lamps were burning in the guest-chamber, and when Fidelis opened the door she saw that Balthasar was awake. He lay like a dead man, but his eyes were alive. They shone upon Fidelis like two circles of dark glass.

"They have caught the girl, father. Hylas has her at the gate. They put her on an ass and brought her here."

Balthasar's eyelids flickered. He seemed to be speaking with his eyes. Fidelis drew nearer.

"What shall be done with her, father?"

Balthasar closed his eyes. His face looked like a wax mask, but behind it his thoughts were working. There was a little blaze of life beneath the wax. Balthasar was subtle. He could think of his world and to-morrow.

His lips moved, and Fidelis bent down. His voice made a sound like the shaking of an aspen leaf.

"Let her be taken to Calleva.—Let—nothing be done to her. Let her be—kept—safe—until I shall come to Calleva."

He opened his eyes and looked steadily at Fidelis.

"I will—choose—matrona."

He closed his eyes, and seemed to smile a little bitter smile, and Fidelis slipped away and returned to Hylas and his crowd.

"Our saint has spoken. She is to go to Calleva, and to be put in prison there until such a time—as God and our saint shall choose to judge her.—Guard her well, Hylas. Let no one snatch this apple of sin from you."

3

Hylas and his people had set out for Calleva, but the chase was over, and they had been on their feet all day, and about three miles from Turris Alba they had turned aside to sleep in the woods. They had not troubled to part Guinevra and the ass, and the beast had laid down and made the best of its burden, with Hylas squatting beside them. Hylas would not be seduced by sleep. He had sat there muttering and scratching himself, and admonishing his prisoner, for the holy madness of Hylas was a busy and thread-picking madness.

"Ha—wretch, the ass is a wiser beast than woman. He eateth clean grass and not the sweets of iniquity. Watch and pray, watch and pray, for to-morrow you shall be with the rats in prison."

Guinevra, so weary that even her aching body was ready to forget itself in sleep, had asked Hylas a question.

"Why are you so bitter against me?"

Hylas had snarled at her.

"You stink—woman; you are an abomination. You stink like a dead dog in the gutter. Out upon you—harlot."

She had sighed; he was a dreadful person.

"Even dead dogs sleep."

"Ha—you would be dead!—But when you are dead you will be in Hell—and demons will burn your body with hot irons.—Out upon you, harlot."

He had sat muttering, and in an excess of weariness and despair she had fallen asleep, but it had not seemed fit to Hylas that sin should sleep, and he had prodded her with his wooden cross.

"Watch and pray—murderess, for your time is short."

And suddenly she had blazed at him.

"Let me sleep, you dog. If this poor ass has a god—I would rather serve his than yours."

After that he had let her alone, as though she had planted some metaphysical flea in his hairy soul for the rest of the night, and he was busy hunting the insect. She had slept for two hours or more, and then her trussed and cramped body had ached itself back to life.—The night had grown pale, and in the dimness of the dawn Hylas had leaped hither and thither striking the sleepers with his piece of wood. "Up—brothers, we must carry the apples of sin to Calleva." He had prodded the ass on to its feet, and by way of a holy and brotherly greeting had spat in Guinevra's face.

So, Geraint, riding like death on a white horse along the road to Calleva, was on the heels of Hylas and his crew, but what Geraint proposed to do was quite another matter. Even one wild lover with a sword cannot prevail against two score fellows of the baser sort, and Geraint was spared this foolishness. He was no hysterical boy to cry—"I will die with her," for he was a man who could hate and hold his hate until his enemies were ripe for slaying. But, to be brief, Geraint on his sweating horse, came in the sight of the tail of Hylas' procession when its head was within a furlong of the west gate of Calleva. Moreover, people were pouring out of the gate to salute the harlot's progress, and throw filth and foul words at the wench upon the ass.

Geraint could do nothing that morning, and his impotence was like a knot of flame in his belly. He got within a hundred yards of the mob's tail and saw the black mouth of the gate swallowing it. Of Guinevra he gained but one fleeting glimpse. He reined in, and to his silent self he promised that if the power should be his, that city mob should pay for the work of the morning.

But Geraint was seen and recognized. Calleva had thought him dead—but there was the girl's paramour, a very live ghost on a white horse. A part of the mob rushed out to take the man as well as the woman, but Geraint was hoarding his to-morrow, and he turned his horse and

rode off. There were men working in the fields, and hearing the shouts of the crowd, and seeing the man on the
white horse, half a score of fellows ran with rakes and reaping hooks to cut Geraint off. Two of them reached the
road ahead of him, but when Geraint rode at them with
drawn sword, they shirked the business and scuttled out
of his way.

About half a mile from the city and before it sank out
of sight, Geraint turned and looked at Calleva. There was
death in his eyes. He saw the great wall enclosing all
those roofs and gables and the pediments of temples, and
the gold figure on its column. The city wall shut him out.
It held Guinevra and anguish and shame—perhaps more
than that, and the heart of Geraint was fierce.

He and Calleva had a debt to settle.

4

And there was Balthasar, a hostage to fate and to
Guinevra. Geraint rode five miles, and though his heart
was fierce in him, he did not forget to be merciful to his
horse. Victor had been ridden hard and fast, and when
Geraint found water he let the horse drink, and leading
him by the bridle into a valley between high woods
he turned Victor loose to graze, and sat down under a
tree.

Yes—Balthasar! If Balthasar was still alive, he might
be useful as a live man to be taken and held as a hostage.
A herald could be sent to Calleva.—"I hold your bishop.
Let the girl be harmed and your bishop shall hang." It
might be possible to barter a bishop against love. Geraint,
watching Victor pulling grass, saw his plan shaping for
to-morrow. He would have Caradoc and Gawaine and
the young Aquilas with him, and more than a hundred
men. He would sweep down upon the White Valley and
make sure of Balthasar.

But was Balthasar live merchandise? A dead bishop, saint or sinner, was either enthroned in heaven or mere food for worms. Geraint sat with his chin on his fist. He was moved to see with his own eyes the thing which most concerned him, to mark down his man for to-morrow, to be sure. He would take the White Valley on his way to the hermitage, and under the cover of the night discover what he could.

Having rested the horse, he rode on, turning south to strike an old grass track. It brought him to the fort on the hills where Coel had pastured his flock. There was nothing here but the wind and the sky and the wild grasses, and Geraint let Victor loose inside the great vallum, and lay down on the bank. The horse was as wise as a dog, and would not leave him. In fact, Victor lay down close to his master, and stretching out his head, let the sun warm him.

Geraint tarried there on the hill-top until dusk, and when the valleys were growing blue he mounted his horse and rode down through the beech woods into the White Valley. He tethered Victor to a tree, and went down towards the pool. He could see lights in the house on the hill-side, and he waited until most of the lights went out. He could suppose that if any lamps or candles were left burning they would be in the room where a wounded man lay abed, or a vigil was being kept over the body of a dead saint. St. Balthasar! Geraint had a grim humour in him that night.

Light after light was quenched, and about two hours before midnight Geraint went up out of the valley to the house. Two windows were still alive, and Geraint knew the room and how one of those windows could be approached. There was no need for him to enter the garden-court. He made for the vineyard and the orchard, and standing awhile to look and listen, he entered the herb garden by a wattle-gate, and saw one of the windows before him. The lattice was open, a curtain half-drawn, and Geraint knew that grass lay between him and that window.

Bending low he reached the wall, and glided along it until he was under the window. He raised himself very slowly until his eyes were level with the sill. He saw a man with a face like wax lying in a bed.

The man was asleep. Geraint was so sure that he was either dead or sleeping that he straightened his body, and drew the curtain slightly to one side. Was Balthasar breathing?—He stood there watching. He was sure that he could swear to a movement of the bedclothes as Balthasar drew his breath. He glanced into the corners of the room to make sure that no woman was sitting watching in the night, and at that moment Balthasar's eyes opened, and remained fixed on the face at the window.

But when Geraint looked again at Balthasar, Balthasar's eyes were closed.

Geraint drew back along the wall.—Balthasar was here for the taking like a fox in a trap, and Geraint returned to his horse, mounted, and rode for the woods.

For a while there was stillness in the room where Balthasar lay. His eyes remained closed, but he was awake, and listening. On a table beside his bed lay a little bronze bell, and the hand of Balthasar groped for it.

A woman, keeping watch outside his door, heard the sound of the bell, and entered. It was Caritas. Balthasar beckoned to her. His voice was no more than a whisper.

"Bring—Fidelis."

Fidelis, wrapped up in a cloak, was with him quickly. She bent over the bed as though fearing the worst.

Balthasar's lips moved.

"I have seen Geraint."

Fidelis thought that his wits must be wandering, and that their bishop was seeing ghosts.

"Geraint—father?—But he is dead and buried."

Balthasar's head moved on the pillow.

"My enemy lives—Fidelis.—I saw the face of death at

the window.—There is great peril here.—Get your men, Fidelis, and let them prepare a litter.—We will go to Calleva."

Fidelis looked incredulous.

"Perhaps you were dreaming, father."

Balthasar's eyes flashed at her.

"Woman, it is no dream.—Do what I bid you.—There will be no mercy for any of us from Geraint."

CHAPTER XXIV

The Coming of the Sea Wolves

¶ In the night shepherds on the downs twenty miles or so west of Anderida saw a light shining at sea like the eyes of an angry cyclops. The men of the downlands were wise as to the meaning of that light. It came from a brazier on the poop of one of the Saxon shore patrol ships, and it warned those on shore that sea-wolves had slipped past the guard at the Straits, and were in the Channel.

These shepherds lit a warning fire, and in the dawn they saw through an opalescent haze a great ship with her sail set, and her sweeps thrashing the water. She was less than a quarter of a mile from the shore, and drawing nearer. There was very little wind, and the shepherds lay on the turf and watched the ship moving in the gradual glitter of the morning. She was the flag-ship of Count Nectarides, with the Chi-Rho in gold upon the belly of her great sail. She shone. Her sweeps churned the water. She was a thing of colour and of pride in the haze and the glamour of the morning.

But the men of the downs were to see more than this one great ship treading the waters. An old man, leaning on his crook, and watching the sun rise above a headland, saw in the shadow of this headland a sight that brought a shout from his lips.

"Look!" and he pointed with his crook, "the sea-wolves!"

There they were, six long ships, black and low in the water, sleeking out of the shadow of the headland from the estuary where they had passed the night. Each long ship held some three-score men, and their oars were whipping the water. The shepherds on the hills were to watch a sea-fight between that floating castle of a Romano-British ship and the raiders, a lion against six wolves. Those on the ship were keeping a poor look-out, and the long boats were well away and making a race of it before their prey woke to its peril. In the stillness of the morning the shepherds could hear the beat of the oars, and the shouts of the steersmen as they urged on the rowers.

A trumpet sounded on the Roman ship. She seemed to falter and hang in the wind, and her sweeps ceased to churn the water. Men were running about her decks. The captain of the watch had taken one look at the raiders, shouted an order, and hastened to the Count's cabin.

Count Nectarides was a haughty gentleman—even in his night-clothes. Being new to his command he had a reputation to make, and he was more of a soldier than a sea-dog. There had been scandals in the service. His predecessor had allowed the heathen their piracy in order that he might fall upon the rogues when they were full of plunder, and share it with his captains and crews. Nectarides was full of a tradition and of fight. What, run away from six sauceboats full of savages? "Full speed ahead, captain. Ram the rogues, tread them into the water. I shall be on deck in three minutes."

The marines were hurrying into harness, the archers crowding into poop and prow. The great ship surged on. The Saxons had spread out in a half-circle, and were keeping station, for there was method in their attack. They were like light troops attacking a phalanx. Nectarides did not wait to put on his armour. With his squire and his secretary he went up to the gilded turret on the poop, and stood there with the ship's captain.

"We will give these whelps a whipping, my friend."

The captain was from Armorica, and having seen more of sea life than Count Nectarides, he was not so haughty.

'They will try to grapple us and board."

"I shall be surprised if one savage climbs our bulwarks. Captain, we'll sink the lot."

The half-circle began to close its claws, and the six long boats shot in towards the ship. They were beautifully handled. The marines lining the bulwarks sloped their spears. Sailors were ready with pigs of iron. The archers began to shoot. In swept the heathen, and turning their shallow boats like fish in the water, crashed into the banks of oars. The slaves at the oars were knocked off the rowing-benches. Men in the bows of the Saxon boats had grappling hooks on poles. To the shepherds ashore it looked an impossible business for the men in those shallow shells to scale the walls of that floating castle, but scale them they did.—Not instantly. Men could be seen falling back into the boats. Spears and grappling poles clashed. A pig of iron heaved overboard crashed through the bottom of one boat. She was sinking, and her crew scrambled into other boats or swam to them. The attack came from all sides, and from a boat alongside the Roman's quarter a big blond giant—Osric himself—got astride the bulwark, and leaping down with an axe, began to deal out death. Others followed him in twos and threes until there were a score or more raiders on the Roman deck, fierce men who fought like wild beasts.

Nectarides, without harness and with nothing but his sword, leapt down from the poop to rally the marines and throw back that boarding party. The fight was bloody and uncertain, but other parts of the ship had been left but thinly defended by the rush to deal with Osric and his band. The Saxons broke in on the other quarter. It was like the storming of a city, and the wild men began to prevail. The Saxon cutlass was a murderous weapon, especially at such close quarters, and the heathen held the main deck. Nectarides was slain at the foot of the steps leading to the poop. The watchers on the cliffs saw the marines in their gilded harness driven from the main deck. Some of them fled below. Others fought to the last on the upper works, or were driven into the sea. The fighting ceased, and the slaughter began.

The shepherds saw men leaping from the great ship into the sea. There were splashes of foam. The ship lay with her sail flapping, her sweeps like broken legs stuck out at all angles. The steersman had been cut down. Presently, nothing was left alive on the upper deck, and the bloody work went below. Men could be heard screaming. Now and again a figure in harness or in the white clothes of a sailor would escape from some bolt-hole and leap into the sea. Men were trying to swim to the shore, and one or two of the white figures reached it, but the men in harness sank like brass pots.

Once more the upper deck swarmed with live men. The Saxons were carrying up their plunder, hutches and coffers, the ship's pay-chest, arms, gear. The stuff was tumbled or lowered into the boats, and when the ship was stripped of its plunder a column of smoke rose from one of the hatches. The sea-wolves were back in their long boats and casting off. They rowed half a furlong or so and lay to on the calm sea watching the great ship burn.

Flames followed the smoke. There were tufts of fire like red and yellow flowers. The oar-ports glowed. Presently, a tall flame licking upwards, caught the great sail and ran up it as though furling it with fire. The shepherds watched in silence, while the great ship burned with all her dead tumbled upon the decks or between them.

The sea-raiders stood in their boats and shouted, all save those who were bloody with wounds and were busy binding them up. Then they took to their oars, Osric's boat leading. He stood in the stern with Nectarides' blue boat-cloak blowing from his shoulders, for a light breeze had sprung up. The long ships went west along the coast, and the shepherds watched them go, knowing that wild work threatened those ashore.

As for the ship, she was like a red brazier. She burned all day, and when night came she still glowed as she drifted east.   About midnight she sank with a sound like the hissing of a thousand serpents, and where there had been light there was darkness.

2

At Calleva the town gaol was situated in a blind alley at the back of the basilica.   The place was empty save for the gaoler and his wife, for Calleva's saint had ordered the doors of the prison to be opened, and three sturdy rogues who had been laid by the heels for highway robbery, had become soldiers of Christ.   The mob conducted Guinevra to this pleasant lodging, and taking her from the ass, pitched her to the gaoler.

"Here's baggage for you."

And sorry baggage she was, with a back that was bruised and bloody, and a face covered with dust.   The gaoler, having heard what the mob had to say—and like most mobs it had had much to say—locked Guinevra into the prison-room which was used for women.   It had no furniture of any kind, nothing but a water-pot and some dirty straw in one corner.   Its window with a criss-cross of iron bars opened upon the alley, and Calleva could put its faces to this window and observe the creature within.   In fact, the cell was like a cage in which a wild animal was confined, and almost Calleva could stir up the beast with its sticks.

Guinevra took to the straw.   It might be foul and musty, but she was too spent to trouble her head about such de-tails.   For nearly a night and a day she had been lashed to the back of an ass; she had been beaten, clouted, spat upon. Her body was both numb and half paralysed, and a thing of smarts and bruises.   The gaoler had had to carry her into the cell, and when he had set her on her feet, she had collapsed upon the straw.

He brought her some bread and water, but Guinevra

seemed beyond such things.   She lay in the straw and was silent.

"Sulky—are you?"

The gaoler pushed her with his foot.

"Get busy.—Put some of this away.—I don't let prisoners die on me, and from what I hear you will have to die in public."

She moaned at him.

"Let me be.—I would sleep."

But he stood over her until she made a pretence of eating and drinking, and when she had satisfied the tyrant in him, he let her lie in the straw as she pleased.   His dinner was waiting for him, tripe and onions, a savoury smell, and he locked her in and left her to make the best of a bruised and bloody business.   He sat at his table with his beard almost in the dish, and fed himself with a knife and fat fingers, and discussed the case with his fat wife.   The wench's back was like a bruised steak.   Do anything for it? Not he.   She was a young wench and could heal by nature. Besides, her neck might be in a noose before her back could heal, so why waste time and labour?

Guinevra slept in spite of the faces at the window—but not for long.   Calleva had voted her a monkey in a cage, murderess, wanton, and all Calleva came to look at the creature who had stabbed their bishop.   Men, women and children, old and young crowded and stared, and flung in foul words.   They flung in objects that were more solid: rotten eggs, fish heads, oyster-shells, stones.   Guinevra was beaten up like some animal.   To save herself she dragged some of the straw into a corner next the street where garbage and stones could not reach her.   Nor could the mob see her here, for the window was deep, and the grille kept heads from intruding.

She sat and cowered there.   Almost, she was beyond feeling the horror of the thing.   Could the world of men do more to her?

It could.

For Hylas came and camped on some straw outside her window. He was both rhetorician and showman. He kept the crowd back, but he entertained it. He maintained for hours a kind of monotonous howling.

"Woe to the harlot.—Woe to the bloody wanton. The wages of sin are death. Take heed, people, and repent and be warned.—God is not mocked. Anathema.—Woe, I say—to the bloody harlot——"

So howled Hylas like a dog baying the moon.

After sundown the prison was visited by Melchior the Deacon. Balthasar, lying on the edge of death at Turris Alba, had thought darkly of certain matters. A less subtle man might have left Guinevra and her story to the mob, but Balthasar was wise as to the fickleness of mobs. A crowd can be fooled by emotion, and by uttering with unction the words—"Child"—"Mother," or by being shown a woman in tears. Balthasar had called Fidelis to him, and had bade her take her tablets and write a letter for him.

"The girl shall have justice."

He had dictated a letter to Melchior, had it sealed up and sent off by one of Fidelis's men.

"Let the man hasten."

Hence Melchior's visit to the prison. He found Hylas beating his chest and howling outside the barred window, with an idle crowd in attendance. Melchior had no great love for Hylas, for Melchior was sleek and kindly and an upholder of the conventions, a man who washed and was careful about his linen. Hylas might howl in the face of God and his people, but he was something of a blowfly. Melchior was admitted by the gaoler, and having presented his purpose and his authority, was taken into Guinevra's cell. The gaoler carried a lantern.

When Melchior saw the girl in the straw the good soul in him was shocked, and perhaps all the more so because the hairy face of Hylas attracted by the gaoler's light, appeared at the window. Balthasar had charged the deacon to make sure that the poor creature was treated decently and with circumspection. She should be judged and dealt with in due season by the law of the Church.

Hylas mouthed at the window, with the crowd at his back.

"Behold the harlot, Brother Melchior.—Woe, woe to the shameful one——"

Melchior was not pleased. He raised two fingers, and admonished Hylas.

"Judge not—brother, lest you be judged."

This set Hylas raving like a dog on a chain, and Melchior, standing upon his dignity, ignored the hairy one, and spoke to the gaoler.

"Have you no better room than this?—The girl is not a wild beast.—The Bishop's orders are that she shall be treated—like a Christian."

The gaoler had another room, an upper chamber in which prisoners of better quality could be lodged, especially if they were prepared to pay. The room had a stout oak door, and a barred window looking on the gaoler's garden; also it boasted a bed.

Melchior exerted his authority. The girl must be moved to this upper chamber. Was not their Bishop a merciful man, even though this poor sinner's hand had been turned against him? Melchior felt pity for the creature crouching in the straw.

But the gaoler was stubborn.

"I receive money for this upper room, sir."

"Do you trade mercy, man?—I will see to it that you are paid, if you are entitled to the money. Are my lord Balthasar's orders—nothing?"

Melchior bent over Guinevra, and by the light of the lantern he saw her nakedness and her bruised and bloody skin. Yes, the mob had not shown her much mercy. This poor, torn Magdalene was a comely thing, and Melchior had a kind eye for a comely woman.

"They have treated you badly, child.—You shall have justice."

She looked at Melchior and shivered, for Hylas was in full blast.

"I am not what they call me, father."

Melchior put his fingers in his ears.

"That fellow's voice—is—beyond—all reason."

She was so weak and stiff that she had to be helped up the stairs—but when the gaoler put an arm round her she flinched and let out a little moan.—"O, my back.—Don't touch me.—I can manage." A rope stapled to the wall served as a handrail, and step by step she drew herself up, and the light of the lantern showed to Melchior her torn and bloody back. Again Melchior was shocked.

"Your wounds shall be seen to—child."

But there were other wounds that no oil could salve. She lay on her face that night in the upper room, and though her wounds had been dressed, and the voice of Hylas had ceased from assailing her, she felt that death and despair were stronger than life.

3

Noon—on the second day—and no Caradoc!

With a great restlessness consuming Geraint he had taken his horse and ridden out from the hermitage, and old Alban had watched him go.

"Blessed are the meek."

But Alban had shaken his head over the text, for there was no meekness in Geraint. And should there be meekness in a man when mobs are vile and merciless? Should the cruel fool be forgiven? Alban had knelt down to pray, thinking of Geraint as a black north wind blowing flames across a city, and Alban—the soldier—understood the heart of man.

Meanwhile, Geraint rode his horse up and down the high road, for, unless Caradoc and Gawaine had ridden elsewhere, and Morgan failed to find them, they would come by way of Vindomis. He posted himself on a hill, and rode to and fro on the brow of it, and about two hours after the sun had passed its full noon he saw a little cloud of dust in the west between two high green woods. Horsemen, and riding fast. Men on foot would not kick up such a dust-cloud. He watched the white road and saw a company of horse appear upon it, and coming at a fast trot. Three figures rode ahead of the main troop, and one of them wore a red cloak.

Caradoc!

Geraint rode down the hill. Yes, Caradoc and Gawaine, with the lad Morgan between them, and fifty men or more following behind. Geraint's grim face showed the beginnings of a smile. In less than an hour he would be leading those horsemen down into the White Valley.

Caradoc was in great spirits. He came cantering up the road on a black horse with his red cloak blowing behind him. He looked into the eyes of his lord, though Caradoc's sword was to make a master of him before another year was out.

"Hail, lord. The boy lost his way, or we should have been with you three hours ago."

Said Geraint, holding out a hand to the smith—"Never was I more glad of any man's face."

Caradoc laughed.

"My black old mug may bring luck.—There are fifty horse behind it, and a hundred and fifty foot on the march behind us. Men seem to like my face, lord. I rode down into the sea country and got nearly two-score fellows. There is even a Saxon among them, a rover who is seeing life and the world.—What's for to-day, lord?"

Gawaine and Morgan joined them, and Geraint turned his horse and rode forward, for he was sacrificing no more hostages to fate.

"Turris Alba.—Balthasar lies abed there.—I want the bishop, my friends."

"What will you do with the bishop, master?"

"Hang him, Caradoc, unless Calleva gives me what I ask for."

When they came to the woods above the White Valley, Geraint halted his men among the trees, and rode forward with Gawaine and Caradoc to see what the valley could show him. Calleva might have sent some of its people to guard the saint, and the house would have to be stormed and taken. Geraint sat his horse under a beech tree and looked down into the green valley.

There was no sign of life in it, no smoke, no movement. The gates of the garden court stood open. There were no men working in the fields.

Geraint's face grew dark.

"Flown!"

He rode hard down the hill with Caradoc and Gawaine at his heels, and dismounting at the gates, drew his sword, and entered the house. The place was silent as death, but in no disorder. In the sisters' dining-room Fidelis and her women had taken a last meal, and left the cloth and cups and dishes upon the table. Geraint, feeling a stranger in this house that was his, went swiftly to the chamber where Balthasar had lain. It was empty. The bed-clothes had been rolled back and left. Curtains waved at the open windows.

CHAPTER XXV

Balthasar Returns to His City

¶ IN the stillness and sunlight of a September morning Balthasar was carried into the city of Calleva. Fidelis and her women walked behind him, grey as to figures and to faces, and for the last mile Urbanus, Melchior and a great crowd accompanied the litter. The walls were thronged with people, and those on the walls and gate saw a bloodless face on a pillow, and a white hand raised feebly to give a benediction.

The crowd was a silent crowd until Hylas the Hermit came leaping from the gate and with his wooden cross aloft, walked backwards before Balthasar's litter. He howled, he gesticulated.

"Death to the harlot, holy one."

The crowd took up the cry.

"Death to the harlot."

Balthasar raised a hand that was like a taper. All this shouting and mouthing and hairy vigour vexed him. He still had a part to play, and so little blood in his body to play it with. His lips moved, but his voice did not carry.

"Peace, good people, peace."

But there was Hylas jigging up and down in front of him, a dog setting other dogs howling. Balthasar made a little gesture with his hand, a peevish gesture, and the debonair Urbanus who was walking beside the litter, bent over him.

"Get rid of that mad fool."

Urbanus stopped the litter and held up a hand.

"Brother Hylas, good people—listen to a physician. Our saint is very weak—my friends.—I charge you—as his physician—let him pass in peace."

The crowd became silent, and Fidelis and her women, moving forward, made a grey screen about the litter. But Hylas was not easily subdued. He shut his hairy mouth, but continued to walk backwards before the litter, brandishing his bit of wood. Fidelis glared at him, and then a mongrel dog, bolting across the roadway and coming in contact with Hylas's heels, overset the zealot.

The crowd laughed. Even the women tittered, for Hylas had sprawled on his back, and the litter-bearers were obliged to pause.

Balthasar looked at Urbanus.

"Why do they laugh?"

Urbanus stroked his beard.

"Brother Hylas fell over a dog—holiness."

"Good dog," murmured Balthasar.

Meanwhile, Hylas had picked himself up, and with wrathful glances at the crowd, went to sulk and mutter in a doorway. The litter swung on. Balthasar had closed his eyes. He was very weary, a bleached body with a brain that could not rest, for Balthasar might lie on a litter and still be an actor upon a stage. This city was his city, and its people his people, and he knew that at all times it is necessary to control a crowd. Had his saintliness suffered? Was there a crack in the white marble? Had he convinced Fidelis?—But Calleva was so much more momentous than Fidelis.

He opened his eyes and looked at Melchior, a Melchior who was walking sedately beside his bishop. He touched Melchior's sleeve.

"Brother—where are they taking me?"

Melchior was feeling suave and self-important. He bent over Balthasar. The people could see that he was the bishop's ear.

"To your house, father."

Balthasar moved his head on the pillow.

"No, no, Melchior—I would be in the midst of my people. Let them take me to the room of the Priests' College in the Forum."

"What you wish shall be done, father."

"Let a bed be prepared there.—I would lie in the midst of my people."

Melchior took charge, a plump and kindly little man who liked to please the world and to look pleasant in public. He spoke to Fidelis and Urbanus. He led the procession through the gateway into the Forum. He was fussy and important and debonair. The doorway of what had been in pagan times the Collegium Sacerdotum, was sufficiently wide to admit the litter. But Melchior remained outside. He ascended the rostrum and spoke to the crowd.

"Good people, our saint would lie in the midst of those who love him.—Let us make him a bed fit for a bishop. Let us soften our voices, and hasten our hands."

The crowd applauded him. It became a race between the matrons as to who should provide their saint with sheets, mattress, pillows, coverlet. Four stout fellows paraded by the wife of Blatho the butcher appeared in the Forum carrying a wooden bed. Fidelis and Caritas became busy in the priest's chamber. The mattress was of down, the sheets of finest linen, and coverlet of wool dyed purple. Urbanus, Melchior, and the two women lifted Balthasar from the litter to the bed.

He groaned a little.

"Good friends—I would sleep."

Urbanus held the door open as a hint to the women, but Balthasar's hand plucked at Melchior's sleeve.

"Let Melchior remain for a little while.—I have a message for Melchior."

When he and the deacon were alone together Balthasar's fingers made a feeble, beckoning movement. The door was shut. the window curtained, and in the court of the Forum the crowd made a respectful murmuring. Melchior knelt by the bed, and the eyes of Balthasar looked at him darkly.

"What of our poor sinner, Melchior?"

"The woman—Guinevra?"

Balthasar nodded.

"I had her well and safely bestowed, father. She is in the prison awaiting judgment."

Balthasar closed his eyes.

"One must remember the Magdalene, Melchior—and mercy."

Melchior looked much impressed by Balthasar's magnanimity.

"The city is very bitter against her, father."

"Bitter?"

"Because of the love they bear you."

"If there is bitterness, Melchior, it should be mine. And if they love me——"

Melchior moistened his lips.

"They would burn the woman."

Balthasar's face seemed to go grey.

"Burn her?—The crowd can be cruel, Melchior. Is not this a Christian city?"

"They are very bitter against the woman, father."

Balthasar closed his eyes.

"This must be thought upon with prayer and fasting.— Leave me, now, good friend.—I would sleep."

Meanwhile, in the shop of Blatho the butcher three men were debating the same problem, Blatho, Hylas and one—Jude the Deacon. Blatho was red meat, a black bearded and bombastic fellow who bulked large in the councils of Calleva and was the captain of one of its companies. He went about with a sword and his butcher's cleaver stuck in his belt, and was thought much of by the crowd. He had a rolling voice, and could roll his eyes. Jude the Deacon was a bitter little man with a sharp nose and a dry and dusty skin. As for Hylas he brought nothing to the debate save his eternal howl of "Let the harlot die." Jude was the most cunning of the three. He had a habit of sniffing and of rubbing his dry fingers together. For many years Deacon Jude had been jealous of Balthasar, and all the more so because he did not believe in the passionate disinterestedness of Calleva's saint. Jude had had no success with the crowd, and he had watched with shrewd and bitter eyes the ascent and splendour of Balthasar. Balthasar was handsome; Balthasar was velvet; Balthasar was beloved of the women. Jude's little, mean, clever soul had snarled in secret. This fellow Balthasar could fool people. What if there was another side to the story of the saint and the sinner? What if Balthasar was very much man? Jude sat and pulled his fingers so that the joints cracked, and he smiled upon Hylas and Blatho. He despised both of them, but they were his partners in a Judgment of Solomon.

"Let the woman burn."

For, Balthasar would have to choose between his heart and his head. So thought Jude. A demagogue could not please both the crowd and his secret self if he was put on a pedestal and hailed as a saint. Jude smirked and cracked his dry finger-joints.

"The feeling of the city should be made plain to his holiness."

So—that evening, the three of them presented themselves at the doorway of the priest's chamber, and were met by Urbanus. Blatho, who was always the spokesman when three people were gathered together, addressed the physician. They had come to inquire for their bishop, and if the state of his body allowed it, to speak with him.

Urbanus demurred, but Balthasar was awake. He had slept, and felt refreshed.

"Let my friends enter."

They stood before his bed, and Blatho, who knew that Hylas would be before him unless he seized the joint, rolled his round voice at Balthasar.

"Father—we men of the city come to you to make plain the feeling of the city.—It is because of the love we bear you that we are bitter against this woman.—We say that an example should be made of such sin, father. The people cry—'Let the woman die.'"

Hylas, hearing the words taken out of his mouth, opened his lips wide and produced his pet epithet.

"Let the harlot die."

Balthasar lay looking at them with half-closed eyes.

"I have been the sufferer, my friends. My blood has been spilt. Shall I avenge it? What does my brother Jude say?"

Jude smirked at him, and put his fingers together.

"It is because our saint's blood is so precious to us that we would punish the spiller of it. What would this city be without its bishop? Who stands between us—and the wrath and darkness and blood of the bad old world? I hold that sin should be sacrificed for the soul of a people."

Balthasar moistened his lips, and lay still.

"My friends—I am very weak.—Let this judgment rest till I am stronger.—We have other enemies than this poor, deluded woman.—Blatho—I trust in you greatly. Look to the walls, Blatho, look to the gates."

Blatho folded his arms and put out his chest.

"I am a rock—father, a rock."

"Brother Hylas—I would have you watch outside the city. See that no wolves come near it secretly."

Hylas bristled.

"I am God's watch-dog. Let sin beware."

Balthasar looked at the deacon and planted a secret barb.

"Brother Jude—preach mercy. Is not the gentleness of your heart known to all men—and women?"

Jude smiled a little bitter smile.

"Especially—to the women, my lord."

Urbanus, the suave and discreet physician, held the

T

door open for them, and they departed, and Balthasar lay with his eyes closed, but Urbanus saw that his fingers plucked at the quilt.

2

That same night a beacon was lit at Old Gwenta in the Meon Valley, but the message miscarried, for those who should have seen it and passed on the signal were keeping no watch. The Saxons had surprised and sacked Regnum; and Venta, hearing the news, had shut its gates, and sent out appeals for help.

Early in the morning two dusty men on sweating horses rode up to the south gate of Calleva. They shouted to the keepers of the gate that the sea-raiders were ashore, and that Regnum had fallen. They came from Venta to seek help from the head of the League of the Four Cities, even from Calleva, and Calleva was Balthasar.

The guards let them in, and since Blatho was acting as the captain of the city they sent the Venta men to the butcher. Blatho was fresh from the slaughter-house when the messengers were brought to him. His hands were bloody, and so was the morning's news. Blatho looked big and self-important over it. Had not Venta walls?— Were the men of Venta afraid of a few savages? Blatho swaggered.

But the business was too weighty for him to swallow. He washed his hands, put on his captain's coat, and went to speak with Balthasar, gathering a small crowd as he went. He found Hylas in the Forum, and hailed him.

"Come—you man of hair and of holiness, we have the heathen on our hands."

Balthasar's wounds were being washed when Blatho, two or three councillors, the crowd, the messengers from Venta, came to the door of the priest's chamber.

Urbanus met them, a linen bandage in his hands. The moment was not opportune.

Said Blatho—"This business is urgent. Let three of us in."

Urbanus kept them in the ambulatory until he had dressed Balthasar's wounds, and then admitted Blatho, Hylas, an elder and the messengers. Balthasar lay abed, looking all eyes in a face that was still white wax.

Blatho rolled off the news, and Balthasar, having listened to Blatho, questioned the messengers. Of what strength were the sea wolves? They had come from six ships?—Assuredly, then, their numbers could not be very great. Was Venta afraid?—Yes, Venta was very much afraid. They were short of arms, and the walls were in bad repair.

Balthasar lay with his eyes closed.

"Leave Blatho and Hylas with me."

When Blatho and Hylas were alone with him, Balthasar spoke.

"My friends—I think the men of Venta are more afraid than in peril. These savages—if they have plundered Regnum, will have their plunder to ship. They will not venture far into the country. But in such a pass as this—we should help our brethren. What think you, Blatho? You are a brave man."

Blatho swaggered.

"Send me to Venta—bishop—and I'll put some spunk into them."

Balthasar opened his eyes and smiled upon him.

"Blatho—the Bold.—There is comfort in your courage, brother. Take fifty men, and Hylas as your chaplain, and march to the help of Venta."

"Let it be a hundred men, bishop."

"Let it be a hundred men, Blatho. I give you them, and my blessing."

So, Blatho swaggered out to get his company together, and Balthasar lay and reflected that Calleva might

be a more dutiful city without the butcher and the hermit.
For, at the moment, he had not the crude strength to over-
bear such men as Blatho and Hylas, but in a few days
his flesh would have shed its weakness. Urbanus spoke
well of his wounds.

Meanwhile, Blatho's voice was larger than his courage.
He assembled his men, but he sat drinking in a wine-
shop until two hours after noon. His men drank to
keep their courage up, and to humour their captain.
The whole city watched Blatho and Hylas lead their
company out of the Venta Gate. Blatho rode a roan
horse; Hylas leapt and shouted; some of the men were
half-drunk and noisy, and the marching was none too
steady. The red-headed fish-porter whose head Geraint
had broken on that day in May was one of the heroes,
and vociferously so.

"We'll skin the Saxons for you."

The crowd cheered, and Blatho slackened his belt,
for he was rather too full of wind and of wine.

3

Less than three hours after Batho's sallying Calleva
was challenged by another enemy. Geraint and six
horsemen appeared upon the road, and came to the west
gate to parley. Geraint had left his men hidden in a
wood within view of the city, and sufficiently near to
support him should Calleva show temper.

The gate was shut, and Geraint rode close and spoke
to the men on the wall.

"Is Balthasar with you?"

They answered him that he was. They were ready
to make a mock of the man on the white horse. What
did his High and Mightiness ask of Balthasar? His
blessing? Or had Geraint come to be baptized? Geraint
was as silent as death. He sat on his white horse, watching

the gate, and waiting for their insolence to spend itself.

"I have a letter for your bishop, and I will wait for his answer."

At a sign from Geraint one of his men rode forward with a wooden letter-case fastened to the throat of his spear. There was room between the top of the gate and the stones of the arch for such a thing to pass, and the man thrust the point of his spear over the gate, and one of the guards unfastened the letter-case. People were crowding the wall, and they began to shout at Geraint. They felt very secure on the top of the city wall, and it appeared that Geraint had only those six men with him.

"Come in and sup with us, my lord."

"What's he here for, neighbour?"

"To get his harlot out of pawn."

It was a rude crowd. It scoffed, and grimaced and snapped its fingers. It attempted a few cockshies with stones and pieces of broken tile and potsherds until Geraint's horse grew restive. Nothing would have pleased the crowd more thoroughly than to have seen Geraint take a toss. Calleva was as bold and as insolent as a lout who howls from a housetop. Geraint drew off for the sake of his horse, and rode slowly up and down the pomerium, and there Caradoc joined him.

"Calleva is very brave, master. A lot of chattering monkeys."

For Caradoc was not in favour of this parleying business. Words, words, and in such a contest a crowd behind a wall was sure to get the better of you. Caradoc was for a night attack, with twenty men swinging a tree trunk against the gate, but Calleva held no hostage for Caradoc.

"We will try words first, my friend."

For Geraint knew that Calleva might be a hard nut to crack. It had those strong walls, a garrison and a vicious mob. They could surprise and storm the city under cover of the darkness, but the very darkness might be their undoing in the confusion of streets and alleys. Geraint was thinking of Guinevra. She would be like a golden fleece hidden in some secret place, and not to be come at easily in the darkness and the frenzy of the fighting.

But the Calleva crowd was shouting at him. A man had returned with their bishop's answer. The messenger was standing above the gate, holding something in his hand.

"Come up, my lord, and get your letter."

Geraint and Caradoc rode towards the gate. The man up above threw something down at them, Geraint's wooden letter case with the seals unbroken.

"Take your answer—Geraint. Our bishop has no words for you."

The crowd shouted.

"That's the stuff to give the fellow."

"Go and get your head shaved."

Caradoc dismounted and recovered the letter. He looked at the people on the wall, and with deliberation and meaning—spat upon the ground.

"Crow on your dung-heap, you fools."

He remounted, joined Geraint, and they walked their horses across the pomerium followed by the howls of the crowd.

Said Caradoc—"You have tried words, master. Now, let it be blows."

But Geraint was deep. He marched his men out of the wood and went west as though confessing that Calleva was too strong for him, but five miles from the city, where a grass track turned south, he halted his horse and foot and waited for the darkness. The horses were watered and rested, and when the moon rose Geraint resumed his march. He went south towards country where down-land and deep valleys ran east and west. You could ride fast on the hills and see for miles over a rolling landscape, but in the deeps of the wooded valleys an army could lie hidden.   Geraint camped his men in one of these valleys, and when the dawn came he sent out his scouts to the north and to the south.   He posted watchers on the hills.   There was water in the valley for men and horses, but Geraint would suffer no fires to be lit lest the smoke should betray them.

CHAPTER XXVI

Ibylas Ibowls no More

¶ A HAWK hovering high over the downland ten miles north of Venta, could have told in bird language of two queer and monstrous creatures crawling up the opposite sides of a green hill. Moreover, the hawk saw the two creatures arrive simultaneously on the grassy plateau and suddenly stop crawling like two gigantic caterpillars confronting each other on a green leaf.

Blatho the Butcher had lodged his men for the night in the buildings of a farmstead on the road to Venta, and since his fellows had broken into the farmer's cellar and emptied it of home-brewed beer, they had been slow in taking the road on the morrow. Venta would not run away from them, and Blatho's men regarded the adventure as a summer festival. The September day was hot and still and cloudless. Blatho had not troubled to send forward a vanguard. His men, marching in a loose and straggling column, were sure of making Venta before sundown with a valiant thirst to be humoured with more beer. They would swagger into Venta, and show its women what stout fellows were bred in Calleva.

It happened otherwise. Blatho, riding at the head of his men, with Hylas beside him, had reached the green plateau of the hilltop when he saw spears and helmets coming over the southern edge of the hill. The plateau covered less than four acres: a carpet of sweet, short turf between beech woods, the road crossing it like a roll of white linen that had been unfurled. Blatho put up a

304

hand to shade his eyes. So, Venta had sent out a company to meet them. He was preparing to salute the men of Venta when the terrifying truth revealed itself.

Blatho reined in his horse. His jaw dropped. His men, closing up behind him, saw what Blatho saw, and went no farther forward. Dusty faces looked very white, for pouring on to that grassy plateau came Osric and his Saxons.

It is a credit to Blatho that he drew his sword. The Saxons had sent up a shout; their harness and weapons flashed in the sunlight. Blatho, looking behind him, saw the frightened faces of his men. They were huddling like sheep, and already the tail of his company was beginning to slide down the hillside.

Blatho cursed. What could a very scared captain do but curse?

"Steady, you dogs. Close up."

But if Calleva's valour was ready to burst and flow away down the green slope, there was one man in the crowd who could play the mad dog. Hylas had fallen on his knees, his wooden cross held at arm's length.

"*In hoc signo vinces.*"

He was up and leaping towards the wild faces of the heathen, like a brown leaf blown towards them by a gust of wind. He brandished his cross. He slavered. He shouted. And the Saxons stood still and watched this madman who came alone across the downland grass. The men of Calleva hung for a moment on the northern lip of the hill. Their faces were like white holes in the sky.

They saw Hylas turn, and look back, to discover that not a man had followed him. His hairy figure seemed to grow small and mean. He gaped at his enemies—as though bewildered. Actually, he put the end of the cross in his mouth—and sucked the wood of it.

The men from the sea began to laugh, and Hylas, still sucking his cross like an astonished child, stared at them dumbly. Laughter, ridicule, all those fierce fresh faces with

their sea-blue eyes!   And suddenly, Hylas turned to run.
But a Saxon had swung his war axe: he whirled it and let
it fly, and the steel blade cleft the head of Hylas.   He went
down soundlessly, his cross under him, his brains showing
white for a moment in an ooze of blood.

The slaying of Hylas let death and panic loose.   The
white faces of Calleva disappeared from the brim of the hill.
Blatho, tangled up in the midst of the rabble, spurred his
horse with the point of his sword.   Calleva threw away its
weapons.   The rout went down the green slope like so
much rubbish shot out of a tumbril.

In the valley below these men of the city were overtaken
by the men of the sea.   The Saxons made a great slaughter.
Blatho, whose horse had thrown him, was slain as he was
trying to crawl and hide himself under a thorn bush.   Some
two score fugitives were saved by scattering into the woods.
There was blood on the high road and blood on the grass
beside it.

2

Melchior the Deacon knocked at the door of the city
gaol.   The moon was up, and Melchior's shadow fell upon
the wall.   His fingers were in his beard.   He looked like
a man who would slip into some dark doorway without
the world being any the wiser.   The gaoler opened the
door to him, and they stood with their faces close, whispering together.

"Bring the woman down," said Melchior, "and come
with me."

Guinevra was standing at the barred window of her
upper chamber when she heard the man's footsteps on the
stairs.   He unlocked the door and spoke to her roughly.

"Come, wench, you are wanted."

For the moment she did not move, but remained with
her right hand touching one of the window-bars.   Life

had made her afraid of everything, of a sound or a shadow or a step upon the stairs. The man saw the white edge of her face in the moonlight.

"Who wants me?"

"Ask no questions and you will be told no lies. Come on, my beauty."

There was a light in the passage at the foot of the stairs, and she saw Melchior waiting below. He cleared his throat and spoke to her like one who felt suavely responsible for a delicate business.

"Cover your face, woman, and come with me."

There was an old grey cloak with a hood hanging on a peg, and the gaoler lifted the cloak and put it over her shoulders. From another peg he took a cudgel, and the three of them went out into the moonlight. Melchior bade Guinevra walk behind him. The gaoler followed at her heels. They went down the alley with the high wall of the basilica rising before them like a cliff. Melchior paused at the end of the alley, and looked up and down the street before crossing it. He had a key which fitted the door of the merchant's hall. He unlocked the door, and waited for Guinevra and the gaoler to enter. A second door led into the great hall of the basilica with its colonnade and screens. The moonlight slanted in and made the dimness strange. Melchior's slippers shuffled; the gaoler's sandals were more noisy. Guinevra seemed to glide without a sound. They passed round a screen, and Melchior unlocked another door.

It was the great door opening into the court of the Forum, and when they had passed through, Melchior relocked it, and bade the gaoler wait there.

"Keep watch, Mr. Gaoler."

The man twirled his cudgel.

"I'm at your service, Father."

Melchior made a sign to Guinevra. He struck across the court towards the southern ambulatory, and under its pent roof she saw a patch of light, the window of the priests' chamber. Melchior ordered her to wait in the ambulatory. He was abrupt, portentous. Standing by one of the pillars she watched him go to the door of the priest's chamber, open it, and disappear.

Balthasar was lying with a lamp burning beside him. He looked like a corpse propped up in the bed, but his eyes burned.

"The woman is here," said Melchior.

Balthasar nodded at him.

"I must save her soul, Melchior, even if she has to die."

Melchior made the sign of the cross.

"You are merciful, father. Surely she deserves hell fire."

When Guinevra saw the face of Balthasar a kind of palsy seemed to possess her. She stood in the doorway, staring at the man in the bed. Her eyes were two black circles. She seemed to fumble with her lips.—Melchior had to push her into the room.—"On your knees, woman." But she stood rigid, and Melchior closed the door on her, and his shoes shuffled across the ambulatory. Melchior was both priest and man of the world, zealous in serving the great. They could hear him walking to and fro in the Forum, buzzing like a bee about the flower of his prayers.

Balthasar's hand made a beckoning movement. It was as white as his face.

"Come and kneel by me, Guinevra."

But she did not move. Her eyes stared at the flame of the lamp.

"What do you wish with me?"

His head seemed to strain forward on the pillow.

"Fool, do you know that you are to die?"

She nodded and gave the lamp a vacant yet consenting smile.

"Yes—I am to die."

"So, you will die—fool! Have you nothing to ask of me?"

Her lips moved. Her hands clasped her bosom.

"What should I ask of you?"

His head sank back into the hollow of the pillow. His pale lips writhed.

"Woman, you will burn.—The people are bitter against you. Yes, you will burn. The crowd does not ask for words. The crowd is cruel. It does not listen to the bleatings of a lamb. And yet, out of my mercy——"

He held out a hand as though he held an apple in his palm. His face was sharp and shining. He moistened his lips.

"Shall we give—lie for lie, Guinevra?"

She understood him. A strange shuddering seized her, and so bitter was her trembling that her hood fell back upon her shoulders. And then she looked at him as though she saw a corpse in the bed, a hideous, stinking thing, corruption that could not be stomached.

"Don't touch me."

Balthasar seemed to writhe. His voice struck at her like the head of a snake.

"Ha!—My mercy—is not the kiss of a lover?—So—so—you shall burn."

She shivered, but looked straight at him. She was mute, and her silence said more than words.

His face had a twisted look, and suddenly he clapped his hands together. His voice rang out.

"You are shameless. No compassion can save you. Unclean, unclean."

Melchior, shuffling swiftly in his slippers, heard those words, and was edified. He opened the door and peered in. He saw Guinevra like a woman who had fallen asleep on her feet.

Balthasar pointed.

"Take the harlot away. She is false and shameless, and beyond all mercy."

Melchior pulled his beard.

"God be gracious to us," said he, having nothing else to say.

He opened the door wide and looked at Guinevra.   She stood for a moment staring at the lamp.   Then, she drew her hood forward and, folding her hands over her bosom, passed out, and Melchior, without glancing at the man in the bed, softly closed the door.

3

Shortly before noon on the third day of the week a watchman on the city wall not far from the Venta Gate saw a number of figures break out of the birch woods where the high road left the shelter of the trees.   The watchman, shading his eyes, shouted to the guards at the gate below.

"Look to it!—I see men on the road."

There had been no news of Blatho and his company, but as this little rabble of a remnant drew near, the watchers on the walls saw that the news it brought had not the bloom of victory.   None of these fugitives carried arms.   Most of them hobbled on sore feet.   One fellow had a bloody cloth wrapped round his head.   Some of them walked like drunken men, staggering and exhausted.

"Lord!" said one of the watchers, "those fellows look as though they had been running all night."

Half-way between the woods and the city wall one of the fugitives turned to look back as though scared of his own shadow.   He saw the white trunks of the birch trees, and his terror turned them into the shapes of men.   He began to run, though his running did not rise above a wearied trot. His feet seemed to go up and down in the same place, but his jogging knees and pawing hands set the whole rout running.   They came in a dusty, dishevelled, squawling mob to the city gate.

"The Saxons—the Saxons!"

"Open the gates—open the gates."

The guards did more than let these fugitives in.   They let in fear, and wild faces and wild words.   When the gates

were closed behind them some of Blatho's men fell on the
stones like runners in anguish at the end of a race. The
man with the red bandage leaned panting against a wall,
and called for water. There was a confusion of voices.
Men reeled about blurting out shreds of news, tidings of
death and of terror. People came running to the gate.
Faces were wild or shocked or stupid.

"Blatho's dead."

"And Hylas. He had his head split with an axe."

"The heathen fell on us like wild beasts."

"There were hundreds of them, hundreds."

The crowd thickened about the gate. There was a
gabble of voices. Someone shouted—"To the walls."
Men rushed up the stairs—peered over, saw nothing, and
came down again. Women caught hold of the survivors,
shook them, asked questions. "Where is my man?"
There were screams, lamentations. Aprons were thrown
over heads. Somewhere in the crowd a voice howled
shrilly—"To the Forum, to the Forum."

It was as though blind Fear took a whip to the crowd
and drove it pell-mell up the straight street towards the
centre of the city. It gathered numbers as it went; it
sucked figures out of doorways: women, children, dogs,
old men, hags. It hobbled and paddled and ran, spilling
into the gutters, pushing its human flood-drift against the
walls. It panted and put questions to its neighbours,
and in gathering more and more frightened faces, it
gathered more fear. Women screamed and chattered,
dogs barked. The Forum was like a turgid and overfilled
heart into which all this terror and clamour and confusion
poured.

In her prison chamber Guinevra heard the uproar, and
was afraid. She stood at her barred window, listening to the
voices of the city, and something in her shivered. She had
learnt to fear the mob; and the mob was out in Calleva.
The city's fear infected her and became her fear. The
crowd-beast was giving tongue. She heard the voices of

the gaoler and his wife below, and the crash of a heavy door being shut.—It seemed to shake both the building and her own, secret, fearful self.

4

The terror of his little world broke at the feet of Balthasar. It seemed that all those faces in the Forum hung like grotesque masks outside his window. Calleva had come to suck courage and comfort from the pale lips of its Bishop.

"The Saxons—the Saxons!"

Balthasar rose on his pillows, and his head strained on its swathed neck. He could see the faces of the crowd, the distracted hands, the jerking heads. The city's panic seemed to blow in through the window. Balthasar's fingers clawed at the coverlet. He drew himself upright in the bed.

Someone was appealing to the crowd, Urbanus appealing for his patient. The door opened, and Balthasar saw the face of Melchior, a face like a full moon with round and staring eyes, and a little circle of flaccid flesh emitting hollow sounds.

"The heathen.—What shall we do?"

Balthasar's hands clutched the coverlet.

"Is the city mad, Melchior? Come in, and close the door."

The deacon's voice shuffled like his shoes.

"The Saxons are upon us, Father."

"Speak up, man—don't whisper."

"Blatho and Hylas are dead. Only a remnant has come back to us. Slaughtered like sheep, sir—slaughtered."

Balthasar's face looked like white metal.

"And you shake like a woman.—Have we no walls? Bring two of the—creatures in to me."

Melchior went backwards, fingering his beard. The

crowd had grown less noisy. It was watching the great man's door. Calleva saw Melchior come out backwards, like a dog out of a rabbit hole, and turn and stare. He raised a hand. His voice seemed to dribble in his beard.

"Our bishop would speak—with two of the—remnant."

The man with the red bandage round his head and another fellow came forward. They followed Melchior through the door in the ambulatory into the room where Balthasar lay propped against his pillows; his lips were tinged with scorn.

"Speak—you.—I listen."

They began gabbling like starlings on a chimney, and Balthasar's hand went up.

"Wait.—Where was this—slaughter?"

Red bandage answered him.

"We were about ten miles from Venta—bishop—when the heathen came over a hill."

"And you ran?"

"We saved ourselves, lord. They were like wolves."

"And where are these—wolves—now?"

The man stared.

"In the woods—sir."

"Man, have you seen a wolf—since you ran from them yesterday?"

"We did not stay to see them, lord."

Balthasar turned on Melchior.

"Deacon, is there any reason left in this city? Are the gates guarded, the walls patrolled? Answer me."

"I cannot say, holiness."

"All of you run like children into the Forum. You cry, 'The heathen are upon us,' and forget the walls and the gates. Is this a mad world, Melchior?"

Melchior looked humble.

"God be gracious to us, lord, but it may be.—I beseech you, do not waste your stength."

Balthasar was like a man possessed.

"Send Urbanus to me," and to Urbanus he said—

U

"Physician, I would rise and speak to my people. They are like sheep. You—Melchior, and you—Urbanus, put your arms about me."

Urbanus protested.

"Bishop—this is madness. You will bleed again."

"Then let me bleed."

So fierce and fixed was his purpose that it constrained them to obey it. His legs trailed as they lifted him from the bed, but when his feet touched the floor his lower limbs stiffened to his will. His face was set like a stone.

"Out—into the Forum."

Between them they supported him into the ambulatory, and when Calleva saw the face of its bishop a great silence fell. Balthasar might look like a corpse in its grave clothes, but the corpse was a live man. A murmur ran through the crowd like a sudden wind through trees.

"Balthasar—Balthasar."

He stiffened himself. That cry seemed to blow colour into his cheeks. He put Urbanus and Melchior aside, and stood alone. His head was proud and high. He raised his right arm.

"My people, are we not God's children? Shall we fear? To the walls.—Guard the gates.—I—your——"

The crowd saw him falter. His eyes seemed to go blind; his mouth fell open; his right hand was pressed to his side. Urbanus and Melchior caught him in their arms. His head fell back as they carried him into the priest's chamber and laid him up on the bed.

Said Melchior—"He has fainted."

Urbanus had the look of a man who saw death on the face of Balthasar.

"The wound has broken. He bleeds again—within. Shut the door, deacon. That wench's knife went deep."

In the Forum people crowded like sheep. Balthasar their Bishop was dying! They forgot the heathen; they forgot Balthasar's words, the city gates and the walls. The white clouds went over their heads, and the little gilded figure on its column glittered up above. The south ambulatory became solid with humanity. Fidelis and two of her women had pushed their way through the crowd, and had their faces to the saint's window.

A woman of the city spoke to Fidelis.

"Can you see anything, matrona?—It will be a fearful thing——"

Fidelis looked grim.

"That the hand of a harlot should have done it.— Anathema."

The crowd saw the door open, and Melchior come out, a very solemn and scared Melchior.

"Our saint bleeds.—Life hangs on a thread. To the walls—good people. Watch and pray."

The crowd strained its thousand heads towards the Deacon to catch what he had to say. Those who were near the door passed the news to those behind them. Death and Balthasar were at grips in that silent room. The Forum seemed to fill with a deep murmuring like the sound of the sea in a cave.

It was Fidelis who dropped poison into the cup.

"The hand of that harlot has done this."

The words were caught up by the crowd.

"Geraint's harlot."

"Murderess."

"She shall die."

CHAPTER XXVII

Geraint Meets the Heathen

¶ A CROWD that is afraid can be a cruel crowd, and Calleva held the victim that could be sacrificed to its fear. Was it not good and right that Guinevra should die? The women were more bitter than the men. Calleva was mourning her dead. The wife of one of Blatho's men climbed the rostrum, and with screaming voice and dishevelled hair, set the crowd howling.

"Burn the she-dog. She has brought death to the city."

Led by women of the gutters the crowd rushed out of the Forum and poured like some filthy flood into the alley where the prison stood. It found the door barred, and howled for hammers and axes. A wagon was standing in the alley, and men and women took the wagon-pole, and using it as a ram, beat in the door. The gaoler, confronting them in the passage, embraced discretion when he saw their faces. This crowd was mad. It would rend and smash anything that flouted it.

"We want the woman."

The man jerked a thumb towards the stairs.

"Take her.—I wash my hands of her."

But this crowd could spice its pound of flesh. Mere killing might be too merciful. Let the feast be spread in public, the tables laid, the benches filled, and the roast be served on a flaming dish. This crowd was convulsed and enraptured with its cruelty. It would gloat and savour the feast, and watch the live thing writhing.

The woman of the rostrum stood on the stairs with her arms spread. She was a dark, lean, bitter creature, with

breasts that hung like shrivelled skins from a flat chest
and a mouth that was a raw wound.   She screamed.

"Don't burn your candle all at once, neighbours.—Let
the wench have her belly full of fear.   Let's keep her on
show to-night, and burn her in the morning."

There was ecstasy on all those faces.

"That's it.—Put her in a cage."

"The Forum's the place to burn her in."

"Pile up the faggots.   We'll light a candle for Balthasar."

She of the shrivelled breasts and half a dozen like her
burst into that upper room.   They found Guinevra sitting
on her bed, white, wide-eyed, dumb.   She had heard the
voices on the stairs and knew that her hour had come.   The
women fell upon her like creatures with claws.   They tore
the clothes from her, dragged her down the stairs into the
room with its barred window opening on the alley.   She
did not struggle.   The smell of the crowd was in her nostrils, and horror of it in her eyes.   She stood naked against
the wall, her face bleeding, her hands clasping her
breasts.

Such was her martyrdom, to stand there through the
hours while the mob howled and jeered, and threw filth at
her through the window.—When twilight came she was
crouching in a corner, her arms over her head.   She made
no sound, and no one showed her pity.

The crowd lit a bonfire in the alley, and mocked her with
its flames.

"That's where you will be to-morrow, murderess."

Calleva was mad all that night.   It rushed from the
Forum to the walls, and from the walls to the Forum.   It
emptied the wine-shops, and sang and boasted.   "Let the
heathen come.   We'll send them to Hades."   It planted
a post in the Forum, and hung it with chains, and carried
in faggots and straw and piled them for the burning.   It
shouted to its saint, who lay in a swoon, too near death to
heed them.

"We'll light you a fire in heaven, father."

Even children carried sticks to the pyre. Urchins squeezed through the crowd outside the prison window, and flung in filth and jibes as their elders. Men held lighted brands to the bars so that the poor caged beast could be seen crouching in a corner.

2

One of Geraint's scouts came riding over the hill, and the news he brought was like a lighted torch.

This man had seen the remnant of Blatho's company flying along the road to Calleva. The countryside was full of a rabble of countryfolk fleeing from the heathen. The scout had spoken with one of Blatho's men, a straggler who had fallen behind with a wound in his thigh.

"The Saxons, lord."

Geraint was sitting under a tree when the man brought him the news. He listened, was silent as death, and then, taking his sword, he let it lie naked across his knees. His men gathered round him—Caradoc, Gawaine, David—but Geraint sat there, silent as death, running his fingers along the edge of his sword.

His men wondered.—What would Geraint do?—Go out to meet the heathen? And that—in truth—was what Geraint proposed to do—but not as his men expected.

He rose, and walked a little way into the deep wood like a man who would be alone with his own thoughts. He put a hand against the trunk of a tree, and leaned against it—head bowed.—And then, his shoulders seemed to straighten; his head jerked back.

"Caradoc."

Caradoc went to him.

"Caradoc—bring Balda to me."

"Balda, lord?"

"Yes, Balda the Saxon.—He is our man in this business."
Caradoc looked strangely at Geraint.

"What do you want with Balda, lord?"

"He shall make peace between us?"

"Peace?" said Caradoc, staring.

"Yes—peace—Caradoc."

"Think you Balda is to be trusted—when his own people are out for blood?"

And Geraint smiled like death.

"I—too—am for blood, Caradoc.   What care I how I come at it?—Who is my enemy?—Calleva.   If the Saxons and I take the city together—my god can march with their god.—I am death on a white horse, Caradoc."

Caradoc looked grim, but his grimness began to laugh.

"Gods of my father, lord, but between us we could storm the place.—I want my crack at Calleva, and I care not greatly how I come by it.—But what will you do?"

"March to meet the Saxons."

"And what—if the wild men will not mate with us?"

"We are not sheep to be savaged, man.   We are as good as they.   When we meet with them I will go forward alone with Balda.—I will give Balda my message to their chief. We two can speak face to face, with Balda to serve us."

Geraint had his trumpets blown.   Caradoc brought Balda to him in the wood, and while his men were arming themselves and harnessing their horses, Geraint spoke with Balda.   The Saxon was a stolid, fresh-faced fellow with a blue-eyed smile that came slowly.   He looked straight into Geraint's eyes, and when he had heard Geraint's plan he smiled.   Balda was blunt in the blows he gave, and in his judgment of men.   My Lord Geraint had a head on his shoulders.

"I would make a three-days' pact with your countrymen, Balda.   We will swear faith and go up together against this city.   When we have dealt with Calleva—your people can fight me if they please."

Balda laughed.

"They come for plunder and adventure, Geraint, and when the spoil is theirs—they go back to the sea."

"Calleva is still a city worth sacking. There is enough for my men and for theirs."

The horse and foot were waiting under the shade of the trees, and David was holding Geraint's white horse. When Geraint had mounted, he spoke to his men. If any of them were pale livered or squeamish let them stay behind. Balda's countrymen were marching on Calleva, and he—Geraint— was ready to call any man brother in the storming of Calleva. The city would be a hard rock to crack and he was ready to share with others the cracking of it. Moreover, Calleva was a rebel city, and had done cruel things. If any man was afraid to join with these sea-wolves or match himself with them when the truce between them was over, let him stay behind.

The men looked at Geraint's face as he rode up and down before them. They were a tough crowd who did not follow him to split hairs or blow soap-bubbles. Let Geraint do what he would. Sundry of them had, like Caradoc, a bloody bone to pick with Calleva. Yes, they would follow Geraint upon the adventure. The young Aquilas, remembering how the men of Calleva had slain their father, had their swords out, and were calling upon Geraint to do what he pleased.

"Lead us against Calleva. We want blood for blood."

Geraint marched east to strike the Calleva-Venta road, keeping to the uplands, with mounted scouts pushed out ahead. The September day was clear and blue, and hill rose beyond hill. The horse went first, and the foot followed after, their painted shields a-row. Half an hour's marching brought them to the high road, and here Geraint halted his men, and waited for news from his scouts, nor had he to wait long. Two of them came cantering over a hill. They had seen Osric and his Saxons in the valley below.

Geraint led his men over the brow of the hill, and marshalled them there, the foot in front, the horse behind. The Saxons should see that he had something solid to bargain with. A stream ran in the valley, with the road dipping to it through woods and meadows, and the Saxons were crossing the stream. Most of them were on foot, but Osric and a couple of score had found horses and were riding half a furlong ahead of the main body.

Geraint called Balda to him and walked his horse down the road. He was trusting Balda and his faith was not misplaced. The Saxons had seen Geraint's men drawn up below the brow of the hill. Their column halted and stood at gaze with the sun shining on their weapons and their harness.

Geraint rode slowly on.

"Go, Balda. Say that I would speak with their war-chief."

Geraint reined in about a furlong from the bottom of the valley, and sat his horse in the middle of the road. He watched Balda gallop down the hill, shouting to his countrymen in their mother tongue. A man on a black horse rode forward to meet Balda. It was Osric in the blue cloak he had taken from Nectarides.

The Britons stood fast on the hill, the Saxons in the valley. Then, Osric and one of his men came riding up the hill with Balda. Geraint's sword was in its sheath, and he had left his spear with David. He raised an arm and saluted the Saxons.

Osric rode his horse within two horse-lengths of Geraint, and these two men sat and looked at each other. Geraint was dark, Osric fair, big men both of them with eyes that did not falter.

Geraint smiled at the Saxon.

"Balda—speak for me.—I am here to swear troth."

And Balda spoke, pointing first at Geraint and his men on the hill, and then at Osric and the Saxons in the valley.

"My lord has a feud against Calleva. He is here—with his sword in its sheath to speak as man to man. My lord says—let us go together against Calleva and share in the fighting and in the sacking of it. And my lord Geraint is a man of his word."

Osric laughed.

"This is a strange blood-bargain.—We—who—should be at each other's throats——!"

He and Geraint were looking upon each other and liking each other as men will. There was no fear in the eyes of Geraint and no fear in the eyes of Osric.

Geraint spoke, looking Osric in the face, while Balda turned his words into the Saxon tongue.

"Osric—I can love and I can hate, and I carry both love and hate on my helmet. This city is bitter to me, and it is a strong city. To-morrow, if you will take me as your blood-brother, we will go up against Calleva, and put it to the sword. I care not who your god is, nor need my god be yours. There is the city. You and I have men who can fight."

Osric's blue eyes still laughed. Here was a man who could dare and who could hate, and the strange love of man for man made them brothers.

"How many men have you, Geraint?"

"Fifty horse, a hundred foot."

"And what shall we find in Calleva?"

Geraint smiled at him.

"You dealt with some of Calleva yesterday. The city may find three hundred men and a mob—to man the walls. We have but to force the gates or storm the walls, and they will not stand against us."

"I trow not," said Osric.

And again he laughed.

"We may love blood-spilling, Geraint—but we love plunder."

"There should be enough for all," said Geraint.—"I want nothing from Calleva but one thing—a woman. My men will want more than that—but we shall not cut each other's throats for a few pots and pans. Let all the spoil be piled where you please, and our men shall share it."

He held out a hand to Osric.

"I do not grudge you anything, brother. There is more than a gold ring between us. We are men of the sword."

Osric pushed his horse forward, and his hand gripped Geraint's.

"There's my troth. Shall it be for three days or for life, brother?"

Geraint smiled at him.

"As long as you please.—But when Calleva is nothing but a great silence—you will go to your ships, and I—to my own place.—And if you come again across the sea—I may be against you, Osric."

Osric embraced him.

"God's truth! But to-morrow we go up together to take this city."

3

There were two women in Calleva who were moved to pity Guinevra, and who pushed their way into the alley after darkness had fallen. A man holding a torch stood outside the prison window; he was playing the part of booth-keeper and showman, and exercising a foul wit. Seeing Pia and Volumna squeezing through the crowd, he hailed them.

"Step up, ladies, and see the show."

He thrust the torch through the bars to light up the cell, and as Pia and Volumna bent to look, a lad pushed his way through the crowd and stood next to Pia. The light of the torch showed them that naked figure crouching against the wall, and Pia was so shocked that she clung to Volumna. As for the lad next her, he stood a moment staring with eyes

of pity and horror, and putting an arm over his face, turned
and broke away through the crowd.

Poor Pia, who was a squeamish creature, clung to
Volumna, and then went off into a faint, and Volumna—
strong as a man, carried Pia out of the press, and sat down
on a doorstep with Pia in her lap.   Another figure crouched
close to them with its back against the wall, its head down
between its knees, but Volumna was so taken up with Pia
that she did not notice her neighbour.   As for Morgan he
had broken away from that window in a kind of fury,
tempted to dash his fists in the faces of the crowd.   He had
squatted down in the darkness against the wall, overcome
by a sudden trembling, and a frenzy that made him sick.

Meanwhile, Pia had come to her senses, and was wailing
like a child in Volumna's lap.

"We must do something, Volumna, do something.   A
woman's a woman, though she may have sinned."

Volumna grunted.

"It is devils' work, my dear, but what can we do?   They
will burn her to-morrow.   This city's mad."

"I must find Fidelis.—Fidelis has a tongue in her head.
She must speak to the bishop."

Said Volumna—"They tell me that Balthasar is beyond
speaking to.—She and Caritas are watching by his bed."

"I must go to Fidelis—Volumna."

The lad had sat listening to their voices, and suddenly
he gathered himself up and disappeared in the darkness.
He ran, but shrewdly so, keeping close to walls, and following the lesser streets.   There was a passion of haste and an
anguish of caution in his movements.   Morgan was no
longer the laughing lad of the impudent eyes, but a fierce
young creature in whom compassion and hatred raged.
But if Morgan had lost control of his heart, he had his wits
in head.   He had managed to enter the city when a gate
had opened to let in a crowd of panic-stricken peasants.
He had a length of light rope coiled round him under his
tunic.   There was enough rope to let him drop over the

city wall. He was to meet his lord at the first milestone outside the north gate of Calleva.

Meanwhile, Volumna helped Pia into the Forum where torches were set in iron brackets attached to the pillars of the covered ways. Brushwood was still being piled for the burning of Guinevra, and when Pia saw the work going on, she shivered and clung to Volumna.

"These are devils—Lumna."

Volumna grunted.

"The city has smelt blood."

"They cannot mean to burn her."

Volumna asserted that nothing but a company of angels descending from heaven could save Guinevra from the flames.

"Then," said Pia, "this city should be treated like Sodom. Fire should come out of heaven and destroy it."

Pia was beside herself. Urbanus and Melchior had placed guards to keep the crowd out of the southern ambulatory and away from Balthasar's window. They stood with the staves of their spears crossed, and would not suffer the women to pass. Pia, beside herself, tried to push a spear aside.

"I must speak with Fidelis. They say she is in that chamber."

The men thrust her off.

"Stand back. We have our orders."

Pia fell a-weeping and hid her face in Volumna's bosom.

"There is no pity—anywhere—in this city."

"Tut-tut," said Volumna; "we will wait here for Fidelis."

Fidelis sat alone beside Balthasar's bed. A lamp was burning, and Fidelis's chin stuck out from under her hood. Even her shadow on the wall looked gaunt and grim. For Balthasar was dying. He might last till the morning; and Fidelis sat like a woman in a bitter spite against fate. Her world was passing with the life of this man.—She sat and looked at his stark, white face, with its closed eyes and pale mouth. Balthasar seemed to know nothing, heed nothing, and his world was falling into ruins.

Fidelis stared at him.—What did those closed eyelids conceal? Had this man—Calleva's saint—been as other men?—Had Balthasar fooled her and Calleva?—And then, she was aware of Balthasar's eyes opening; they looked at her strangely, with a kind of dark and glassy anguish.

His lips moved.

"Fidelis——"

She bent close.

"I listen——"

"Guinevra—let them not——"

Fidelis glared. She sat rigid.

"The city has judged her—father."

Balthasar's face twitched. He stared at Fidelis like a sick child who has asked for some cooling drink and been rebuffed. He put out a hand as though to touch the woman. Then, the hand dropped on the bed; his face seemed to fall to pieces like a broken mirror. The jaw sagged, the mouth hung open, the eyes were empty. Balthasar had ceased to breathe.

Fidelis stared at him. She bent down and put her ear close to that flaccid mouth. Then, she got up from her stool and gathering her cloak round her, went to the door. —So—Balthasar had been—— Fidelis made a noise in her throat, opened the door, and turning to look at the dead man in the bed, gave a bitter jerk of the head, and passed out.

The soldiers raised their spears, and in the ambulatory Fidelis found a passionate Pia clinging to her.

"Fidelis—she must not burn.—Plead with our saint. Save her."

Fidelis flung Pia off.

"Fool—our saint is dead."

CHAPTER XXVIII

Calleva Howls

¶ GERAINT had marched his men after dark into a deep valley less than a mile from the north gate of Calleva and hidden them in the woods. With Gawaine and Caradoc he had held a war-council with the Saxons in a deserted villa on the Venta road. It had been agreed between them that they should attack an hour after sunrise, Osric at the south gate with the main body of his men, Geraint at the north gate. But Osric was to send some fifty of his men to surprise the east gate. Calleva, if it was on the alert, would be expecting the enemy to come from the south, and the north and east gates might be lightly held. Geraint had offered to place fifty of his men under Osric's orders to fight at the south gate as a proof of his good faith, but Osric had laughed at him.

"Tell your captain, Balda—that I see death in his eyes, death for these skulkers behind walls."

Geraint had his plan. He set his men to fell young trees and make six rough ladders. Fifty of his fellows were to scale the walls, force the north gate and let in the horse. Geraint would lead a charge of horse down the broad street straight through the heart of the city. The Calleva mob would not stand to meet such a charge, and if Osric's men were being held up at the southern gate, Geraint and his horsemen would ride through and take the defenders from behind.

With his outposts placed, and his men lying down to sleep in the fern, Geraint took David Red Head with him, and went down through the woods to the road. A great

327

stillness held, and there was a faint sound of water running in the valley. Calleva was hidden by the dark swell of a hill, but the sky above it quivered with pale light, and out of the hollow night came a vague murmuring.

Geraint saw the road white and dim in the valley. It crossed a stream by a stone bridge, and on the hill beyond the bridge stood the first milestone.

Geraint looked at the sky.

"Calleva is burning torches, David."

David had his hand to his ear.

"You can hear the city like a wasps' nest, master. They are afraid of the darkness."

Said Geraint—"We may catch them yawning at sunrise."

But if Calleva was restless, so was Geraint, and his torch was not a pine bough. He went down to the bridge with David and stood leaning on his sword. He knew that Morgan should cross this bridge to reach the milestone on the hill above, but what if the lad should cut across country? He sent David up the hill to watch for Morgan.

He heard David's footsteps dying away up the hill, and the water making a faint gurgling as it flowed between the abutments of the bridge. The road climbed towards that patch of light in the sky. The distraught city sent to him the sound of voices merged in a confused murmuring. What did Calleva hold for him? The night was passing, and Morgan tarried. Had anything untoward happened to the lad? Geraint was restless, but he stood motionless, leaning on his sword.

Someone came running down the hill from the direction of Calleva, and Geraint drew back against one of the stone walls. On such a night as this no chances were to be given or taken. The footsteps came fast, and Geraint could swear that they were Morgan's, but he held his sword ready.

"Morgan."

The lad pulled himself up, and then sprang away with a sharp cry.

"Who's that?"

"You should know my voice, lad."

"Lord!"

Morgan fell on his knees at Geraint's feet. He was panting, almost beside himself. He clasped Geraint's knees.

"She is in prison, lord!—The mob!—Beasts—beasts! They will burn her to-morrow."

Geraint held Morgan by the shoulder.

"Burn her?—God!"

"Balthasar is dying.—They will burn her in the forum —as a murderess.—But if you had seen her, lord, as I saw her."

Geraint straightened. He looked at the haze of light over Calleva.

"By my sword—that shall not happen.—Is the city keeping watch, Morgan?"

"It is like a cage full of wild beasts, lord. Some of the men are on the walls—others guarding the forum. She is in the town gaol, with a foul crowd keeping watch. The faggots are all ready in the forum."

Geraint stood thinking. Should he gather his men, and cut his way into the city by night? Osric and his Saxons were feasting; they had roasted an ox and were full of strong drink. He might hazard too much in a bitter battle in the dark streets of Calleva. He might lose the very thing he sought to save. Morgan, shivering, knelt and looked up into the dim face of Geraint.

"I heard someone say, lord—that the fire would be lighted three hours after sunrise."

Geraint put his sword away in its sheath.

"I am both mad and wise—Morgan. We shall be in Calleva before they light that fire. One should not be mad too soon."

But Geraint was not going to wait on that bridge all night like a dog on a chain. He sent Morgan running for David, and when David and the lad joined him, he spoke quietly to them like a man who was master of his soul.

v

"I go to warn Osric.—They will be heavy with food and drink.—David—I have a trust for you."

David looked at him and waited.

"I would have you stay and watch with Osric's men. See that there is no late sleeping. Pull Osric by the beard, if needs be. Will you take that hazard on you? These men are rough."

David gave a jerk of the head.

"I have nothing much left to fear in this world, master, I will kick those wolves up, if needs be."

"Good man.—Come, both of you. I have things to say to Osric."

They went up to the wood, woke Balda, harnessed three horses, and leaving Morgan to sleep, rode south round Calleva. The city had taken the storming of Regnum to heart and was keeping a night watch on the walls. But it appeared that the men of Calleva were afraid of the darkness. Cressets had been lit, and the sentinels carried torches, but these lights flared against the dark sky more thickly in the south. Geraint, watching these tufts of fire sprouting on the black walls, was wise as to their significance. The city corporate was a body lacking a head. It crowded to confront the southern sky, leaving the north to God and the illusion that no enemy would come from that quarter. Geraint looked grim. In the morning Calleva's eyes would be fixed on the south. It would bristle against Osric and his sea-wolves, and forget that it could be struck mortally between the shoulders.

They found the Venta road, and riding on the grass beside it, met no one. Calleva had no stomach for night-work outside the walls. A grove of trees rose like a black cliff, and beyond the trees, and hidden by them, the deserted villa sent up a spume of smoke and light. The Saxons had lit fires in the courtyard, eaten their ox, and filled their bellies against the morrow. Some of them were still drinking; hairy men, their heads like yellow fleeces. Others were asleep with their arms beside them. Osric had had a

bed carried out into the courtyard. He was sitting on the
bed in the midst of his men, his sword across his knees, a
gold chain round his throat.

There was a guard at the gate, but when Balda had
spoken with them, they let the horsemen through. Osric
laughed when he saw Geraint, but there was no laughter
in the eyes of the lover. He dismounted, and stood with
Balda to speak for him. Osric was still laughing.

"Are you afraid that we shall be fuddled at sunrise?"

Said Geraint through the mouth of Balda—"I am a man
and a lover, Osric, and three hours after sunrise the city
will burn that which I love. Should I sleep? The woman
is very dear to me."

Osric called for a cup of wine.

"I drink to the lover, Geraint.—You can drink from the
same cup to the brother in me. We shall not fail you."

Osric drank and rising, gave the cup to Geraint.

Said Geraint, when he had drunk—"You will find all
the city crowding the walls on the south against you.—Be
cunning with them. Keep them in play—I shall break in
on the north."

Osric took the cup and sent it whirling into the fire.

"That's enough strong drink for to-night. I shall sleep
three hours under the stars.—Will you sit at the foot of my
bed to awake me, brother?"

Geraint smiled at him.

"I go to my men."

But he left David Red Head behind him, and David
sat with his back against a wall on a floor of flint cobbles
that did not tempt him to sleep.

2

Calleva's wakefulness was more than the wild mate of
its fear. Two hours before midnight, Melchior the deacon
and Urbanus the physician, stood regarding each other

across the dead body of Balthasar. Should not the city be told that its saint had ascended into heaven? Both Melchior and the physician were sleek and comfortable men who liked their world well larded. Melchior might be a zealot, but discreetly so, and when zeal was in fashion. Urbanus stood with his paunch out, stroking his beard. Was it not Balthasar who had taught him that a crowd is an uncomfortable complex of crude forces that must be bamboozled and controlled.

"The people should be told."

He looked at Melchior. Assuredly it was Melchior's duty to inform the city that death had come to its bishop. Moreover, might not Melchior step into the dead man's shoes. He hinted as much to Melchior.

"You were his right hand—deacon."

But Melchior's hand was feeling moist and flabby. This terrible night found his belly quaking. He could deliver an eloquent discourse on brotherly love, but as to holding an angry dog at the end of a chain—that was another matter. Melchior was no hero. Like many fat little men he quaked when the world shook under him.

"They will go mad—Urbanus."

Said the physician—"Well, let them sweat out the fever. Let them purge their passion.—I have done all that a man could do. I am weary, and shall go on a holiday."

Melchior's mouth fell open.

"Leave the city?"

Urbanus busied himself with closing the dead man's eyes. Balthasar's eyes, like those of the frightened Melchior, stared too hard. Simple souls might conceive the city to be a sure sanctuary, but Urbanus had a sensitive skin. He too was no warrior.

"I think you should tell them, deacon."

Melchior, climbing the rostrum, and standing under the stars, announced to Calleva the passing of its saint, and Calleva took the news as Urbanus had prophesied it would. Torches tossed; voices raved; faces grew more wild.

Calleva saw death and mouthed at it.   Urbanus had scuffled off, almost expecting to hear the crowd cry—"Death to the physician."   But Calleva had its victim.   The woman should burn; she should burn in the midst of the city while Calleva's men of war kept the walls; she should be a torch to light a dead saint into paradise.   Let her writhe in the flames.   Calleva would howl her a requiem.

It was Deacon Jude who followed Melchior on the rostrum, and with his vulture's head shining in the torch-light, exhorted the people to do honour to the dead. Jude's bitter lips were smeared with balm.   Almost, it was possible to forgive your enemy when he has done you the courtesy of dying.   Jude had his thin tongue in his cheek, and his eyes on the dead man's shoes; he could wear more eminently than that shuffling sentimentalist—Melchior.

It was Jude who took charge of the death-chamber. Women brought candles and they were set about the bed. Acolytes stood at the foot and the head of it, and in Balthasar's dead hands Jude placed a little silver cross.   Calleva crowded in the ambulatory.   It would look upon the face of its dead saint, and Jude, standing by the doorway, ordered the procession.   Calleva, like an endless snake, writhed into the chamber and round the bed and out into the torch-flare.   Women knelt and kissed the cross in the dead hands. Some of them wept; others cried out that even in death Balthasar was a handsome and a memorable man.   Jude, standing by the doorway, suffered them to flatter the dead. Balthasar's fleshly magnificence would soon be with the worms.

Meanwhile, the scum of the city betook itself to Guinevra's window and pelted her with the news.

"Balthasar is dead."

They told her how she should burn for it—how the flames would lick her feet and run up her lascivious body.

"By noon, to-morrow—murderess—you'll be no more than a handful of ash."

Guinevra sat with her chin on her knees, eyes staring with a kind of dumb and consenting horror at the evil faces that filled the window. She was half-dead already, cold, congealed. Her heart beat, but somehow it was not her heart. Her feet would be so cold when the flames licked them. Terror, anguish, fire, smoke, wild faces, cruel shouts! Would she smother quickly? Was this world real? If only she could die before they dragged her out to that flaming horror.

She could not call on her God, but in her heart she called on her lover.

"Geraint, O, Geraint!"

But she had no hope of any rescue. She was shut in by the mob and the city walls, and yet, for a little while, she fell asleep. Strange, tragic sleep, the pale flower of utter, stricken weariness. She slept with her head on her knees, her hands trailing on the floor, and for a time the crowd at her window did not suspect her of sleeping. But presently the stark stillness of her challenged their spite.

"The slut is asleep."

"Stir her up."

A wanton and malignant hand threw a potsherd. It struck one of her knees, and with a little gasp her head jerked up.

"Geraint——!"

The crowd howled.

"She calls on her lover."

They laughed and mocked her.

"Geraint's got another wench by now, my beauty."

"Geraint—Geraint—your harlot's calling you."

"She'll be hot stuff—all right—in the morning."

So, the night wore away; torches burned themselves out, but that filthy mob could not rest. It boiled and seethed like a pot. It hung like a pagan crowd round the gates of an amphitheatre, lusting for blood and violence and death. Men came down from the walls and joined it. The night was passing, and a faint greyness began to spread over the city, and Guinevra saw the day like a grim face taking shape at her window.

The alley was packed with people. She heard a woman's voice raised like a rusty knife held aloft.

"We'll put this smock on her."

"Is she to be taken out now?"

"Let her stand at the stake for an hour."

The women came into her cell.

"Here's your burning-shirt, you harlot."

Almost, she was like a dead thing in their hands. They had to hold her up and scuffle the smock over her head and shoulders. Someone spat in her face. She did not feel their hands as they dragged her towards the door.

In the Forum the little gilded figure on the column seemed to be waiting to catch the first rays of the rising sun. The Forum was a sea of faces, stupidly expectant faces. From the ambulatory came four men carrying the dead saint upon his bed. Fidelis walked before them, Melchior and Jude behind. And when the crowd saw this procession it began to howl. Balthasar's face might be still in death, a faintly sneering mask of wax. The crowd swayed and struggled. The dead saint's bed seemed to float in a viscid, glutinous liquor, a kind of human sludge. It moved a little, stuck, swayed, moved on again, until the bearers planted it at the foot of the pyre.

Calleva was howling for its victim, and Balthasar lay with his face to the dawn, white and vaguely sneering.

CHAPTER XXIX

The Storming of Calleva

¶ STANDING under an old thorn tree less than a furlong from the city, Geraint saw the dawn break over Calleva. Behind him the ground fell away sharply into the shadow of the valley. His "foot" were drawn up for the attack on the slope below, and he could see the points of their spears. The "horse" waited in the bottom of the valley, lest the jingling of harness or a beast's snorting or pawing the ground should be heard by the sentries on the walls.

Geraint stood close to the trunk of the thorn, shield slung round his neck, his sword set in the grass. There was a great silence without the walls, but Calleva itself made a sound like vexed water. The sky was clear and pearl grey in the east. The top of the city wall cut it like the blade of a sword held flat. The ground near him was feathered with fern, the fronds growing grey as the light increased. Geraint's face was as grey as the dawn.

What was the luck of the morning? He could see three dark objects on the battlement of the north gate, and two more on the curtain wall to the south. They looked like posts, but Geraint knew that they were the sentinels. Five men! But how many more were there in the guardroom, or asleep at the foot of the wall? He saw the three dark objects above the gate draw together, and in the stillness of the dawn he could hear their voices. A harsh laugh drifted to him. He saw two of the figures disappear. The third man stood motionless, leaning on his spear. Manifestly, the watch at the north gate suspected nothing, nor guessed that the hillside bristled with spears.

Geraint felt his heart beating fast and hard, and the dawn was cold on his lips. He had but to turn and raise his sword to his men, and they would come charging after him across the level ground where the road made for the gate. The sky in the east changed from pearl to gold. The walls and roof-tops of the city were very black. Wisps of yellow light tangled themselves in the fern fronds. The sky was deeply blue above, and under the thorn tree the face of Geraint seemed to grow white and strange.

Caradoc crept up through the fern and joined Geraint under the tree.

"What luck, master?"

Geraint pointed to the three figures on the wall.

"I have counted no more than five of them. Osric has a mile to march.—And yet——"

Said Caradoc—"Lord, let's at them now."

Then, in the stillness of the dawn they heard a sound of tumult in the city, the shouts and howls of the mob. It was the moment when the body of Balthasar was carried out into the Forum, and a frenzy seized Calleva. Calleva was howling for the woman to be brought out, and as Geraint listened to those cries his heart seemed to leap in him. He looked into Caradoc's eyes. It was as though the nearness and horror of some tragedy was revealed to him.

He turned, plucked his sword out of the grass, and held it aloft. Not a word was spoken, not a cry raised. The line of spears came up the hill. Helmets and shields caught the sunlight. The ladders stuck out like the horns of strange beasts. Geraint and Caradoc went trampling through the fern. Geraint saw the figures on the wall come to life. One of them was jerking its arms like a wooden puppet pulled by a string. He heard the men shouting.

But there were not a dozen men on the gate and the wall when the ladders were reared against it. Geraint took pride of place on the first ladder, Caradoc, the second.

Their men swarmed behind. Geraint had a glimpse of two fellows with spears trying to prize the ladder away from the wall. It swayed and jerked, but the weight on it held it sure. Geraint saw the two stupid, frightened faces above. One fellow thrust clumsily at him with a spear, and the point slid off Geraint's shoulder-piece. He thrust with his sword and caught the fellow in the belly. The man went backwards, and Geraint was on the wall.

He cut down two more men and found Caradoc beside him. The others did not wait. They ran for the stairs and went tumbling down them. The ladders were spilling men upon the wall. Geraint went leaping down the stairs with Caradoc and a dozen more at his heels. In the mouth of the gateway they met three sleepy guards rushing out wildly and slew them. The bar was thrown down, the bolts pulled back, and as the gate swung open Geraint saw his horsemen galloping over the grass.

Morgan rode in with Geraint's white horse and spear. The lad looked bleached with excitement. He tumbled off the horse, and Geraint mounted, sheathed his sword and took the spear.

His voice rang out.

"Get together—you horsemen—knee to knee.—Caradoc —come after us—as quickly as you can run."

Geraint put himself at the head of his cavalry and went galloping down the straight street into the centre of the city.

2

It so happened that matters were to go well with the storming of Calleva. Osric and his Saxons, afraid lest Geraint should break in ahead of them and get the glory, and the first push at the plunder, were astir before sunrise. Moreover, Osric sent a hundred men instead of fifty to the east gate, which happened to be lightly held, and these

Saxons were swarming up their ladders at the moment when Geraint mounted his horse. Geraint's men wore bands of white linen round their right arms so that they should be known to the Saxons. Meanwhile, Osric and his other hundred shouted and beat their shields in the south, and behaved as though they were the vanguard of the main host. Calleva, crowding the south gate and the walls saw Osric's men marching up the Venta road with ladders and a tree trunk for the battering of the gate.

Calleva, seeing no more than a hundred men, and having jammed the gate with a barricade of sacks filled with earth, danced on the walls and mocked Osric. Let him bring his ladders to the walls. Calleva had beams and stones ready to hurl at their enemies. Some two hundred citizens held this part of the city, and numbers and their wall made them boastful.

Meanwhile, Geraint thundering down North Street, saw half a dozen fleeing figures ahead of him, the men who had fled from the north gate. They were running for the Forum, but the pursuit was so close on their heels that the crowd in the Forum were to be caught like sheep in a pen.

These wild fugitives rushed in through the passage that led from the street on the north of the Forum between a shop and the high wall of the basilica. They tossed their arms and shouted.

"Geraint, Geraint is upon us."

"He has taken the gate."

Upon all those people fell a sudden silence. The gilded figure on the column could look down upon that mound of brushwood and in the midst of it, and crowning it—Guinevra in her white smock. Balthasar lay stretched on his bed. The heads of the crowd were as close as peas in a pod, the faces all turned one way towards the men who had rushed in with the alarm. For some seconds that strange, stark silence held. The man with the torch, who was to light the fire, let the burning brand droop and splutter.

In the stillness the crowd in the Forum heard the rush

of Geraint's horsemen, the clash and clangour in the street.
Death was upon them. The crowd swayed; cries seemed
to rise like dishevelled hair blown by the wind. There was
a rush to shut the great gate of the Forum, but the space
between the pillars of the vestibule was so jammed with
humanity that the leaves of the gate were clogged.

That was what Geraint saw—when riding down the
east street, he turned his white horse at the gate—a mass of
wild faces packed in the entry, a mass of heads, that dark
mound of brushwood, and crowning it—Love in a white
smock.

For an instant Geraint sat facing the mob. His
horsemen were knee to knee behind him. Caradoc and
the foot were not a hundred paces behind and shouting
as they ran. Geraint's face looked death.

He rode straight at the mob.

"Kill—kill!"

The crowd bulged back from the gateway like a great
sack at which a man has struck a blow, but it was stuck
so solidly in the narrow space that it could give no further.
Geraint threw his spear into the crowd and took to the
sword. The charge was like a chariot crashing into
wheat. Terror could not run. The people went down
under the horses feet, and under those flails of iron. The
crowd screamed, struggled, fought, trampled itself, was
bestial in its panic. A part of it, rushing to escape by
the northern slype, met some of Caradoc's men and recoiled—to be slaughtered. The doors of the basilica
were open, but so wild was the struggle to escape that
the crowd writhed there like a great beast stuck in the
mouth of a cave.

Geraint and his men slew until there was no live
thing left in the court of the Forum. Such of the crowd
as survived was crouching in the ambulatories, or hiding
in the shops or offices, or on the terrace above them, or
fighting to escape from the basilica by way of the merchant's
hall. Melchior the deacon lay dead across the feet of the

dead bishop. Fidelis's grey hair was a drabble of blood.
A few stupid dumb faces looked up from the shambles
at the man on the white horse. And the white horse's
legs and chest were bloody.

Geraint's men stood leaning on their weapons. They
saw him ride his horse close to the pile of brushwood.
Three or four pairs of legs stuck out from under the
faggots. Geraint was looking at Guinevra, and she at
him, but the wall of brushwood rose between them.

Geraint was silent as death. He pointed with his
sword to the legs of the skulkers under the faggots.

"Pull them out."

Geraint's men dragged out three screaming men.
One of them was the fellow who was to have fired the
pyre, and such was his terror that he still clutched a
smouldering torch.

"Ha," said Geraint, "you carried the key to Hades."

He made a sign to Caradoc. Caradoc swung his
sword, and the fellow's head rolled from his shoulders.

"Clear me a path," said Geraint.

His men dragged the faggots aside, and made him a
lane, and Geraint rode his horse to the stake where
Guinevra stood with a chain about her. She looked in
his eyes, seemed to droop; her body fell forward over
the chain. Guinevra had fainted.

3

It was Caradoc who broke the chain—an old rusty
thing which snapped when the smith's huge hands wrenched
at it. Geraint was off his horse. He took Guinevra in
his arms, and before them all he kissed her. The dark
lashes lay shut; she was white as milk; her head hung
down. Calleva had left its stigmata upon her, but Geraint
saw nothing but his dear love a-swoon with closed eyes
and lips that were pale and poignant.

Yet—this bloody business in the Forum was but the beginning of things. Calleva's armed men had yet to be dealt with. Geraint stood looking into the face of Guinevra. A man could not fight with a woman in his arms, and this pale, blind thing was still in danger.

Under the pent-roof of the southern ambulatory he saw the strong door of the Vectigalis. He bade his men burst it in. Stepping among the dead with reddening feet he carried Guinevra into the chamber. There was a bench in the room, and he laid her upon it. He called Caradoc to him.

"Caradoc, take twelve men, and hold this doorway."

Caradoc looked blank. Was he to be left to guard a girl?

"Have you not had enough slaying, man?—This charge I lay upon you——"

Caradoc grinned.

"Have it your own way, lord.—You must lead."

And he called twelve men by their names, and posted them in the ambulatory outside the door.

"Find something to put under her head, Caradoc, and to cover her."

"If I'm to be nurse, lord—I'll do it thoroughly."

And Geraint mounted his horse, and rode out of the Forum with his men storming behind him.

The strangest thing of all to him was the emptiness of the streets and their silence. Here and there a figure scuttled along a wall, or dived into a doorway. Calleva had gone to earth. But from the southern quarters came the sound of battle. Osric and his Saxons were at grips with the garrison there. Geraint swung his horse into South Street and as he came to the cross-roads close to the Christian church, he saw the body of Saxons who had forced the East Gate close upon him. Geraint pulled up and waved to them with his sword. He had Balda beside him.

"To the South Gate—Balda. Bring those fellows after me."

He rode on. The south street ran straight as a spear shaft, and down it remnants of the garrison from the west gate and the walls were running to join the main body who were holding the southern quarter against Osric. Geraint waved his men on and rode hard after these gentry. Some he and his men slew; others fled into the alleys or over walls. Geraint galloped on. He could hear the shouts of the sea-rovers behind him.

Half-way to the Venta Gate Geraint saw a mass of men before him, shields, spears, a banner. A part of the garrison, wild with the bloody news from the Forum, had faced about to recover what was lost. And Geraint's blood whimpered in him. Here were men with arms in their hands, men with wild faces, men who were as fierce for blows and blood as he. Calleva, the Calleva that he scorned and hated, was there for the slaying in that open street. Geraint lay back till men and horses were close behind him, and then rode at a gallop at those spears and shields.

He saw them waver and sway, but the men of Calleva stood, stuck like a bone in gorged throat. Geraint and his horsemen crashed in, and tore a lane through the mass, and into that bloody rent his footmen and the Saxons slashed their way. Calleva thrown back against the walls of houses and of gardens, fought for its life and lost it.

4

From the shambles about the Venta Gate Geraint, Osric and Balda rode up towards the centre of the city. All three of them were bloody with the blood of other men, but at the Venta Gate they had made an end of Calleva and its communism.

Osric looked at Geraint, for from Geraint's face the grimness was passing, and Osric smiled in his eyes.

"I see a man who has come by his heart's desire."

And Geraint understood him without using the ears and lips of Balda, but he answered Osric through Balda.

"I have—what I have—thanks to you, Osric.—What more can a man say?"

Osric laid an arm across Geraint's shoulders, and they rode with their knees touching, the white horse and the black together.

Said Osric by the mouth of Balda—"All cities bring evil, brother, and should be destroyed. They are maggot heaps. They breed chatterers, little vain fellows with swollen bellies, envy and wind. What say you, Geraint; shall we burn this city?"

Geraint was silent for a little while.

"Nay, let us leave it empty and silent."

And Osric laughed.

"My men and yours will empty it.—But let us speak of the spoil. I would have no quarrelling between your men and mine."

"I have all that I desire.—But my men will want their plunder."

"The strong will always plunder the weak, brother. It is a law of nature, let the mealy mouthed say what they will. Come now, let us agree to have all the spoil gathered together in one place, and you and I will apportion it. We will take our gold and our silver and our raiment, and such women as we choose, and go back to our ships. What say you, Geraint?"

They had come to the cross-roads near the Mother Church. A few dead lay about, and a dog was licking the blood in the gutter. There was an open space round the church, and it lay in the heart of the city.

Geraint reined in.

"Let the spoil be gathered here, Osric.—I will send out a trumpeter and warn my men."

"Balda shall go for me—and blow his horn. All shall be fair and honest between us."

Geraint sat looking at the red ears of his horse.

"Am I bloody, Osric?"

Osric smiled at him.

"Somewhat bloody, brother."

Said Geraint—"I would wash."

He rode into the open space about the church, and dismounting, looped Victor's bridle over a rail, and going to the labrum he washed his face and hands and throat. Osric also washed at the labrum, dashing the water into his blue eyes.

"I smell the sea.—What of your god, Geraint? Does he ask for a sacrifice?"

Geraint was wiping the blood from his harness with a cloak that Balda had found lying in the church porch.

"My god—Osric, is—I know not what. Sun and moon and water, green trees and the dew on the grass."

Osric's eyes were merry.

"And—love—brother."

"Yes, a man should love," said Geraint, "and hate as fiercely as he loves."

CHAPTER XXX

Geraint and Guinevra

❡ WHEN Geraint came again to the Forum he found a great silence there, and looking in through the gateway he saw all the dead lying in the sunlight, grotesquely twisted and grotesquely still. Nothing moved in the courtyard. There was not so much as the flutter of a garment, and in the centre of it all Balthasar lay dead on his bed beside the pile of brushwood.

One live face peered round a pillar. It was Morgan's, and the magnificence and the horror of the slaughter stared in Morgan's eyes. Geraint saw the lad and called to him.

"Come and hold my horse."

The lad looked at his lord with awe, for Geraint was like the wrath of God, and this merciless slaying had silenced a city that had shown no mercy. Geraint dismounted, and picking his way over the corpses and the bloody stones, he stood at the foot of Balthasar's bier. He looked long and steadily at Balthasar without rancour and without regret. His enemy was dead, with dead Melchior sprawling across his feet. Nor had the city finished with death. The Forum might be silent, but from the outlying streets and houses came the sound of the spoiling and the slaughter. Osric's and Geraint's men were making an end of what was left. A remnant of the city had saved itself, flying in wild panic through the west and north gates into the woods and fields.

Geraint faced about. He saw Caradoc leaning on his spear and watching him; and behind Caradoc in the

346

shadow of the ambulatory were those twelve men. Geraint beckoned to him, and Caradoc came striding over the corpses.

"All's well, master."

"All's well, Caradoc."

"She is—awake—in there—but strange and dumb. For a day and a night they filled her poor belly with fear. And that's no food for a woman."

The grimness came back to the face of Geraint.

"Calleva has paid.—Go, you and your men. Take your plunder and your pleasure."

Geraint went and stood in the doorway. After the sunlight of the forum courtyard the room looked dim to him, and Guinevra was part of its dimness. She was sitting on a bench against the wall opposite the door, her face afloat, her throat showing. Her hands clasped the edge of the seat, and her arms were like two pale cords taut from shoulders to hands and holding her erect. She looked at Geraint with weary, half-closed eyes, and the mouth of her was dumb.

Geraint's love grew very gentle. He went in and stood before her, and all the grimness had gone from his face.

"Guinevra—for you—there is no more fear."

Her pale lips moved.

"Yes, lord."

He went on his knees, for she was like one still palsied with fear, wild and pale. He drew her hands to him, and they were cold. He put his mouth to them, and began to chafe her fingers.

"My beloved is still afraid."

He saw her face wake to life, but in the very feeling of things there was anguish. She seemed to come up out of deep water. She shivered. Her lips fell apart. Her eyes were both bright and blind. And suddenly the man in Geraint was wise. She needed his arms, the warmth and the strength of his body, the tumultuous and tender words of a lover.

He rose and lifted her up.

"Cover your face, child.—It is not good out there."

She clung to him, her face against his shoulder, her lips touching the steel shoulder-plate.

"O—my dear lord."

He stood a moment, holding her.

"Am I not more than lord, Guinevra? Am I not man, a man who is free to love you."

She drew her head back and looked at him, and there was pleading in her eyes.

"Do not speak soft words to me, dear lord."

He looked at her steadily.

"She—who was my wife—is dead, Guinevra, but let us not speak now of the dead. I hold life in my arms. Shut your eyes and trust me."

He carried her out through the ambulatory to the gate where Morgan was waiting with the horse, and as he went he looked at her closed lids. He saw the bruises on her forehead, and the marks of Calleva's claws on her face, and his love found a strange beauty in them. He thought —"Whither shall I take her and let her rest until the bloody business of this day is over?" and he bethought him of the house of Cornelia. He would try it, let the wheel come full circle. He gave a jerk of the head as he passed Morgan, and Morgan understood him. He followed Geraint into the street, leading the white horse by the bridle.

There were dead lying here and there, and Geraint had a glimpse of four of Osric's men with a great oak coffer on their shoulders, their round and painted shields hanging on their backs. He found Cornelia's gates standing open, and the courtyard with its garden empty. Someone had dropped a grey cloak on the stones. But there was a strange peace about the place. The women had fled, and plunderers had come and gone.

Geraint carried Guinevra into the vestibule. She lay in his arms, and her eyes both met and avoided his.

Said Geraint—"Half a lifetime can be crowded in a day or a summer.—Do you remember how I carried you into this house?"

She gave him a gleam of the eyes.

"I remember."

"But there are no women to-day to take you from me. This house is ours, though the plunderers have been here. Let us see what they have left us."

He carried her into the summer-room where Cornelia had sat to have her beard plucked. The place was in disorder, a coffer lying on its side with its lid wrenched off, drawers pulled from a chest, curtains torn down, but the same couch stood by the window. Geraint carried Guinevra to the couch and laid her upon it.

But she sat up, knees together, her hands over her bosom. Love might stand and look at her devoutly, but she was a woman who had been dragged through the streets, and she felt like one. No need for her to ask for a mirror. And Geraint understood.

He smiled. She was trying to huddle her feet under the couch. But for her hands the clumsy smock would have showed her breasts.

"There is some wisdom in man.—When I knock upon your door, my dear, open and see what you will find."

He left her. He went out into the courtyard where Morgan was letting the white horse drink the water in the basin of the fountain. He looked mysteriously at Morgan.

"Lad, can you thieve?"

Morgan twinkled.

"Try me, lord."

"I saw shops with their shutters still up.—Run, or the world will be before you. Break in. Bring clothes, shoes, linen, stockings. Run."

The game was to Morgan's liking, and he ran back towards the Forum, and falling in with two of Geraint's fellows, he shared the adventure with them.

"Come on.—I want women's clothes."

"You'd make a poor girl," said one of them, "you need a razor."

"Ass of my fathers," quoth Morgan, "the clothes are for someone who can wear them. Come and smash shutters."

Meanwhile, Geraint had closed the gates, and fastened Victor's bridle to the latch ring so that any plundering gentleman of discretion might be met by the horse, and mount his own conclusions. The Sign of the White Horse consecrated the house. Caradoc, happening to pull himself up to look over the gate, saw Victor, grinned, and dropped back into the street.

"Elsewhere, you fellows. Our lord lives here."

Geraint had gone exploring, and common sense—even in a lover—took him to the kitchen quarters. Even fair women must wash and eat. And in the kitchen he found the embers of a fire still glowing under a copper cauldron full of water, and in a pantry he discovered milk, bread, fruit and a jar of honey. Geraint filled a basin from the cauldron, and carrying it through the house he set it down outside the door of the summer-room. He knocked, and stole away. In a passage leading to the women's bath he found a clean napkin hanging on a peg, and taking it, and going out into the courtyard he tossed the thing through Guinevra's window, and it fluttered in like a white bird.

Geraint went back into the house, and taking a great salver of pewter, which some plunderer had tossed aside when he had realized that it was not silver, he put bread, fruit, milk and honey on it. If the spirit of love was hungry, so was the flesh. He cut himself bread, and spread honey on it, and he was standing in the portico, eating, when he saw a bundle tossed over the gate. Morgan followed the bundle, and picking it up, he carried his plunder to the steps of the portico.

"I had first choice, lord."

"Let us see the spoil," said Geraint.

Morgan went on his knees and untied the knot. He showed what he had to show—aping the shopman.

"A blue under tunic, lord. A gown of saffron. A girdle of purple silk. Two pairs of leather shoes; one pair red, one pair brown. A cloak of homespun dyed green. Three pairs of hose. A hat of white straw with blue ribbons. A mirror, a comb—an unguent box.—A new strigil—but that is for myself, lord. Two bronze pin-brooches.—A pair of garters——"

He looked up, laughing at Geraint, and Geraint smiled at him.

"You are a good thief, Morgan. Take out the strigil, and tie up the bundle.—What's that you have stuck in your girdle?"

"A dagger, lord.—I left two swords and a shield outside the gate."

"Arms for Morgan?"

"I am a man, lord, now."

"You shall be my man—Morgan."

Geraint took the bundle, and going to the window of the summer-room, he put it over the sill and let it drop.

"Woman's gear, Guinevra."

2

Calleva called to Geraint. He had left Guinevra sleeping, with Morgan watching the gate, and he mounted his horse and rode through the city. There was not a live thing to be seen in Calleva save a few dogs, and the pigeons on the roofs, and the men who were sacking the city. But the dead were everywhere, for many of Geraint's men had been as rough handed as the Saxons and had spared neither young nor old. From the Hospitium in the south-east to the silver-refinery in the north Calleva had been stripped, deflowered, plundered. Geraint met two of his own fellows looking as black as charcoal-burners, each of them carrying a sack. He reined in and questioned them.

Yes, they had been exploring the furnaces of several likely-looking houses. They were shrewd fellows. The hot-air chambers under the floor made good rabbit-warrens, and they had caught no less than four of Calleva's old cronies hidden with their hoards among the hypocaust pillars. They opened their sacks and showed Geraint their spoil; silver and copper coins, a few pieces of gold, rings, fibulæ, plate, and one or two ingots of silver. The owners?—O, well, to be sure, if the furnaces of Calleva were lighted there might be a smell of baked meat under the floors.—Geraint never saw the rascals again. They walked out of the city with their plunder, and went their way.

Geraint remembered his own dead and wounded. He had lost no men in the storming of the north gate, but riding down to the south gate he counted seven dead, and found five lying wounded. The wounded were calling for water, and Geraint dismounted, entered a house close to the town bakery, filled a water-pot and gave the wounded drink. There were Saxons also who called for water, and Geraint refilled his water-pot twice. As for the men of Calleva—there were no wounded among them; they needed earth or fire, not water. Geraint had left his baggage wagons at Turris Alba, but there were wagons and horses to be had in Calleva. As for his dead they should not be left in the city, but should be carried to the White Valley and buried under sweet turf.

Riding back up South Street he met David Red Head. Osric was calling for Geraint, and Geraint rode up to the Christian church. He found Osric here, and Gawaine, Caradoc, the young Aquilas, and a crowd of men. Both the young Aquilas were bloody, and still fiercely pale. They showed Geraint their swords.

"We have sent many shades to serve our father."

The place looked like a market-square on market day.

The plunder had been piled here, all the strange and multifarious things that men covet: hutches, strong-boxes, raiment, fabrics, plate, arms, braziers, vessels of copper and of brass, pewter dishes, cups, beakers, furniture, bed-gear, and in the narthex porch of the church a dozen young girls. Osric's Saxons had got together a number of horses, wagons and tumbrils to carry their share of the spoil to their ships, and when Geraint looked upon this scene he feared that the sharing of the plunder might set men quarrelling.

But he had Osric with him, and Osric could honour a bargain, and hold his wild men to it. Geraint and Osric, with Balda between them, sat on their horses by the porch of the church. Four men were chosen from each party as porters, and the business began. All the spoil was halved and piled in two different places. There were shouts, japes, laughter. The sea-rovers wanted no bed-gear or pots and pans. Geraint's men could take what they pleased for the household. But the young wenches were for the ships.

Osric looked at Geraint.

"Shall we quarrel over the women, brother?"

"I take none of the women, Osric."

When the sharing of the plunder was finished, Osric bethought him of his wounded and his dead. He sent two wagons down to the south gate and had both the dead and the wounded brought up to the church square. Osric would have burned the city, and the dead with it, for nothing cleanses like fire.

Geraint remembered the pile of faggots in the Forum.

"There is a pyre ready for your dead, Osric."

He sent wagons for his own dead and wounded, and rode with Osric and Balda to the Forum, and when Osric saw the slaughter that had been made here, he smiled grimly.

"This is a good sight, Geraint. This city will pull no more faces at you."

He rode his horse among the dead, and seeing Balthasar lying there on his bed three spear-lengths from the pile of brushwood, he sat and gazed at Calleva's saint.

"Who is this man, Geraint?"

"My enemy."

"By my gods, he too should burn."

"Let him lie," said Geraint, "a dead man in the midst of a dead city."

The pile of faggots pleased Osric. Assuredly, his dead should be burnt here in the midst of the city they had stormed. He had those warriors carried in and laid upon the pyre with their arms and shields. Balda brought a torch, and Osric took it and lit the fire. He stood holding the torch, and when the flames rushed up through the wood he and his Saxons sent up a great shout and beat their shields with their swords. The smoke rolled high about the little gilded figure on its column. The white face of Balthasar seemed to glow.

Osric mounted his horse and called to his men.

"Load the wagons. The sea calls us."

Geraint rode with him out of the Forum.

"You go to your land, Osric; I—to mine. Honour has stood fast between us."

Balda passed the words to Osric, and Osric gazed steadfastly at Geraint.

"Maybe—the sea will bring us again to this island."

Geraint smiled at him.

"You might find me against you, Osric, in battle."

"That's on the knees of the gods, brother—in the lap of the gods."

Osric's men loaded the wagons with the plunder and the wenches. There was some screaming and struggling among the women. They called on Geraint, but Geraint sat his horse and was silent. Calleva had not pitied Guinevra, and strong men take what they will. Nor did Geraint's men murmur, for they too had had their will of the city. There were no virgins left in Calleva, none save

Guinevra, nor had some of the girls taken unkindly to the adventure. Next day Geraint was to see a score of them pranked up in the wagons, and making no moan over being loved by a soldier.

Osric and his Saxons marched out of the rebel city of Calleva by the east gate, for the south gate was still barricaded and the roadway cumbered with corpses. Geraint rode to the gate with Osric, and there they kissed each other and said farewell.

"It has been a great sacking, brother. The gods give you good days, and many children."

Osric took the golden torque from his own neck, and fastened it about the neck of Geraint.

"There is a wedding knot for you, my friend."

And there they parted, never to meet again.

CHAPTER XXXI

Sunset Over Calleva

¶ IF Rome had taught the world one virtue, it was the virtue of cleanliness, and though the world might proceed to shed that virtue, when Geraint looked upon his men after the storming and sacking of the rebel and Christian city of Calleva, he could swear that both he and they needed washing. There were the Public Thermae, and baths at the Hospitium, and when Caradoc asked his master for orders, Geraint looked at the smith's red hands.

"Take the men and wash them, Caradoc."

"All of them, sir?"

"They need it."

Caradoc might scoff at the softness and the effeminacy of cities, but both the morning and the work had been hot, and there was water to be had in Calleva. "To the baths —you fellows." He marched fifty of them down to the Thermae, and in the peristyle he found one citizen left alive in Calleva, an old man in a white tunic sitting on one of the seats of the ambulatory with a clean towel across his knees.

Caradoc hailed him.

"Hallo—you, I thought we had not left anything on two legs alive in this city."

The old man stood humbly before Caradoc.

"Would my lord wash?"

"There are more than a hundred of us who are foul with fighting. And who are you, old man?"

"Sir—I am the keeper of the baths.—I have worked in the thermae for forty years. My attendants have run

away. I, sir, am too old to run away. And—after all—
the world must wash."

Caradoc laughed.

"I have always held, old man, that good sweat keeps a
man clean. But is the water hot?"

"I—myself—fed the furnaces at dawn. My lord shall
be served."

"Lord," thought Caradoc, "I am getting on in the
world. And why not?" His men were crowding behind
him into the court, and he addressed them.

"Gentlemen, the water is hot. Go to it. Assuredly,
Calleva owes us a bath."

He took the old man by the arm. He, Caradoc, had
never explored such a temple of civic luxury as this. Let
the keeper show him the place.

"For—I have a friendly feeling for you, old man. You
stuck to your towel, and did not run to see a pretty wench
roasted. Lead on."

The old man seemed to recover his spirits and his
colour. He was somewhat proud of the city's thermae, and
he seemed to forget that there were no citizens left to
bathe in them. With some dignity he conducted Caradoc
into the apodyterium, and pointed to the great coffered
roof and the painted walls and the niches in which the
bathers hung their garments.

"This is the apodyterium, sir."

"Ha, the apodyterium," said Caradoc; "I'll have one
in my new house when I build it."

The old fellow became garrulous. He said that in the
good old days he had seen a hundred bathers stripping
themselves in the chamber—but the city had become less
clean. Yes, sir—too much chatter about souls, and less
care of bodies. And this was the frigidarium. There—
on the right—my lord could observe the cold bath. That
room was for service. There were strigils and towels for
those who had not brought them. The gentleman would
hardly credit it—but of late the lewd fellows of the city

had been demanding free oil for the anointing of their bodies.

"Free oil?"

"Yes, sir."

Caradoc spat on the floor, and then passed his foot over the spittle.

"Free funeral will be more in the fashion."

The old man sighed, and led the smith through the caldarium into the sweating-chamber.

"This is where you sweat, sir."

"Sweat—my friend?—I have done that all the morning. But—let us out of this, and wash."

Ignoring the ritual of the establishment, Caradoc stripped off his harness and his clothes in the caldarium, and soused himself in the hot bath. The old man fetched a strigil and a pot of oil, and he dealt with Caradoc's hairy body. When he had scraped and dried him, he made Caradoc lie on one of the marble benches and rubbed him with oil.

"This is a strange business," said Caradoc, "but not unpleasant.—Come on, you fellows.—One should go clean to the ladies."

So thought Geraint. After taking leave of Osric he had ridden back through the silent streets to the house of Cornelia, to be met at the gate by Morgan who had found other feathers and had girt himself with a sword. Morgan was both the man, and mysterious. He pointed to the window.

"She sleeps, lord."

Geraint did not ride into the courtyard lest the sound of his horse's hoofs should wake Guinevra, but he sent Morgan up the lane to stable the beast. It was the very same lane in which Morgan and Guinevra had changed clothes.—Geraint went to the window of the summer-room. He saw Guinevra asleep on the couch, one hand under her cheek, the other across her bosom. She had put on the new clothes which Morgan had brought her, the

saffron and the blue, and then had folded her petals.—
Geraint left her sleeping.—After all the rough work of the
morning he could tread gently while his tired love slept.
He had other work for Morgan, and between them they
rekindled the fire under the copper cauldron in the kitchen,
and carried the thing to Dame Cornelia's marble bath.
Geraint stripped himself and washed, while Morgan sat on
the steps of the portico and polished his lord's lorica, greaves,
and shoulder-pieces, his helmet and sword.

He heard Geraint calling him.

"Is there clean linen to be found in Calleva?—I have
worn this tunic a week under my harness."

Morgan was on his feet.

"If there is one I'll find it, master."

Morgan ran, and in one of the plundered shops near the
Forum he found six plain linen tunics on a shelf in an inner
room.   He took two of them, one for himself, and one for
his lord, and returned to the house of Cornelia.

2

Guinevra slept till the fifth hour after noon.   She woke
to find the westering sun shining in at her window, and for
a moment there was fear in her eyes.   Death and the shadows
of it had been so near her, that this window might have been
that other window full of the faces of Calleva's mob.   She
started up with a hand to her throat—but this window had
no bars.   It was a sheet of silent sunlight.   Her old smock
lay on the floor.   Her body was sheathed in saffron and
blue

Her colour came back.   She sat and smiled with her
arms clasping her bosom.   Her eyes grew deep and dark.
She seemed to listen to some sound within herself as a
woman listens to the singing of birds in the greenwood on a
morning in May.   The sweet stealth of the dawn.   The
surge of the young year, meadows in flower, the smell of

the thorn blossom, the white lace of wild weeds in orchards, the poignant song of a blackbird, yellow broom ablaze, bluebells in the green gloom of the woods. She sat and clasped herself and dreamed. Her face was mysterious. Her glances seemed to slant this way and that.

The window of Cornelia's summer-room. She had stood at it on that afternoon in May when Geraint had ridden away, but had turned at the gate to look back. But how silent everything was! Had she been plucking hairs from Cornelia's Roman chin the uprooting of one small hair might have been audible. Dear, admirable, downright Cornelia with her hair piled like a fortress!—She heard the beating of wings, and going to the window she saw Geraint sitting on the stone seat by the fountain, feeding pigeons with pieces of bread. The birds were round his feet, and he smiled as he tossed the crumbs to them.

Her lover! And the transfiguration! She had seen him ride into the Forum like the north wind on a white cloud. She had seen him kill; she had seen the crowd roll away from him like smoke. The man on the white horse. She looked at him dearly and steadfastly. Yes, a man should be strong and fierce in the face of a crowd, but compassionate to dumb things.—And, suddenly, Geraint seemed to feel her eyes upon him. He turned his head and saw her at the window.

"Guinevra."

The birds fluttered from his feet and settled again behind him.

"Guinevra——"

She looked both at him and beyond him, her face mysterious, her hands resting on the sill of the window.

"The city is very still, lord."

He said—"It is a dead city, Guinevra. It lies at your feet.—Is there any other thing that you would ask of me?"

Her hands went out to his.

"To be—that which my lord desires."

He looked at her deeply.

"To-morrow we will go and stand under Alban's cross, and take what life can give us."

3

When the sun was setting, Geraint mounted his horse and rode again through the city. The sunset was on its red roofs and its painted walls and the fluted pillars of its temples. Windows glimmered, and here and there a tree rose above the houses like a green dome. And to Geraint Calleva had a strange, grim beauty with its dead lying where his vengeance had overtaken them, and the walls and pavements painted with dark stains. The silence of death was everywhere. It seemed to tremble at the trampling of his horse. The empty streets echoed. Almost, he expected to see white faces peering from windows, but the windows of Calleva were dead eyes. Doors and gates stood open. Geraint saw a pair of legs sticking out of one doorway, and in another a hag lay clutching the fragments of a broken jar.

He rode to the south gate and looked again at the slaughter that he and Osric had made. The dead lay tumbled upon each other, or sprawling upon their faces, but here and there a man showed his face to the sky, mouth open as though uttering a cry of fear, the whites of the eyes staring. Nothing moved here, and the street smelt of blood. As the sun sank the bodies and the faces of the dead grew grey.

Geraint turned his horse and rode up to the Forum. Not for a generation would Calleva wax arrogant and vex its neighbours. Those who had fled from the city might creep back to it, or Calleva might remain a city of the dead. There would be no hot and howling mob in its Forum, no one to throw potsherds and foul words at a woman. The sword had cut the throat of Calleva's insolence.—

The court of the Forum lay in the shadow, the basilica loomed black; the plundered shops were like open mouths. The ashes of the fire still glowed, and a smell of singed cloth and hair and flesh hung in the air. Geraint dismounted, and leaving his horse in the gateway, walked amid the dead to look again at Calleva's saint. The heat of the fire had scorched the bed-clothes, but the white wax of Balthasar's face was firm. In his hands rested the little silver cross.

Geraint gazed steadfastly at his dead enemy.

"My friend," thought he, "if your cross had been the cross of Alban, you would not have been lying here, dead in the midst of a dead city."

He took the cross from Balthasar, looked at it, and then replaced it under the dead man's hands. Balthasar seemed to sneer. Thus, would he leave Balthasar with his people about him, clasping a symbol of saintliness.—What did the dead eyes of Balthasar behold? A god, paradise, hell, or nothingness? Would man ever know?

Geraint, riding from the Forum, met Caradoc and some of his men carrying wine pots, and butcher's meat, bread and fruit in baskets of osier.

"We have shared out the spoil, and we go to feast, lord," said Caradoc.

"Under the stars, Caradoc?"

"We have lit our fires under the stars, but the church of the Christians will serve us to feast in."

"Take your pleasure," said Geraint to the men, "for, to-morrow we leave this city."

He beckoned Caradoc to him, and Caradoc stood beside the white horse, and listened to Geraint's words. He nodded his big head and smiled.

"Love rides where it pleases, lord. Leave the men and the march to me."

Geraint rode back to the house of Cornelia, stabled his horse, and fed and watered him. He stood awhile under the stars in the garden court, and the night was sweet to him, like the face of his love. To-morrow they would go out together into the green country where cities did not rage, and the smell of death was not. The woods should spread their green glooms for Guinevra.

And Geraint slept on a mattress of straw across the doorway of Guinevra's room, with his sword and his shield beside him.

CHAPTER XXXII

Alban is Called from the Plough

¶ A RED dawn saw Geraint's men march out of Calleva. There were clouds coming up from the west, and the wind smelt of rain. Geraint sat his horse at the west gate, with Guinevra beside him, wearing a green cloak over her blue tunic. The men saluted Geraint and his lady, and laughed in each other's eyes. Said one fellow to his neighbour— "Calleva was worth sacking—for that," and his comrade replied—"I guess Geraint thinks so.—But what will the lady think of our wenches?"—"Lord," quoth the first, "she'll have other things to think of to-night."

Gawaine led the main body which was bound for Vindomis. Only Caradoc and twenty men, with David and Morgan among them, were to ride with Geraint to the White Valley. The spears went tossing along the road, and Geraint looped the bridle of Guinevra's roan horse over his arm, and rode out with her through the right-hand arch of the gate. He made a sign to Caradoc to lead on his twenty men, for lovers do not ask to be stared at.

About a furlong from the city Geraint reined in and turned the horses' heads towards the east. Calleva loomed dark against a stormy sky. The little golden figure above the Forum, shining against a blue-black cloud, was like a finger raised above the city.—"Silence!" And Calleva was as silent as death. Not a live thing was left in it save the dogs and the birds, and the old keeper of the thermae. Geraint's face was stern. In the Forum Balthasar lay with his people about him in the midst of a strange silence.

He looked at Guinevra and his eyes softened, for Guinevra's face was the face of a woman to whom the day would
be as mysterious as the dawn. She was in a mood to divine
mystery in the simplest of things, and her eyes were deep
and dark.

"Calleva will trouble us no more."

He turned the horses and glanced from her face to the
sky.

"Rain before night. Shall we care?"

Her face dreamed. She thought of rain in the woods,
a wind shaking the wet branches, the sweet smell of the
earth.

"I shall not care, dear lord."

"Now—or ever?"

Her eyes went to his.

"Never—while my lord is with me—in rain or shine."

For ten miles or more they rode behind Caradoc and
his men towards the wet west, with a wayward wind snatch-
ing the dust from the feet of the horses. The green trees
were ruffled, the grass aslant. Ever and again Caradoc
would draw aside and look back to see that those two were
behind him. Not far from the Shrine of Sylvanus standing
amid the old thorn trees, Caradoc looked back and saw that
the road was empty. He gave a toss of the head, laughed,
and led his men down through the woods to the White
Valley. Caradoc had had his orders, and with him rolled
a wagon full of household gear from Calleva. The White
Tower was to be garnished against the coming of the
night.

In the woods the silence was complete, save for the
soughing of the wind in the tree tops, but the green glooms
below were like deep water. Sometimes the sun broke
through as the clouds drifted, and there would be a glitter
of light among the tree trunks. The two horses moved
like one, as though in sympathy with their riders. Geraint's
arm was about Guinevra. Her head rested against his
shoulder, and her pale face dreamed.

"You will make a Christian of me yet, my dear, you and Alban."

But to Guinevra love was her faith, and these green woods her sanctuary.

"If Alban is Christ's man, his Christ is not the Christ of Calleva. And, in our faith, dear lord, there is but one man—and one woman."

He smiled down at her.

"You would have it so, Guinevra?"

"I would have it so," she said.

When they came to the forest stream and saw Alban's valley in a sudden shrine of stormy light, Geraint reined in and kissed his love's lips.—Alban was at work in his field, ploughing up the stubble with a wooden plough drawn by two oxen. He borrowed his plough team each year from a farmer over the hills in the river country. Geraint, riding down with Guinevra, raised an arm and hailed Alban.

"Alban, leave your ploughing. Here are two people who would be yoked."

Alban thrust his goad into the earth, and leaving the team standing, he put his cloak over his shirt, and came to them with the face of a man who was warm with labour.

"God give you joy, Geraint. So, the tale ends well in spite of Balthasar."

"Balthasar is dead," said Geraint, "and Calleva humbled. You preach humility, Alban.—I will humble myself before you, if you will, now that I have left my enemies in their blood. But this child is innocent."

Alban smiled upon them both.

"Have I not been a man of blood?—When you left me I saw death in your eyes, Geraint. Some men come not to Christ until they have struck down Satan.—You would be joined together, you two?"

Geraint looked at Guinevra.

"If the woman will take me. She has seen me fierce, and she has seen me gentle."

Guinevra put her hand in his.

"I take my lord fierce, and I take him gentle.—I take him in shadow, and I take him in sunlight, for better or for worse, as life may show."

Alban crossed himself.

"What answer do you give to that, Geraint?"

And Geraint looked proud.

"She is gentler than I am, Alban, but in this love of ours I see good things, faith and honour and sweet living, children, and the fruits of the earth, and peace for my people."

"That is a good answer," said Alban.

So, they went to the wooden cross, and there Alban joined them as man and wife. He signed Geraint with the sign of Christ, but he kissed Guinevra on the forehead.

"Be gentle to your man, child, for that is the way to keep him. Strong men do not accord with turbulent women. But, peradventure, your heart is wise as to that. Men come to drink where the waters are deep and still."

He blessed them both, and watched them mount and ride into the woods, and then went back to his ploughing, with a little flock of birds following at his heels for the sake of the worms and the grubs the ploughshare uncovered.

2

There was a moment of sunlight over the valley. The White Tower shone, and the wind was in the apple trees, and fretting the water. The sky was as grey as the smoke from the chimney of Geraint's house, and even as they gazed, the sunlight passed and raced along the woods.

Geraint held his wife's hand.

"Is the place fair to you, Guinevra? Can you remember that which is good——?"

She took the words from his lips.

"And forget that which is evil? The evil has passed, dear lord, with the passing of those who made a business of being good."

Geraint pondered those words of hers, and then he smiled at her.

"That is a wise saying for one who is so young.—And it would seem that their business failed them."

Morgan had been on the watch outside the great gate, and he came running up the hillside to meet them. He went on his knees before the horses.

"Welcome home, master."

Guinevra gave Morgan her hand to kiss.

"We owe much to Morgan.—But never more will I borrow his clothes."

Geraint's men, with Caradoc at their head, came out to greet him and his lady. Caradoc had put on fine clothes and great manners, as befitted a man of the sword. The smith had become the captain, and Caradoc's sword was to carve him a place in Britain.

"All is as it should be, master. The smell of good women is out of the house. It is ready for a fair one."

Geraint dismounted and lifted his wife from her horse. The men made way for them, and Geraint led Guinevra across the courtyard to the house. On the steps of the portico he kissed her, and taking her in his arms, carried her over the threshold.

"When love comes in, fear flies out of the window."

Tables were laid. Caradoc had brought with him a man who was a comely cook, but of the feasting neither Geraint nor Guinevra had much thought. They drank wine out of the same cup, and Caradoc made a speech like a smith hammering heavy metal. Geraint and his men pledged each other. Presently, Caradoc came and whispered in his lord's ear, with a hand laid to his mouth.

"The boat lies by the bank, master, and the bed is made."

Geraint took his wife by the hand, and they went out and down towards the water, leaving Caradoc and the men to empty the wine jar.

Geraint looked at the black barge lying amid the water-flags and sedges.

"This craft has served us ill and well, beloved. For your sake I will have it painted white."

He took her in his arms and lifted her into the boat.

"There is no wound in me to-day—save the wound of loving you too much."

She put her fingers on his lips.

"I can heal that wound, dear lord."

When the twilight came they were standing together in the doorway of the tower, and in the twilight rain began to fall. The wind had dropped, and the rain fell straight upon the water, the leaves and the grasses. It blurred the hillsides, and they stood and listened to it with their arms about each other.

Said Geraint—"There is a beauty in all things, Guinevra.—Peace is not yet, but because I love this green world with its woods and fields and waters, I would bring peace to it. I have been fierce to Calleva, but I can be gentle here. Will you grow old with me in this valley, Guinevra?"

She looked up smiling into his face, her eyes aslant.

"Am I so very old, lord?"

He laughed and kissed her and drew her into the room. It was clean and sweet and strewn with herbs. They left the door open to the night, and the rain played upon the water and the trees. In the darkness Geraint held love in his arms, and Guinevra gave him all that a woman can.

CHAPTER XXXIII

Cornelia has her say

¶ GERAINT dispatched a horseman with a letter to Leo, Prefect of Britannia Prima at Corinium.

"Your Excellency—the bishop is dead, and Calleva humbled."

Such was the succinctness of Geraint. Leo Gallicus, supporting his white head with his hand, and with one eye shut, blessed such brevity and was wise as to its wisdom. Emperors and statesmen can be grateful to a man who—instead of honouring them with a golden oration, presents them with a bloody head on a charger. The indiscretion of the sword may tear rents in the web of statecraft, but if the wasp is in the web, the thing is reality.

Leo questioned the messenger. Yes, my Lord Geraint was at Turris Alba. He had taken to himself a wife, but matrimony would not prevent him from marching in person to present his respects to his Excellency. Leo dismissed the man with a present and a letter to Geraint. The letter said very little, for Leo was not a man to commit himself on paper. Would the Emperor Valentinian be pleased? It was very necessary that the Emperor should be pleased.

Leo ordered his litter and was carried to the house of Rhadamanthus. His bearded sybil should be presented with the news. Probably, she would have something to say on it, suggestions to make, for Leo was responsible for his province, and if a city in it had been stormed and

370

sacked, the accomplished fact would have to be served up delicately on a golden dish.

"Matrona—your Geraint is a forward fellow. I set him to stable an ass and he has slaughtered a whole city."

Cornelia's blue eyes blazed.

"Does that inconvenience you, my friend?"

Said Leo, smiling down his nose—"It might be—deucedly—inconvenient. Geraint shared the game with a pack of Saxons.—The Saxons have gone, but an empty city remains.—The problem is—what shall I say to the Emperor?"

Cornelia was prepared to write his Excellency's dispatch for him, and to add a dossier of her own. Were there not many notable people who had suffered at the hands of Balthasar, eminent citizens of Calleva who had been displaced and plundered? Let the lawyers draw up a document—"We—the undermentioned servants of the Emperor who have suffered at the hands of this rebel prelate and his mob, wish to express our gratitude to the Prefect of Britannia Prima for restoring peace and property, and to record our appreciation for the valour and loyalty of my Lord Geraint.—We, the undersigned humble and devoted servants of the Emperor, salute him——" Cornelia would procure the signatures. She herself would head the list. And would any Emperor doubt her good faith?

"My dear Leo," said she, "when a pot is in danger of boiling over, some credit is due to a man who begins to rake out the fire.—What has Count Benedict to tell the Emperor? Has he recovered the Wall, or pacified the north country?"

Leo looked sly.

"Poor Benedict is stuck in York. The heathen can do what they please north of the Trent."

"Great news for the Emperor, my friend!—And have we not trouble nearer home.—You told me only yesterday that the Cymri were out again, and that they have beleaguered Caerleon."

Leo nodded.

"That is beyond my province, at the moment."

"Nonsense," said she—"will not the Emperor be grateful to any man who can help to return him that which is his?   When the house is burning, do we stand on the threshold and say—'By your leave, sir—but the prerogative is yours.   Go first.'—Give Geraint the command of such forces as you can raise, and send him against the Cymri.   Let him—pacify—the Welsh.—That will be butter to spread on Calleva's loaf."

Leo stroked his chin, and looked at her wickedly.

"By the way, matrona—Geraint has a wife."

"Ha," said Cornelia—"my golden girl?"

"I know nothing of her colour, madam—but when a man has a new wife—he is apt to bid farewell to arms until such a time——"

"Proceed—my dear."

"Until such a time as he is sated."

Cornelia wagged a finger at him.

"Cynic.—I will look after Geraint's wife for him. He is not one of your fat and uxorious fellows who ride nothing but—woman.   And if the woman is wise— which I think she is——"

"Proceed, my dear," said Leo.

"She will send him out on horseback and know that he will come back the fresher.   War and love accord well, my dear sir."

"So—Geraint is to live in—harness?"

"Double harness, Leo.   Man is a restless creature, if he is worth marrying."

"Then—my worthlessness—must be apparent to the world."

"Bachelors are other fish," said she.   "I don't know which it is—boiled or fried—but send Geraint to fry the Cymri."

2

Geraint left a dozen men to watch the White Valley, and gathering his company from Vindomis, he marched for Corinium.

On the last day of September he rode into that city and was met by Leo and the notables in the Forum. Geraint had his wife with him on her roan horse, and when Leo had looked upon Guinevra he smiled and murmured—

"So—Troy fell."

But if Corinium gave a public welcome to Geraint, and wondered between whiles if his men would behave themselves, Geraint had no municipal manners. Councillors might smirk and make speeches, but Geraint was remembering a certain formidable old lady with grey hairs on her chin.

Cornelia, at her window, saw Geraint and Guinevra riding together down the street, and Cornelia's blue eyes stared hard. Assuredly, they made a comely pair, proud of each other and proud of their love. Poor Placida. —But Cornelia caught herself up. The dead should not be dissected. She leaned out of the window and showed to the wedded pair the jocund and stately head of a Roman matron.

"Hail—children."

Geraint saluted her.

"So, it is you, matrona. We were coming to this house—for your blessing."

Said Cornelia—"By the look of you, my dears, it is a little late in the day for my blessing, but you shall have it for what it is worth."

She looked at Guinevra, and Guinevra's eyes were deep.

"We owe you everything, matrona."

"Well, well—I must send in a bill."

In the garden of Rhadamanthus the three of them sat under a lime tree, and Cornelia, having listened to their story—as Geraint chose to tell it, took Guinevra into the house, for Guinevra had been on the road since daybreak. The bath and Cornelia's Martha were at her service, and Guinevra kissed Cornelia.

"I am very happy, matrona."

"Ha," said Cornelia, "you will pull no more hairs from my chin."

She went back to the garden and Geraint, and sat herself down and looked grim.

"Now, my dear, let me hear the whole truth."

"The truth, matrona?"

"You spoke—delicately—because of your wife.— What did you do to Calleva, my friend?"

Geraint told her the whole story, and Cornelia's blue eyes were fierce. She clapped her hands together.

"I am a good hater, Geraint.—That fellow Balthasar lying dead in the midst of a dead city!—Ye gods, and they would have burned the girl!—I should like to have seen the faces of that crowd—when—you rode in. Yes— I must go and look at Calleva."

"It will be a city—of ghosts and of silence, matrona. —There may be a few who will come back.—But, my hatred has passed."

"Ha," said she, "you had your feast, my dear. Life is like that. Do not let us be sentimental.—I am a wicked old woman, Geraint, but I love what I love, and I hate what I hate. Will the world ever be otherwise, unless man learns to live on slops like a slave?"

3

Geraint, with his company reinforced with levies from Corinium and Gleva, marched against the Cymri who were beleaguering Caerleon, routed the little dark men, and freed the city. And there, David Red Head took his revenge.

But greater happenings were to ripen in Britain before the leaves fell from the trees. The Emperor Valentinian, growing wise as to the desperate state of the island, sent his general, the great Theodosius, to Britain. Theodosius landed at Rhutupiae with veterans of the Rhineland legions, and was met by the prefects and the notables. The Vicar of Britain was dead, and Count Boniface beleaguered in York, and the Emperor had sent a letter of authority appointing Leo Gallicus Vicar of Britain. Geraint was with Leo on the great stairway leading from the pharos to the quay when Theodosius landed in state at Rhutupiae.

Leo presented Geraint to the general.

"Here is a man who would serve with you, sir."

Theodosius had heard of Geraint as an amateur soldier who was rather rough in his methods.

"Ha—the gentleman who sacks cities."

Said Leo, smiling down his nose—"When you have heard the story, general, you will wish you had shared in the sacking. Our friend Geraint took Troy."

Theodosius, like all great captains, had a liking for a man who could cut a crisis in twain with a sword, and leave the official world to patch up the pieces. In the pretorium he dined with Leo and Geraint on his right and left, and the three of them were well matched.— But to be brief, Theodosius chose Geraint to be the leader of his light horse in the campaign for the recovery of the island. History has it that Theodosius gave six months to pacifying the southern provinces—but Geraint had performed much of the pacifying before the coming of Valentinian's general.

Theodosius cleared the forests of their wild men. He rode through Calleva, a Calleva to which a miserable and humble remnant had returned to clear away the dead bones of Balthasar's dream. Calleva was a city of old women and old men, of starveling children and fleabitten dogs. Its shops were empty, its basilica a place of ghosts, and from the day of its sacking Calleva was a dying city. The woods began to march up to its walls. Its wells grew foul and rotten. The glass fell from its windows. Its baths became waterless. Grass and brushwood began to cover its walls.

In the spring of the year Theodosius marched to recover the north, and Geraint went with him. Boniface had died of dropsy in Eboracum, and Theodosius, gathering the ruins of the legions, and using an iron hand, drove the heathen over the Wall. Its forts and towers were rebuilt and garrisoned. Thence, Theodosius marched by way of Caerleon into Wales, and the Cymri humbled themselves before him.

Britain was herself again for a generation, and Geraint found peace among his fields and woods.